HIGH PRAISE FOR CATHI HANAUER'S "POWERFUL"* FIRST NOVEL, *MY SISTER'S BONES*

"ELEGANT . . . Hanauer has her finger precisely on the pulse of the rising generation, and she writes with a sensitivity and authority regarding teen experience that is unrivaled among her literary contemporaries."
—*The Capital Times* (Madison, Wis.)

"A VIVID, SPIRITED PORTRAIT . . . One of the richest and most satisfying qualities of this novel is that harmonious balance between the many aspects that make up Billie's life."—*The Village Voice*

"RIVETING . . . A PERSUASIVE, WELL-RENDERED AND RICH FIRST NOVEL ABOUT FAMILY . . ."—*Kirkus Reviews**

"A BEAUTIFULLY WRITTEN FIRST NOVEL."—*Library Journal*

"HONEST PROSE, WRITTEN FROM THE HEART."—*Essex Journal* (West Orange, N.J.)

Please turn the page for more extraordinary acclaim. . . .

my
sister's
bones

a novel by

cathi
hanauer

Delta
Trade Paperbacks

A Delta Book
Published by
Dell Publishing
a division of
Bantam Doubleday Dell Publishing Group, Inc.
1540 Broadway
New York, New York 10036

ISBN: 0-385-31704-2

Reprinted by arrangement with Delacorte Press

Manufactured in the United States of America
Published simultaneously in Canada

To my parents,

  for their love and for believing in me

And to Denise,

  wherever you are

acknowledgments

My heartfelt thanks go to the following, without whose help this book would not exist as it is: First, to my agent, Elizabeth Kaplan, and my editor, Marjorie Braman, whose talent, energy, and encouragement set everything into place. To Roberta Myers and Amy Hanauer, who saw this through from the start and said all the right things, and to the others who so generously gave their time and wisdom: Adrian LeBlanc; Rory Evans; Kristin van Ogtrop; all the Hanauers; and everyone at the MFA program at the University of Arizona, especially Jonathan Penner, Robert Houston, Karen Mockler, Jeff Barnet, Vicki Broach, and Deb Jane Addis. To Vivian Gornick, who helped me realize what was worth writing about, and to Catherine Hiller, who supplied moral and editorial support when I most needed it. To Gerri McNenny, Neal and Erica Hartsough, Karen Offitzer, and Harriet Silverman, for graciously providing places of inspiration in Tucson. To Tony Imbimbo, for help with the Italian; Johnny Herr, for help with the wrestling terms; Leslie Morgan, for the optimism way back when; and K.A. in Tucson, for the honest and open talk over lunch. And to Gary at The Copy Room at 850 Third Avenue, for the breaks.

Most of all, to Daniel Jones, my partner and best friend. For everything.

my
sister's
bones

YOUNG LOVE, AMERICA

Beside the Pepsi vending machine, red
white and blue he's kneading her left buttock
through her bleached jeans hard enough
to bruise but she's kiss-tonguing
his ear, in play, you can tell
it's play since the orange facade
of HAROLDS TIRES $14.95 is hot as the summer sun
at the horizon and the sky, at dusk,
is just too blue.

He's wearing a shirt with sleeves rolled tight
to his biceps, an EXXON cap on oily curls,
her right arm crooked easy around his neck
like Susan Hayward used to smiling teasing
hurting, in play, you know it's play
since the red-finned Plymouth at the edge
is distended as in a funky photograph
and the horizon's spiky, palms and eucalyptus
foreshortened at dusk: You know what? his white teeth
are saying, Us two could die together, sometime.

—JOYCE CAROL OATES

Suffering is the necessary prelude
to the re-establishment of the self.

—HAYDEN CARRUTH

M y sister Cassandra borrows our mother's car and drives us both to the mall, which is good. But when we get there, she wants to go off by herself, to get stuff she needs for college. "You know we can't shop together, Billie," she says. "We'll just fight."

"No, we won't."

"Yes, we will." She swings her head, spilling corn-blond hair down her back. "See?"

"But you're not leaving for college for two months!" I don't want to wander the mall alone. This is not something you do in New Jersey when you're fifteen. Not when you're seventeen, either, unless you're Cassie, who doesn't care what people think.

"I need to start getting organized," she says. "I want to start studying in advance."

So I agree to meet her at two o'clock, outside Bamberger's prom department.

For an hour I wander the mall alone, feeling like the biggest dork alive. To kill time, I try on sneakers, then buy cherry bubble gum and chew the whole pack. I examine the displays of blue flowers, trying to decide if they're real or fake. In the bank, I read a sign in front of the teller: If I don't use your name at least once during this transaction, I will give you a dollar. *At one thirty I go to Baskin-Robbins and get myself a double choco-late-marshmallow cone. One half-hour left.*

A bunch of girls are hanging outside Baskin-Robbins, smoking ciga-rettes and leering slit-eyed at whoever walks by. They have maroon nails and streaked hair, combs protruding from back pockets of skin-tight corduroy pants. There are four or five of them, about my age. One has on a jacket that says Bloomfield—the only town with tougher girls than my town, West Berry.

They watch me go into Baskin-Robbins.

They watch me come out with my cone.

Rather than lick it in front of them and risk whatever comments that might bring, I let the top scoop, which wasn't on tight to begin with, orbit dangerously to one side. As I step out of Baskin-Robbins, it plops to the floor, inches in front of their spike-heeled shoes.

One of them bursts out laughing—the one with black hair with two white streaks in front and a palm-sized crucifix hanging between her tits. Another one puts her hand over her mouth and snickers. The third one sneers, showing her tongue. "Oh, gr-oss," the fourth one says.

What I should do, I know, is laugh with them—one good laugh at my expense—then leave the ice cream on the ground and get out of there. In-stead, I freeze up. Then I curse: "Oh, shit!" Then I try to clean up the mess. But I don't have enough napkins to get it all up at once, and when I go to throw the bulk of it in the trash, someone steps in the rest. Some old guy, trailing chocolate marshmallow footprints on the tan tile floor. Fluorescent lights beam down on it.

The Bloomfield girls lose it. They hoot with laughter, doubled over, their bodies wriggling. The more they laugh, the more people look to see what's going on. Soon we've made a small scene. Before I can stop myself, I shoot White Streaks a dirty look. "Shut up," I say.

First they just trail me, their spike heels clicking the floor, their bangle bracelets jangling. Past Smuggler's Attic, past No Name, past Seafood Eat Food. So close, I smell one of their Love's Baby Soft, another one's pot pipe, or maybe pot breath.

Then they start to say things. "Bitch, bitch, bitch," one chants softly. Another says, "Hey, slut, you got your period. Look at the back of her!

*Look at her ass!" The third one just laughs. The fourth says, "I bet she's a
kike, the little snot. Hey Snot, you're a kike, aren't you."*

*I go into Bamberger's. They follow me. "Who do you think you are,
looking at me like that, dog-face?" White Streaks says. She shoves my back.
I turn around. She sneers. "Hey slag, I'm talking to you."*

*Behind her, powder-blue prom dresses swish gently on their rack. White
lights hum overhead. I could run for it, but if they catch me, I'm dead. Blood
throbs behind my eyelids. Where are salespeople when you need them?*

"What?" I say to White Streaks, and my voice sounds like gravel.

*"You heard me," she says. "I asked you a question. Who were you
looking at back there? Huh?"*

I swallow. "Nobody."

She pushes my chest, hard. "You calling me nobody?"

I roll my eyes. "No."

*"That's what I thought." They have formed a ring around me now,
like lions circling a lamb. I'm the tallest, but there are four of them. Behind
me, one taps my shoulder. When I turn to her, she takes a step back and
beckons. "C'mere," she says. "I want to show you something."*

"What?" I say miserably.

"I said, come here," she says.

*"Listen, I've got to go." I try to run. White Streaks sticks out her foot
and trips me.*

*I fall against a rack of clothes, one hand sinking into carpet. I get up
quickly. And that's when Cassie shows up. Early, as usual.*

*She swings around a corner, three notebooks clutched to her chest,
pencils and pen and a pencil sharpener in one hand; you can always see what
she bought right away, since she never lets the salespeople give her bags. Her
hair is a curtain almost to her butt, her round green eyes are narrowed.
"Hey," she says to White Streaks.*

*White Streaks backs up a step. "Hey what?" she says, but you can
tell she's thinking. Cassie's taller than she is, and bigger, and stronger. And
older. And beautiful, too.*

*"Hey, that's my sister," Cassie says. "That's what." She grabs my
arm like I'm luggage and begins to pull me. "Come on, Billie."*

"Wait a minute," White Streaks says. She takes a step toward us.

Cassie stops. She turns around. "Don't you have anything better to do with your life?"

"Fuck you, whore," says White Streaks.

So Cassie slaps her, hard, across her cheek. Crack! *White Streaks stumbles back. My mouth falls open.*

They don't follow us to the car, but we run anyway, back past Smuggler's Attic and Hotdog Hovel, past blue flowers, breathing fast. I am laughing and laughing, floating, flying through the mall. "I can't believe you did that!" I keep saying. "I can't believe you hit her."

At the car—parked at K-11, Cassie remembers, of course, though I'd forgotten to check—she opens her side and gets in. She places her stuff neatly in the backseat, then leans over and opens my door. I slide in. "God," I say, "that was perfect."

She stares out the windshield, keys in her hand. Clots of white clouds block the sun. "I've never hit anyone," she says.

"What do you mean? You hit me all the time." I laugh.

She turns to face me. "What happened back there?"

I tell her the story. As I talk, she watches me, mouth closed, eyes fixed to mine, something not completely happy on her face. At the end, she says, "You shouldn't have said anything to her. You should have ignored them."

"I tried," I say, "but they kept—"

"Why stoop to their level, Billie?"

"I didn't, Cass. I—"

"Forget it. I don't want to hear it, okay?" She starts the car and drives over to join the line of cars pushing out of the mall parking lot.

I turn away from her. Out my window, on a white cement road barrier, someone's painted, "Fresh paint calls for fresh graffiti." Underneath it, in thick lime-green script, are the words "Life Is Corruption."

"Can I turn on the radio?" I say after a minute.

"No," Cassie says.

So we drive home in silence. I have the moment, the memory, to keep like some jewel you carry in your change purse just to know it's there, but I see now that that's all it is, a moment. She smacked a girl for me, and now it's over.

So we drive home in silence, me and my older sister, back to the way we are, the way we always were.

chapter
one

A week before Thanksgiving—three months after she leaves for college—my sister calls on the phone in our room. "Billie?" she says, sounding very far away. "Don't tell Mom and Dad it's me, okay?" She waits. *"Okay?"* she says, a little louder.

Downstairs, at top volume, my father is watching *Masterpiece Theatre* on PBS—a rerun of the show he made my mother and me watch with him this past Sunday night. My mother is in the kitchen cleaning up from dinner, feeding the dogs, scraping roast beef scraps off our plates.

"Okay," I tell my sister. "How are you? How's college?" I'm surprised she's calling up here, and glad for the distraction. I'm supposed to be studying for my PSATs. Any minute my father will walk in and ask me what page of the booklet I'm on, what words I've learned.

"I called to tell you I got rid of all my clothes," she says. "I would have told my roommate, but she's not here anymore."

"Thanks a lot." I reach for a bottle of nail polish—lavender, one of West Berry High's colors. "So where is she?"

"She went back to Indiana, to her mother. She didn't even tell me. The dorm director had to do it." I hear her shift the phone around. And then I hear her crying.

I put down the nail polish and hold the phone tightly. I can't remember the last time my sister cried. "Cassie, what's wrong?" I say. "What do you mean you got rid of all your clothes?"

She takes a deep breath. "I gave them to a clothing drive, at the mall."

"The mall?"

"A guy on my hall talked me into going, he said we both needed a break. But when we got there, there was all this *Christmas* stuff already—underwear with Santa Clauses, red rubber reindeer, glittery stockings—and all these big plastic toys. And people all over the place, pawing through everything. They knock something down and just step on it, like it's—like it's *ruined* or something. And buying things, just buying. Wrapping paper, shiny boxes—they couldn't buy it all fast enough."

"Well, yeah," I say slowly. "I mean, that's sort of what Christmas shopping is, isn't it?"

She's quiet a few seconds. "I had to go," she says. "I made Tim take me back and get all my clothes, and I gave them to this clothing drive in the parking lot." She sniffs. "After that I felt much better."

She doesn't sound better. I picture her standing, nothing but her underwear on, in the lot of some mall, hurling her clothes into the wind: her pink sweats, her white cotton shirts, those old turquoise shorts that she'd let me borrow if she was in a good mood. They sail over cars, like small parachutes. For a second I'm happy: now I'll have nicer clothes than she does, I'll look better than her, for a change.

But then I picture her huddled in some freshman dorm room at Cornell: dull green carpet, textbooks all over the place, and my sister, naked, crying into the phone. Something tugs at my heart. "Oh my god," I say.

"No, it's okay, it's good." She sounds convinced now. "People don't really need so many clothes, you know? We only really need one thing."

I think about what would happen at my school if you wore the same thing every day. You'd die. If you didn't die of humiliation, people would kill you. "What about when you're washing it?" I say. "Or at night?"

"I don't know. Tim will let me borrow something, probably."

I have to say it. "So this guy's in love with you, right?"

"Who. *Tim?*" She sighs. "Billie, no one's in love with me."

She's either wrong or lying, I'm sure, but I don't give her the satisfaction of saying that.

"I look terrible, anyway," she says then. "It's the food here. It's too—I don't know, there's too much of it, or something. I can't eat it. All I do is study. And take showers. I don't even play tennis anymore. I used to go to the pizza place, just to get out of here, but now the waitress there hates me. I always leave a huge tip, even though I only have coffee, but she gets this look on her face when I come in, like—" She stops, breathing fast. "Oh god, someone's here," she whispers. "Billie, someone just knocked on my door. What should I do?"

"Answer it?"

She fumbles with the phone. "I've gotta go. I'll call you back." She clicks off.

I stare at the receiver. I want to call her back but I don't have the number, and I can't ask my parents or they'll want to know why I'm calling Cassie. My father will say, "I'll call down here," and then he'll stay on the line while we talk, interrupting whenever he wants —or giving advice, as if we're one of his patients he can tell to take some Mylanta and go to bed.

So I hang up and wait, watching a silver half-moon shine through my bedroom window. It lights up the leaves of the big oak tree that towers over our house—the ear tree, I call it, because of the knot in the trunk shaped like a huge human ear. Cassie used to say the tree listened to everything our family did, all the time. During storms, she said, when its branches whapped our windows, it was warning us we'd better behave.

I watch the moon shimmer down the leaves—ten minutes, then ten minutes more. Downstairs, the TV goes off. The moon shifts slightly, so I can no longer see it. And Cassandra doesn't call back.

★   ★   ★

My sister is someone who makes life harder than it has to be; that's what I think. In high school, Friday nights, she'd sit home and do schoolwork, her fingers twisted like branches in her hair. She wouldn't answer the phone if it rang, and she'd tell me not to either. Of course I would anyway; I have a life, too. But it was almost always for her, and always a guy. Then I was supposed to say Cassie wasn't home and I didn't know where she was. One time this kid called for her twice—once at eight, once at ten—and the second time I felt so bad for him, I said, "Yeah, she's here, I'll go get her." She killed me for that. Like it would have been so fatal to talk to some guy who worshiped the very air her presence had graced.

I get nervous just being around my sister sometimes, the way everything has to be perfect. In her notebooks, she reserves one page for doodling, and there's so much scribbling on that page it's like the color of the paper is black lead, but the rest of the pages are white and perfect, every line used, both front and back. It's unreal. I mean, when you get bored in a class, you draw on your notes, right? When you love a guy, you write his name a thousand times. You draw it in bubble letters, in script, inside hearts. My ninth-grade notes say "Greg" all over them.

With Cassie, if a page gets messy, she'll copy it over. On the rare chance she ever slips. Then, before a test, she highlights furiously, a rainbow of streaks over everything. That part's cool, I have to admit.

Sometimes, I'll catch her watching me out the side of her eye, and I know she's thinking I look like a sleaze, just because my bra strap is showing a little or I have on a lot of lip-gloss. So I'm always surprised when she compliments me or laughs at something I say. She told me once that I'd do fine in the world, that it was herself she was worried about. That made me feel great for a minute or two. Then I wasn't sure if it was a compliment or not. But I decided to take it that way, since it didn't seem like she was trying to be harsh. Another time, in the dressing room at some store, she told me I had muscular calves, and that made me so happy, I stared at them in every store window all day. Later, I said, "Cass, do you really think my calves are muscley?" She made a face and said, "What's *muscley*? What's *muscley*? Just because Tiffany Zeferelli can pull off that dumb act doesn't mean you can." She couldn't erase the compliment, though. I still like my legs better ever since she said that.

Last year, we had a party—all her friends and mine in the house at once, plus a bunch of people neither of us knew. My parents were in Europe; my grandmother was supposed to check in on us periodically. So Cassie got some guy to buy liquor, and I made drinks in the blender with amaretto and vanilla ice cream, and we all had a huge water fight, all over the house. The carpets got drenched. Later, Cassie's friend Ardelle Johnston asked me if she could borrow a blanket, so I gave her an old one of Cassie's from the closet, this cream-colored quilt with pink roses on it. Ardelle smiled and thanked me and took it down to the basement, with this guy Walter McCann following her. Next day I found the blanket down there with a pinkish-brown spot on it. I brought it up to show Cassie. "What happened to him?" I said, and she laughed and said, "It's more what happened to *her.*" "Oh," I said, and then I got it and I felt pretty stupid. It was bad enough still being a virgin in West Berry without actually demonstrating it.

But Cassie was looking at the blanket. "We'd better get rid of it, before they get home," she said, "since we'll never get it clean." So we took it up to the woods in my father's old brown BMW; we got the keys out of his underwear drawer, where he always hides them. And Cassie waited in the car while I got out with the blanket and ran in and left it under a tree.

When I came back, I was still laughing, but then I saw that Cassie looked upset. "Where did you put it?" she asked as I got in the car. I told her.

"Why?" I asked.

"Well, did anyone see you?"

"Of course not, fool."

She bit her bottom lip. "*Which* tree?" she said. "I mean, near the entrance or far in?"

"About halfway in, I guess. Why, already?"

She shifted in her seat. "What if Mom's walking the dogs sometime, and she walks by the woods and sees it?"

I rolled my eyeballs. "She won't."

"How do you know?"

"Because! I put it far in. God, what is your problem?"

She stared at me. Then she started picking at her cuticles, which she does sometimes. The same person who saved exactly one notebook page to draw on. "Cassie, that's revolting," I said.

She pulled her hands apart. And then she got out of the car and slammed her door and ran toward the woods. Barefoot and everything. "Where are you going?" I yelled, opening my window, but she just ignored me. So I sighed and sat in the car waiting, listening to the motor hum. It was starting to get dark outside, and cool. My parents would be home by tomorrow morning. I put my feet up on the dashboard, then took them down again. I checked myself in the rearview. I rubbed my arms underneath my T-shirt. For some reason, I felt suddenly sad.

After a few minutes, Cassie came back with the blanket. "I don't believe you," I said, but she just tossed it in the backseat and got in. Then she drove us home and took the blanket upstairs, and while I finished blow-drying the hall rug, she started scrubbing at that bloodstain. By the time my parents came home the next morning, that blanket was perfectly clean. Tiny little roses on an eggshell background, like nothing ever happened. Like the incident was erased and Ardelle Johnston was still a virgin.

Except that Cassie's hands were pink from the scrubbing and her eyes were slitty and tired. And she looked totally stressed. A bundle of nerves, my grandmother would have said.

I couldn't get mad at her, though. Because I knew she couldn't help it. Everything has to be perfect with my sister. That's what I mean.

Thanksgiving Day, late afternoon, and Cassandra, who's getting a ride home from college, hasn't gotten here yet. My parents alternate complaining. "Where the hell is she?" yells my father, pulling his navy sweater over his head. It's a sweater he looks good in. It matches his blue eyes, which set off the pink glow of his cheeks, and it hides the slight gut that even swimming every other day can't make disappear. Not that he cares, anymore than he cares about his nose, which is sort of hawkish. He's six foot three and a half, and he wears it, all of it, with confidence. He looks the way he acts. Sometimes I wonder which came first.

My mother dumps a handful of sliced red peppers into a pan. "I'm sure she's on the way, Michael," she says. She wipes her palms on her apron, stirs a whisk through a pot of something.

But ten minutes later it's my mother at the window: "I can't imagine where she is. Did she say what time she *thought* she'd be home?" And my father: "She said she'd be late. She didn't give me a time. She'll get here when she gets here."

After that the relatives arrive—my grandmother Zelda and her brother Myron and my father's sister Nancy and her kid Emily—and everyone gets busy sipping wine and making hungry small talk and hovering in the kitchen, the smell of turkey thick in the air. My father's answering service calls, and he curses, then calls the patient back in the kitchen so we all hear him talk. When he gets onto "urine" and "loose stools," my aunt Nancy makes a face, then asks me loudly what books I've read lately. I give her the list, and which ones I liked best: one by John Updike, one by John Irving. "When are we eating, Aunt Jane?" Emmy finally pipes up. My father hangs up. *"Now,"* he answers, looking at my mother. "I'm not waiting all night for her, Jane."

My mother glances at the clock. She pulls in her lips, then smooths back her short dark-blond hair. My mother's five eight or nine, with short nails and strong hands and very little makeup, even on Thanksgiving. She has green eyes—the same color as mine and Cassie's. Only my father's are blue. "Okay," she says. "Dinner's served."

All through the meal, my sister's plate sits empty and sparkling while the rest of ours pile up with food: turkey and sweet potatoes with marshmallows, cranberry sauce and string beans. Later, my aunt brings out apple pie and ice cream. "Cassie's ass is grass when she gets here," I whisper to Emily, and she laughs. My mother gets up to check outside for the third time. "She'll be here, Jane," my father says. "Sit down and eat your cake." My aunt Nancy shoots me a glance. She and my father have had their spats over the years.

But it's not until almost ten—just after Uncle Myron, the last one to leave, takes off—that my sister shows up. She comes in quietly, like maybe she thinks she'll get by us and up to bed before we notice her. But I want to see if she really gave away her clothes, and my mother wants to fix her a plate, and my father, I'm sure, wants to ask her what the hell took her so goddamn long to get here. And I want to know, too.

When she comes in, though—same old black coat she's always had, zipped all the way to her chin—all he says is, "Next year, try to make it for dinner, please," and then he kisses her. My mother does the same. "Ooh—you're freezing!" she says. "Didn't the boy who drove you turn on the heat?" Cassie leans in to kiss me, avoiding the question, and when we touch cheeks, she really is freezing. Her lips are tinted blue, and I realize she wasn't in a car at all—not recently, anyway. She was outside somewhere, walking or hanging around, waiting until the relatives left.

"Let me get you some hot dinner," my mother says, heading for the kitchen. "Take off your coat. You must be starving."

Cassie shakes her head quickly, and her leg begins to vibrate, like a plucked guitar string. Something about her looks different, though I can't tell what yet. "Thanks, Mom," she says, "but I'm so tired, I think I'll just take a quick shower and go to sleep, okay? I'll tell you everything in the morning. Okay?" She heads upstairs, a big lumpy knapsack slung over her shoulders, no suitcase or duffel bag. Our two boxer dogs follow, wagging their half-hotdog tails and snorting wet spots onto her.

My father hesitates for about fifteen seconds, and then he goes upstairs anyway. And then my mother goes up, too.

I stay down—in the kitchen, since the sight of my sister's unused plate in the dining room makes me feel sorry for my mother. I hear the shower go on. I pick some crust off the pie, read my horoscope and the advice columns in the newspaper. I wash a few dishes and leave the rest. The shower goes off. I finish clearing the table and put away Cassie's place after all. Then I go upstairs, too.

I'm hoping she'll notice I've cleaned up the room—so she won't have to tell me my half's a sty, like she always used to. But she's sleeping already, or at least faking it, and when I turn on a light, she doesn't budge. Her long, wet, gold ponytail lies on her comforter. Her knapsack sits neatly on the floor, fully zipped.

I watch her a minute in the faded light from my small bedside lamp. When we were young, we could wake each other up just by staring. Now the covers rise and fall with her sleeping breaths. I hear the dogs sniffing outside the door, their nostrils pressed to the base like vacuums, and even though I'm in here and they're not, I feel just as gypped as they do. I want to see how she looks, ask her what's in her backpack and why she hung up on me last week and why she didn't come in for dinner. I want to see what she's wearing.

Anyway, she's the one who ends up waking *me,* halfway through the night. At first I think she's telling me something, but then I realize she's talking in her sleep. "But I can't, but I can't, but I *can't!*" she moans, her voice getting louder each time. "I don't know, I don't—"

I sit up, half-panicked. "Cassie! Wake up."

Silence.

"Cassandra?"

But she rolls over and sleeps. And I lie there and pull the pillow over my face. I remember her friend Steve once telling me, "Cassie is tortured, in a way." I'd pictured her tied up being whipped, and I'd laughed and said, "Steve, give me a break."

In the morning, I wake to the smell of coffee and homemade waffles and the sound of the news on my father's old black radio. It feels like Sunday. My sister is still buried in covers. I watch her a minute, then go downstairs.

My father turns from the newspaper when I walk in, and I wonder if he's disappointed I'm not Cassie. "Morning," he says, his mouth full of waffle. He reaches out and changes the radio station to some opera.

"Morning. *God,* that's loud, Dad."

He nods and goes back to the paper. He's half hard-of-hearing and half just likes it loud and doesn't care if we don't. I slide into my place, which is already set with a big and small glass (milk and juice), two plates, full silverware. On the table in front of me is a bowl of fresh cut-up fruit. I pick a few bananas out of it with my fingers. "Guess what?" I yell over the music. "Cassie talked in her sleep."

"Two more minutes on your waffle," my mother says. "What did she say?"

My father raises the volume. "Listen to this," he says. "This part is beautiful." He begins to sing loudly, making his voice waver like he's a real singer, which he's obviously not. I stand up to get my waffle, then carry it back and sit as far away from him and the radio as I can. "Pass the butter," I say, not looking at him, and then add "please" before anyone reminds me.

The dogs cock their heads, listening to my father sing. Their eyelids waver. And then Mollie, the mother, begins to moan, and soon Ethan starts in. My father laughs and sings louder. Mollie moans louder, singing along. It's funny but it's not, and I try not to laugh.

"Michael! Cassie's still sleeping!" my mother tries. Even when she's not exclaiming, she puts an exclamation point at the end of most things she says.

My father glances at her. He reaches out and lowers the volume ever so slightly. "I'll have one more waffle," he says. "And then I've got to go to work." He looks at me. "Go wake your sister, please. It's past eight thirty. I want to see her before I leave."

Cassie appears in the doorway. "Do you honestly think I can sleep through that?" She steps into the room, rubbing her eyes. She's wearing a big old sweatshirt of my father's, long johns I don't recognize, and black slippers that look like she pulled them out of the trash. Her hair escapes in scattered strands from her ponytail, which has grown almost down to her butt. Her lips are no longer blue, but they're too pink—deep pink, like cherries—and so chapped they're peeling.

My father laughs again. He lowers the music a little more. "Good morning," he says.

"Morning," Cassie says, her voice croaky. Her eyes dart to the counter, then to the table. She looks both tired and hyper at the same time, if that's possible.

"Perfect timing!" my mother says. "Ready for your first waffle?" She slides a hot waffle onto my sister's plate.

My sister stares at the waffle. I stare at her. Under the table, the dogs jostle each other for her attention. She still hasn't greeted them properly since she came home, and they know it.

Cassie reaches out to pick some fruit out of the bowl, then changes her mind and doesn't take anything. The dogs nudge at her feet. And then she does something I've never seen her do: she sticks out her foot and kicks Mollie away. Not hard—Mollie doesn't even flinch—but still, I can't believe she did it. "Cassie!" I say.

She turns to face me. And then something else happens that hasn't happened before: a dog growls, long and loud and mean.

"What was *that*?" my mother says. We all look at each other. And the sound comes again, like an earthquake.

For a second I'm afraid; maybe Mollie is about to get back at Cassie for kicking her, maybe our dogs aren't as gentle as we think. I bend down to look under the table. As I do, the table jolts; milk and orange juice and coffee splash all over the place. And the dogs emerge, snapping and snarling—but at each other, not at my sister. They rise on their hind legs, backing into the counter, knocking off my mother's bowl of gathering compost heap. Eggshells, banana peels, orange rinds rain onto the floor. The dogs don't even seem to notice. They just go on attacking each other.

"Jesus H. Christ!" my father yells, smacking at them with his newspaper. Saliva flies from their jowls and sticks to the walls in threads.

My sister moves to a chair that's farther away. She closes her eyes and covers her ears. I scream. My father sticks his foot out to separate them, but they cling together, lunging at each other's face and neck.

What finally stops them is my mother. She emerges from the laundry room crashing together two metal pan lids, like some crazy marching band cymbalist. The sound is thunder in our little kitchen, and we all turn to look at her. The dogs stare, panting and wide-eyed and cowering. My father grabs Ethan's collar. "Get Mollie!" he yells.

He is yelling to Cassie—she's the oldest, the closest, the one who always takes the lead. But Cassie just sits there, her hands still sandwiching her ears, so I grab Mollie's collar instead. My hand slides in dog spit. "Put her upstairs!" my father orders as he drags Ethan outside.

I pull Mollie upstairs to our room and close her inside. Then I stand outside the door awhile, my heart pumping fast, trying to figure out what happened, what's happening.

Back down in the kitchen, my family is freeze-framed. My sister is slumped in the corner chair, looking down at the table; I can't see her face, just the top of her head. My mother stares at the mess like she wants to say something—something optimistic, probably—but can't think of anything. My father stands in the middle of the room, one hand pinching his chin, the other dangling at his side. It makes me nervous, him standing there doing nothing like that. Unbelievably, the opera still shrieks away, like the background for some creepy play.

My mother bends down, gathering the bottom of her purple robe in one hand, and picks up an eggshell. "That was *disgusting!*" she says. "I'll throw them out in the street before they'll behave that way in this house again—Michael, would you lower that radio, please?"

I think for once my father is actually glad to have someone give him an order. He lowers the radio—not quite all the way, but enough so the music now sounds like trapped bees. He picks up a few orange peels, just for show. Then he sits down at the table. He looks at my sister. "That enough excitement for your first day back?" he asks. And he laughs.

We're all hoping Cassie will laugh back, I think, even though nothing's funny. My sister has the greatest laugh, like tinkly bells, or the top few notes of a xylophone, and sometimes when she laughs, it's contagious. She lost Best Laugh in the yearbook only because Maria Scozzio laughed loud as a shriek. Or maybe also because she got other stuff: Best Looking, Best Athlete, Most Likely to Succeed.

But Cassie doesn't laugh this time. She just looks at her waffle, now hard as a Frisbee. And we all look at her—examine her, really—for the first time in four months, since she's left. She's pale as sour cream, and her skin looks too thin; two blue veins cross her forehead like train tracks. I remind myself that my sister's always been pale in the winter. And the nervousness—blinking, biting her bottom lip—makes sense too, considering our dogs have just turned vicious. But I still think there's something different about her, and as I watch her, it comes to me: She is smaller. *Thinner.* Not by tons, and maybe something someone else wouldn't even notice, but when you share a room with someone for sixteen years, you know what she looks like. I know she has a scar on one calf—she fell down ice skating once—and a heart-shaped birthmark on the back of her neck. I know her bottom teeth are crooked, because my father doesn't believe in braces unless they're "necessary." And I know she's always been bigger than this. She's tall and muscular and flat-chested—like my mother, like me—and stronger than half the guys in her class. But she looks almost small now, buried in that sweatshirt, her neck sticking out like some scrawny bird's. And her face is less round than before. Sucked in under the eyes, tighter on her head.

I can't help thinking about the girl at my grandmother's country club who got anorexia last year. She'd swim up and down the pool for hours, her sharp elbows pushing at her skin. I couldn't bear to watch her. "Cass," I say, trying to sound casual, "you look skinny, or something. They feed you up there or what?"

"*Do* they feed you up there," my mother corrects, but her heart isn't in it this time. She's watching my sister, her mouth closed, her forehead slightly creased.

Cassie glances at me, then stands up. She flicks a strand of hair off her face. "Mom, I'll have my waffle in a little while, okay? I'm not hungry yet." She glances toward the sliding door to the hallway, the one I dragged Mollie through. Then she turns and walks the opposite way, into the laundry room and out the back door.

Through the window, the sky is the color of cold: dull and purple and heavy. The room is quiet except for the radio buzz. "Where's she going?" I say.

"Where *is* she going?" my mother asks my father. "It's freezing out, Michael! She'll freeze!" She speeds to the door and yells outside, "Cassandra, come back and get a coat, at least!"

"Let her go, Jane," my father commands. "She's in college

now. She knows enough to come back if she's cold. Close the door, before Ethan comes in." His theory has always been, If you don't make a big deal of something, it isn't one—except maybe at the hospital. He's a cardiac surgeon.

My mother stays at the door a second longer, maybe for spite, then comes back into the room. "She didn't even eat her waffle!" she says. "She hasn't eaten a thing since she came home." She sounds like she does when she's just found out someone she knows is getting divorced, or a kid in her second-grade class pulled a knife on another kid. Sort of surprised and sad and worried all at once.

My father flips through the paper again. "Where's the sports page, Jane?" he says. "I have to go in a minute." My mother hurries over to find it. And I tell myself, Well, if he's not worried, why should I be? He's the doctor.

So I finish my waffle. I think of volunteering to eat Cassie's, since it seems pathetic just lying there on her plate. But I don't really feel like eating a whole cold hard one just because Cassie didn't. So I say, "Mom, can I have another waffle? I'm still starvin'."

"Starv*ing*," she says. "In this family, we put the *g* on the end of words." What she means is, "You will not talk like Tiffany Zeferelli in this house." Tiffany is my best friend, who lives three blocks up the street.

But she goes over anyway, my mother, and ladles in some batter to make a fresh waffle for me. She likes to feed us, which is fine with me. I like to eat.

For an hour, my mother alternates between worrying about my sister and worrying about the dogs, who break into another fight as soon as she lets Ethan in. My mother and I manage to separate them and lock them in different bathrooms. Immediately they both start to whine. Ethan scratches at the door so hard you can feel the paint peeling off in strips. My mother calls the vet, watching out the window for Cassie as she holds the phone to her ear. "He's away until Sunday," she tells me, hanging up. My sister walks in the back door.

She waves and smiles a little at my mother as she passes us—probably because she feels guilty—then goes directly upstairs. My mother looks at me. "I think she should have some breakfast," she says. "Don't you?"

"I think something's wrong with her."

"What do you mean?" Her eyes focus on me—the same bright green eyes as mine and as Cassie's, almost the color of fresh peas.

"I told you," I say, "she had nightmares, she was yelling in her sleep. I had to yell at her to stop, Mom. And she's much skinnier. You can't tell because she's wearing sweats, but I can see it." I'm about to say that her roommate left her all alone at college and that she gave away her clothes at the mall, but I decide against it.

My mother observes me. I can tell that half of her believes me about Cassie, but the other half doesn't want to. And then the phone rings. She answers it quickly, and I listen until I know it's my father, calling to see if Cassie came back.

Upstairs, my sister is hunched over some fat black book, marking things with a pencil as she reads. More books spill out of her knapsack. The front zipper compartment is open, and I notice a few tubes of Chap Stick in it. I sit down at my desk. "You gonna tell me why you gave away all your clothes, Cass?" I ask.

She turns to face me. "What?"

"Your clothes. Why did you give them away?"

"I told you. I don't need them."

"So you're gonna live in sweatpants the whole year?"

She shrugs and looks back at her book.

"Isn't that sort of tacky?"

"I don't think so." She doesn't look up.

"Cassie," I say, "is something wrong with you?"

Now she looks at me suspiciously, pencil poised in her hand. "Like what?"

"I don't know. You're acting weird."

She looks back at her book, but I see her close her eyes for a second. "I just have a lot of work," she says. "I'm so far behind. I'm always behind. I can't—"

"What?"

She shakes her head. "Nothing. I sound like I'm on the rag. Sorry."

Was this *my* sister, apologizing to *me*? "No," I say. "Tell me. Come on."

"I just—I don't know anything."

"About what?"

"About anything."

This isn't what I'm looking for. "You're being retarded, Cassie. You know you're smart—"

She shakes her head again. "If there's one thing I've learned this semester, it's how ignorant I am. We all are."

I roll my eyes. "Oh, okay."

She shrugs. Then she turns back to her book. "Sorry. I've got to study. I've got to read thirty pages an hour, or—"

"Or what?"

But she's reading now, like I'm not even there.

I get up. The hell with her. "I'm going to Tiffany's," I say.

Later, when I get home, Cassie's off walking Mollie, and after that she takes Ethan out for about an hour. Then it's dinnertime, and my mother makes fettucine with creamy shrimp sauce, and Cassie pushes it around on her plate. "I'm stuffed," she says when she notices the three of us are all done. "I'll put it in the fridge and have it later." She gets up. And my parents don't say anything, not even my father, and I realize then that being in college is the ticket to freedom in our house.

That night, I find Cassie's plate cleaned and dried and returned to the cabinet. I smell the dogs' breath to see if she fed her dinner to them, but I don't smell anything but dog breath. Outside, I turn on the back light and check the compost heap to see if she threw it in there. I don't find it. I don't find it anywhere.

The next night, though, when she tries it again, my father clears his throat. "Just finish," he says, though he doesn't sound mad. "I only gave you a small portion."

Cassie stands up. Her face is red, and she's breathing very fast. "You can't tell me what to eat!" she yells. "I'm eighteen. I'll decide what to put in my body."

My father blinks in surprise. Then he laughs, though it's the sort of laugh that comes just before he gets really mad. "I think you should eat your dinner when it's served," he says. "Not an hour later."

"I don't care what you think!" Cassie yells. She storms out of the room and upstairs. China rattles in the cabinets.

I look at my mother and raise my eyebrows. "She hasn't eaten all weekend," I say. I'm half-hoping to get my sister in trouble and half-hoping to make them see that something's really wrong with her.

"She really hasn't, Michael," my mother says. "She didn't eat her cereal, and she didn't eat her toast, and she didn't eat any of the tuna fish I made—"

"All right," my father says. He pushes his empty plate away and clears his throat. "She's under a lot of stress now, that's all. Freshman year is very hard at Cornell. She'll get her appetite back after exams."

I'm sort of amazed he's defending her like this. But I know, too, that my parents will watch her at breakfast tomorrow, and I'm glad. And then I feel a pang of guilt, remembering how Cassie stuck up for me the night before she left for college. No big deal, I just wanted to go see a weight-lifting competition and my father was hassling me, but she said, "Oh, just let her go already," and he considered a minute and then actually did. He'd get mad at her more than me, definitely, but he also trusted her more, I think.

In the morning, the dogs have another fight, just before I come down to breakfast. I hear my parents running to separate them. "They can't be together, that's all," my mother says. She locks Ethan in the downstairs bathroom. In the kitchen, Mollie paces the floor restlessly, toenails clicking all over the place.

Later, my mother tries the vet again while my father and I eat apple pancakes. From the kitchen, I can hear her talking. "Uh-huh. But it's—uh-huh. Uh-huh." She hangs up and comes back into the kitchen. My father and I have finished the stack. Cassie hasn't come downstairs yet.

"Well," she says, "Dr. Aiello says Ethan is trying to establish dominance over Mollie, and Mollie isn't ready to give it up yet. He says it can happen when something in a household changes—like Cassie coming home. He says we should keep them separated until she goes back to school. They'll probably stop fighting once she leaves, but they could always start up again. Now that they know they're capable—"

My father waves his hand. "Pish tosh. Dogs don't *know* things." He'd never been a fan of psychology, even for humans. And he hadn't wanted my mother to call the vet. "Next time," he says, "I'm not gonna separate them. Next time I'm gonna let them fight until they stop."

"Or kill each other," I mumble. I don't want to do that, not at all. Already, the dogs have scratch marks all over them, and their eyes sag, droopy and red. I love my dogs. And I have my own theory about what's making them act this way: I think they know something's wrong with my sister, and it's making them nervous. And they don't know what else to do.

Cassie comes down then, finally—still in sweats, but her hair is brushed neatly and she's holding her coat and knapsack. "My ride is coming in twenty minutes," she says. "He wanted to get an early start." She looks at my mother. "Sorry, Mom."

What can my parents say? They're the ones who decided she didn't need a car, who urged her to find a ride home from school with someone from the area. My mother sighs. "At least have some breakfast first," she says.

And my sister does, for a change. She vetoes the pancakes, but she pours herself a bowl of Rice Krispies and eats the whole thing. My parents watch her, and I can tell they're relieved. And my father's glad my sister is studying hard, and glad she's at Cornell, his alma mater. My mother's glad she's eating. And she's happy *he's* happy, which always makes things easier.

Cassie's ride arrives shortly. He honks, and she jumps up. "I'll be back in a few weeks," she says. And then she's gone again, and it's just me and the dogs for my parents to worry about.

In the dogs' case, the vet turns out to be right. Cassie leaves, and they stop fighting. They glare at each other a little, but that's it. It's sort of amazing. As for me, I eat plenty, no problems there, but my report card makes my father wig out: mostly B's—A's only in English and gym—and a C in chemistry. "Cassandra *never* got a C," he reminds me. He thinks I'm an underachiever. My mother thinks my friends are a bad influence.

My father monitors my studying. I'm to learn twenty new words a day—words like *zenith* and *protectorate* and *maw*—and do ten pages of SAT math, along with my other homework. I'm to read *The New York Times* at least twice a week, and "The Week in Review" section on Sundays. I'm to watch *Masterpiece Theatre* whenever he tells me to, just because he likes it.

Meantime, there are patients with failing hearts to be seen, and operas and football games to be listened to. So he goes back to the hospital, and my mother goes back to her second-grade class at Jefferson Elementary, and I go back to West Berry High. And for a little while, life goes back to normal, more or less.

chapter two

In December, things start to happen to me. I get through my PSATs. I start wearing makeup. My hair grows past my shoulders, finally. And my chest grows—for the first time in two years, and after I'd pretty much given up on it. "Christ, you're bigger than Cassie!" my father says one day. Not that that's any huge accomplishment, but he likes to compare us.

I buy a pair of shoes like Tiffany's—come-fuck-me shoes—with heels high as candy canes. "West Berry babes," she says, smiling at us in her mother's three-way mirror, though we got the shoes in South Berry, where Main Street opens up and extends like a throat and both sides are lined with big, crowded stores: the Wig Gig, Rocky's Records, Killer Klothes. We walk down there on Saturdays, try on tight sparkle shirts and spike heels to match. Sometimes we're the only white girls on either side of the street. Afterward, we walk the mile or so back to West Berry to get pizza at Giuseppe's or cannolis at Maria's Caffe.

Guys on both sides, south and west, are checking us out. They've always checked out Tiffany, with her softball-sized boobs and plenty of cleavage on display, but now they look at me too, their eyes zipping up and down. I smile at one of them in school—a senior named Vincent DiNardio. Two days later he asks me out.

"Really?" I say, thinking maybe he's kidding. He's a varsity wrestler with a waiting list of girls and biceps as thick as my thighs. He laughs. "What, you're calling me a liar?" I tell him no, not at all. Then I accept.

About this time—mid-December—Cassie calls to tell my parents she's not coming home over Christmas break. She wants to get ahead for next semester, she explains. She'll get more work done if she stays in Ithaca.

I'm on the extension in my parents' room; my mother's on the phone in the kitchen, my father's on in the den, TV in the background. This is how we do it. Cassie calls collect, then my father refuses charges and calls her back—cheaper that way—and while he dials, he yells, "Jane, Billie, I'm calling Cassandra!" and we're supposed to get on. Then the two of us sit there listening while my father tells her things: weather patterns, how much money he's put in her bank account, what movies he and my mother have seen.

Tonight, after Cassie says she's not coming home, he yells, "What are you talking about? You stay at college over Christmas if your family lives in Taiwan, not New Jersey."

My sister is quiet a minute. "I thought you wanted me to study," she says softly. "I thought you'd be glad."

"Of course I want you to study," he yells. "You'll study here. You'll bring your books home with you. That's what I did, I'd bring all my books home, and—what?" Pause. "When's your last exam?" Pause. "Jane, talk to her a minute while I get her schedule." I hear him run upstairs.

"Are you worried about grades?" my mother asks. "Because if it's grades, you know, you're in college now, and you don't need to—"

"Exams end December seventeenth," my father interrupts, picking up in his study. "You can stay an extra day if you want, but then you're to find a ride home. If you can't, I'll buy you a bus ticket—"

The other phone rings, in my room. I place the receiver on the floor and run to grab it before it rings again.

"Hey, babe," Vinnie says. "Did I catch you at a bad time? You sound out of breath."

"No—no." I listen for my father. And then it hits me: My sister doesn't want to come home for Christmas.

"So how are you doing?" Vinnie says.

I sit down at my desk, trying not to sound freaked out. "Okay," I say. "How are you?" I'm a little nervous, too. This is only the second time we've talked on the phone.

"I'm good," he says. "I'm great, to tell you the truth." Silence a minute, and then he says, "Don't you want to know how I did?"

"What? Oh god, of course! Sorry."

"That's all right. I pinned. Thirty-eight seconds. The kid was a fucking fish, excuse my language."

"Thirty-eight seconds? That's fantastic." In spite of everything else, a small thrill goes through me. This guy is my boyfriend.

"Thanks," he says, and I can see him smiling into the phone—slightly overlapping front teeth, sneakered feet on a desk, brown hair combed back in a perfect D.A. He gives me a play-by-play of the meet then. "I wish you'd of been there," he says.

"Me too."

"Your father won't let you come though, right?"

"I can go to the home matches," I say, embarrassed. "Just not the ones far away. He likes us to be home before dinner."

"Uh. How come?"

"I don't know. He likes us to eat together. I'm supposed to study afterward." I kick my door open a little farther. My father is still yelling at Cassie.

"Well, as long as you come to a few of them," he says. "I want you to see us. We're hot this year. Plus, you know, I'm captain, and everything—" Someone picks up an extension in his house. "I'm on, asswipe," Vinnie says. The person clicks off.

"So what were you doing?" he says to me. "When I called?"

"Nothing, really. My sister's on the other phone." I hesitate. "She doesn't want to come home for Christmas."

Silence, and then, "You're kidding me. Wait, where is she again?"

"Cornell. In Ithaca. About four hours from here."

"Right. What'd she go all the way there for?"

I shrug. My parents' friends' kids go to college all over the place: Stanford, Duke, Berkeley, Yale. "It's a good school," I say, but then I stop. I don't know anything about Cornell, except what my father's said. "To tell you the truth," I say, "I think the pressure's getting to her."

"Probably is. Isn't Cornell the school with the highest suicide rate? Corn Hell, they call it. I heard there's some gorge that kids are always jumping in—"

"Is that true?"

"I don't know. That's what I heard. You wouldn't catch me near the place." He laughs. "Nuh, I'm sure it's fine. Your sister's a brain, right? She was always on Honor Roll and shit. She'll do fine there. I have to say though—I can't personally see not wanting to spend Christmas with my family."

I want to defend Cassie, but I can't. "Me either," I admit.

"Oh, but wait. You celebrate whaddayacall. Hanukkah. Right?"

"No. Christmas."

"You do? But you're Jewish, right? Weinstein. That's Jewish."

I think about lying, like I did when I met Tiffany and told her I'm part Italian. My mother's father, I said. She didn't call me on it, but I think she knew I was full of crap.

"I'm Jewish by birth, but we weren't raised Jewish," I explain for the millionth time in my life. "My father doesn't believe in religion."

"Then how come you celebrate Christmas?"

"I guess because we like it. We don't celebrate it in a religious way."

"Huh." He's quiet a second. "Is that why you live here instead of Berry Jews?" Berry Jews is the way kids in school refer to North Berry, the town where my father grew up and where my grandmother, Zelda, still lives. The same kids call South Berry "Black Berry," and our town "Berry Wop"—home of the best sausage pizza, Italian delis, and weight-lifting team.

"We live here," I tell Vinnie, "because my father didn't want us to be JAPs. And, you know. My parents like it."

"What's a JAP?"

I pull the phone to my bed and lie down. "A Jewish American Princess. Like, a girl who drives a red car with a license that says 'Daddy.' Or has tons of clothes and a diamond bracelet and her own tennis coach."

"Oh." He pauses. "My cousin's like that. She's Italian, though."

"It's worse if you're Jewish," I say automatically.

"Why?"

"I don't know. I mean, which would you rather be?"

He laughs. "No offense, but I'm proud of what I am."

Well, I'm not, I almost say. The Jewish people I know call the town council to question the length of traffic lights, return things, use coupons, complain about the rising price of steak. In class, we're the ones who raise our hands and talk too much. That's why I try to keep quiet when I can.

"You know," I tell him, "once, when I was little, my grand-mother ripped open a package of hamburger in Shop Rite and tried to make the butcher rewrap just the amount she wanted. When he wouldn't do it, she left her cart of food in the aisle and dragged me out of there."

"No!" Vinnie laughs once more. "Tell you what," he says. "As far as I'm concerned, you're Italian. Okay? I mean, it's not like you act Jewish, anyway."

"Thanks," I say, not sure if I should be flattered or insulted—though I'm glad he said it.

"Well, except I'd probably guess you were just because of how good you do in school. I heard you get like straight A's. Is that true?"

"No. Who told you—"

"Yeah? What'd you get on your last report card?"

"Two A's. That's it. And a C in chemistry."

"Chemistry! You've gotta be a genius to take that in the first place."

"Listen, I didn't want to take it. My father made me. If it were up to me, I wouldn't take anything hard. Just English, shop, and lapidary. And maybe gym. That's it." I remember then that Cassie took physics and French and, for electives, stuff like shorthand and journalism. I lean out the door and try to hear if my father's talked her into coming home after all, but I don't hear anything.

"Okay, okay," Vinnie says. "I'm only kidding. Don't get all hyper-dermic about it. Listen, I think it's great that you're smart. I wish I was smarter."

I wish I *were* smarter, I think without wanting to. "You are smart," I say. I pick at my pillow nervously. "You have to be smart to wrestle, don't you?"

"Hell yeah. I mean, you gotta know the moves, and whatnot." He sighs. "But I'd still love to come home with A's. My mother'd shit her pants."

I smile. "So what's your mother like, anyway?" Somehow I can't picture him actually having a mother.

"My mother?" he says. "I don't know. I mean, she's my mother, what can I say? You'll meet her."

"I will?"

"Of course. You're my girlfriend, aren't you?"

Neither of us talks then. I hear him tapping on the phone with something—a coin or a pen. "Well, I guess I should go," I say. "I'm supposed to be studying." I'm thinking of Tiffany's theory: Guys get hard from girls who play hard to get.

"Aw, don't go," Vinnie says. "Stay on a little more. My mother's making macaronis. If I get off, I'll go eat them and then I'll have to make weight again next week. It's torture. She's torturing me."

"Poor baby," I joke, but I mean it, too. Vinnie's cut six pounds this week for wrestling, eaten almost nothing, run six miles a day in three pairs of sweats. "Okay," I say. "Two more minutes."

"Ah. Two whole minutes. I better use 'em right." He pauses. "So tell me what you're doing right now, so I can picture you."

"Now? I'm lying on my bed."

"Yeah? What are you wearing?" His voice is softer.

I glance at my clothes: jeans, sweatshirt, socks. "Just a T-shirt," I say.

"What else?"

"What do you think?"

"Let's see. Pink panties with lace, the kind that go up your crack in back."

"Nope."

"Okay. Black ones, same thing."

I smile. "Nope."

"I guess I'll have to come over and see, then. Can I?"

"I don't know. Can you?"

"Aw, man." He sighs. "You're making me crazy over here, you know that?"

Again I feel a thrill: the power of talking without him seeing me, of saying whatever I want. "So when can I see you?" he says. "We've been going out a week already, and we haven't even had any fun yet."

"Depends what you consider fun," I say, smiling, thinking of the first day he kissed me, the day he asked me out. After school, he came to my locker, and we stood awkwardly for a minute, him looking at some couple making out behind us, me trying not to fixate on him. It was hard; every time I looked, I noticed a few more details. He was my height—maybe even a little shorter—with a wrestler's body to the extreme: thick neck, huge arms and shoulders, a back that angled in a sharp V to a tiny waist and butt and toothpick legs. He had a small bump at the top of his nose and round brown eyes that seemed tough and sexy and sad all at the same time. He wore a varsity jacket, navy blue Levi corduroys, and a thin tightly fitting gold chain with a small Italian horn dangling from it—the same horn worn by all my friends, not to mention just about everyone else at West Berry High. His skin looked slightly tan even though it wasn't, and his cheeks were sunken in from cutting weight, which made his cheekbones stand out. He was beautiful, everyone said. I couldn't believe he was standing here with me.

He peeled his eyes away from the couple making out. "Well, I got practice in a minute," he said. "Want to walk me to the gym?"

I wanted nothing more. I shrugged and slammed my locker. "Okay," I said.

We shuffled silently down the hall, past a water fountain with a sandwich stuffed in it, past dozens of lockers—gray, metal, vented, the same. I thought maybe I should be saying something, but I didn't know what to say. Kids glanced at us curiously. And I thought, Yes. It's Vinnie DiNardio. And me.

We stopped outside the gym doors. He stood facing me a minute, looking into my eyes till I had to look down. The wrestling coach came out, smiled at me, and knuckled Vinnie's arm. "DiNardio, you got five more seconds," he said. He went back inside. Vinnie kicked lightly at my shoes. I watched his sneakers, my palms wet. I tossed my head, trying to do it the way Cassie did.

"Hey, Billie," he said. "Billie. That's a cool name for a girl. How'd you get that?"

"Um—my parents thought I was gonna be a boy. Then they decided to keep the name anyway." He was chewing green apple gum; I could smell it.

"Yeah?" he said. "Well, I'm glad you're not a boy." He took a deep breath, watching me. "Do you like wrestling?"

I nodded. "I just read a book about it. *The World According to Garp*. Do you know it?"

Immediately, I wished I hadn't said it. "Can't say I do," he said.

We were both quiet then. "Do you have any more gum?" I asked.

He laughed. "Whatsamatter? You got bad breath?" He squinted at me. "Or is that for you to know and me to find out? Come here." He dropped his bag of wrestling stuff and put his hands on my arms and pulled me to him. His hands slipped to my hips, and he held me a second. "I like you," he said, "you know that?" And then he kissed me on the mouth, very gently, and I thought I knew then what people meant when they said they melted. I thought I'd slide down and seep right into the tiled green floor, burrow right into the cracks.

Vinnie let go of me. He smiled. He picked up his bag and opened the door to the gym. "Gotta go," he said. "I'll call ya later. Okay?"

I resisted an urge to palm sweat off my forehead. "Okay," I said.

Now, a week later, I pull myself back to our phone conversation. "Why?" he's saying. "What do you consider fun?"

"Um—I guess you'll find out."

"I guess so," he says. "So, like, when?"

"I don't know. You're the one who has wrestling every day."

"Well, you're the one who has the father."

I laugh. "You have a father, too." I pause. "Don't you?"

"Yeah, but mine don't give a shit what I do." He laughs. "Nuh, that's not true. But he lets me go out, anyway."

"Mine does too, on weekends."

"Okay, so what about this weekend? Saturday night. Let's go to the movies."

"Okay," I say.

"Yeah? Okay, good. So what do you want to see? Want to see *Rocky* or something?" He's being so nice, I almost can't believe it.

I hear my father walking around then. I sit up. "Sounds good. You pick. I really should go, though. My father—"

"Okay, okay. I'm gone. Good night, babe. Dream of me." He clicks off.

Before I can hang up, my father knocks once and walks in. "What are you doing?" he says.

I stand and drop the phone in the cradle. "Nothing. I was—"

He reaches for the phone, unplugs the receiver, and puts it on the dresser. "Dammit, Billie! I didn't put that phone in so you could talk on school nights. Did you finish your homework?"

"Yes," I lie, sitting down at my desk.

"Did you learn any SAT words?"

I stare at him. "What do you mean? PSATs are over."

"Right. And SATs are in three months."

I shake my head. "No—it's next fall," I explain. "Senior year. That's when everyone takes it."

"Well, you're not everyone. I let Cassandra wait to take hers, and then she hardly had time to improve her scores. Just plan to take them in March, with the seniors. Then you can take them three times if you have to."

I sit back, amazed. But I force myself not to say anything—not just because I hate fighting with him, but because it's easier to keep quiet and then just do what I want anyway. The opposite of Cassie, who yells and screams at him and then does exactly what he says.

My mother comes in then and stands behind my father, where she looks almost small, almost like a kid. The two of them stare at me. "What?" I say to my mother, sort of snotty, even though she hasn't done anything. Ethan trots in, looks at all of us, and goes out again.

Finally my mother says, "Well, that's crazy, her wanting to stay at school," and I realize she's thinking about my sister, not me. She sounds sad. "What do you think's come over her, Michael?" she says. For a second, despite my anger, I feel sorry for her.

"She's nervous," my father says. "That's all. She's got exams coming up. She'll come home. I'm not worried." He turns around and walks out of the room, I guess to prove it.

I glare after him, then get up from my desk and sit on my bed, furious. My mother looks at my desk chair like she wants to sit but then she doesn't. "Did you know anything about this?" she says. "What did she say in that letter she sent you?"

I'd sent Cassie a postcard I found in our room just after Thanksgiving, a monkey dressed in a miniskirt. Two days ago, I got a short letter back. *Dear Billie*, it said. *Thanks for the card. It actually really cheered me up. Even with all the studying I do, I still fuck up constantly here. It's weird, how you think you're sort of smart in high school, and then later you realize you didn't have a clue. I got back two tests last week. I'll spare you my grades. Let's just say they're beyond pathetic.*

Sometimes I get so scared, thinking this is how it's gonna be from now on—working my butt off all the time, and then screwing up anyway. Then I remind myself this is only temporary, college. But then I wonder. Maybe this is just what life is. It makes me want to close myself off in a room. I have to remember that John Donne quote I've always loved: No man is an island, entire of itself; every man is a piece of the continent, a part of the main; if a clod be washed away by the sea, Europe is the less, as well as if a promontory were, as well as if a manor of thy friends or of thine own were; any man's death diminishes me, because I am involved in mankind; and therefore never send to know for whom the bell tolls; it tolls for thee.

Do you believe I know that thing by heart? Only because we had to memorize it in Flynn's class junior year. Hey—did you get to that yet? Did you have to memorize it, too? Though, knowing you, you probably just wrote it on your hand for the test. Well, maybe you have the right idea. Anyway. See you soon. Love, Cassandra

I had put the letter in my drawer—Cassie sounded so much nicer in it than she does in person—but now, for some reason, I don't want to show it to my mother. So I tell her, "All she talked about was her grades. She's freaked out because she did bad on two tests."

"Bad*ly*," my mother corrects. "What did she get?"

"She didn't say. Probably A-minus or something. She probably thinks Dad will disown her if she gets a B." I glance at the SAT book, filed on the shelf above my desk. I'd thought I wouldn't have to touch that thing again for months—at least until my PSAT scores came back. "That's what happens when you study too hard for SATs," I say, my voice rising. "You end up at the school with the highest suicide rate. I'll tell you one thing, Mom. I'm not going to Corn Hell. If he thinks so, he better pray."

My mother looks out the window, into a starry black night. She doesn't like it when I pit her against my father. "Well," she says, "I'm sure it's not Cornell's fault she's upset. College is hard. It's a big change for her."

I want to tell her about Cassie's roommate leaving, but I don't want to betray my sister either. I wonder if Cassie's told anyone else. I wonder if she has more friends in college than the few casual ones she had in high school. It doesn't sound that way.

I scrape at my nail polish. Lavender chips land on the bed, on the carpet. "Who called before?" my mother says.

I look up. "You heard the phone ring?"

She nods.

"Did Dad?"

"I doubt it. His hearing is awful these days."

"Oh." I shrug. "Well, it was Vinnie. DiNardio. My boyfriend."

"Your boyfriend?" She smiles, then shakes her head.

"What?" I say, smiling too, but I know exactly what she means: Why can't you go out with someone whose last name doesn't end in a vowel? "He's nice," I say. "He's captain of the wrestling team."

"I'm sure he is."

"What? Nice or captain?"

"Both. How old is he?"

"He's a senior. Cassie knows him. I'm going out with him this weekend, to the movies. Saturday night."

She turns to pluck a dead leaf off my spider plant. "Did your father say you could?"

"I didn't ask." I sigh. "God, why wouldn't he?"

She shrugs. My mother doesn't like fights either. "Well, I'd better go finish my lesson plan," she says then. She bends down to kiss me good night—a quick, cool kiss, more business than affection. Then she turns and heads out, dropping the plant leaf in the garbage on the way. "Good night," she says. "See you in the morning."

"Good night. Mom?"

"What?" She pauses in the doorway.

"I'm sure Cassie will come home for Christmas." I'm reassuring myself as much as her.

She stares at me a second. Then she smiles. "Of course she will." She pulls the door closed behind her. "Sleep tight," she says through the crack.

Friday morning, I lie in bed listening to the sounds of our house at seven A.M.: the dogs already barking and whining to be let in, my mother grinding coffee beans, my father's electric razor humming. His radio is turned up so loud, I can hear the full weather report through my closed door. Sunny, high in the forties. I get up and go to my parents' room.

He's shaving at the window, his back to me, peering into a small round mirror perched on the sill, and wearing boxer shorts and an undershirt and black socks. His legs are long and muscular—from his tennis, his swimming—and he has to bend them to see in the mirror. I wonder why he doesn't just put the thing on his dresser, but then I see that it's covered, as always, with the various trinkets Cassie and I made him over the years: an acorn with his initials painted on it, ceramic animal paperweights, a clothespin letter holder with a red felt heart glued to it. He notices me and turns halfway around, still shaving. "Morning," he yells.

From downstairs I smell melting butter, and I know my mother is making scrambled eggs, because it's Friday. Monday and Friday is scrambled, Wednesday we have them over easy, and Tuesday and Thursday we can have cereal if we want. "Morning," I say back.

My father turns off his razor. He goes to his closet and picks out a shirt, holds up two bow ties to me. "Which one?"

I point to the brighter one, not bothering to tell him that no one wears bow ties in December, that hardly anyone wears them anymore at all. He already knows this.

He nods and puts the rejected tie back. "Dad," I say quickly, "I just want to tell you I'm going to the movies tomorrow night, okay? With this guy Vinnie. He's Cassie's friend. Okay? He's a wrestler. The best one on the team." If I ask for permission, he can say no. But if I don't, he can stop me at the last minute and ruin everything. This is halfway between.

My father laughs, which gives me hope. "I'm not impressed," he says. "What movie do you want to see?"

"I don't know. Maybe one of the *Rocky*s or something."

He glances up at me, buttoning his shirt. "One of the *Rocky*s?" he repeats, and he laughs. "Why don't you go see *Casablanca*? It's a wonderful movie. Have you ever seen that? 'Louis, I think this is the beginning of a beautiful friendship.' That's the last line. It's very famous."

I feel the aggravation rise inside me, left over from last night. "No—Dad, we want to see *Rocky*. Vinnie does. And I do."

He puts his hand on his hip. "Where's it playing?"

"I don't know. I think Willowbrook."

He pulls a pair of pants out of his closet, steps into them. "You don't need to go all the way to Willowbrook when there are six good movies right around here. *Casablanca* is at the Greenmont. Right up the street."

I want to kick him. I grind my toe into the carpet, waiting. He sits down on his bed to put on his shoes. His back is to me again, but I see him glance in the little round mirror, and I realize he can see me in it. "Your mother and I are seeing *Casablanca* tonight," he says. "I thought you might want to come with us. Tiffany can come, too, if she wants."

"Michael," my mother calls up, "your eggs are ready."

"I'll come with you tonight if I can go with Vinnie tomorrow," I say. "Okay?"

He finishes tying his shoes. "He has to drive you halfway across the state to see dreck?" He sighs. "Next time, tell him to take you to see something decent, will you?"

Is that a yes? On the radio, the announcer is talking about a bank holdup in northern New Jersey, two people shot. My mother's voice rises up over it. "Michael?"

"Coming," my father yells down. He turns to me. "Does he drive better than he picks movies, this kid?"

"Yes," I say, relieved, though I have no idea how he drives.

"What?" he says.

I turn to leave the room. "Yes!" I yell. "Yes already, Dad!"

Second period, I get a bathroom pass and go look for Tiffany in her algebra class, but she's not there, which makes me mad: she's failing algebra and a couple of other classes because of absences. I think about calling her house, waking her if she's still asleep, telling her to get her butt to school and try harder, like she promised me she would. But one of the two pay phones has a wad of purple gum stuck on the receiver and in the other phone booth some football player has his hand up some cheerleader's shirt, so I go back to class. I haven't seen Vinnie yet either, though that's not unusual; he has study hall first period and gym second with the wrestling coach, which means he doesn't have to come in until third.

Tiff shows up just after fourth period, almost lunchtime. I find her at her locker taking off her coat. Her hair falls in perfect black curls to her shoulders; her lips sparkle like fresh snow tinted pink. She's wearing a royal blue shirt with puffy shoulders, gathered at the waist. It's unbuttoned low enough so her bra shows. I undo one more button on my own shirt. "Nice and early today, huh, Tiff," I say.

She smiles. "Sorry, Bil. I overslept."

"You're an asshole, you know that?" I want her to go to college when I do, maybe even the same one. Sometimes I think this could happen. One in three days, maybe.

Today is one of the other two. "I was so exhausted," she says as I follow her into the bathroom. "I went to sleep at like four in the morning. My father's selling shoes, everyone was over."

"What do you mean, selling shoes?"

She shrugs, digging through her sack of makeup. "He has this friend, he got a deal, all these shoes like half price. So he figured what the hell." She looks at me. "You gotta come see them, you'll love 'em, Bil. They are so sharp."

"Are those them?" I point at hers—rust-colored spike-heeled pumps with tiny leather bows on the back. They look okay on her, though I can't imagine them on me.

She nods. "I got four pair. He said I can have more at the end, if anything's left. Do you love 'em or what? Here, try one on."

She kicks it off, and I shove my foot into it, growing taller. "Nice," I say. "Too high for me, though, maybe."

"Nah," she says, but I'm thinking about her father, how he's always getting "deals" on things. They moved here a few months ago —from Bay Ridge, Brooklyn—to open a deli, Tiffany tells me, but that doesn't seem to be happening. Sometimes he works in the city, leaves early in the morning, and comes back late at night or the next day. I don't know what he does there. I've stopped asking.

"I tried calling you, but the line was busy," Tiffany says. "Why didn't you call me? How's Vinnie?" She finds a compact and brushes on blush, sucking in her cheeks like a fish. On the mirror next to her, things are scrawled in blue felt-tip pen, orange lipstick. *Mike V. has a pencil dick. Get me the fuck out of here.*

"My father," I say, answering the first question, and when she nods, understanding, I say, "Tiff, I think my sister's losing it."

She stops brushing and looks at me, concerned. "What do you

mean?" Tiffany barely knows Cassie, but she has sisters, too. And a brother. Dominick. He's older, and looks like a man—not as old as a father but like someone you'd see in a commercial for aftershave or razor blades.

I tell her about Cassie's call, and she tells me not to worry, she knows she'll come home, she can feel it. I tell her about my plans with Vinnie. "I have to go see *Casablanca* tonight with my parents, though," I say. "Want to come with?"

She closes her blush. "Okay. I heard that movie's great."

"Really?" I'm surprised—both that she thinks the movie will be good and that she wants to come out with my parents.

She doesn't answer; she's penciling black lines on the inside of her eyelids, which makes me wince. But when she's done, I say, "Can I use that?" Her eyes are even rounder and darker now, with thick black rims, long eyelashes.

She hands over a pencil stub labeled *charcoal*. "Hurry up, though. Hawkins killed me last time I was late. Do I look like a whore?" She turns to me, displaying one side of her face.

"Of course."

She laughs. Tiffany has gone all the way with two guys—one when she was fourteen and one when she was fifteen, last year. In Bay Ridge, she says, you can't be sixteen and be a virgin. We're not sure if you can here, though I still am.

"No, really," she says. "Whore?"

"Well—just right there." Her skin is the one thing on her that I wouldn't want on me. She hides it well, though—covers it with makeup, cuts school to lie in the sun, uses a sunlamp.

She rubs one cheek to blend in the cranberry powder. "Now?"

"No, that's good. How do you do this?" I'm trying to put on eyeliner the way she does, but it's coming out blurry, like a caterpillar.

"You have to pull down your eye," she says. "Like this."

She takes the pencil and tries to show me, but I'm laughing too hard. "Forget it," I say. "Show me later."

She waves the pencil away. "Keep it, I got like ten more. I gotta go." She's on her way out.

I smile and drop the pencil in my bag. If I accumulate enough of Tiffany's things, maybe I'll turn into her. "Thanks," I say. "Wait, though. I'm coming." We teeter out together, clomping our heels, laughing.

After dinner I walk up to her house to make sure she'll be ready when my father comes to pick her up. A full moon washes white light over the streets, and I'm glad; normally I'd take a dog with me if I were walking this late at night, even though our neighborhood is pretty safe. I look at each house as I pass it, thinking about the people who live inside: Frankie, the autistic kid who stares red-eyed at the TV all day; the old man who rides his rusty old bike back and forth every afternoon. At Ronnie Beetle's old house the garbage cans have been put out and there's a car in the driveway, and I wonder who moved in after Ronnie and his father and sister moved down to Main Street last year. I think of Ronnie in grade school, spitting constantly, like he couldn't keep saliva in his mouth. His father would beat him if he let his hair grow out even half an inch—milk white hair, so short his pink scalp showed through, like a tint.

I turn the corner onto Tiffany's block, crossing the street to avoid walking too close to Cindy Laker's house. Two years ago, Cindy's brother—a senior in high school—hanged himself in their attic. Cindy was a sophomore at the time, same grade as Cassie, and I remember, about a week after it happened, being in the car with my mother and passing Cindy walking by herself up the street. My mother stopped and backed up and rolled down her window and asked her if she wanted a ride the rest of the way, but Cindy shook her head and stared at us till my mother waved good-bye and pulled away. A few minutes later, at a stoplight, I noticed that my mother's eyes had tears in them. I didn't say anything. By the time we got to Shop Rite, she was fine again.

I walk faster, not wanting to think about Cindy and her brother. The houses are a little closer together now, four to a block instead of three. They're painted normal West Berry colors: gray with white shutters, blue with dark blue, beige with brown. I see Joey DeMao's minibike, glistening silver and black in the floodlight spilling over his driveway. I pass the Walters' house, and then the Skoles', where they put down sod last year and dyed it lime-green when it started to die. My mother thought that was hideous—said she'd rather see a pile of mud than painted grass—but I thought it looked sort of neat. Passing it always made me want to run through it barefoot; it was thick and even, like carpet, no rocks or sticks to cut your feet.

I can see Tiffany's sisters' cars as I approach the Zeferellis' house: two little Datsuns, one red, one white—Michelle's with the sun roof, Bambi's the cassette stereo. Their father brought them home one night just after they moved in, as a surprise. I can just about make out his black El Dorado in the driveway—its windows tinted so dark that Tiffany uses them to put on lipstick—and I wonder why it's outside and not in the garage next to their mother's, its white twin. I look for Dom's motorcycle but don't find it, and I figure he must be down at the Shell station, where he works. First I'm glad—I don't have to be nervous—and then I wish he were here anyway. When he is, I can't stop staring at him.

The Zeferellis' house is cotton-candy pink, which makes it stand out on this block like a Good & Plenty in a pile of grass. I met Tiffany the day they painted it, a couple weeks after they moved in. It was a summer day, just after lunch, and I was running with Mollie, but when I got near their house, I slowed down to stare. Four guys, shirtless and tan and holding pink paintbrushes, were yelling to each other in Italian and dancing on their ladders to disco coming from speakers on the lawn. Tiffany was painting the front door, which was also pink—only the trim was white—and she was dancing too, and singing. She wore a tight blue tube top and high-heeled sandals and the tightest jeans I'd ever seen. Another girl, dressed in terry-cloth shorts and sunglasses and a bikini top, was lying on the lawn in a reclining chair, applying baby oil to her thick tan thighs. Her fingernails were cinnamon, so long and bright I could see them from the street.

Both the girl and her father, who stood on the front lawn drinking a beer, were yelling things up to the guys—"Joey, you missed a spot, honey," or, "Watch the window, Ricky, I don't need a lawsuit now, you know what I'm sayin' to you?"—and a sort of excitement started to build up in me, like I'd stumbled onto something incredibly exciting. But suddenly I got embarrassed, just standing there staring, and I tugged Mollie and started to jog away. And then Tiffany shrieked. I saw her pointing at me—at Mollie, really. She dropped her paintbrush in the grass and ran over, her chest bouncing like potatoes in a sack. "Ooh, I love your dog, hi doggy," she crooned, kissing Mollie's snout. "What's his name?"

I tried not to act too thrilled. "Mollie," I said. "It's a she."

She turned toward her father. "Daddy," she called, "this kind is *exactly* the dog I want. A boxer, right? Oh my god, he is *gaw*geous."

"Thanks," I said. I wanted to return the compliment. "I love the color of your house."

"What, that?" She pointed. "Oh. It was the color of our house in Brooklyn, so we figured what the hell, maybe this way we wouldn't get homesick." She laughed. "We have like a hundred cans of paint or something, my father got them cheap. Help yourself if you want some for your room or whatever."

I pictured my father's face if I brought home pink paint and started slapping it on my walls. I smiled. "Thanks. Is that what your accent is? Brooklyn?"

She nodded. "Bay Ridge. Oh yeah, I'm in New Jerrrsey now. I gotta say my r's." She laughed. "No offense, but Jersey accents are so queah."

"I never knew we had accents."

"What are you, kidding me?" She looked at me. "Hey, you want some Kool-Aid or something?" She glanced at her father. "Or a beer?" she said, lowering her voice. "Come on in—you can bring the dog, my mother would probably love to see it, if she's up yet. What's your name?"

We introduced ourselves. "That's my sister Bambi, the fat pig in the chair," she said, pointing, "and that's my father. And that's Joey, Ricky, Carlo, and . . . Ricky's cousin, I forget his name. They're from Bay Ridge, too. Come on."

Inside, she led me to the kitchen and then to a walk-in pantry. I dropped Mollie's leash and stared. Virtually every inch of shelf space was covered with the sort of food you'd never find in my house:

Fritos and Ring-Dings and Cheez Whiz, Rice-A-Roni, Jiffy Pop, Froot Loops. On the floor were cans of Hawaiian Punch and Tab, and some yellow containers of something. "What's that?" I asked.

"That?" Tiffany pointed. "Oh. It's Nutra-diet. It's this thing, you mix it with water and drink it like six times a day. The more you drink, the more weight you lose." She picked it up. "It's my sister Michelle's. Want some?"

"No thanks. How many sisters do you have?"

"Just three. Well, I mean one's a brother. Dominick's twenty-two, I think. Then Bambi, then Michelle, then me. I'm sixteen. What are you?"

"Same."

She nodded. "Don't worry, I'll drive you to school. You can't get your license here till seventeen, right?"

"Yeah. Do you have yours?"

"Not really, but I know how to drive, so . . . you know. No big deal." She pulled down a box of chocolate-frosted Pop-Tarts, then ripped open the silver packet and broke one in half. "Want one of these? Or something else? Help yourself."

I reached for a jar of peanut-butter-and-jelly-in-one. "Can I have this?"

She shrugged. "Suit yourself." She moved to the refrigerator. I followed her, peering in. It was filled to the brim, mostly with brownish things: a large sausage, a package of cheese dogs, half a chocolate cake. Tiffany pulled out a capless can of Reddi Whip, shook it furiously, and shot a wad into her mouth. "Open," she ordered, and when I opened my mouth, she sprayed some in for me too.

I swallowed, savoring the taste of chemicals and preservatives. My mother wouldn't buy canned whipped cream if it were the last product on earth. A wave of guilt breezed through me. "Do you have any milk?" I said.

Tiffany found a can of Yoo-Hoo. "That's the best I can do," she said, dumping it on the table with her half-eaten Pop-Tart. She went back to the stove. It was covered with pots and pans, still full of food, sauce cooked onto their sides in red and orange streaks. Tiffany stuck her finger in a pot and sucked it clean. "Mmm," she said. "Nyawkies." I had no idea what that meant.

Now, months later, I know, if not what it means then at least what it tastes like. Fantastic. Thick soft little noodle-things covered with tomato sauce. I know now what "govadells" taste like, too, and "pasta vazool"—though I still have no idea what they're made of, or what's inside them.

I glance at my watch and then hurry a little, approaching the Zeferellis' door. I can smell cooking, tomato sauce heavy with parmesan cheese. "Gravy," they call it, though to me gravy was always steak juice or something brown you pour over meat loaf or pot roast. I ring the bell, and then, knowing they won't answer it, I open the letter slot and yell, "Tiffany!"

I hear her mother's voice. "Someone's at the door. Michelle, get the door, would you?"

"Ma, we're sleeping, Ma. Let Tiffany get it."

I wait. Nobody comes. I open the slot again and peer in at deep red carpeting. On the wall I can see the picture of Jesus they've hung, even though the only time any of them ever goes to church is on Ash Wednesday. He's on the cross in the picture, two drops of blood oozing out of his chest, and I wonder—not for the first time—why people always display pictures of him suffering. Once I actually asked Tiffany. "Don't you want to remember him in happier times?" She shrugged and laughed. "Beats the fuck out of me."

I ring the doorbell again; it chimes eight times. I can hear a television in the background: "Only six more of these beauties left, genuine opal rings, get 'em while you can. . . ." One of Tiffany's sisters appears in the upstairs window. "Billie! Oh my god, she didn't let you in yet? Wait a minute." She disappears. I hear her yell, "Tiffany, ya retard, Billie's here!" and then she's back again, and I can see it's Michelle. "Sorry, honey," she says. "I'd let you in myself, honey, but I'm not dressed. See?" She presses a huge bra-covered breast to the window and laughs.

I smile and look away, straight at the door. Her sisters are always doing things like this to me. I can't tell if this is just how they act or if they play it up when I'm around because they know it embarrasses me. And even though it does, I still envy them—their boldness. This is where Tiffany got some of hers, I think.

The door opens. Tiffany grabs my arm and pulls me in. "Sorry. I was downstairs with the shoes. You gotta come see this."

She drags me through the kitchen. Her grandfather is sitting at his usual spot at the table, drinking red wine. I wave to him. He waves back with his glass, sloshing wine over the edge. He looks at the splash on the table, then back at me, and we both smile. I like the old man. Sometimes Tiffany and her sisters complain about him behind his back—that he smells, or that all he does is sit around drinking wine. And I think, So what? He doesn't criticize, he doesn't complain, he hardly even speaks, at least not in English.

Mrs. Zeferelli is standing at the stove, dressed in a bloodred bathrobe and high-heeled sandals. Her hair is freshly dyed, gold as butter. "Hi, honey," she says to me. She's sipping from a glass with an olive in it. In front of her, tennis ball–sized meatballs crackle in oil in a pan.

She puts down her drink, forks a meatball out, and places it on a paper towel. From behind her, Tiffany grabs the meatball with two fingers and runs toward the basement, blowing on it.

"Tiffany!" she yells "What am I, a shade darker, slaving away over here? And there's hardly enough meatballs as it is, between the old man and everyone carting all their friends here to eat." She looks at me. "I don't mean you, Billie, you know you're welcome." But I know she's saying that because she has to. And I know I'm the only Jewish person that comes here—practically the only non-Italian—and I'm here a lot: using their pool table, watching TV, eating meatballs that are really for them.

But when Tiffany offers me a hunk of one, pulling me into the basement stairwell, I take it and scarf it, even though I've already eaten and she hasn't. I swallow fast when I see the shoes, though. Hundreds of white boxes, spread out all over the room: extending in stacks five or six high from the back wall to the pool table, around to the pile of clothes spilling off the washing machine. Michelle's boyfriend Ricky is stepping around them to get at the pool table. He's playing with another guy, someone I don't recognize.

They stop and look up when they hear us. The other guy picks up a beer from the bumper and sips, looking at me. "Spiffy Tiffy and Billie babe," Ricky says, glancing at his friend. A cigarette dangles from his lips.

In the back corner, Bambi's friend Laurie, who's Ricky's cousin, parades in circles in mustard-yellow pumps. Her hair is teased about five inches and cemented in place with hair spray. "What about these, Rick?" she says.

Ricky peers over. "Well, they don't exactly move me to tears or nothing."

"Oh, shut *up,* Ricky." Laurie turns to us instead.

"They're gorgeous, Laur," Tiffany says. "Unreal."

The shoes have the highest heels I've ever seen. Like walking on icicles. "They're great," I lie.

Laurie smiles. "Shit, now I've gotta take these, too. That's four pair. There goes my friggen paycheck."

Tiffany's putting on black and purple platform sandals. "Go ahead, try on whatever you want," she tells me. I remind myself that these are what people are wearing in the hottest clubs, and that they must be fantastic if the Zeferellis wear them. I open a few boxes, trying to find a pair I can see myself in. "Where'd your father get all these?" I ask Tiffany.

"I don't know, his friend has a shoe store, I think. Hey Ricky, pool hog, when do we get to play?"

Ricky's leaning over the table, aiming. I watch the tattoo on his bicep: Betty Boop, but with blond hair, red lips, cleavage. She dances as he shoots. The three-ball smacks in. He straightens up, cigarette still dangling. "Is there a mouse squeaking in here?" he says. "Man, I coulda swore I heard a peep—"

"Shut up, Ricky," Tiffany says, laughing. She whips a shoe at him. He ducks, and the shoe smacks the wall behind him.

The door upstairs opens, and Mr. Zeferelli fills the doorway, wearing a T-shirt and slippers and sweatpants. "Hiya, honey," he says to me, beaming. "You like the shoes? Tiffany, did you help Billie find something? Maybe the blue ones? They'd look real sharp on her."

Tiffany glances at me. "I don't know, Dad, most of them aren't really Billie's style."

"No—" I protest, but her father says, "Honey, let *her* decide, will you? Maybe she'll see something she likes. Come on up, kids, any minute we're gonna get started eating up here." He disappears.

I know what will happen if I asked my mother for money to buy a pair of these shoes; it makes my heart heavy to think about it. She'll ask me why Mr. Zeferelli is selling them, and what, exactly, it is that he *does*. But I know, too, that I should buy a pair; if I don't, it'll only confirm their theory that my family is cheap. They know my father's a surgeon, that my grandmother belongs to a country club. They know I can afford a pair of their shoes. I think of the time, before they knew I was Jewish, when Michelle called someone a cheap Jew in front of me. I laughed along with them, trying to cover it up, but later, when I came back from the bathroom—Tiffany told her while I was gone—Michelle apologized like crazy to me. She was only kidding, she said. She actually *liked* Jewish people, she had a good friend in Bay Ridge who was one. I told Michelle forget it, don't worry about it, I don't care, and I wished Tiffany hadn't said anything. The apologizing was always much worse than anything people said—not just because I didn't believe it, but because then I knew that in the future they'd have to be careful what they said around me.

Ricky pushes by us and goes upstairs, his friend close behind him. When they're gone, Tiffany says, "Don't worry, you don't have to buy any of the shoes if you don't have the money or whatever."

"I know," I say, but I'm glad she said that. I glance around for a clock. "Tiff, are you almost ready? I told my father we'd be outside waiting at eight forty-five. What time is it?"

"I don't know. Come on, let's go up."

The clock in the kitchen says 2:15, so Tiffany goes off to call Dial-the-Time. At the table, Mr. Zeferelli is dishing out spaghetti and passing around the plates. Meatballs are piled high in a huge bowl in the middle of the table. Michelle forks one onto her plate. She's wearing a pink silk bathrobe with silver trim and hot rollers in her hair, even though Ricky's sitting right there. The grandfather is

there, too, and Mrs. Zeferelli and Laurie. And Dominick. I stare at
him, my palms suddenly clammy. I haven't seen him in weeks, except when my mother drives by the Shell where he works. I don't let
her go in, of course; I'd rather die than have him fill our car with gas
while we sit there. Instead, I study him secretly as we pass by, if he's
outside. He'll be pumping gas, or leaning into someone's car, his
hands propped on the roof—explaining something, maybe, or staring
off into who knows where. He never looks at you, Dom—not for
more than a second. And he's the only Zeferelli who's serious all the
time. Maybe because he's the oldest, like Cassie.

The second time I ever saw him—before I could stop her—
Tiffany asked him if he could drop me at home, since he was leaving
just as I was. He shrugged, then said, "Sure," and went and got me a
helmet. He kick-started his motorcycle. I was dying of nervousness; I
couldn't believe I was actually supposed to touch him. I got on the
bike, trying desperately not to shake it. Tiffany laughed. "You look
like a bug," she said, and then, "Grab him, you gotta hold on, fool,
unless you want to fall off." I touched the shoulder of his jacket. He
reached back and took my hands and wrapped them hard around his
waist. And then he took off, and for three blocks I got to hold him
like that, to breathe in the smell of him: clean clothes and clean skin,
leather jacket, a hint of gasoline.

Since then he'll say hello to me if he's around, and once he
offered me a cigarette before he lit up. He waves now—just once,
quickly, and probably because I'm still staring, but my insides start to
churn anyway. He has dark-brown hair, sort of long, and his skin is
the color of caramel, smooth as a girl's. But what I'm looking at are
his eyes: they're amber, almost orange. He's looking behind me, at
the doorway, it seems—or maybe he's just thinking about all the stuff
he has to do, between school and work and everything else. I wave to
him fast and then act interested in Tiffany, embarrassed to be just
standing there. She's peering in the fridge. She takes out a bottle of
orange soda, throws her head back, and swigs.

Mr. Zeferelli has finished serving. He winds pasta around his
fork and takes a dainty bite. "Oh my god, can this woman make
gravy," he says, kissing fingers. "I mean, when she cooks, she

cooks. . . ." He looks at the grandfather. "Daddy, there's your plate, go on! Billie, Tiffy, pull up a chair. Where's Michelle?"

Tiffany's done swigging soda. She wipes her mouth with the back of her hand. "Bambi's not eating, Dad, she's on Nutra-diet. And I'm going to the movies."

"The movies! Well, good. More food for us, then." He winks at me, then smiles at his wife. "Oh, *ho*-ney," he croons. "You have outdone yourself once again. . . ."

I love watching him—the way he talks, the things he says. Sometimes I think he's the nicest man I've ever met. Michelle's talking, too, telling about her friend who ran over her father's foot when she backed out of her garage. "She was putting on her mascara in the rearview," she says. "Can you fathom it?" She laughs, a long hoarse laugh from deep in her chest. A cigarette laugh. Ricky shakes his head, and I wonder if that laugh is part of what he sees in her. "Jesus Mary," he says. Mrs. Zeferelli is shrieking with laughter, a fresh martini at her place. I want to sit down with them, watch Dom eat spaghetti, have Mr. Zeferelli hand me a plate—but there are no more chairs, there's no place to sit anyway.

A horn honks outside. Tiffany glances at me, her eyes widening. "Oh my god, your father! I just gotta get my bag, it's upstairs, Billie, my coat's in the family room, I think . . ."

I'm nervous now, a different kind of nervous than I am around Dominick. My father hates to be late for movies. He hates waiting for anyone, especially me. I run to the front door and flip the light three times, so they'll know we're coming. Then I run to the family room. The door's half-closed, and I burst through it, not bothering to turn on the light, and get halfway to the couch before I realize someone's lying on it. Two people, in fact, buried under a blanket. I stop short. "Oops—sorry," I say, turning around.

Bambi laughs. "No no, honey, it's okay. Come in. What do you need?"

"Sorry," I say again, not looking at her, heat seeping into my face. "I just need Tiffany's coat." I glance around frantically. On the table is a full ashtray, a mug of gray coffee, a bag of Doritos. The place smells like cigarettes and something both fresh and slightly sour. Maybe sex.

"Try over there," Bambi says, and she reaches out with a satin-bathrobed arm and points to a pile of clothes on the floor. I dig through the pile, searching for Tiffany's coat. "This place is such a mess," Bambi says, "you must think we're such pigs—ow! Tito, that's my *tit* you're grabbing!"

"Aw!" a man croons. "Am I hurting your titty? Poor thing."

I want to die. I dig harder—an electric blanket, a scarf, two other coats—and then, finally, Tiffany's jacket. I grab it and bolt out of there.

In the hallway, I stand for a second panting, the fake-rabbit coat dangling from my hand. From outside, my father's horn sounds again —loud and long this time, like a foghorn. "Tiffany!" I yell, and I run for the front door just as she clomps down the stairs.

"Okay, okay, okay," she says. "Sorry, Bil. Here I come, here I am."

As we run from Tiffany's house to my father's car, the night is cold and star-filled and velvet black, and I want to stay in this halfway point, hide in the dark, never get to the car. But my mother is out and walking toward us, calling, "Hurry up, girls!" I turn to Tiffany. "Shit," I say. "Get ready."

We slide in, to classical music and my father's fury. "Jesus H. Christ, Billie! What the hell were you doing? You said you'd be outside waiting!" The car lurches forward.

"Sorry," I say, drowning in violins, oboes, French horns. And humiliation. Tiffany's father never yells at her.

My apology makes him madder. "Don't *be* sorry! Be on time, dammit!" Our car speeds down the street.

My mother turns around. "Hi, Tiffany," she says a little too quickly. "I haven't seen you in a while. How are you?"

"All right," Tiff says. "How are you?" Her thigh tightens on the seat next to mine. The only time she's ever nervous is around my parents.

"Fine thanks," my mother says. "And how's school? Do you like West Berry?"

Tiff shrugs. "It's all right, I guess."

"Different, I'll bet," says my mother. I can't tell if she's prying or being polite or talking so my father won't yell—maybe some of each. Whatever it is, I wish she'd turn back around.

"Have you started studying for your SATs yet?" she asks, and then I'm pretty sure she is prying, trying to find out if Tiffany plans to take the test.

Tiffany senses it, too. She picks up on stuff like that; she knows how to read people. She knows what they like, too. And I'm learning from her. I laugh now when boys joke, even if it's not funny. I laugh at myself if I can. Guys like girls who laugh.

Tiffany's struggling for an answer for my mother, so I answer for her. "She doesn't need to study. Her vocabulary's ten times better than mine." It's true; she comes up with words that amaze me sometimes: *bizarre, utilize, indispensable, imbibe.* "Mom, can we please talk about something else?" I say then. "SATs make me nauseous."

"Nause*ated,*" says my mother.

I turn to Tiffany to roll my eyes but she's picking at a nail and not looking at me, and I want to smack myself for inviting her along, for ever letting her and my parents be together in the same place. Two elements that don't mix, never have, never will. And me in the middle, trying to make everything okay.

My father is making an illegal left turn. My mother looks at him, frowning, but doesn't say anything. She turns back to Tiffany. My chest tightens. Leave us alone, already, I'm thinking.

"And how's your mother's job in New York?" my mother asks. "Does she like it?"

This question wouldn't be bad if Tiffany's mother hadn't been fired already, for showing up late so many days. I widen my eyes at Tiffany—our signal to lie. She leans forward. "She doesn't work there anymore," she says. "It was exhausting her to commute into the city every day, so her and my father decided it wasn't worth the money."

"*She* and my father," my mother says.

I am horrified. "Mom, that is so *rude!*" I yell. "God, who cares how she says it, if you know what she means?"

"All right," my father warns. "*We* care, that's who. Jesus! Learn to drive, spastic!" He blares his horn and swerves sharply around the car on his right.

I cup my hand in front of my face and give my father the middle finger behind it. I hold it until I'm sure Tiffany sees. She smiles a little—just a split-second, but at least it's something.

And then my father's pulling around a barrier and onto the new highway that's not open yet. Smooth black pavement, no white lines, no other cars. Rules are made to be kept, unless he's the one breaking them.

"Michael!" my mother says, but he laughs. He speeds up to seventy, then seventy-five. His old BMW does it easily; it's not a great-looking car, but it is fast.

"Oh my god, I can't believe we're on here," Tiffany says, impressed.

My father laughs again. "Want to do a hundred?"

"Sure," Tiff says, and he cruises to ninety. We fly through the night, no cars in sight, blasted-out rock on both sides of us.

Tiffany shrieks when he hits one hundred. And then everything's okay again. He's happy because he's back in control, she's happy because it's fun, I'm happy because nobody's mad. My mother's the only one not loving all this, I think. But she's not about to say anything.

When we get there—on time, since he's made up for some minutes on the way—he tells us to get out and get on line while he parks. "Look young," he says. He wants to get us in for under fourteen. I'm way too tall and Tiffany looks about twenty-three in her makeup, but we do it anyway—bend our knees, and she covers her chest—and the cashier doesn't say anything when my father buys the tickets. I'm sure she knows, though. I avoid her eyes on the way in, hoping she doesn't go to West Berry High.

My father picks a seat, front and center, and we follow him like a line of ducks. The place isn't packed, and the crowd is quiet. I don't see anyone I know. I settle in.

Halfway through the movie, though, someone lights a cigarette
—as always. And as always—even though the kid's rows away from us
—my father stands up and yells out, "There's no smoking in here."

Tiffany nudges me, her eyes wide on the screen. I nudge her
back, like, don't worry, he always does this. But I pray the person
will just put the cigarette out, and my heart's beating fast.

Instead, the kid takes another drag—a black kid, I see now,
about my age.

"Put out that cigarette," my father yells. A couple of people
turn around. Tiffany and I sink lower in our seats.

"Oh, fuck you, man," the smoker calls back, and I think, This
is it, this is the time he gets his ass kicked. I look around for a cop,
just in case. But the cigarette goes out, and the kid doesn't light up
again, thank god.

After the movie my father takes us for ice cream, to a little place
up a big hill in North Berry where my parents used to go when they
were dating. "Get whatever you want," he says, and I know it's his
way of apologizing to Tiffany, and to me, for yelling at us before. He
never stays mad too long, maybe because his life moves too fast. I'm
still mad, though. It takes me longer.

My mother is nice now, no more bogus questions. She orders
her usual, a vanilla fudge cone. My father gets a coffee scoop with
hot fudge. Tiffany orders a banana split—after I say I'll share it—and
I'm glad; I want my parents to have to pay for something expensive
for her.

On the way home my father jokes with her about her lip-gloss,
a glass vial of pink gel that, when she rolls it on, sends the smell of
strawberries wafting through the car. "Do you wear that or eat it?"
he says, pulling up to her house.

"Wear," she says. "Want some?"

"No thanks." He laughs, then turns around to see her. "Next
time be a little more prompt, would you please?"

She nods. "Okay. Thanks for the movie."

"Did you like it?" he asks.

"It was interesting."

He laughs again. "Good. Next time I'll take you to see *Gone With the Wind.*"

"Wait—wait." She thinks a second. "Scarlett O'Hara, right?"

"*Very* good," he says, clearly impressed, and I could almost hug her right there.

She nods coolly. "I'll call ya tomorrow, Bil."

She slams her door then and shakes her butt walking inside. And I'm filled with relief. It's okay for me to hate my parents, but I can't stand thinking Tiffany does.

chapter three

Saturday morning I wake up after ten, and I lie in bed wondering why my father didn't wake me, remembering my date tonight with Vinnie. I can hear the shower going, and the dogs' collars jangling. And then my parents' phone rings.

I'm not ready to get up yet. I let it ring again, and then a third time. Then, feeling guilty, I jump out of bed and run to get it, but my parents' door is closed. I run downstairs to the den.

By the time I get there the machine has answered. "This is Mary Joyce Goodman, the director of Cassandra's dorm at Cornell," a woman's voice says. "I need to speak to Dr. or Mrs. Weinstein about Cassandra. We have a little problem—no emergency, but there are a few things I think you should know about. If you could call me back as soon as possible—"

I grab the phone. "Hello—sorry. This is Billie, Cassie's sister."

"Oh! Hello. Do you expect your parents in soon?"

"My mother's just in the shower. I can get her out—"

"No no, that's okay. Can you ask her to call me when she gets a chance? The number is—"

"Is my sister okay?"

The woman pauses. Something tightens inside me. "She's fine," she says then. "She's—"

"Because I knew, I mean I thought over Thanksgiving something might be wrong with her. She wouldn't eat, you know, and she gave away all her clothes—"

"Sorry. She did what?"

I know I probably shouldn't be telling her these things. But I can't stand this person knowing things about my sister that I don't, and I figure she'll trade information with me.

So I tell her how Cassie called me crying that night, how she went out in her slippers in the cold. At the end I say, "Is her roommate still gone? Does she have anorexia or something?"

She hesitates a second. "She's probably just a little overwhelmed. But I really should talk to your parents about this—"

"Okay, wait, hold on." I put down the phone before she can refuse, and I run up to get my mother.

She comes to the phone with a towel wrapped around her, her hair dripping wet. "Uh-huh," she says. "She did—uh-huh." She sits down on the bed and turns slightly away from me. Her hair drips onto her shoulders and arm—little streams of water, like tears.

After a minute she reaches into the wastebasket, pulls out an envelope, and writes something on it. I strain to see. A phone number, some notes in script I can't read. I slide down on the floor in front of her, waiting. She looks without seeing me.

"I'll tell my husband," she says finally. "We'll call you back this afternoon." She hangs up the phone.

I jump up. "What did she say, Mom? Tell me."

She looks at me curiously, then touches her hair lightly, as if it hurts. "Cassandra's roommate left school," she says. "She had some sort of breakdown. Did you know that?"

I don't know what to say. I've never lied well to my mother.

"Did you?" she insists.

I nod, and her eyebrows flicker. "Why didn't you tell us? Why didn't Cassie?"

"I think she thought she'd come back. She didn't want to worry you, I guess."

She takes a quick breath. "When did she tell you?"

"Right after. That night she called. Mom, what's wrong with her?"

She stares at me a second. Then she sighs, like she's trying to dismiss the whole thing. "Apparently some girls on her hall are worried about her. She doesn't go to very many meals, and she's lost some weight, I guess. She spends a lot of time in her room alone. Sometimes—sometimes when they knock on the door, she won't answer."

"Maybe she's just being a snot," I say hopefully, but I remember that night on the phone, how she'd freaked out when someone knocked on her door.

"She wrote an essay that upset one of her professors," says my mother. "It had apocalyptic overtones."

"Maybe it's just some weird intellectual thing, then. She's always been weird like that."

My mother cocks her head. "The teacher gave her an A, then suggested she talk to someone at the health center. She won't go, though. She says nothing's wrong with her." She pauses. "This Miss Goodman, her dorm director, wants us to think about taking Cassie home now. So she has an extra week for Christmas break. She says she can get take-home exams if she talks to her professors, and classes end this week anyway."

"She won't come." I'm about to remind her Cassie didn't want to come home at all, but I stop myself.

"I'd better call Daddy," my mother says. She reaches for the phone, then stops. "No. He said he'd be home early for lunch. I'll just wait." She dresses quickly—wool slacks, a turtleneck, a sweater —then goes downstairs.

I take a slow shower, dry my hair, put on jeans and a V-necked T-shirt, a sweatshirt jacket over it, and a pair of spike-heeled, fur-lined blue suede clogs. Then I go downstairs, too.

When my mother is nervous, she's like a windup toy: she starts doing things and doesn't stop. When I get to the kitchen, she's cleaning cabinets, unloading the dishwasher, straightening things. "I'll make you breakfast," she says to me. "Brunch, really, at this hour. Want scrambled eggs? Cinnamon-raisin bagel? Corn toaster cakes?"

I place my order. Within minutes it's on the table in front of me, yellow and steaming. "Honey?" she asks. I nod, and she brings over the plastic honey bear, then watches to make sure I'm eating. "Do you need a ride to the library?" she asks. She knows I have to write a speech for speech class. I've been putting it off all week.

But I shake my head. "I'm not going anywhere until I find out what's wrong with Cassie."

My mother frowns. Then she goes to the refrigerator and takes out a brown paper bag. Inside are four tomatoes, big and red; she gets ripe fruit and vegetables year round from an expensive fruit store in North Berry. She washes the tomatoes, dries them, slices them into thick slices, arranges them on a sky-blue plate. She adds vinegar and oil, garlic salt, fresh parsley. She puts it all in the fridge. The whole thing takes about a minute.

I stand up to bring my empty dish to the dishwasher, but my mother grabs it before I pick it up. She whisks it to the sink and washes it. Then she sponges off the table and resets it with three places, even though I just ate.

I sit back down. For some reason, I don't want to leave my mother; something about watching her comforts me. She's making macaroni and cheese now. She heats up butter and flour, adds milk and hunks of cheddar cheese she got at the cheese shop. She stirs it with a wire whisk, the muscles flexing in her forearm. Her hair is almost dry. It dries with a nice little wave, like lasagna—unlike mine, which is thick and stick-straight.

She lowers the flame to a flicker and glances around the room, like a kid looking for something to do. The dogs lie like logs at her feet—not fighting today. She gets two dog biscuits out of the pantry and feeds one to each of them, patting their heads.

"Mom," I say. "Why don't you sit down with me a minute?"

She nods once, like she might, but instead goes back to the fridge and takes out a bag of carrots. She peels one and slices it into small neat sticks. Then she does another. Then a third. Carrots pile up, flowing off her cutting board. Orange all over the place. "Mom," I say.

"Hm?" She's still cutting. The knife flies through the air.

"That's enough carrots, don't you think?"

"What? Ow!" She drops the knife and brings her finger to her mouth.

I stand up quickly. "Did you cut yourself?"

She shakes her head, sucking her finger. "It's nothing." She takes her finger out of her mouth and looks at it. A drop of blood falls onto the carrots.

"Mom, god! Put it under water." She moves to the sink. "What are you cutting so many carrots for anyway?" I'm yelling at her, even though I don't mean to. "Let me see it!"

She holds her finger under water. Red runs into the stream. "God! I'll go get a Band-Aid," I say.

"No—I'm fine." But she'd say that if she were dying. I run upstairs for a Band-Aid and peroxide. When I come down, she's holding a paper towel over her cut. "It's not even bleeding anymore," she says, then mumbles, "That was stupid of me, just stupid." She sounds like Cassie.

"Be quiet. Press hard." I put the Band-Aid on for her, forgetting to use peroxide.

The garage door rumbles open then, vibrating the house. "Good," I say. My mother sticks the peroxide in a cabinet. She piles the carrots on a plate quickly. "Put these on the table," she says, handing them to me.

I can hear my father's car radio from all the way up here, tuned to the news. At a commercial, he'll bound upstairs and burst in here and turn on this radio, so he doesn't miss anything.

My mother starts to flag him as he comes through the door. Then she changes her mind. She lets him pick up the mail and flip through a few letters. The dogs leap all over him. He bats them around a little, talking to them. Then he feeds them each a dog biscuit, too, making them sit and lie down and shake his hand.

"Michael," my mother says finally. "Cassie's dorm director called."

He rips a letter open. "What?" he says over the radio.

"And Mom cut her finger," I say.

He looks up.

"I nicked it, it's nothing," she says.

He puts down the mail. "Let me see."

"I have a Band-Aid on it," she says. "It's fine."

He examines her finger around the Band-Aid. A spot of blood shows through the gauze, but otherwise it looks okay now. "Did you wash it out first?" he says, and when she nods, "Jesus, Jane! Would you be careful, please? What were you cutting?"

"Nothing. Carrots. Michael, Cassie's dorm director called. She's worried about Cassie."

She tells him all about it. I hover over them, waiting for my father to seem upset. But he doesn't, even when she mentions Cassie's roommate leaving. "That's not so strange," he says. "Lots of kids leave freshman year."

"She's skipping meals, though," my mother says.

He thinks a second. "Maybe she doesn't like the food. I couldn't stand it either." He laughs.

My mother shakes her head. "I don't know, Michael. I'm worried." But she looks less worried than before he came in, and I feel the same way. Relieved. Like if he's not worried, there must not be anything to worry about.

"Aren't you gonna call her back?" I say. "She said to call back, right, Mom?"

"I'll call her back," he says. "But I'll eat my lunch first, if you don't mind. I have to be back at the hospital in half an hour. What are you doing today, Billie?"

"Going to the library," I mumble. My mother hands him macaroni and cheese. She brings out the tomato salad, all red and pretty on the plate. Somehow the sight of it makes me sad. She serves him some, and I sit down and watch him eat.

When he's finished, he tells her, "Good lunch, Fly." Then he leaves his dishes and goes upstairs.

My mother clears his place, and the two of us wait in the kitchen, trying to hear if he's calling Cornell. Minutes later he's back in the doorway. "I don't know," he says, as if he does. "This lady Goodman sounds like a bit of an alarmist." He folds his arms across his chest. "She's doing fine in all her courses and says she feels fine, so I don't see the problem. Her professor said her essay was great." He laughs.

My mother shakes her head. "Well, I don't like her living alone, without a roommate. And skipping meals. I think we should just go up and get her."

My father clears his throat. "I'm not gonna drop everything and rush up there just because of some paranoid dorm director," he says loudly. "She's not sick. She's a little nervous, that's all. She's always been a high-strung kid." He turns and walks away from us, down the hall, toward the stairs.

My mother watches him go. She unties her apron, not looking at me. I stand up. "Mom?"

She hangs up the apron and turns to me. "What, Billie?"

"*Tell* him if you're pissed! Don't give in." I don't know why I'm saying this; normally I'd stay out of it, just go open a book or go to Tiffany's.

My mother regards me a second. Then she turns and picks up a sponge and begins to wipe the counter very fast.

"Then *I'll* tell him!" I yell. "Okay?"

My mother keeps wiping. Her Band-Aid flashes back and forth.

I turn to go upstairs. But my father's coming back. He reaches the kitchen doorway and stands there once more, looking at my mother. Then he says, much more quietly, "I'll call her this afternoon. If she asks me to come get her, I'll go get her. Okay?"

My mother finishes wiping the counter. She looks at me then at him, and I wonder if she thinks she's won. Has she? "Okay," she says.

My father drops me at the library on his way back to the hospital, after promising my mother he'll call home as soon as he talks to Cassie. "What time, do you think?" I ask, getting out of the car, shivering in my sweatshirt jacket.

My father tells me not to worry about it, to concentrate on my work. He thinks I'm staying here till three or so and then calling home and hanging up after one ring, to signal my mother to pick me up—so I don't spend the dime. What I plan to do is call every hour to see if my mother's heard from him about Cassie yet. Inside the library, I check the pay phone to make sure it works. I'm tempted to call Tiffany, but I don't let myself. She'll probably be asleep anyway, and I want to get this speech done so I can stop thinking about it already.

I head toward the shelves, then browse them, looking for something I can demonstrate to the class—"something that interests you," the teacher said, though I'd rather do something that makes people laugh. On the magazine rack, *Cosmopolitan* is displayed; a brassy-haired woman leers through bronze pillow lips—the kind of lips that leave prints on mugs, people's cheeks, cigarettes. She wears a sheer white shirt over a skimpy gold bra. Skimpy on her chest, anyway. I pick up the issue and flip through it, stopping at an article titled "Big-breasted women: Why we love/hate our chests." At the end is a box of tips on how to enhance your own breasts.

I read a few. "Wear a wire-rimmed bra for a more pronounced shape." "Do push-ups three times a day." "Tape your breasts together with masking tape, for cleavage." I imagine Vinnie reaching into my shirt at the movies and peeling off masking tape, and I smile. But then I wonder if Vinnie likes big breasts, much bigger than mine —if he's secretly a breast man, just killing time with me until someone bigger comes along. Tiffany's boyfriend in Brooklyn was a breast man. He told her that the day they met. Luckily, she qualified.

I glance around, then read on. "Before sex, sneak away and rub blusher into your nipples." "Run cold water over your breasts before getting dressed, to make them perky and alert." I picture breasts with little smiley faces, bouncing like cheerleaders. I picture myself standing in front of the class rubbing blush onto my naked chest. I close the magazine and put it back. Then I tiptoe to the card catalogue, trying not to let my heels clomp, and look up anorexia.

There are a bunch of books listed. Back at the shelves, I pick one out—*Starving to Death*—and slide onto the floor with it.

Some of it is stuff I already know, maybe from things they've told us in health class: that a lot more women than men get it, that victims are often overachievers. "Anorexics tend to be introverted, emotionally reserved, perfectionistic, self-deprecating, and socially insecure," it says. "They seek approval from others and tend to have a compulsive personality. As the disease progresses, they may experience hair loss, sleepiness, pallor, gastrointestinal distress, depression, and anxiety. They may have a lack of energy and feel apathy and a decrease in sexual interest." One researcher, it says, found that five to fifteen percent of patients hospitalized for anorexia die in treatment, giving it "the highest fatality rate of any mental illness." Another researcher found that up to nineteen percent die. I flip the page and skim paragraphs, stopping at one. "The family of an anorexic, like the anorexic herself, may deny that a problem exists, the former for the very reasons that lead to the disorder in the first place: an emphasis on the external, on success and achievement and maintaining a 'perfect' appearance." This is news to me. I reread it, then turn the page again. There's a before-and-after shot of a girl who died at age fifteen, weighing sixty-nine pounds.

I close the book quickly. Then I open it again and stare at the picture for about five minutes straight. I remind myself that my sister is far from emotionally reserved or introverted—though she's not exactly social either. I think about the fights she had last year with my father, the fights they always have, the screaming and yelling. My sister would say anything to my father. Then she'd feel bad afterward, sad and guilty.

I put the book back on the shelf. There's no way Cassie has anorexia. She's nothing like the people in this book. Why am I even reading this stuff? I go into the children's room to get away from it.

I check out the tiny tables and chairs, the construction-paper wall art, the corner of toys. In the center of the room is a display of the most popular children's books of all time, and I'm surprised at how many of them I know: *Green Eggs & Ham, Madeline, In the Night Kitchen.* When we were young, my mother read us a story every night. My father would come in at the end and tell us jokes or read us poems. I think of how Cassie and I were the only kids who could recite "Casey at the Bat." I still can.

Then I think about how, just when you start to get some freedom in your life, everything gets so much more complicated; just when you're finally allowed to have a little fun, you get bogged down in all kinds of things. Schoolwork, SATs, college. Sometimes the more I know, the harder it is to have a good time. "Ignorance is bliss," Tiffany says when she doesn't feel like learning something, and I wonder if that's true. Maybe what's happening to Cassie is that she's learning too much, she knows too many things. Depressing things about the world. I don't want to know them. I want to keep that from happening to me.

I pull out a copy of *The Bears' Picnic* and take it to a miniature table, to read as soon as I think of an idea for my speech. The room is pretty empty for a Saturday. A few kids are reading books here and there; a toddler in a star-scattered hat wobbles around like a hard-boiled egg with legs. His mother trails after him. He shrieks for a cookie, his shrill scream breaking the quiet, and his mother hands it to him fast and glances around. I think of the power little kids have just because they have no shame, and I envy them in a way.

But I'm avoiding work, as usual. I write down *Interests/Talents* on my pad. First I list *Music,* since I had tons of lessons as a kid: guitar, piano, trombone, tenor sax. We had swimming lessons, too, and gymnastics and ice skating. Since I wouldn't be caught dead demonstrating any of those things, I move on to interest number two. *Pool,* as in Tiffany's pool table. But of course I can't demonstrate that. I put *Astrology* for three, since Tiffany's aunt from Brooklyn read my chart last month. She said I'd live a rich and varied life and travel far away, but eventually return to live near home with several exotic pets and two kids.

The "after" picture of the anorexic flashes in my mind. Tonight, I will call my sister and try to talk some sense into her—but I'm supposed to see Vinnie tonight. For some reason I don't want to now. The thought of it makes me nervous.

I glance down at my list and add Vinnie's name to it, trying to psych myself into the date. And it works, a little, just the idea of him, and his name: Vinnie DiNardio. Even Tiffany would love to go out with him. I write his name again, in block letters. Then I write it on the table. I erase it before the librarian sees, then scribble it all over the page.

Through the glass wall into the adult room, I can see a guy and a girl studying from one book. His hand rests on her thigh. I watch them a minute. And then, from behind me, someone touches my shoulder. I swing around. Vinnie's standing there. I jump about a mile in my seat.

He laughs. "Sorry. I didn't mean to scare you. What are you doing in the kids' room? Hey, is that my name?"

"God, what are you *doing* here?" I grab the list and crumple it.

But he grabs it back and moves away from me, smoothing it out. "It is my name!" he says. "Man, that is so cute. I love that, I really do."

I do something I've learned from Tiffany then; I tell him I'm embarrassed—"I am *so* embarrassed!" I say—because if you admit you're embarrassed, things aren't nearly as embarrassing, sometimes.

"Don't be, hon," he says, smiling, but I still am, it never works for me.

"What are you doing here?" I say again.

"What, you think I never take out books?" He laughs. "I take out books. Maybe I came to get that Garp thing you were talking about." He pulls up a tiny chair and sits on it. "Nuh, okay, I called your house and your mother told me you were here. Doing a speech or something." He picks up *The Bears' Picnic.* "What's this? This isn't for the speech or anything, is it?"

I feel myself blush. "No. I just—I used to love that book."

"Yeah?" He flips through it and puts it back down. "So you want to get out of here? Go for a ride or something?"

I glance at the clock. My speech is due in three days.

"No, forget it," he says. "I shouldn't bother you, you're studying." He stands up. "I'll just see you tonight, okay?" He bends down and kisses me on the cheek. Then again, on the mouth.

His lips are soft and gentle, like last time. And suddenly I don't want to be in this place anymore, thinking about my speech or about my sister. "No, wait," I say. "I'm coming, I don't know what to demonstrate anyway."

"Oh, you're on demonstration? I remember that."

He smiles, and again I notice his teeth, the way they overlap just a little in front. A lock of clean hair falls sweetly in front of his eyes. "You took speech too?" I manage.

"Yup. Got an A, too. Kalemba loved me. Know what I demonstrated?"

"What?"

He stands up. "I'll show you. Come on."

"Where?"

"Somewhere good." He takes my hand. "Trust me, would you please?"

He takes me to school, of all places. We pull into the parking lot, and it's emptier than I've ever seen it, like a black sea under us. Above, the sky is gray and overcast. The whole thing makes me feel very small.

He walks me past the empty football field, up the big cement steps, to the big red front doors. "Where are we going?" I say, shivering in my sweatshirt. "Isn't it locked?"

"Not to me, it ain't." He dangles a key ring with two keys on it. And then we're inside, and I know that the wrestling coach hooked him up, and I wonder if the coach could get in trouble for that—or if we could, for being in here. But I love it. It's a different place without lights and voices yelling, without lockers being slammed. The hallways are dark and cool, so big and empty our footsteps echo down the hall. "Whoa," I whisper.

Vinnie smiles. He touches my hand. Then he nudges me up against a locker. "You are so cute," he says. He kisses me again, like he's tasting something delicate and sweet and savoring the taste. He hugs me in closer, pushes his body against mine, and his hand moves up my arm to my neck, and I feel his breath grow deeper—and I love that, knowing I've done that to him. I put my hand inside his jacket. But he pulls away suddenly. "Come on," he says, motioning.

We head toward the gym, but when we're almost there, he takes me down a staircase I've never even thought about going down, never had a reason to. At the bottom is a door. He opens that with the second key. "Take off your shoes," he says, leading me into a room. "No heels in here. And close the door behind you, okay?"

The room is pitch black, very warm. I can feel my feet sinking into something—like soft wax or wet sand. Vinnie kicks off his sneakers and disappears into the black; seconds later a light bulb comes on in the corner, and then I see that I'm standing on a mat—a thick blue wrestling mat, covering the floor from wall to wall. A big white circle is painted on it. The room's about half the size of a tennis court.

Vinnie tosses his jacket over near his shoes. He's wearing loose Levi jeans that used to be tight and a short-sleeved gray T-shirt not quite long enough to tuck in his pants. His biceps roll in the sleeves, like grapefruits. I have to take a deep breath, he looks so good.

"Come here," he says, but he comes to me anyway, touches the zipper of my jacket. "Here, take this off, too—you'll sweat your butt." He lifts the jacket over my head and tosses it away.

I have on just my T-shirt then, thin and white and V-necked. I catch him checking it out quickly then looking away. And then I'm nervous again. Maybe he doesn't like what he sees, maybe he *is* a chest man. Maybe I don't turn him on after all, now that he's finally got his chance. And suddenly I wish I hadn't come here, I wish I'd stayed at the library, where I belong.

But he leads me into the middle of the room, and then he's down on his hands and knees like a dog. "Get like this," he says.

"What for?" I do it, though, relieved to be doing something other than waiting for him not to kiss me.

He gets down behind me. "Because I'm gonna show you some moves. You'll have something to demonstrate for your class."

I laugh. *"Wrestling?"*

"What, you got something against it?" He smiles. "That's what I demonstrated. Thing is, you'll need another person. I can come to your class, if you want. Kalemba would think it was funny. Okay, ready?" He grips my upper left arm with one hand. Then he brings his right arm over my back and puts his palm on my stomach. "Okay. When the ref blows the whistle, I chop your arm, grab your hand, and flip you over. Like this." In two seconds, I'm lying on my back pinned, laughing, him lying over me. "Got it?" he says.

He shows me again, then a third time. He does it fast, without hurting me at all. Then he tells me to do it to him.

I get down behind him. With my left hand, I grip his thick upper arm. My fingers barely go halfway around. "Harder," he says. "Come on, scare me." I dig my fingertips into his flesh. "Good," he says.

I bring my other arm over his back and around his waist, like he did to me. I flatten my palm on his stomach. I can feel the warmth of him through his T-shirt, feel his body move as he breathes, and I feel like this is the closest I've ever been to him, even closer than kissing. He smells like fabric softener. A tingly feeling waves through me. I press my cheek to his back. "You smell good," I mumble.

He laughs. "So do you."

I hadn't thought he was smelling me. The thought turns my muscles to jelly, and I want to lie down then, just sink into the mat and feel him warm and heavy over me. But he makes me do the move, and then do it again, and then he teaches me another one. He's touching me all over, our hands are all over each other, but not in the places that count, and somehow that feels even better, in a way. Except that the more he does it—the more it's all business on his end—the more I want him to do something, kiss me or push against me as hard as he can, so that finally, in the middle of one of our moves, when he whispers in my ear, "Oh, I want you so bad," I almost die of relief. We kiss at last, and then he has our shirts off, and we tumble around in that hot room, roll together on those warm sinking mats.

His kisses are long and intense now—but soft, too, like it's an effort to hold back and be gentle but he does anyway. And I love that too, knowing he's holding back, knowing he wants to be rougher but he won't. His hands wander on me—the sides of my chest, all up and down my jeans—touching me like I'm something he doesn't want to break. My breathing gets deeper. I can tell that turns him on even more by the way he breathes back, by the pressure in his hands. And I want to stay there forever like this, never doing any more or any less. This is perfect, the perfect amount of pleasure without giving—losing—anything in return.

So when he tries to get down my pants, I stop him without even thinking too much about it. I've always worried about stopping a guy—what you say, whether he'll listen to you or not, what to do if he won't. But Vinnie stops when I say to. He makes himself roll away, then lies on the mat and breathes up at the ceiling. His chest rises and falls. For a second I feel power, like I did on the phone that day: this guy will do anything I say. But I also feel regret, and I roll back to him, wanting another kiss, wanting to know he forgives me, he likes me anyway.

Afterward, we go upstairs to the boys' gym locker room; he needs some vitamins from his locker, and he wants to show me something. I'm carrying our coats—my sweatshirt, his big wrestling jacket—and we're holding hot clammy hands, and I feel incredible. Sort of beautiful, I think—maybe for the first time in my life. I wonder if this is how Cassie always feels. Or used to, anyway.

When he opens his locker, the first thing I see is a Bible. I drop our coats on the bench and pull the book out. "You read this?" I say, flipping through it.

He finds his pills, then gives me a look. "No, I just keep it there to hold the locker room down." He shakes his head. "You're funny, you know that? Don't you read the Bible? Or—no, wait. You read the Koran, or something, right?"

"The what?"

He laughs. "I'm only kidding. Nuh, I'm not one of those religious freaks, or anything, but the Bible's cool, it's awesome. I read it before I wrestle. I swear to God, sometimes it's the only thing that gives me the willpower to get out there."

This seems both absurd and fascinating. "How?" I say. "I mean, in what way?"

He thinks a second. "I can't explain it right now. You gotta read it to see. I'll let you borrow mine. After wrestling season, though, okay? Or you can take it out of the library." He laughs.

"Are you making fun of me or what?" I say it the way he would to me.

"Aw, I'm sorry," he says. He cradles my head and kisses my cheek. Then he reaches into his locker and pulls out a black and gold harmonica. Vinnie's locker of tricks.

He blows a few tinny notes on it and then starts into a song I recognize, though at first I can't remember the words. And then they come to me: *You can't always get what you wa-ant* . . . The Rolling Stones. The notes waver in the locker room, linger in the air, liquid and metallic.

I sit down on the bench, amazed at how good he is. For all the music lessons I had as a kid, I can't play anything that sounds nearly this good. I have to smile at the song, too. He closes his eyes for the finale. When he's done, he tosses the harmonica back in the locker.

I stare at him. I know he's showing off, but I don't care. "Who taught you to play that?" I say.

"No one. I just learned. You don't always have to be *taught* stuff, you know."

I shake my head. "I *love* that."

He smiles. "Figured you would."

"Play something else. Please?"

"I don't know nothin' else." He laughs. "Nah, I know a couple other ones. One song per visit, though. That way I make sure you keep coming back."

I wonder if he means that. And I wonder what I have to offer him, then—besides the obvious, I mean. But he can get that from half the girls at school. More than half. We both know that.

"What time is it?" he says then, and I realize as he says it that I've been gone from the library a long time, much too long. We leave quickly, jog back through the halls, through the parking lot, back to the car.

He drives fast to the library, though he goes a block out of the way to show me his house. It's a small, two-story house near South Berry, with a tiny lawn and peeling beige paint. He shows me the window to his room. I stare at a clothesline in the side yard. Socks, T-shirts, jeans the color of the sky float from it, like flags. It looks colorful and vibrant and bright, and sort of romantic, in a way—

though I wonder how the clothes don't freeze in this cold, and what they do when it's even colder.

Back in the library parking lot, he takes off his wrestling coat and hands it to me. "Put this on, would you? So you don't freeze to death on me." I snuggle into the jacket, imagining what Tiffany will say. Even Cassie might be impressed, though she'd never admit it. It's gold and lavender, West Berry colors, with Vinnie's name sewn in script on the front. His weight is on the sleeve: 158. And underneath it, "Captain."

I lean to kiss him thanks, but he waves me away. "Give me a pen, I'll write down those moves for you."

So I hand him paper and a pen instead, and he writes for a minute and hands me the list. He's put down the three moves he taught me, each with its own little diagram. At the end, he's written, "I will come to your class to demenstrate if you want, just let me know when."

I laugh, feeling cocky. "Demonstrate," I say. "It's spelled with an *o,* Vinnie."

His face clouds. He shrugs and looks away.

"I mean, I *think* it is," I stammer. "I mean, I don't even know. It just looked wrong for a sec."

He laughs once, just breath, his mouth closed—like nothing's really funny. "Whatever. Doesn't really matter much, you know what I mean?"

Right then I am everything I never wanted to be. I open my car door and step out, his jacket heavy on my shoulders. "See you later?" I say.

"I'll pick you up at seven thirty." He doesn't look at me.

"Okay. Thanks, Vinnie." I want him to kiss me. "Well . . . 'bye," I say.

" 'Bye." He waves once, staring out the windshield. I slam my door. He pulls away behind me.

But as soon as he's gone, I'm thinking about other things. My mother, my sister. I rush into the library. Someone's on the phone, a girl I recognize from Cassie's class. "Ma, I did—Ma, I *did* tell her," she shrieks. "I tol' her, I says, 'Mary, you need to pri-or-i-tize'—" I glance at the clock. Three seventeen. I pace back and forth, trying to think of another phone in the area. And then I see my mother, striding through the library toward me, looking furious. My heart sinks.

"Where were you?" she calls, throwing up her hands. A couple of people turn to look at her, then at me.

"Mom, shh—"

"I've been looking all over for you! Daddy's going to Cornell, he wants you to go with him. He's home waiting for you. *Hurry!*"

We jog to the car. "Did you get your speech done?" she says as we run. She's already less mad, now that she's found me.

"Some of it. How's Cassie?"

She opens her car door without answering. I wait for her to slide over and open my side. Ethan's in the car, slobbering all over the place. "Where did you go, anyway?" she says when I get in. She starts the car.

I think of rolling on the mat with Vinnie in that wrestling room. "For a walk," I say, looking away.

"In this cold? Without a scarf or gloves?" She sighs. "To *where?*" The car stalls, and she starts it again.

"Just around. Mom, what's wrong with Cassie? Does she know Dad's coming up there? What changed his mind?"

My mother pulls onto the main road. "I don't know. She says she's fine. She told him she doesn't want him to come, but—" She sighs again. "I guess he'd just as soon have her home, if she's so upset."

I watch her make a turn. "It's because of you," I say. "He's going because you told him to."

"Well," she says, like she doesn't believe that. She never gives herself credit for anything.

"Is he gonna kill me?" I ask.

"Probably." Now it's her chance to get back at me, to make me sweat—like I did to her at the library.

"When does he want to leave?"

"He wants to get there in time for dinner. Eat on campus, then drive back home."

"Mom! It's already like three thirty."

She shrugs.

"And Cassie said she'll come home?"

"I think that's part of why he wants you to go. He thinks she'll be less angry if you're there."

"He does?" For a second I feel flattered. And then I think about barging into Cassie's dorm room, trying to drag her out of there. I don't want any part of it. I look out the window. We're back on our street. "Okay," my mother says, sounding nervous again. "When you get upstairs, just put on a sweater and a coat and some gloves and get in the car fast."

But he greets us calmly—his anger, as always, unpredictable. He's standing at the kitchen table looking at a map. "I think I'll take that other route, the one we took last time," he tells my mother—as if she cares. He looks at me. "Do you want to come?"

Do I have a choice? "Do you want me to?" I ask.

"Sure."

"I will, then."

"Good." For a second he looks relieved. And then it's over. "Let's go, then, please. Get whatever you need. I'd like to be out of here in fifteen minutes."

It's not until we're at least a mile from our house—the whole thing happens so fast—that I remember my date tonight with Vinnie. I suck in my breath. "Dad?" I say after a minute.

"Hm?" He's watching the highway, his blue eyes fixed on the road.

"Do you think we'll stop at all?"

"What for?"

"I don't know. To go to the bathroom or whatever?" Somewhere with a phone, I'm thinking.

"Don't tell me you have to go already."

"I don't." Even when I do have to go, I almost never ask him to stop. He'll tease us or get mad. Sometimes both.

He sighs. "It's a four-hour trip, Billie. I'll stop if there's a reason to."

I keep quiet then. I think about Vinnie and the mat room again, and I replay his hands on my neck, on my jeans. The same feeling from before washes over me. The thrill. I replay it a few more times, till it starts to lose effect. Then I make myself stop, to save some of it.

After a while I take out *The Great Gatsby,* glancing at my father. Usually he doesn't like us to read or even do homework in the car on family trips; he likes to quiz us—on state capitals, rivers, presidents— or he talks about politics, or movies, or whatever. Once, when Cassie took out a book, he said, "I didn't have children so I could be their chauffeur."

But this isn't really reading—the book is for English class—and this isn't a family trip, is it? My father's eyes are on the road. He's driving only slightly over the speed limit, and the radio isn't even on for a change.

And then I open the book and lose myself in it. Gatsby has just fired all his servants. I love the book, like I love almost everything we read in English class—though I'd never admit it to anyone, my parents because it would make them too happy, Tiffany or Vinnie because they'd think I was weird. I think of Vinnie's harmonica song. After a while I close the book and drift off to sleep.

When I wake up it's five forty-five and dark out. My father's pulling into a gas station. "Morning," he says to me, noticing I'm awake. "We're making great time."

I rub my eyes. "Where are we?"

"About an hour and a half from Ithaca."

"That far still? I'm starving."

My father looks around. "There's a McDonald's over there. I'll pull in after I get gas, if you want."

"Really?"

He doesn't answer, just gets out of the car to watch the guy pump, like he always does.

But he takes me to McDonald's. He parks the car, comes in, and gets out his wallet. "What do you want?" he says, looking at the menu.

"I don't know." I glance at the burgers in their crackly wrappers, breathe the greasy, salty smell of the place. "I want fries or a hot fudge sundae. I can't decide which."

He smiles. Like, at least I don't have to worry about *you* losing weight. "Get a hot fudge sundae," he says. "I'll have a bite."

"Okay."

He places the order and asks for two spoons. "Here or in the car?" I say, collecting the sundae.

"Here, if we hurry."

"Good. I love McDonald's."

"You *love* McDonald's?" He laughs. "Christ! How'd I raise a kid who loves McDonald's?"

When he takes us out for dinner—two or three times a month —it's always to some expensive restaurant in New York, French food or Chinese. "Everyone in West Berry loves McDonald's," I answer.

But he's not listening. He takes a bite of the sundae and passes it to me.

I eat my share quickly, then tell him I'll be right back and head for the pay phone, back near the bathrooms.

But when I get there, I realize I don't have enough change to call Vinnie. For a second I think of calling collect, but I talk myself out of it. I don't want to risk Vinnie thinking I'm cheap—and what would I say to him, anyway? That my sister won't eat even though she's not fat, even though she doesn't have to make weight for some team? That we drove four hours each way to bring her home and I had to go along so she wouldn't get mad? He would never get it. I decide to let my mother explain when he calls before he comes to get me. If he calls first. I go back to the table, trying not to think about it.

Back at the table, my father's looking at the map. "Ready?" he says.

I nod. "Thanks for the sundae."

He stands and dumps the cup in the trash. "Let's go, then," he says.

★   ★   ★

I know what to expect when we get to Cornell, at least in terms of the place, since I was here last year when we all drove up after Cassie got accepted. It was cold and raining, fat icy drops, and I remember wet grassy hills everywhere. Students in colored raincoats and duck shoes ran in different directions, like ants. Inside, they wore wool sweaters, khakis. Total preps. I remember thinking I wouldn't be caught dead wearing any of that stuff.

It's still gray out when we pull in now, a deep thick gray that makes me wonder if the sun has come out at all since last time I was here. The roads are lit pretty well, well enough for my father to point out his fraternity house once again. I wait for him to tell how it had the highest grade-point average on campus when he was there, how he had the highest grade ever recorded in advanced calculus—one hundred five, with extra credit. But he doesn't say anything this time; maybe he knows I know the story by now. I know, too, that my grandmother had wanted him to join a different fraternity, the all-Jewish one where the richer kids were, even if their grades weren't as great. I'd heard her say more than once, after he swore in public or chewed like a pig, that it was "that fraternity" that ruined him. "If he'd only joined the one I told him to," she'd lament.

We pass a couple more buildings, and then he points out Cassie's dorm. "Why don't you run in and tell her we're here?" he says.

"What for?" I don't want to be the one to get to her first.

"What *for*?" He laughs. "She's in room seven-oh-eight. Go on, I'll park and meet you up there."

I get out, zipping my coat, and teeter up to the door, suddenly conscious of my shoes. The heels plunge deep in the mud as I walk, come out gluey with wet dirt.

But inside nobody seems to notice or care. In fact, no one notices me at all. A few kids are sitting around on couches or chairs, reading or studying. A couple of guys play Ping-Pong. A girl walks by eating an ice-cream sandwich. I head toward the elevator.

Someone comes and waits with me, a tall guy with blond bangs that hang in his face. I can feel him looking at me. When the doors open, he holds them till I get in. "Thanks," I say, pressing seven, feeling shy. The doors close.

He turns to me. "You live here?"

"My sister does." I still don't look at him, and I wonder why I'm being such a dork.

He smiles. "Is your sister Cassie Weinstein?"

I turn to face him. "How did you know?"

"You look like her."

"I *do?*"

"Totally." The door opens, and he gets out. "Party on three tonight," he says, flicking hair out of his eyes.

When he's gone, I try to see myself in a thin metal strip in the corner of the elevator, but it doesn't work. I wonder if Cassie was planning to go to that kid's party tonight. He was cute. Tall and preppy, though. Not my type.

On Cassie's floor, I walk slowly—past doors with message boards, some of the markers torn off. Cassie's door doesn't have one. I wonder if her roommate took it when she left. I take a breath and knock once.

"Who is it?" It's Cassie's voice, slightly tense.

"Me!" I say, relieved to hear her.

"Billie?" She opens the door, pulls me in, closes the door behind me. "God, that was fast. What'd he do, go eighty-five the whole way?" She looks me up and down. "I didn't know you were coming, too. Where is he, anyway?"

"Parking." I examine her carefully for signs of something. Her eyes are slightly bloodshot, slightly puffy, and she's got on no makeup whatsoever, but otherwise she looks okay. Meaning, great. I'm always blown away by how pretty she is when I first see her after a while. I don't look anything like this, really. Who was that kid?

Cassie smiles at me, finally, then pecks me on the cheek. I smell shampoo, slightly stale breath. She's wearing the same big sweatshirt she wore all Thanksgiving, gray sweatpants, ratty sneakers. "Well, you look okay," I say. I'm suddenly glad I came. "I mean, you don't look sick or anything."

She rolls her eyes. "I'm not sick. This whole thing is absurd." She turns around and reaches for a tube of Chap Stick on her dresser, and then I can see: She is skinny, even thinner than at Thanksgiving. Her sweatpants hang like a sack, held up by their drawstring.

"You're skinny, though, Cass. Really skinny. Like, gross."

She applies Chap Stick, then caps the tube. "Please," she says. "I could gain ten pounds in a minute." She glances in the mirror, then turns away. "So tell me something real. What's new?"

I shrug. "I don't know. I'm going out with someone—"

"Who?"

"Vinnie DiNardio—" I pause. Maybe not after tonight.

Cassie smiles. "DiNardio? You're kidding."

"No. Why would I be?" I fold my arms. "He's nice."

"I know he's nice. He's really nice." She laughs a little. "Meg Roberts used to say, 'With a body like that, he doesn't need brains.' Have Mom and Dad met him yet?"

I shake my head.

"That's good." She sits down on her bed. "So how long has this been? Wait, is that his coat?" She touches the sleeve. "I mean, is this a *thing* or what?"

"I don't know. I mean—I really don't know him yet."

"Give it time," she says. "You will." She smiles. "Vinnie DiNardio. Holy shit. My sister and a BMOC."

"A what?"

"Oh. A Big Man On Campus. You know, a stud."

I stare at her, almost suspicious. Cassie and I have never been cheerleaders for each other. But now she's being nice, and I want to be nice, too. I look around the room trying to find something to compliment. The walls are empty, except for a poster-sized monthly organizer taped to the wall, filled in neatly in blue pen. Her dresser top is bare, and her night table is empty except for another Chap Stick and a small wind-up alarm clock. Her bed is perfectly made. On the other bed, a naked green-and-white-striped mattress sits generically on its box spring. For the first time I'm aware of her roommate being gone, of Cassie sitting all alone in here every night, not answering the door. I sit down on the mattress. "How come you never got another roommate?"

She's biting her nails. Chewing her fingers, really. "What for?"

"I don't know. So you're not all alone."

"I like to be alone. I get more work done."

"Well yeah, but—don't you get bored?"

"Bored?" She shakes her head. "I never understand people who get bored. How do they have time?"

"Okay. Lonely, then."

She stares at me a second, then shakes her head again. "No."

The way she says it, I'm not convinced. "I'm glad you're coming home," I say then.

She smiles a little. "You'll have to share a room again. At least for a couple of weeks."

"So what? You're the one who always wanted your own room. I couldn't care less."

She turns away from me, so I can't see her face. Then she gets up and opens a drawer.

"Do you need help packing or anything?" I say after a minute.

"No thanks." Inside the drawer is a single pair of jeans. She opens a second drawer, takes out a duffel bag, and shoves the jeans inside it. The third drawer holds five textbooks. She sticks them on top of the jeans. "There," she says, closing the drawers. "I'm packed."

"That's all you're bringing?" I remember then that her clothes are gone.

"What else do I need?" she says. "We're not seeing anyone over Christmas, are we?" She looks at me suddenly. "Who's having Christmas dinner? Is Mom?"

"I don't know. We're going to Zelda's tomorrow night, though."

"Oh god. We are?" She sits down again, looking panicky.

I feel like I should apologize. "Are you mad?" I say. "I mean, that we're here?"

She shrugs. "I don't know. At first I was. Now—" She sighs. "I just don't know how I can, like, just *leave*. Exams are next week."

"They said you can get take-homes."

She closes her eyes and shakes her head, as if electricity is going through her. She makes two fists and digs her knuckles deep into her eyes in a way that makes me cringe.

There's a rap on the door, and my father walks in. "Jesus, it's freezing in here! Hello, child. Don't you have any heat?" He kisses her cheek and smiles at her, like he's amused to find her here.

"Yes, I have heat," she says. "I just use it sparingly. Dad, what did Mary Joyce tell you?" She sighs. "You didn't have to come here, you know."

"I know I didn't *have* to come here. She said you weren't going to meals. Are you going to meals? Where's your meal card? I didn't put you on three meals a day so you could sit in your room." He looks her over. "You look okay. A little tired. How do you feel?"

"Fine. I can't sleep, that's about it. Hardly a reason to blow off my fucking exams."

Fucking? I wait for my father to explode. But he just raises his eyebrows slightly and says, "Watch your mouth. Just relax, and don't worry about your exams. They'll get taken. Why can't you sleep? Do you have a sore throat? Any pain?"

She shakes her head.

"Let's see," he says, stepping over to her. He places his two fingertips on each side of her neck and presses. She rolls her eyes toward me and smiles, but I'm glad he's doing it. If something's wrong with her, he'll find it. "Swallow," he says.

She swallows.

He shrugs. "Your glands are fine. You look thin. Have you had dinner yet?"

"Yeah. I had a late lunch."

"Come on, then. Finish packing. We'll go get some dinner in the dining hall, and then I want to come back and talk to that lady, what's her name? Goodman. She said she'd be here at eight." He looks at his watch. "We have thirty-five minutes. Where's your valise?"

Only two people on the planet call a suitcase a valise: my father, and his mother, Zelda. Cassie points to her duffel bag. "I'm all packed."

"That's it?" he says.

"All she has is one pair of jeans," I say, but I realize as I say it that this is something he'd be happy about, not upset. He's always encouraged us to pack light. He'd think she was being thrifty or practical.

He's wandering around the room now, examining things. From behind the curtain he pulls out a large bottle of Evian. "Christ, Cassandra, there's a water fountain ten feet right down the hall." He's not criticizing, just kidding, I can tell—trying to keep things light, make somebody laugh.

But Cassie's face falls, and I see something pass through her eyes, some sort of pain. "It's not mine," she says. "It's my roommate Shona's. Was." She turns away from him. "Anyway, people piss in that fountain. Boys."

"Oh, pish tosh," my father says. "I went here for four years and never saw anyone piss in any fountain."

"Well, I guess it didn't happen then, if you didn't see it." Cassie bends down to zip her bag. "Anyway, I don't buy water. I don't buy anything. Okay?" She looks up at my father, and her face is terrible then, pale and twisted.

But he laughs, determined to make light of it. Of everything. "Good," he says. "That's the way it should be."

We get to the dining hall just as it's closing. Kids pass us coming out, laughing, holding books, holding hands. I look at Cassie to see if she knows any of them, but she's averting her eyes.

Inside, she strolls off. I go to the grill and ask for a cheeseburger and fries. At the hot food counter, my father's ordering lasagna, flirting with the server. Do I get a discount if I buy two? They didn't have girls behind there when I went to school here, just old ladies. I see Cassie glance at him and turn away in disgust, though it doesn't seem to me he's doing anything so bad. Just being corny. The girl smiles at him politely. Cassie flashes her meal card at the cashier and disappears into the dining room.

I find her at a table in the back corner, sitting with a small, slightly bruised red apple in front of her. "That's all you're eating?" I sit down next to her, deposit my tray, take off Vinnie's jacket, and hang it on the back of the chair.

She looks at my burger. "I had a late lunch." Then she looks at my shirt—Tiffany's shirt, actually, a tight silver thing with a zipper down the front. Something Cassie would never be caught dead in. "I know, you hate my shirt," I say. "Well, I like it."

"Actually, I was looking at your chest."

I look down. "What about it?"

"It's bigger."

"Oh. I know." I laugh.

"So don't you think you should dress a little less—"

"What?"

She shakes her head. "Never mind."

"No, what? Tell me."

But my father arrives then. He sits down and butters a roll quickly, like he's painting it with the knife. He takes a large bite, then looks at Cassie's apple. "Cassandra," he says, mouth full of bread, "that's not dinner. That's fruit."

"I told you, I just had lunch."

"Well, now it's dinnertime. Go get some dinner."

"I'm not hungry."

He shrugs. "We're not eating again before we get home, you know."

"Good." She touches the apple. "People don't need three meals a day anyway. We don't need anywhere near the amount of food we consume."

My father laughs, chewing. "Oh, no?" He swallows. "At least have a little protein," he says. "You'll be hungry in an hour. Here, you want some lasagna?" He pushes his plate toward her.

We've always been a family that shares food. In restaurants we pass around forkfuls and samples on butter plates as if we're playing Go-Fish. By the time we start eating, our plates look like an artist's palette—a little taste of each thing, each person's.

Cassie studies his lasagna, then takes a forkful and swallows quickly. "Thanks," she says.

I hold out my cheeseburger, relieved. "Want a bite of this?"

She hesitates, then takes a small bite and hands the burger back. She closes her eyes and swallows. "Mmm. That's good." I wonder if she really had lunch. I push the fries toward her. "Have fries, too. I can't eat all these."

"No thanks." She glances around. The room is almost empty now; there are trays of garbage, crumpled napkins, dirty plates on tables. Cassie gets up and walks to one of the tables. She picks through a tray. "What's she doing?" I ask my father.

He glances over his shoulder at her for a second. Then he looks at his watch and takes another bite of food. Cassie's moved on to the next table now. She has a small stack of clean napkins in her hand.

She works her way around the room, then comes back and puts the napkins on our table. "Look at this," she says. "Look at this."

My father glances at the napkins. He stands up. "I'm getting dessert," he says. "Anyone want some? Cassandra?"

She looks from the napkins to him, then shakes her head slowly.

"Okay, then," he says, walking away.

Cassie's staring at the napkins, like she might cry. "I hate people," she says. She looks at me puffy-eyed. "Did you know they can make pantyhose that don't run? They can make light bulbs that last a hundred years."

"Who?" I say, feeling nervous for the first time since we got here. Maybe she doesn't have anorexia. Maybe she has something worse.

She touches the napkins with one finger and laughs once, without a sound. Then she takes the pile over to the napkin dispenser and puts the napkins back in. She turns around to come back. But she stops, reaches into a tray on a table, and removes an apple with a couple of bites taken out of it.

I push my last bite of burger away, feeling sick. Cassie wipes the apple on her pants as she approaches. "Cassie," I say slowly. "What are you doing? Whose apple is that?"

She reaches for my knife. "Can I use this?" She slices out the part with bites in it, then sets the rest of the apple down next to her other one. "I knew I shouldn't have taken my own," she says, shaking her head.

"Cassie. You are *not* eating that apple."

She looks at me. "Wrong." She picks up the sliced apple and takes a bite, chewing slowly.

And then my father's back, carrying a plate of lemon meringue pie. He sits down and begins to eat it quickly.

Cassie takes another bite of apple, then stands up. "I'm going to the bathroom," she says. She picks up both apples and shuffles away.

I wonder if she's going to throw up. I watch her from the back —her blond ponytail, her baggy gray sweats. Should I go after her?

"I have to go meet the Goodman lady," my father says. "I'll meet you two back in Cassie's room."

I swallow. "Dad. Did you see what she just did?"

He forks the last bite of pie into his mouth. "What?"

"She took that apple off someone's dirty tray and—she *ate* it! God, what the hell is wrong with her?"

"Watch your mouth. *What* did she do?"

I tell him again.

He looks at me a minute—half-smiling, like I'm kidding. But he sees that I'm not, and his eyebrows shoot together, and I feel him register confusion, disbelief, discomfort . . . and then his face relaxes. He doesn't want to deal. He can't face that his daughter's sick —just like the library book said.

I stand up. "She's so skinny, Dad. She must have lost twenty pounds. Do you think—I mean, I was reading about anorexia—"

"She'll eat again when she's home," he says confidently. He stands too then, towering over the table. "She'll be more relaxed there. Your mother will cook all her favorite foods. She'll be fine." He watches me a second. Then he reaches out and ruffles my hair. "Don't worry about it. Okay?"

I shrug. How can I not?

He glances once more at his watch. "I've gotta go, I'm already late. I'll meet you in a few minutes. Okay?"

"Okay."

He smiles. "Help your sister get ready to leave."

★   ★   ★

Going home, Cassie wants to sit in the backseat, which is fine with me; more leg room in the front when my father's driving, since he pushes the seat back as far as it goes. Almost immediately she falls asleep. I stay awake, watching taillights ahead of us bleed into the dark, thinking about how for years I loved being driven somewhere by my father at night. I'd watch the blue and green numbers light up the dashboard, the speedometer needle waver back and forth. Late at night he'd turn off the radio, and the car would float along the highway, and soon the hum of the motor and swish of the tires would lull me to sleep. He'd carry us up sleeping and put us straight in our beds until we were nine or ten. After that, though, Cassie always forced herself to stay awake. She told me once it was because she couldn't stand the thought of having to wake up from deep sleep and climb stairs—that she'd rather struggle a little the whole time than relax and then suffer at the end.

Now, she sleeps deeply. I keep looking back at her, checking her out. I can't stop thinking about that apple.

My father turns around and glances at her, too. "Don't wake her," he says, as if I'm planning to jump on the girl. And then he says softly, "Poor kid."

It's the kind of thing he'll say about us when we're not around to hear; he'll give us sympathy or credit or even brag about us, but never to our faces. We have to hear it from each other or from other people.

But this time his sympathy makes me nervous. "Why is she poor?"

"I don't know. Freshman year is rough. It's tough to leave home." He smiles. "Do you know what her last words were to me when I dropped her off in the fall?"

"What?" I remember how she packed everything a month before she left, how she wrote letters to her roommate. "What?" I say again.

"I'd walked her to a meeting, all the way across campus from her dorm. She kept walking ahead of me, like she wanted me to go. But when we got there, she turned around and said, 'Daddy, I can't believe you're leaving me here.' " His eyes stay on the road, but the speedometer fluctuates slightly. "I almost didn't," he says.

"Maybe you shouldn't have." I'm not trying to make him feel bad, but I think I do, in a way.

He looks at me a second. And then he turns back to the endless road, to this endless day. A minute later, though, he flips on the radio. I stare out the window as a man's voice comes on, reciting the latest news, filling our car.

chapter four

My father lets Cassie sleep in on her first morning back, but by eleven we're all getting impatient for her to wake up. My mother lingers in the kitchen over blueberry pancake batter, obviously hoping to cook her up a huge batch. My father's laid out a purple-topped tube on the kitchen counter to draw her blood into; he wants to test her for mono. And we all want, I think, to check her out now that she's back on our turf. Even I'm starting to feel like maybe we overreacted yesterday—whizzing up to Ithaca, whipping her away before classes end.

I also want to get in my room and call Tiffany. I want to tell her about Cassie and ask what I should do about Vinnie, whether I should call him or wait for him to call again. Whether blowing him off for our first date still qualifies as "hard to get." I can guess the answer, and it fills me with panic. What have I done?

To distract myself, I play solitaire at the dining-room table. My father takes off for the hospital. "Get dressed," he tells me on his way out. My mother cleans up the kitchen and goes upstairs, but she leaves the electric frying pan out on the counter and a bowl of fruit on the table. I start to think about lunch.

A horn honks outside, and I hear a car radio somewhere. I wander into the kitchen and eat a strawberry and a raspberry, then wander back out. I twirl hair around my finger, totally bored. I can't bear the thought of doing homework. I want to get dressed; I'm wearing a pink nightgown and sweatsocks with holes, and my hair is pulled up messily with a sock. The dogs follow me, bored too. I think about walking them up to Tiffany's. But she'd be asleep, her whole family would be asleep, except Dominick and her father, who'd both be gone.

A horn honks again, this time more insistently. I shuffle to the den and peer out between the curtains. Vinnie's green Plymouth is idling in front of our house. "Oh, *shit*," I whisper, ripping the sock out of my hair. I run to the front door and crack it. "I'll be right there," I yell out.

In our room, Cassie's awake, sitting on the edge of the bed looking at her hands. "Hi, Cass—what are you *doing*?" I say, bursting in, and then, "Vinnie's here! God, what am I gonna do?" I pull on jeans and a bra and a tight V-necked red sweater.

Cassie stares at my shirt. "What do you mean?"

"Because look at my hair!" I push my feet into silver-sparkled socks and high-heeled clogs. I fluff my hair. "Oh, forget it. That's what he gets for not calling first." I grab my purse, pull out a tube of lip-gloss, and roll it on, thick as shellac. In the mirror, I can see Cassie watching me, squinting, as if she's never seen me before. "What?" I say, finally.

She bites her bottom lip and shakes her head.

I turn to face her then, about to make a snotty comment. But something about the way she looks makes me stop. She's got her arms folded, like she's cold, and her eyes are puffy and tired. Her face looks very small. "Are you cold?" I say. "I'll tell Mom to turn up the heat if you want. . . ."

"What?" she says, because I'm talking a mile a minute.

I force myself to slow down. "Cass, do you want me to stay here with you?"

She shakes her head quickly. "That's okay."

"Are you *sure*?"

She nods, and I can tell she's lying. But I don't want to stay. I throw the lip-gloss on my bed and run downstairs.

Outside, I can hear a song I like coming from Vinnie's car. I want to run to him, but I force myself to walk slowly, trying to look casual and sexy. It's cold out and I don't have a coat, but I'm sweating anyway.

Halfway to the car, though, I stop. What if he wants to kill me? Obviously he hasn't come here to tell me I'm a babe. I take a deep breath and make my way slowly to the passenger-side window. "Hi, Vin," I say.

He's not smiling. "Get in," he says. "I got a bone to pick with you."

I open the door and slide into his car, not looking at him. I stare at the dashboard, and then at a large bronze crucifix hanging from the rearview mirror.

I can feel him watching me, his face tilted slightly, like there's something he doesn't get. "Just tell me this," he says. "Did we have plans for last night? Or am I deaf? Because if I am, you know, I probably should do something about it."

He's not yelling, just asking. I shake my head. "No, we did, Vinnie. I had to go somewhere at the last minute. I tried to call and tell you, but . . . your line kept being busy."

I hate myself for lying. He looks out the windshield, mouth closed, nodding like *Oh, right.* His leg shakes the seat.

"I figured you'd just go out with your friends or something."

He looks back at me. "Is that what you think of me? Well, you're wrong. I sat home trying to call you. No one answered, so I drove up here. I thought your phone was broken." He palms back one side of his hair. "I honked like twenty-eight times. I took off when your mother came out. She looked pissed."

"Vinnie—"

He shakes his head. "You blew me off."

How could I have thought I'd get away with this? "No," I say. "I didn't blow you off, Vinnie. I swear."

"Nuh? What would you call it?" He pushes the base of his palm gently against the steering wheel. "Where were you, anyway?"

"Okay, listen." I tell him the whole story then, except for all the details about Cassie. I tell him my father made me go to Cornell at the last minute. I swear on my mother's grave, so he'll believe me.

He considers all this, studying my face. "What's wrong with your sister, anyway?"

I picture Cassie pulling that apple from the tray, slicing off the eaten part. "I don't know. She might have mono." I touch Vinnie's crucifix. I can't help it. I want to see what it feels like.

"Really?" he says. "That's too bad." He means it, I think. He watches me awhile. "What's that shit you got on your mouth?"

"What? Oh. Lip-gloss." I wipe some off, embarrassed.

"Smells like bubble gum."

"It's bubble gum flavor."

"C'mere, let me see." He leans toward me and sniffs. "Mm," he says. He leans closer. "Let me taste." He kisses me.

I feel extremely grateful to him right that second, and sort of amazed, too: I can't believe he's forgiven me this fast.

"Mm," he says again. "That stuff is delicious." He kisses me again, and I close my eyes, feeling my shoulders and legs relax. When we stop, he draws the back of his hand across his mouth. "Got any more?" he says.

"Any more what?"

"Lip shit."

"It's inside. In my bag." I never call it a pocketbook anymore; Tiffany told me that's corny, just like it's corny to use the word *supermarket*. You say you're going food shopping and leave it at that.

"Well, why don't you go get it," he says. "Get your coat, too. Get *my* coat, I should say. We'll take a ride or something."

We're supposed to spend Sundays with the family; my father plans trips to New York or the shore, some museum or ballet. But today we have no plans, and I know we won't leave for Zelda's till late afternoon. For a second I think of Cassie, all alone in our room. But she'd never stay home just for me. And anyway, I can't say no to Vinnie now. "Okay," I say. "Let me just tell my mother."

Inside again, I grab Vinnie's coat from the closet and yell upstairs, "Mom, I'm going out for a little while."

She comes to the top of the steps. "Where to?" She doesn't like
to give me permission to do things that might piss off my father.

"Just around," I say. "With Vinnie." I find my leather clutch
bag under the piano, where one of the dogs dragged it, and wipe it
off on my jeans. "I'll be back by two or three."

"Make it two," she says, but she doesn't try to stop me, maybe
because she's got enough to worry about with my sister. Cassie still
hasn't come downstairs for breakfast. I picture her sitting on her bed,
staring at her hands.

And then I close the front door and head for Vinnie's car and
try not to think about any of that.

"Where to, hon?" Vinnie says. He pulls me over next to him,
clamps one arm around my neck, starts to drive.

"I don't know. Oh, I love this song."

Vinnie turns it up and starts singing, off-key. *Friday night I
crashed your party, Saturday I said I'm sorry. . . .* I want to sing, too,
but I don't have the nerve. Instead I half-dance against him, looking
out the window. House after house of lawns, turning brown with
winter; a white Trans Am with a fiery orange stencil on the hood,
parked the wrong way in the street. On Northway Avenue we pass
the Chinese restaurant, the West Berry drugstore, the haircut place,
and the cleaners. "So where do you want to go?" he says again.

I kiss greasy pink lips onto my window. "How 'bout the mall?"

"Okay."

"Really?" The mall is one of those things—like Tiffany—that
my mother doesn't fully approve of, so she doesn't take me without a
hassle. And when Tiffany drives us, we always have to get whoever's
car she "borrowed" back fast—or I have to be home.

But Vinnie's taking me now, in his car, and we can stay as long
as we want. It occurs to me that he'll drive me wherever I want to
go, and for a second the thought makes me want to ask for something outrageous. Just to see if he'll do it. I think about walking
through the mall with him then, his big arm around me. And me
wearing his jacket, feeling normal for once. The thought fills me
with joy.

But when we get there and park and go inside, I'm not really sure what to do. We walk aimlessly, no real destination in mind. We're not holding hands, and I wonder if Vinnie's still a little mad from before. The mall's filling up fast with Christmas shoppers. Decorations hang down from everywhere: glittery stockings, red-nosed reindeer, sparkling five-pointed stars.

In the center of the mall, kids are lining up to sit on Santa Claus's lap. Vinnie takes my hand. "Let's go see Santa," he says, pulling me over, "You can get your picture taken with him."

I laugh. "Oh, right."

"Why not?" he says. "I'll pay."

I stare at him to see if he's kidding, but he doesn't seem to be. "Aw, come on," he says. "I want the picture. For me."

But I don't want to do it. I shake my head, a slight tightening starting up in my chest.

"Not even for me?" he says. He tries to pull me to him then and kiss me, but I squirm away. "No!"

He lets me go. "Oh, I get it. It's against your religion, right? Sorry."

I hadn't even thought about that. "No, it's not. I told you we celebrate Christmas."

"Then why won't you do it?"

"Because! I'm not lining up with a bunch of three-year-olds to get my picture taken with Santa Claus. I'd feel absurd." It's a Cassie word, *absurd,* and I'm surprised to hear myself use it.

His brown eyes open wider and the pupils seem to darken, like he's both hurt and surprised. "I don't get you sometimes," he says.

I don't know what to say. Sometimes I don't get myself. Why can't I just take the stupid picture for him? I touch his name on his jacket, on my chest. "Want to go to Seaquarium?" I ask.

The purple lights of the place soothe me; we can't see each other that well, and there's other stuff to look at anyway. He follows as I walk through the rows of tanks. "Those are tetras," I say, trying to be nice. "And those are mollies, those black ones. They eat their babies if you don't separate them as soon as they're born. The beta fighting fish eat each other even when they're adults. You can only have one in a tank." I realize I sound like my father—explaining things, acting like the resident expert of the world.

"How do you know?" he says.

"We used to have a fish tank."

"Oh." He points to the arm-sized piranhas in a huge tank in the front of the store. "Man, my brother'd go for that."

"How old's your brother?" I'm glad he's talking again.

"Which one? I got three."

"You *do?*"

"And two sisters."

"There are six of you?" I think of his little house, the clothes-line full of clothes. His father's a plumber, I know. "How old are they all?"

He tells me their ages—all older except his little brother, Rudy, who's eight. He tells me his one sister lives in South Berry. "She brings her kids over every day and stays a friggen month," he says, though I can tell it doesn't really bug him. I listen, half-interested, but when we leave Seaquarium, my mind wanders. I think about what we look like together. I watch people who pass us, to see.

He wants me to try on a shirt he sees at No Name, a black shirt with a high neckline. It's not something I'd ever wear, but I do it anyway to make him happy. When I get it on, though, it looks terrible; in the mirror, a teenage nun gawks back at me. But when I come out Vinnie smiles. "You look incredible in that," he says. "Like really pure or something. C'mere, let me see."

I take a step toward him. I can see a salesperson watching us, a girl around my age. She starts to walk over. "I'm gonna take it off now, Vinnie, okay?" I say.

"Wait, turn sideways first."

I turn once, then escape back to the dressing room, wondering what my problem is. Most girls would love a guy like Vinnie admiring them. So what's wrong with me?

I pull on my sweater and go back out, determined to chill out and have fun the rest of the time. Vinnie's leaning against a wall, waiting. In a mirror behind him I can see the back of him. He looks short and wide-topped, like a triangle. I move my eyes to the actual him. "Let's go somewhere else," I say.

We go to Smuggler's Attic, where I got the bubble gum lip-gloss. I tell Vinnie how Tiffany rips the glosses out of the cardboard to try the different flavors, then puts them back. He laughs and flips through the packages. "Which one do you want? Pick one out, I'll buy it for you." He pulls out Wild Passion Berry. "Ha!" he says. "How 'bout this? Perfect for us."

"That's okay," I tell him. "I have two already. You don't have to buy me anything." In a way, though, I want him to buy me something. Not this, though. The flavor sounds bad.

"What, you don't want it?" he says.

I shrug. "I sort of like bubble gum the best."

So he buys me another bubble gum. He hands it to me on the way out. "Try it," he says.

I take it out and roll it on, and he kisses me again. I don't know why, but I don't feel like kissing him. But I like the idea that people will see us, so I let him do it anyway. "Want to get something to eat?" I say afterward.

We head toward the food corner, past Hotdog Hovel and Seafood Eat Food. "How 'bout some mussels?" he says.

"Mussels? Ugh!"

He laughs. "Then what do you want?"

I look around. "How about Italian Kitchen? Spaghetti and meatballs or something?"

He sticks out his tongue. "I couldn't go near the food there. They use horse meat in their sauce."

Now it's my turn to laugh. "How do you know?"

"I just do. You never eat spaghetti in a place like that. I can't eat sauce unless my mother makes it. Or my wife, if I had one."

I remember then that Tiffany won't eat spaghetti either unless it's homemade. "So what should I get, then?" I say, feeling dumb for suggesting it. "How about pizza? Is that okay here?"

"You want pizza?"

I shrug.

"Let's go to a real pizza place, then," he says. "Come on. We're out of here."

He drives us back to West Berry, past the high school and down toward South Berry. But a few blocks before it, he turns right and drives down a street I don't recognize. He pulls up outside a restaurant. From inside the window, a green and red and white sign says "Johnny's Pizza and Pasta." Vinnie parks. "My cousin's part owner," he explains. "You're gonna love this. None of that cardboard mall crap."

I'm trying to peer in, but it's too dark to see inside. Vinnie opens the door, and as we walk in, I feel like I'm entering a warm pizza cloud, swelling with sausage and garlic. I inhale deeply. Eight or ten red booths, all empty, line a wall with a mural of Venice painted on it. Behind a small counter, a short thin guy with dark curly sideburns is slapping around a pizza. He flips it in the air, spinning it like a record, and catches it on his fingertips.

He stops when he sees us and smiles a crooked-toothed smile. "Vinnie!" he says. He turns around and yells into the kitchen, " 'Ey, John, you'll never guess what the wind blew in." He puts the dough down and spoons tomato sauce in a circle onto it. "So how ya doin', Vin?"

Another guy comes out then, shorter and chubbier, a bowling-ball gut under his T-shirt. He slaps his cheek when he sees us. "Vinnie! Where you been, you stranger?" He comes around to shake Vinnie's hand.

Vinnie shrugs one shoulder, smiling. "Been busy as hell, that's where—"

"What, you're too good for us now that it's wrestling season? Now that you're pinning half the state, you forget your own flesh and blood?" He knuckles Vinnie's chest. "Don't worry, your brother keeps me posted. I'll be at the states watchin' you kick some ass, even if you forget we exist down here."

Vinnie's grinning. "Ah, come on John, I can't come down when I'm cutting weight, I'll die. What are you making now, huh? It smells fantastic."

"Nothing, just pizza, nothing. Sit down, I'll feed yas. What do you want? Who's this, anyway?" He points to me, smiling. "Where you been hiding her?"

"That's Billie. My girlfriend," Vinnie says. He turns to me. "That's my cousin John, and that's Rocky. Tell him what kind you want, he's the prince of pizza. He can make anything."

Rocky's shaking handfuls of shredded white cheese on top of the tomato sauce, and I want to stay here forever just watching him. I've always wanted to be a waitress in an Italian restaurant; I love the dark and the smells of garlic and parmesan and the way everyone always seems to be having a good time. And I like the idea of serving people food and making them happy—Italian food, and Italian people.

Once, I actually asked my father if I could waitress down at Solano's, just to see what he'd say. He said I couldn't work during the school year until I was a senior, and then only in his office, like Cassie did—spinning blood in a centrifuge, testing urine samples with a dipstick. "I don't need you waiting tables," he said.

"She was ready to eat Italian Kitchen, at the mall," Vinnie's telling Rocky and John.

John shakes his head. "Good thing you rescued her, huh, Vin?" He winks at me. "Whaddaya want, sweetheart? We got everything. Pepperoni, meatballs, Sicilian, extra cheese. Or calzones, or linguine and clams . . ."

I turn to Vinnie. "What do you want? We can share." It's the first thing I've said since we got here.

Vinnie shrugs. "You pick. I've had it all already, anyway."

Rocky and John watch me, Rocky's pizza waiting to be topped, and for a second I wonder if this is a test. I wonder if these guys met Angela, Vinnie's last girlfriend, and if they liked her. She was Italian. I'm pretty sure they can tell I'm not. "Um—pepperoni?" I say.

Rocky scoops a handful of pepperoni from a metal bin and tosses slices all over the pie. He pushes it in the oven.

Vinnie disappears back into the kitchen. Rocky's kneading a new ball of dough. I watch him a minute, then turn away, not sure what to do. "Do you need help or anything?" I ask.

He laughs. "No thanks, hon. We're between rushes, as you can see. Sit down, make yourself at home."

I slide into one of the booths, smelling pepperoni. Vinnie comes out with a carafe of red wine. He pours me a glass. I take a small sip. It tastes okay—a little like vinegar but not too bad.

And then Rocky's there with our steaming pizza, loaded with orange pepperoni and dripping with cheese. Vinnie serves me a piece. "Be careful, that's hot as fire," he says. He waits, watching me.

I blow on it impatiently. "What's wrong?" I say when I notice he's not taking any.

He shakes his head. "I can't, I'm five pounds over. Only three days till the next meet. Coach'll kill me if I cut all the weight at the end, like last time."

I stare at him. "You're not eating *anything*?" Hungry as I am, I can't imagine sitting here scarfing without him. Plus, there's enough pizza for five people. "Vinnie, you've gotta have one piece, at least." I'm starting to feel like a pig, between Vinnie and my sister both starving themselves.

From across the room, John calls, "I don't know, Vin. You ask me, you're gettin' small. You gotta feed your muscles, at least."

Vinnie considers. "All right, half a slice. Now you know why I don't come here during season." He cuts himself a sliver of a slice and puts it on his plate.

I dig in. The pizza slides down my throat, cheesy and fantastic. "You like it?" John says.

I nod, my mouth full. "It's unreal."

He looks pleased. "Not like that rubber shit you get at the mall, huh?"

I laugh. "Vinnie calls it cardboard." I wipe my face with a napkin, feeling warm and excited, buzzed with wine and food. I'm not nervous or shy anymore. I want to thank these people for being so nice, for making it easy again between me and Vinnie.

Vinnie serves me a second slice. "Be right back," he says. He goes back to the kitchen and comes out with a huge glass of water. He stands at the counter drinking it.

Rocky's smoking a cigarette, and I can hear Vinnie giving him a hard time about it, telling him it's a cancer stick, he's polluting his system. I make a mental note to tell my father Vinnie hates cigarette smoke, too. Vinnie and Rocky are chatting now, slinging around Italian words: *cavone, compare, marrone a mi*. Rocky looks over at me. He says something to Vinnie. "Couple weeks," Vinnie replies. He comes back to our table. John drifts over, and I thank him again for the food.

"What, that's all you're eatin'?" John holds his palms toward the ceiling. "Jeezus, Vinnie, she eats like a bird."

Vinnie gets a box from behind the counter and slides the pizza into it. "She'll take it home to her mother. Come on, Billie, I better get you home." He reaches into his back pocket and pulls out a twenty. "What do I owe you?" he says to his cousin.

John waves his hand. "Forget about it."

Vinnie shakes his head. "You forget about it. Come on, what? Fifteen? Twenty?" He holds out the bill. I dig for my wallet. "I'm the one who stuffed my face," I say. "I'm helping, too."

John waves me away. "Come on," he says to Vinnie. "What do you think, I'm some kind of Jew?"

There's a second of silence, and my heart seems to stop and wait, to pause for a beat. When it starts up again, it feels painful, like a hammer. I can feel blood pump through me.

Vinnie laughs once and looks at the table, his face slightly red. I pray with every ounce of energy I have that he won't tell them I'm Jewish.

He glances at me, and I widen my eyes as a signal, like I would with Tiffany. He looks back at John. "You really won't take any money?" he says.

John plants his feet apart and folds his arms over his gut. "Vinnie. Don't embarrass me, okay? Come on. This is family."

I know Vinnie wants to get out of there before he says anything more. He shakes John's hand, then picks up the pizza box. "Thanks a lot," he says. "I owe you."

"You don't owe me nothin'. Just come around and see us, okay? Bring your beautiful girlfriend back, too. Billie. She don't look like a boy, though." He smiles warmly at me. "Come back and see us again, huh, Billie?"

I plaster a smile on my face. "I will," I say.

In the car, Vinnie can't stop apologizing. "They don't mean it," he says. "They talk about everyone like that, even Italians. Even *gumbahs*."

"Forget it," I say. I snap on my seat belt, then unsnap it again, feeling like a dweeb. "It doesn't bother me." But it does, more and more every time. I want him to start driving, already.

"What do you mean it doesn't bother you?" he says. He starts the car and pulls onto the road. "It has to bother you."

I shrug. "I'm used to it." I turn to face him. "It's true, anyway. Jews *are* cheap. If that had been a Jewish restaurant, they would have taken your money."

"So what? Italians are pigs, some of 'em. So what? If someone called me a pig, I'd beat the fuck out of him."

I feel tired, suddenly. "Don't worry about it."

"You should be proud of what you are," he says. He turns to look at me. "*I'm* proud of you." He puts his arm around me and pulls me over. He plants a wet kiss on my cheek.

I want to squirm away. I keep my eyes on the road and stay still. It's starting to snow a little, just a flurry. I watch the flakes land on the windshield, melting into drops of water as they do. I'm glad to be going home, though I wonder if my father's there, and whether he's mad that I'm not.

But Vinnie turns left a few blocks before my street, onto a dead-end road.

"Where are you going?" I ask.

He drives to the end, then turns off the car. He puts his arm around me again. He kisses my cheek, then my ear, then my neck. I turn to face him finally, and he kisses my lips.

I kiss back a minute, then pull away gently. Through the box, the pizza is hot on my thighs. "Vinnie," I say.

"What, babe?" He kisses my eyebrow. "I like you so much, you know that? You are so perfect for me."

I force myself to smile. I don't know what to say.

He goes for my mouth again, and I let him, feeling like I have no choice. I don't want him to think I'm some spoiled Jewish girl who's using him to buy me things. I don't want to make him mad, either. His hand slips into my jacket and down the front of my shirt. I laugh uncomfortably, stiffening. "Vinnie."

"What? What's the matter?" He pulls his hand out—not mad, just confused.

"No—it's just—I really have to get home. I've been gone for a while, and my father doesn't even know I left, and I'll probably—"

"Okay, okay." He lets go of me slowly, sighing. "Sorry. It's just that you turn me on, that's all. You turn me on so much."

For a second that familiar tingle goes through me—like in the wrestling room. If he comes back right now, I might give in.

But he turns on the car and backs out of there, like I asked. "I'll take you home," he says.

Cassie's sitting on the front steps when we pull up, wearing a huge coat of my father's and at least three scarves—one of them wrapped around her head and covering her mouth and nose. She's holding a thick textbook open on her lap, but she's not reading it.

"Is that your sister?" Vinnie says. "What's she doing?" He waves to her.

Cassie waves back quickly with one hand but doesn't get up.

"Should I go say hi?" he asks—a little nervous, maybe.

"You better not. She might be contagious. Next time."

I watch his car pull away, and then I walk toward my sister, the pizza box in my hand. "What are you doing sitting out in the snow?" I call, but then I hear the opera coming from the house and I know. He has it on all the radios, even the stereo in our room. Cassie hates it as much as I do. "Oh," I say. "Bet you missed that at school."

Cassie squints up at me. Her green eyes are pink, filled with tears.

My hands tighten on the box. "What's wrong?"

"The dogs had another fight."

"Oh." I sit down next to her, dropping the box onto my lap. "They fight all the time now."

She shrugs and looks at me, just her big bloodshot eyes above the scarf, so I can't see her expression. "How's DiNardio?" she says. "Did you have fun? Where'd you get the pizza?"

"Johnny's. Down on Oak. Do you know it? His cousin owns it."

"I guess." She looks at the box.

I push it toward her. "Want a piece?"

"No. We're going to Zelda's for dinner."

"I know." I try to see what she's thinking, but I can't tell just from her eyes. I stand up. "Well. I better go in. I'm probably dead, right?" I touch her head as I walk past her and inside.

My father's sitting in front of the television, which is turned on despite the opera. The newspaper is spread on his lap. "You're just lucky," he says to me. His eyes shift back to the TV. "We're leaving in twenty minutes."

"I'm ready. Dad, look. Vinnie bought us pizza."

"Ah, *shit,* Redskins!" He picks up the remote control and presses it. "What?" he says to me.

My mother comes down the stairs, a pile of books in her arms. "Oh, good," she says. "I realized, after you left, I don't even have Vinnie's number . . . pizza?" She raises her eyebrows.

I nod. "Vinnie bought it. For all of us. How's Cassie?"

"What?"

"*God,* that music is loud. I said, 'How's Cassie?'"

My mother glances toward the den. "Michael, can we at least turn it off upstairs?"

My father looks at us over the paper. "No," he says.

He's beyond obnoxious. But my mother just rolls her eyes and smiles at me. "Cassie's fine," she says. "You'd better get ready to go. Want me to take that?"

I hand it to her as she moves past me, down the stairs, toward the kitchen, and then I clap my hands over my ears and go upstairs.

★   ★   ★

It's sleeting by the time we leave for my grandmother Zelda's. In the backseat, my coat almost touching my sister's, I listen to the windshield wipers click. Outside, nearly every West Berry house has a Christmas display: rainbows of lights, elaborate Baby Jesus scenes. The decorations dwindle as we approach North Berry. Just houses now, bigger. The road widens to four lanes.

Zelda lives in a large house, near the border of North Berry, that she bought with my grandfather years ago. My father pulls into the round driveway, and I think of Cassie and me running around it endlessly as kids, like balls on a roulette table. Later, when Cassie was learning to drive, Zelda let her practice her K-turns and parallel parking on it. I wonder if she'll do the same for me when I get my learner's permit in a few weeks. I think about asking Cassie if she'll help me learn, too. But she's scrunched down in the seat, still drowning in scarves, looking cold and sulky.

So I concentrate on Zelda's house. It's just like her: big, beautiful, overstated, well manicured. We run to the door, trying not to get wet. My mother carries a platter of shrimp and cocktail sauce. She rings the bell. It chimes long and deep throughout the house, like a gong. And then Zelda's there, ushering us out of the rain and into her warm familiar smells: flowery perfume, lime and tonic, raw steak. She hugs me hard. My cousin Emily rushes up, her hair in tight pigtails that bob like two springs. She's wearing a tight little green pants outfit that makes her look like a string bean. I give her a hug, wondering if Zelda dressed her and how long she's been here. Coats are coming off everywhere. My grandmother's hugging Cassie now, asking her how school is.

I go into the kitchen to say hello to Celia, the black woman who cooks and cleans for my grandmother. She asks me about school, and I give her a brief update, then ask if she needs help. She smiles and tells me no thanks, as usual. And then my father's at the bar, cracking ice cubes, making drinks, and I follow everyone to the living room.

My grandmother sits down, then stands again. "It's so dark, I want to see you all." She dials the lights to full power. "How's that?"

"Fine," my mother says.

"Too bright," my father says at the same time.

My grandmother laughs and turns it down a little. "Now?" We nod. "Help yourself to some shrimp," she says. "Jane, those look scrumptious. You didn't have to do that, but I'm glad you did." She's dark tan, as always, wearing orange lipstick and dark blue eye shadow that makes her eyes very blue. And lots of big gold jewelry. Her long splashy skirt is red and orange. Her nails glitter the same red, like polished jewels. "I like your skirt, Zelda," I tell her. "Is it new?"

"It is. Thank you, sweetie." She beams.

My father takes a bunch of shrimp, and I take one, too, even though I'm not hungry yet. When I sit down, Emily climbs on my lap. Cassie's sitting in a plush armchair with neon fruit printed all over it, and I hope it's the chair design or the black coat she's got draped over her shoulders that makes her face seem so white. My grandmother's looking at her, too. "Cassandra, are you sure I can't take your coat?" she says.

"No thanks." Cassie smiles uncomfortably and crosses her arms.

"Or I can turn up the heat. Are you cold?"

Cassie shakes her head. "I'm fine, Zelda. Thanks. I just want to keep my coat on a minute." Silence. Emily climbs off me and leans across the table to take a shrimp. She turns to me, then bites off a corner tentatively and chews once without closing her mouth. Then she makes a horrified face and spits the bite into her hand.

I crack up. Emily giggles. "Oh, Emmy," my grandmother says. She sighs. "At least use a napkin." Cassie holds one out to her, but she runs out of the room, I guess for solace from Celia.

Zelda leans back, then purses her lips. "You look thin, Cassandra. Your face. Mikey, does she look thin to you?"

My father glances at my sister. "Does she look thin," he says slowly, like he's contemplating. When he doesn't want to answer a question, he repeats it slowly, like that.

My mother takes a shrimp and a napkin. "That's a nice sweater, too, Zelda."

"It better be," Zelda says. "After what I paid for it. And it's too big, I think. The salesgirl talked me into buying it this size. Don't you think it looks baggy?"

My mother shakes her head. "I think it looks just right."

Zelda looks at the sweater. It's purple with a strip of the same orange as her skirt. Everything coordinated, everything perfect. I picture her sashaying into the country club. My father's wearing old-fashioned khakis and a sweater she knit him fifteen years ago. "Well, how do you think I should wash it?" Zelda asks.

My mother examines the material. "In cold water, by hand. Lay it out flat to dry."

"But won't it shrink if I wash it?"

"It shouldn't. Not if you use cold water."

"What if I use warm?"

My mother shrugs. "It'll probably shrink."

"Well, I *want* it to shrink. Just a little, though. How much will it, do you think?" She sips her drink and makes a face. "Ooh, Michael, this is strong," she says before my mother can answer.

My father shrugs, takes another piece of shrimp.

My grandmother's watching him, waiting for a response about the drink. When she doesn't get one, she looks back at Cassie. "Sweetie," she says. "You're not eating."

Cassie shifts around. "I don't want any right now. I'll have some in a little while. Thanks."

Zelda frowns. "I thought you *liked* shrimp. Don't you like shrimp?"

"Yes. I just don't really—"

"I'll fix you something else." Zelda leaps up from her chair. "I have chopped liver, chopped egg—or I could open some pickled herring. You like that, don't you?" Her voice is loud and deep, big and strong, just like her, and I want to defend my sister, tell Zelda to back off for a change.

Cassie shakes her head, hard and fast. "I really don't want anything, Grandma. Don't worry, okay?"

Zelda sighs, hands on hips. "Well, you're too thin." She looks around. "Can I fix something for anyone else? I have applesauce, Ritz crackers, melba toast—"

"Mother," my father interrupts, "we're eating shrimp. Sit down and relax, would you please?"

Zelda sits. "I just thought you might want something else. Is that so bad?" She crosses her legs and sips her drink. The grandfather clock ticks loudly. In the kitchen, Celia's shoes clack against the linoleum floor, and I know she's shuffling around, opening pots and pans, adding butter or seasoning. Celia has heart problems. She comes to my father's office occasionally. Afterward, I always ask to make sure he hasn't made her pay anything.

Zelda leans forward again, this time scrutinizing me. "Your hair looks different," she says. "It looks lovely. What did you do differently?"

"Thanks. Nothing. It's just longer, I guess."

She turns to Cassie. "You should do yours more like Billie's—not so tight back like that. You have such lovely hair. Though with your face, you could wear just about anything. You've always had good bones. . . ." Her voice fades. She jumps up again. "Oh, sweetie, let me hang up your coat, already. It spoils the look of the room."

"Jesus, Mother!" my father explodes. "Let her keep it on if she's cold!" I want to cheer him for saying that.

But I can't help feeling sort of sorry for Zelda, too. She looks sad and less pretty now, like she always does after he's mean to her. But she's just as bad to him. Why can't they both chill out, why can't we all just relax? Celia appears in the doorway. "Dinner's ready," she says in her soft little voice, and I wonder how she can stand any of us.

We sit at our usual spots, my father and Zelda at the ends, Cassie and I on one side, Emily and my mother on the other. Emily flicks at the chandelier, icy crystal diamonds, until my grandmother says, "Sweetie, don't touch." And then we sit quietly, watching Celia shuffle in and out from the kitchen with platters and bowls of steaming food—a thick steak, red potatoes, glazed carrots, hot rolls in a cloth-covered basket—until Cassie and my mother both get up to help her carry things in. They bring it to my father, who takes a portion and passes it. He stands up to carve the steak. "I want the bone," Emily announces.

I pile food on my plate, watching to make sure my sister puts a few things on hers. And then I eat my dinner and tune out the voices and replay being in the car with Vinnie. He was so sweet and gentle, the way he touched me, the way he always touches me. Why was I so anxious to get out of there? I love having Vinnie to think about at times like this—sometimes more than I love being with him. In my mind, I map out the phones in this house and pick one to call him from later—in my grandmother's room.

Zelda passes my father a basket of rolls. "There's a house for sale four blocks from here," she says. "Did you see the sign?"

"No," my father says. He takes a roll.

"Oh. Well, it's Pensen Realty. I've got the number." She pauses. "Do you want it?"

"What for?" my father says. "Pass the butter, please."

Zelda shrugs, already defensive. "I just thought you might think about moving to North Berry." She passes him the butter.

"Mother, why would I do that?" he says.

"I don't know. I always thought you'd move here eventually." She sighs. "I never did understand your living in West Berry all these years. Everything really is much nicer here. The temples, the grocery stores . . ."

My father laughs. "What do I care about the temples?" he says, buttering his roll.

"Well, you should care," Zelda says. She folds her arms. "All my friends' children have settled here—"

"And all your friends' children's kids go to Hebrew school and take tennis lessons and go to summer camp."

"So?"

"So that's not what I want for my children."

"Me either, Zelda," I say. "I like West Berry."

My father sighs. "Mother, could we please change the subject?"

I glance over at my sister. She's using her fork to make a carrot design on her plate.

"How are your card games, Zelda?" my mother says.

Zelda flaps her hand and smiles. "Terrible. The Rothmans are in Italy this week, so the Morgans are filling in, and they're atrocious players—"

"Where in Italy?" I say.

"A place called Anzio, near Rome. It's not so nice now, though, Italy, apparently. Not like when your grandfather and I went. They don't feel they can walk around at night, Agnes said. But the hotel's beautiful, they say, so that's good—"

"Did you go to Sicily?" I ask. Tiffany's family is Sicilian.

"Oh, we went all over. Sicily, Venice, Florence. Florence is where I got my gold bracelet and my elephant ring. I'll show you after dinner. The gold is wonderful there. Aggie said she'd bought quite a bit." She glances around the table and sighs. "Well, I had my time there, I was lucky. You girls will, too. Someday you'll have husbands who will take you to all kinds of beautiful places."

"Someday we'll take ourselves," Cassie says. It's the first thing she's said since dinner started. We all turn to her.

My father laughs. "What are you, some big women's libber now?"

"Well, that doesn't sound like much fun to me," Zelda says, "going off to Italy without a husband."

"Depends on the husband," I say.

Everyone laughs. "That's true, I guess," Zelda says. "Although, if he's your husband, I'd hope he'd be a good one."

"Well, what if you thought he was at the time, but later he turned out not to be?" I look around at them. "I mean, how can you tell?" I'm thinking about Vinnie. Every time I see him, I feel something different. Sometimes it even varies from hour to hour.

"How can you tell? You just *can*," Zelda says. "If you can't, he's not the right one. You don't really love him."

"That's not true," says Cassie. "My women's studies teacher says that any woman who goes into marriage absolutely sure hasn't thought about marriage realistically. She says any woman who's not ambivalent about marriage is in for a rude awakening." She looks around at us. "That goes for having kids, too."

I'm not sure exactly what she's talking about, but I'm glad she's talking, anyway. But my father laughs loudly, like it's not really funny. "Did I *pay* for that course? Women's studies? Jesus!"

"What's the matter, Dad," Cassie says. "Do you feel threatened?"

"Threatened?" He laughs again. "Hardly."

I believe him, too. If he really felt threatened, he'd just stop paying for the course.

My mother watches Cassie; maybe she's wondering where she got so smart. Zelda touches her earring and looks around. "Who wants more?" she says.

Emily stands up. "I do. Can I ring the bell for Celia?" She pops up and reaches for a tiny silver bell sitting on the bureau.

"Don't you dare," Cassie whispers.

Emily looks startled. "Why not?" But the door opens and Celia is there anyway, holding the refilled platter of steak.

"Oh, good," Zelda says. "She read our minds." She smiles at Celia. "Everyone needs more, please, except me, I'm stuffed. You can leave the platter on the table afterward, if you don't mind."

Cassie stands up. "Excuse me." She heads back toward the bathroom. Her plate is still mostly filled, of course. I fork up some of her carrots and eat them quickly, trying to avoid a scene.

Emily inches over to my grandmother, peering at the platter of steak. "Can I have a spoonful of gravy?" she asks. It's another ritual, as old as ringing the maid's bell. Zelda spoons pink juice off the platter with her teaspoon and feeds it to Emily, like medicine. When did Cassie and I stop doing this? "For good blood," Zelda says happily. She looks at me. "Want some, Billie?" I shake my head. "No thanks."

Zelda shrugs and kisses my cousin and pulls her up onto her lap. "I tried on Zelda's jewelry before," Emily announces. "And Zelda's shoes." It was Cassie who started calling my grandmother Zelda; the rest of us followed her lead. Emily jabbers on, telling how she went shopping with Zelda, how Zelda polished her nails, how she watched Zelda get her hair done. My mother's asking all kinds of questions, to keep Emily talking. My father's joking with her. He likes little kids.

I help Celia clear the table, then go see what Cassie's doing. She's not in the guest bathroom. In Zelda's room, I can see a light under the bathroom door. I knock once. "Cass?"

"What," she answers.

"Are you on the bowl or what?" I want to make sure she's not throwing up—though I don't think she ever really does. There's never anything in her stomach *to* puke, anyway.

"No," Cassie answers me. "Come in, if you want."

She's standing in front of the mirror looking down, her long ponytail—gold in the bright bathroom lights—flowing down to her jeans. When I come around, I see that she's looking into one of my grandmother's cosmetic drawers. It's packed from one end to the other with blushes, eye-shadow compacts, mascara, colored pencils. I reach for a plastic container full of bath oil beads. "Remember these?" I say. "Once I dumped the whole package in, just to watch them swirl around in the bath. Zelda called me an oil slick when I got out. She wasn't mad, though."

Cassie nods absently. I put the beads back, thinking of all the things I've seen Zelda do to keep her skin from wrinkling. Once a week, she swathes her hands and feet in Vaseline, covering them with cotton gloves and socks to sleep. When she touches you, her fingers have the cool silky feel of a snake.

My sister pulls out a bottle and examines it. " 'A hydrogenized biolytic glowing potion for the skin,' " she reads. She sets it on the counter and takes out another bottle, and then another. She lines them up until there are five of them, standing like soldiers. Next to them she's lined up lotions, bath oils, perfumes. "Stuff," she says. Like it's some horrible thing.

For some reason, I feel the need to defend my grandmother. "She needs it," I say. "She's old, Cass."

Cassie looks at me bleary-eyed. "What is *need*?" She closes the drawer and opens a second one. There are cans of hair spray, rollers of all sizes, a hairclip shaped like a seashell. I take out the clip, open and close it a few times.

Cassie picks up a large pair of scissors and puts it on her right hand. She stares at the mirror, blinking at her face. With her left hand, she reaches for her ponytail. She extends it from her head, like she's about to cut it. I laugh. "I dare you," I say, still playing with the clip.

With a single snip, she chops off half her ponytail at the roots. I gasp and grab at her hand, dropping the seashell clip. "What the fuck are you doing?"

But she steps away from me, and the scissors snip once more, and the ponytail swings from her fist—a long silky gold rope, completely separate from her. On her head, short jagged hair juts in all directions. Her eyes are huge in her skull—deep, round green eyes that don't like what they're seeing, outside or in.

I feel panicked. For eighteen years she had that hair. All her life. She looks at me, half-smiling. "Holy shit," she says.

For a second I wish I could freeze time right there, before anyone else finds out. I take a step away from her. "You're crazy," I say. "I'm going to get Mom." I fly out of there.

Hours later, in bed, my scruff-headed sister breathing sounds of sleep across the room, I remember everyone's reactions. Emily cried, then asked if we were keeping the hair. My grandmother ran around like some drugged insect, crying, "It's all my fault, I shouldn't have told her it didn't look nice pulled back." My mother tried to say it would look fine once it was all evened out, but she talked much too fast, the words somersaulting out of her mouth. We were standing in the hallway, me, my mother, and Zelda. "Why would anyone want to just *ruin* herself like that?" Zelda said. Celia peeked out of the kitchen, and I knew she was wondering what all the fuss was about—why we were all gathered there, standing, when there were so many rooms with so many chairs.

Cassie was in the den. She had walked down the hallway, mumbling something about hair being nothing but dead cells anyway, then gone into the den and closed the door. My father had gone in after her.

I heard Cassie talking to him behind the door, her voice rising in pitch. "I can't believe you let me leave, Dad! God, I didn't even talk to them about my exams."

And my father: "I'll call your professors tomorrow morning, okay? Don't worry about it. Try to relax."

I knew he would call, too; he would never lie about something like that. He came out of the den, and we all stood there looking at him, waiting for him to say something. In his shirt pocket, his glasses case made a lump at the heart of his sweater. "Calm down," he said finally. "She cut her hair, that's all. Hair grows back."

And a part of me relaxed, just hearing him say that. Some surface part of me just unwound and let go, free. But deep down another part of me knew much better. My sister wasn't okay. And for all that I wanted to hear my father say she was, when he finally did, I couldn't believe him.

chapter
five

Christmas vacation I'm home almost every day with Cassie, which amazes me even as it happens—not least of all because she's anything but fun to be around. When she's not sneaking her food to the dogs or back to its boxes and jars as soon as my mother leaves the room, she's walking round and round our block or sitting with her face buried in some thick textbook or, worst of all, spewing out depressing facts for my benefit. Looking like a match—stick body, little cropped yellow head—she sits there and tells me how many trees die to make a day's worth of newspapers, how many bags of garbage a family produces in a year. She describes how we're living off our planet's capital, not its interest, then launches into how much waste results from the average airplane flight. Last time she flew, she tells me, she returned her snack bag and told the flight attendant it was untouched, but the woman smiled politely and then trashed it all anyway. "Company policy," she said, dumping sealed peanut butter crackers, unopened blocks of cheese, and a fresh orange straight in the trash.

Each person got three drinks with a new cup each time, she tells me, even if they were drinking the same thing. And everything— plastic utensils, plastic earphones—had been swaddled in clear plastic wrap. She tells me all this in minute detail, bold blue quarter-moons

under her eyes, and I sit there and listen, even though it's information I don't really want. I don't want to become a person who can
never get on a plane or stuff a cup in the trash.

Listening to her makes me want to call Tiffany, or go hang out
up at her house. And I do, sometimes; we see each other at least
every other day. There's always something new going on at her
place, and people smoking and drinking and having fun, and there's
Dominick—or rather, the *feeling* of Dominick: his shoes, the door of
his room. But I never stay there as long as I want, because I can't
bring myself to leave Cassie for too much time. For one thing, I'm
the only one who seems to know what a mess she is, or at least to be
worried about it—which means, I think, that I'm the one who has to
help her. My father relaxes after her blood work comes back and
shows her to be slightly anemic but otherwise okay; he brings her a
bottle of multivitamins plus iron and orders her to take one every
day, and that's that. My mother watches her a lot—her lips tight
together, like she's worried—and she cooks good things and pushes
her to eat all the time, but my sister has her fooled. She has ways to
empty a plate without eating a thing, ways my mother would never
dream of—not that it would occur to her that my sister didn't eat the
stuff anyway. And my mother doesn't realize how skinny Cassie is
either, since my sister hides under sweats all the time. I'm the only
one who knows what she looks like. I'm the one who sees everything, and I feel like I need to be there with her, seeing it.

And my sister seems to need me, too, in a way she never has
before—which is another reason I hang around. I guess it gives me
some weird sort of satisfaction, knowing she finally appreciates me.
Plus, I still like to look at her: the way her eyes widen when she talks,
the way her mouth twitches just a little, like a tic. I look at her and
see myself sometimes, in a more perfect version. Then, other times, I
look at her and I'm so sick of her, I want to scream.

I almost can't wait to go back to school by the end of my
vacation. But the day I get back, I find myself calling home to make
sure she's okay, and that goes on all week. Sometimes I even call
twice. She acts like I'm crazy when I call, and I act like I'm annoyed
to find her there, though the truth is I'm relieved to hear her voice

and I think she's relieved to hear mine. "Why don't you *go* some-where?" I ask her. She tells me she has to study, she wants to get ahead for next semester. I let that one go for now, though I know I can't much longer. No one, herself included, has said that she isn't going back to Cornell, but I feel like I can't let her go back there— not like this, all skin and bones and acting like she might jump in that gorge at any second.

So another week passes, and Saturday we're there again, two sisters on two beds in one room. I'm half reading *Heart of Darkness,* half trying to decide what to wear to Donna Pizarro's party, which I'm going to with Vinnie tonight. Cassie's sitting cross-legged on her bed reading some Christmas card, her bony chin pressed to her bony, flatter-than-ever chest, and even though it's gone, I see her gold ponytail, a ghost limb, spilling forward like a fountain from the top of her head. Falling sadly over her sweatshirt, sweeping the string of her sad gray sweatpants. "Hey, Cass," I say, mostly just to say something to her, "did you ever read *Heart of Darkness?*"

She looks over at me, then back at the card. "Of course."

"I don't get the line about 'The horror, the horror.' At the end."

She doesn't look at me this time. She says, "God, I can't believe I wrote this just last year."

"What?"

"This card to Steve. I never sent it."

Steve Zucker was Cassie's friend all through high school, even though he lives in Connecticut. "Why not?" I say.

She shrugs.

"Let me see," I say.

She tosses the card over, then lies down on her back. On the outside of the card is a stick-figure Santa, looking jolly. I open it up. *Dear Steve, Jamie and I are over, with many promises to be "good friends." Though I seriously doubt that. He and I will never truly understand each other, only you and I can do that.* I glance over at her, debating whether to feel offended that she wrote that. But it's true, I *don't* really under-stand her. And last year, I didn't even try. I read on. *No one else here gets me at all, in fact—so please come visit me soon. Put it on your new calendar. "Visit Cassandra." Then let me know what day, and I'll be here waiting, just like that. Okay? Merry whatever. Love, Cass. P.S. Mail me a kiss, my applications are done. The grand tally: Cornell, UVA, Princeton, Yale, Swarthmore, and Boston College—just in case the God of the Ivies doesn't think I'm worthy and dooms me (alas) to "More Competitive" land.*

The last part is a reference to a category in the *Barron's Guide to Colleges,* which my father consulted like the Bible during Cassie's application process. The book ranks the colleges into categories— "Most Competitive," "Very Competitive," "More Competitive," and so on—and by the end he knew the lists by heart, along with the better schools' SAT averages. "Most Competitive" schools were the only ones he'd considered for Cassie. I know the same will be true with me. It's something I try not to think about.

I pass the card back to Cassie, imagining what she might write now: *Dear Steven, You wouldn't recognize me, inside or out. I cut off my hair. I weigh about a pound. Can you tell me how to stop the planet? I want to get off. . . .*

The thought makes me sad—like everything seems to these days when I'm around my sister. She's staring at the ceiling now, palms under her head. I stand up. "See you later," I say.

She sits up quickly. "Where are you going?"

"I don't know. Tiffany's, maybe. I'm so *bored.*"

Her eyes fill up with tears. "Sorry."

I sigh. "Why are *you* sorry, Cass? I'm not leaving because of you." But I am, and she knows it, and the worst part of all is that she actually cares. I wish then that she'd be her snotty old self again. It was so much easier to hate her sometimes than it is to pity her, like this.

I pull the door closed again and step back in the room with my sister. I sit on the floor, against the shelves that hold games we played as kids: Stratego, Yahtzee, Monopoly, Careers. She always beat me, mostly because I never cared if I won and she did. "Tell me about your roommate," I say.

She turns toward the wall. "What do you want to know?"

That's better. Snottier. I smile. "I don't know. Was she nice? What did she look like?"

"You mean what *does* she look like. She's not dead, Bil. Anyway, what does that matter?"

"I don't know. I'm just curious."

She shrugs. "Tall, skinny, red hair. She wore black work boots all the time. She looked like a boy. Really beautiful."

"Did you ever talk to her again after she left?"

"Once. She called me from work. She works at a movie theater. In Galesburg, Illinois." She smiles. "She had all these ticket stubs in her hand, and she was telling me she couldn't stop thinking about who'd handed them to her. She was wondering how many of them were good people and how many bad. I told her there's no such thing as a good person."

Her roommate sounds as ridiculous as Cassie. But after a while I ask, "So what makes someone a 'good person,' anyway?"

She looks at me. "What do *you* think?"

"I don't know! Cassie, why does everything have to be so philosophical these days? I swear, I think you learned too much at college. I think it ruined you."

"Is that what you think?" She smiles a little.

I shrug, losing confidence. I hear my mother then, scurrying around downstairs. She's baking something—cherry pie, I think. One of Cassie's former favorites.

"Did you ever notice," she says then, "that Mom and Dad are always, like, *doing* something? They're hyper. I mean, they never stop."

I want to refute her, but it's true really. "I wonder why," I say.

"Because they can't," Cassie says. "If they ever stopped, they'd be overcome with sadness."

I turn to face her. Does she really think that? Maybe my mother —*maybe*. Not my father, though. "How do you know?" I demand.

"I don't. But I think so."

"Why?"

She sighs. "You always want an answer, Billie. Sometimes there just isn't one." She tenses up, suddenly. "Who's here?" She turns and kneels to look out the window.

I climb up next to her on her bed to see out, too. A red

Mercedes—familiar, but I can't place it—has pulled up in front of
our house, but it's backing away now, down the hill. It rounds the
corner, out of sight. I watch the branches of the ear tree blow in the
wind. "Probably no one," I tell my sister.

Through the branches the sky is a thin silver-gray, and it looks
like it might rain. I turn around and rest my back against Cassie's
headboard, my legs straight out in front of me. She turns too, finally,
and sits next to me the same way. The left leg of her sweatpants is
pushed up almost to her knee. Her calf pokes out, a bone with no
meat. "Look at your leg," I say, pointing. "You're a rail. You're a
railroad." I touch my finger to her calf and push in.

She laughs. "Stop."

I do it again.

"*Stop!*" she says, laughing. "That tickles." She tries to push me
away, but she's weak as a butterfly. I do it a third time, then a fourth.
It's been so long since I've heard her laugh.

She tries to slap me then. "Dream on," I say, catching her hand,
but I stop tickling her anyway. I rest my hand on her calf. Her legs
are a little hairy, but the hair is thin and soft, like a baby's. "You're so
soft," I say. I run my finger up and down her calf. She lets me for a
second, then giggles again. "*Stop* it, already."

I get up and walk over to my desk and sit down on my chair.
Up on our shelves there are trophies all over the place, Cassie's trophies from all her tennis tournaments—local ones, school ones, ones
from the tennis camp she went to for a couple of summers. She
probably couldn't even beat me now. She probably wouldn't last one
set.

I remember, then, something she said to me, on one of her first
days back home from school. She told me she was afraid of people
now sometimes, in a way she never had been before. On the street,
she said, she'd keep turning around, checking to see if anyone was
there. She felt like someone was behind her all the time, just waiting
to jump out. One time, she said, she broke into a run just because
some guy was walking nearby. He'd caught up to her later, on a main
street corner, and asked her if she was okay—some young guy, just a

kid, with glasses and a sweatshirt and jeans. She'd felt incredibly stupid then.

I swing around on my desk chair and face her. She's rubbing Chap Stick on her lips. Her hand moves back and forth, and I wonder which came first, her fear or her weakness from not eating. Now the two seem to feed each other. I watch her a little longer. And then, almost suddenly, something opens up inside me, and a glimmer of understanding seeps in—some small idea of what she's going through. I don't know why. But I know I don't like it, and I want to get out of there. "I have to go to the bathroom," I say, leaving the room.

I'm not in there a minute before the doorbell rings and the dogs start to bark, and then Cassie's outside the bathroom door, knocking to come in. I open the door. "Who's here?" she says in my face. Like I have ESP, or something.

We can hear the dogs rush to the front door, their toenails scratching furiously at the floor. And my mother: "Stop it, dogs! Sit! Both dogs sit!"

The door opens, and the voice of Frannie Greenbaum, one of my mother's oldest friends, pierces the air. "Jaane! Oh god, do I have to pee. . . ."

Frannie lives in North Berry, not far from my grandmother, and pops in occasionally uninvited, which my mother doesn't mind. She doesn't mind anything about Frannie, though they're as different as two people can get. Frannie has four kids, all boys, the middle two —Dean and Jeremy—Cassie's age and one year older than me. "You will not believe what I went through to get here," she's screaming to my mother. "Do you have coffee, Jane? I need a pot this instant. Before I even take my coat off. I am not kidding. I'm frozen solid, the heat in the Mercedes is out again, I'm utterly incensed. Are you busy? Are the kids here? *Cassandra!*" she shrieks. "*Billie!* Oh god, I have to go so bad, I can't stand it. Wait. I'll be right back." The bathroom door downstairs slams.

Cassie looks at me wide-eyed. "I'm not going down there," she says.

"Why not?" But I'm relieved in a way.

"I'm just not," she says. "Say I'm sleeping, Bil. Please?"
I shrug. "I'll try."

Frannie sits at the kitchen table, stirring Sweet'n Low into a mug of coffee and blabbing like some endless radio broadcast. She's telling my mother about some kid in one of her sons' school whose parents tried to disown him. "Jeremy wants to adopt him," she says, laughing, like she does at everything—though in a different way than my father. To Frannie, everything's a riot or a disaster. And no event in New Jersey goes unknown to her, especially if it has to do with kids.

My mother listens, nodding, as she loads the dishwasher. This is their routine: Frannie sits and drinks potfuls of coffee and talks, and my mother runs around the kitchen doing things.

Just the sight of the two of them in there makes me feel better about life. "Hi, Frannie," I say, giving her a quick hug. "Mm. I like your perfume."

She laughs. "Do you? Jesus, *look* at you! You're absolutely *stunning!* God, Jane, that's good coffee. Jeremy gave it to me. The perfume, I mean. It's Heartbreak, or Heartburn—I don't know, one of those things. Anyway, I can't decide if I adore it or if it nauseates me. Janie, what do you think—oh my gosh, I can't *believe* I didn't ask, Billie! How did you do?" She stares at me expectantly, looking a little like the grinch—bulging eyes, slightly buck teeth—but with short orange hair.

I slide into a chair. "How'd I do with what?"

"PSATs! What else? Jeremy's SAT scores came yesterday, he got 1540—but he doesn't count, he was always fabulous on all those tests, he gets it from his uncle Solly, Janie, you remember him. He weighs four hundred pounds now. What it is is he has to have a quart of Häagen-Dazs butter crunch every day—but anyway, we're all ecstatic about Jeremy. I mean, he's pretty much *into* Princeton now, we think, we hope"—she pauses to gulp coffee, waving her free hand wildly to keep the floor—"which is a huge relief for all of us, considering what hell the past month has been. His latest thing was, if he didn't get into Princeton, he wasn't going anywhere, so he wouldn't even *look* at the Harvard app—"

"*App?*" I say.

"Application. David was beside himself. I mean, we figured he'd *probably* get in with anything over, oh, 1430, but you can never be supersure, not these days, not when his extracurriculars weren't great. They were *not* great, Jane. I told him all along, I said, 'Jeremy, editor of the school newspaper just isn't enough anymore, not without sports awards or community honors or something.' I said, 'Now, if you were Black or Vietnamese or Iranian . . .'" She shook her head. "Anyway, those SATs—my god, did that kid obsess. He took Stanley Kaplan three times, Jane. He said to me, he said, 'Mom, I'm going to break 1500 if it kills me.'" She grins. "What could I do? It was his money, he earned it cleaning pools last summer, and anyway it paid off, thank God. He'll get in now. He's got to. Icky Steinberg had only 1230 last year, and he got in, and he was only twelfth in his class—no, I'm wrong. Eleventh. Jeremy is second. He'd have been first if he hadn't had that confrontation with his algebra teacher." She looks at me. "But anyway, that's neither here nor there. What about you, sweetie?"

I slouch lower in my chair, suddenly miserable. "My scores didn't come yet."

"No? That's strange. I thought they all went out at once. Oh well, yours'll probably come today." She smiles. "Don't worry, it doesn't really matter this time, PSATs aren't the real thing. Anyway, you can always do Kaplan to improve. I know for a fact that both Dean and Jeremy went up—mm, a lot. I mean, a *lot*. And Jake Hoffner went from 1060 to 1300 just from sitting in on the course a couple of sessions, after he got back from Israel. Both his brothers are at Yale, and his sister's at Brown. . . ."

"I'm not taking a course," I say, standing up. "I don't want to go to any of those schools, anyway."

Frannie raises her eyebrows and looks at my mother, who's washing dishes, then at me. "No? Where do you want to go?"

"I don't know. Somewhere with a good wrestling team."

My mother sighs and picks up another soapy pan, but I wonder if, deep down, she isn't just a tiny bit glad I said that.

"Well, what about Cornell?" Frannie says. "Have you been up there to visit Cassandra? Where *is* Cassandra, anyway? Out with her friends, probably, if she's anything like Dean. That child hasn't been home for five minutes since he walked in the door. I am absolutely convinced I will never see him again. Although maybe it's different with girls, maybe it's—"

"She's upstairs," I say. "Sleeping."

"Sleeping?" asks my mother.

"She was really tired this morning. She's always really tired lately, Mom. Because she never eats anything—"

"What do you mean?" my mother says. "She ate a whole plate of spaghetti last night." She looks at me for confirmation.

What Cassie did, I'm almost sure, is feed some spaghetti to the dogs and pitch the rest under the thick pine trees way in back of our house, and I want my mother to know this. But I can't tell her. At first I convince myself this is because of Frannie; I couldn't possibly say it in front of her. But if it were just the two of us, just my mother and me, I still wouldn't be able to say it; I couldn't bear the expression on her face (shock, confusion, sadness) and knowing that I was the one who caused it.

But I know, too, that not saying anything only makes everything worse. So I opt to hint. "Are you *sure* she ate it?" I say, and I hate myself for being such a wimp.

My mother stares at me. "What do you mean, am I *sure*?" She turns off the sink and goes into the hallway. "Cassandra!" she yells upstairs. After a second I hear her go up.

Frannie rises and pours more coffee into her mug. She slides it into the microwave. "So how's your love life?" she says. "I hear you have a new boyfriend. An Italian wrestler, right? Your father told me."

"What?" I turn reluctantly to face her. And then what she said registers. "He *did*?"

She nods. "He says this kid's the best wrestler in the school. Is that true? God, Dean wrestled once for about a week. The nightmare of my life. Absolutely animalistic." She sniffs.

"Well, I like it." I'm glad to be off the topic of SATs and amazed that my father said that about Vinnie. I smile, thinking about how he came to my class on Tuesday to help me demonstrate wrestling moves—just like he said. The class loved it. Then on Wednesday, in a home wrestling meet, he pinned a kid in twelve seconds. Afterward, people congratulated *me*.

The microwave buzzes, and Frannie pulls out her mug and blows into the puff of coffee steam. And then my mother walks in, with my sister behind her—shuffling in, one hand buried in her hair, the other clutching a Chap Stick, of course. Frannie lurches around, nearly spilling her coffee. "There she is!" she shrieks, rising to hug Cassie. Her mouth drops when she notices the hair. "Oh my god! Let me *see*! Look at this, Rapunzel goes to college and turns into— what? A modern woman, I guess. I think I like it . . . yeah, I do like it. I do. It's sort of punky. What made you cut it, Cass? You needed a change?"

Cassie nods, her eyes glassy. She tries to smile. "Yeah. Probably."

Frannie cocks her head, assessing. "God, you're skinny, though. You were never that skinny, were you? I thought girls *gain* weight at college. Christ, Jane, she's a rail."

My mother frowns at Cassie, and I wonder if she asked her about the spaghetti upstairs. "She never eats," I say. I can say it in front of her, when she's there to defend herself—or not to, if she can't.

"I do so eat," Cassie says, glaring at me. She moves to a chair, sits down in it, then gets up again. She leans her back against the wall, grips her sleeve. She bounces on her toes, little bounces, a million times a minute. Behind her, my mother's ASPCA wall calendar shows a mother leopard and two baby leopards frolicking.

Frannie beams at Cassie. "So? Do you love it? Is it fabulous?"

"What?" Cassie says.

Frannie rolls her eyes. "Cornell!"

"Oh. Um—yeah, it's okay. It's hard. It's okay."

My mother's back at the sink but watching Cassie. "Does anyone want a cookie?" she says. "Or a piece of fruit? Cassandra? I just
bought some green grapes—"

"Not for me, thanks," Frannie says, and then, to Cassie, "I hear
your roommate left. What happened?"

Lines work their way into Cassie's forehead. "I don't know. She
didn't like college, I guess."

"You're kidding!" Frannie sips coffee. "Were you close?"

"Sort of." Cassie shifts her feet nervously. "So how's your family and everything?"

This is what you ask Frannie if you feel like tuning out for an
hour or two. "Ugh!" she shrieks. "My family! They're lunatics.
David's married to his job." She sighs, looking pleased. Her husband
is the CEO of a bank in New York. "Dean is nonexistent, and
Douglas wants to go skiing in Switzerland with the Millers. He's
driving us insane, Jane. Should I let him go? They want to take him
and pay for the whole thing."

"When does his school start?" my mother asks absently. She's
still watching my sister, who's still bouncing on her toes, as if they're
a spring.

"Thursday," Frannie says. "He'd miss two days. But I've already
talked to his teacher, she said he has A's in everything, so it shouldn't
be a problem."

My mother shrugs and sighs. "Well, Michael wouldn't let Billie
go. Then again, Michael doesn't ski, and David does."

"David thinks he *should* go. I mean, it's all free."

"So he would have lessons?" my mother asks. She moves to the
back door and lets in the dogs. Outside they don't fight, but in here
she closes Ethan out of the room, just in case. As soon as he's out,
though, he scratches the door and whines to be let back in.

Frannie opens another packet of Sweet'n Low and dumps it into
her coffee. She's taken a mound of them out of her bag. "Apparently
they're flying two ski instructors over with them, boys who used to
teach them at Deer Valley, in Utah. Have you been there? It's fabulous. Anyway, it still makes me nervous, though. Knowing Douglas,

he'll break his rib cage, or puncture a lung, or rupture his spleen. . . ."

My mother's bending down, looking at Mollie's paw. "It would make me nervous, too. Oh Mollie, what did you do to your nail?" She dabs at Mollie's front paw with a wet cloth.

"Well, none of us are going skiing anytime soon, so you don't have to worry, Mom," I say. I glance at Cassie. Her lips are two red apple slices. She still hasn't sat down.

"God," Frannie says, "my kids can't get enough of skiing."

"We're not allowed to go," I say.

Frannie's eyes widen and bulge. "You're *not?*" She looks at my mother. "Since when?"

My mother, finished with Mollie's foot, walks to the pantry and takes out a box of milk bones. "Michael feels it's an expensive, dangerous sport that they really don't need," she says thoughtfully. She feeds Mollie a bone, then walks over and cracks the door and hands Ethan one through the crack. She turns to look at Cassie again. "Cassandra, have some grapes."

"Oh, Michael." Frannie flaps her hand. "He should take a chill pill."

"Actually," Cassie says, ignoring my mother, "I don't feel a need for skiing in my life. I mean, I don't miss it. I mean—there are more important things." She looks at the table.

Frannie blinks a few times. Then she says, "Johnny Weller's son wants to open a ski camp for kids. In Vermont. As soon as he finishes at Wharton."

We all stare at her. I don't think any of us has a clue who Johnny Weller is. "Really?" I say finally, embarrassed at the silence. I look at my mother, wondering whose side she's on here—because there does, suddenly, seem to be sides.

"So I hear," Frannie says. She pushes her coffee into the microwave again and presses numbers. The motor whirs on.

No one says anything then. We all just sit there for what seems like much too long, and then the upstairs phone rings. "I'll get it!" I yell. I run out of the room.

★   ★   ★

It's Steve Zucker, which makes me glad. I haven't talked to him since he came to visit us last year, and I like him, or at least I did then. He was funny, and he didn't make me feel shy the way some other guys do—maybe because I knew I'd never fall for him. He was too smart, too tall, too Jewish; something about the way his voice escalated into authority brought my father to mind.

I decide to flirt with him, the way Tiffany would, just to get my mind off this day. So I laugh loudly and say, "Steven, this is so weird, but we were just talking about you." I've never called him Steven, but Tiffany does this all the time—calls guys by a more formal name than what everyone else calls them, even if it's not their real name. Guys seem to go for it.

And Steve does laugh. "Oh yeah? Well, I'm not sure I want to know what you were saying, since your sister hasn't called me in months. What's the deal, Billie? Is she blowing me off?"

"Not at all." I tell him about the Christmas card she found that she "forgot" to send. Then, to make sure he doesn't think she's mad, I tell him she's lost some weight lately and isn't feeling so hot. I picture her downstairs, refusing to sit. I wonder if my mother's managed to make her eat a grape.

"Wow," Steve says. "How much weight has she lost? She doesn't have anorexia, does she?"

"No—I mean no." But his words shock me. It's the first time I've heard anyone else suggest the possibility. "She's just being ridiculous," I say nervously. "She's sort of obsessed with recycling things. I think she took some earth class at Cornell—"

"*Recycling* things?"

"I know. No, but you know Cassie. She's just a space case." I force a laugh.

"Actually, it seems to me that's the one thing Cassie *isn't*."

I laugh again. "Oh my god, Steven, you kill me!"

I hear him shift the phone around. "Billie," he says, "are you nervous, or something?"

As soon as he says it, I am. "What do you mean? Why would I be *nervous*?"

"I don't know, " he says. "Forget it. You just sound different, that's all. I mean—Billie, you don't have to put on an act for me."

The whole room seems to grow hot then. "What are you *talking* about?" I say.

"Nothing. Sorry. Forget it."

I squeeze the receiver. Why does it work for Tiffany but not for me? "I'll go get Cassie," I say.

"Wait. Billie? Listen, I didn't mean anything. I'm just—I'm sorry, okay?"

"What for?" I put down the receiver. "Cassie, phone!" I yell from the room so Steve can hear.

I head downstairs slowly, past the fading wallpaper, and stop altogether halfway down. I don't want to go back down there. I don't want to talk about SATs, or skiing, or any of Frannie's kids. I don't want to go back upstairs, either. I don't ever want to talk to Steve Zucker again. I sink down on the stairs, wishing I lived in California, wishing I had my license so I could drive myself out of here.

Cassie appears at the bottom of the stairs. "Did you call me?"

"Steve Zucker's on the phone. Believe it or not."

She stares at me a second. Then she reaches for my mother's purse on the banister and pulls out her key chain. "Come on," she says. "Let's go somewhere."

"What do you mean? Cassie, Steve's on the phone—"

"I don't want to talk to him. I've gotta get out of here, I can't breathe with that perfume Frannie's wearing." She's rummaging through the coat closet now. She takes out my father's old black overcoat and slips it on. It dwarfs her.

"You're just gonna *leave* him there?" I ask.

She looks at me like she's considering, just for a second. Then she says, "I don't care." She turns away. "Are you coming or not?"

I glance back toward the kitchen. Frannie's voice babbles on, rising and falling hysterically, punctuated by laughs. I think of Steve, sitting waiting somewhere. Looking at his watch and thinking about what a fool I am.

Cassie's opened the front door already. "Stay then," she says.

She steps outside and moves down the stairs. Through the screen, I see her drift past the ear tree and toward the driveway. A yellow-headed stick in black under a gray sky, getting herself out of here.

I grab Vinnie's jacket. "Wait, Cass, I'm coming," I call. My shoes are on the floor of the den. I slip them on, then run out after my sister. To hell with Steve. To hell with all of it.

My mother's station wagon is parked in the driveway. We get into it fast, as if someone might come down and stop us if we take our time. My sister turns on the motor and backs out. Smells fill my head—dog fur, vinyl seats, library books, potting soil my mother's been carting around. I breathe it in deeply, glad now to be in here with my sister, wanting her to take me somewhere.

And she does. She holds the wheel with one hand, cruising like she's been driving forever. I watch her enviously. "Just a few more weeks," I say. She nods, knowing I'm talking about getting my driver's permit when I turn sixteen and a half. In the dirt on my window, I draw a faint heart with my finger. "Will you take me driving?" I ask.

"If you're nice to me."

"Oh. Forget it, then."

She gives a small laugh, then turns right. There are clumps of snow here and there, an occasional bike or deflated basketball or battered doll lying in between. In front of the junior high, dead brown stalks are all that's left of the tulip garden that bloomed pink and yellow just a few months ago. We pass a woman holding a newspaper under her dog so he poops right onto it—careful not to let it touch her red mittens—and I laugh, until we pass the Lakers' house and I think of Cindy's brother, dangling above a tipped-over chair, his tongue blue, his eyes bulging like a frog's. I turn away. "Jeremy Greenbaum got his SAT scores yesterday," I tell Cassie.

"Yeah? What'd he get, ten thousand?" Cassie rubs at one eye. Then she turns to me. "Oh—does that mean yours are coming, too?"

"I don't know. I didn't check the mail."

"Let's go check it, then. We don't have to go in. Mom won't have gotten it yet, we'll just take it out of the box—"

"No," I say. "I don't want to know what I got. I don't care."

Cassie glances at me. "Of course you do. Just because you wish you didn't care doesn't mean you don't." She turns the car around, back in the direction of our house, then says, "Wait, is that the mail carrier?" She won't say "mailman" anymore, even if it is. "Wow," she says, "look at that. We don't even have to go back home."

Up ahead, he trudges along dressed in blue, his big brown bag over his shoulder. Cassie drives toward him, then pulls up to the curb. "Go on," she says. "Just ask him for our mail. He'll give it to you."

I shake my head, my heart already beating faster. "Cassie, forget it. I really don't want to know what I got."

"Why? You're gonna find out eventually."

But she regards me a second, and I know she's remembering when her own scores came. She'd opened the scores in the afternoon and put them back in the pile of mail, and they were in there, next to my father's plate, when he sat down to eat his dinner. He slurped grapefruit noisily, ripping open letters between bites, tossing junk mail on the floor, bills in a pile. Cassie ate quietly, avoiding anyone's eyes. My father glanced at the scores and swallowed a mouthful. "What are these?" he said. He looked at my sister. "These scores can't be *right,* Cassandra. Can they?" He stared at her. "*Can* they?"

Cassie shrugged miserably. She bit her top lip hard, showing her crooked bottom teeth.

My father put down his spoon and got up. He went into the kitchen. We all listened as he picked up the phone and called the SAT testing service, which of course had closed for the day. He hung up and returned to the table. "You've had straight A's for two years, Cassandra. What happened here?" His voice was rising; his face was red. "Did you read the practice booklet? Were you sick the day of the test? A *cretin* would do better than this."

Cassie took a deep breath. "I wasn't sick. I was nervous. I always am for those kinds of tests, Dad. I always screw them up."

My mother and I had stopped eating. We sat and waited, and I remember wondering, even through my fear, why Cassie didn't tell him to take a long walk off a short cliff—or something to that effect, like she usually did. Could he really be mad at her for doing badly on a standardized test? For once I wanted to defend her, even if it meant fighting him.

I didn't say anything though, of course; I sat there like a wimp, and my mother and Cassie sat there, too. We were waiting for him to smack the table, to explode and let loose on my sister.

But he sat back down. He stared at Cassie for a minute, and you could see the muscles working in the sides of his jaw. He took off his glasses, placed them down on the table. "It's my fault," he said. The three of us stared at him. "I should have had you take a course, like every other kid did. I'm sorry."

"Don't be *sorry*, Dad," Cassie said.

My father rubbed his eyes. "Maybe I *should* have moved to North Berry. Maybe I should have listened to my mother for a change."

"No way," I said. "I like West Berry." Of course, everyone ignored me.

Things changed in our house after that. Every night there were two hours of enforced SAT study time for Cassie. Radios and TVs were lowered, and the dogs were put outside. I was to leave our room and study downstairs at the dining-room table. Our bedroom phone was unplugged.

At the end of each session, my father knocked on our door and asked Cassie what she'd learned. Sometimes he'd quiz her. He'd write down ten of her words and have her use them in sentences.

The worst part was, she didn't seem to mind. "I *am* pathetic," she'd said to me one night, and she told me how, as she sat in some classroom with her number-two pencil taking her SATs, all she'd been able to think was, "This is a test, this is a test, this is a test." But the second time she took the test, her scores did improve. Enough to get her into Cornell, anyway.

Now, sitting in the car with her, I dread any part of it happening to me. "Just pull away, Cass," I say. "Please? I'm not into this."

Cassie looks at me. She shakes her head, then shifts the car into park and gets out to approach the mailman. And I'm thinking, You bitch.

She comes back with a stack of mail and tosses it on the seat next to me. "There," she says. "Now at least it's your choice. If you don't want to open them, don't." She puts the car back in drive and pulls onto the street again, waving thanks as she passes the mailman.

My anger slips away. She's trying to help me, not to make things worse. I pull a *New Yorker* from the pile, and then a lingerie catalog with a big-boobed woman in a red lace bra and underpants on the front. There's a letter from Chemical Bank, addressed to my father, and a letter from Con Edison—two of a zillion companies he has stock in. He has a zillion bank accounts, too. Like my grandmother, he likes to play with them, see how they're doing, switch them around to get more interest.

I glance at people huddled in the bus stop on Northway as we pass it, then flip through bills from Exxon and the phone company, letters from the Fresh Air Fund and New Jersey Public Interest Research Group—both of which my father gives money to. There are still a few of what look like Christmas cards in the stack, most of them from my father's patients—more for my mother to cram onto the piano top and living-room table. A smiling, round-eyed toddler with pigtails stares up at me from a Missing Children postcard. And then I'm holding it, a thin white envelope with my name in furry computer type on the front. "Today sucks," I say.

We're stopped at a traffic light now. Cassie glances at the envelope. She blinks a few times, like something's stuck in her eye. The traffic light turns green, and someone behind us blips their horn. Cassie jolts and steps hard on the gas. The car lurches forward.

"Whoa!" I steady myself against the dashboard, then turn to stare at her.

But her eyes are shining. "You should get rid of them, Bil. Rip them up. Or—no, I know! *Burn* them! Make it symbolic. Here, use this." She pushes in the cigarette lighter to turn it on.

We're approaching the highway, and she slows down—too much—to merge onto it. Another car blares its horn behind us. "Oh god, sorry, sorry," she says. She jabs at her left cheek and eye.

"What's wrong with your face?" I say. "Cassie, you're driving like shit. Do you have something in your eye or what?"

She shrugs. The lighter pops out, and she gestures toward it with her chin. "There. Go ahead."

The scores aren't even in an envelope, really; the whole thing is just a Xerox copy form you have to fold and tear the edges off. "In the car, though?" I ask Cassie. We're on the new highway now, which finally opened at the end of last month. Trees and jagged brown rock whiz by. "Where are you going, anyway?"

"I don't know. Anywhere. I can't pull over now. Here." She pulls out the lighter and holds it toward me, her eyes on the road.

The ring glows inside it, a yellow-red Life Saver, never used. For a second I'm tempted. I picture myself touching the ring to the corner of the paper, watching my name melt away. And then another corner. The smell of burning paper would fill the car—sweet, like marshmallows—and my PSAT scores would be gone.

But something holds me back. Maybe curiosity, maybe just the knowledge that my father will find out the scores anyway. "Oh, forget it," I say, ripping open the scores. "Math sixty-seven, Verbal seventy-three. There. Done. End of story." I drop the sheet on the seat between us. My hands are shaking.

Cassie turns to me, her eyes big as nickels. "*Seventy-three?* You're kidding, right?" She looks back at the road, but she feels around for the sheet and picks it up. She looks at it quickly, then drops it again. "Seventy-three," she repeats, shaking her head. She laughs. "You don't even try, do you. God, wait till Dad finds out."

My heart's beating fast. I picture myself being shipped off to Cornell or Princeton—to waste away, never to see Tiffany or Vinnie again.

And yet now that I have the scores—now that my sister's clearly jealous of them—I don't really want to wish them away. I turn to Cassie. She's rubbing her eyes again. "You think he'll be happy?" I ask.

But she's pawing at her face again. "God, I'm so spaced out all of a sudden," she says. She grips the steering wheel with both hands, then closes her eyes tight and opens them again. Our car veers to the left.

I glance at the road and then back at her, alarmed. "What are you *doing*? Cassie, what's wrong with you?"

She doesn't answer. She's fighting to straighten the car, blinking back tears, and my whole body starts to shake then. I grip my armrest as our car swerves again. More cars are honking. I hold my breath and wait for whatever's about to happen.

And then, up ahead, I spot the sign for the exit to Wayne—where we get off for Five Oaks, my grandmother's country club. And suddenly I'm sitting up coaching my sister, acting like I know what I'm doing. "Just slow down," I say, breathing fast. "There's an exit right up there. Can you get to it? Should I help you steer?"

She shakes her head no. She's peering out, blinking, clinging for control.

"Keep going, Cass, you're doing great. Can you make it to the first exit? You're almost there."

My sister nods, a dozen teeny little nods, and then somehow the cars around us back off and give us room, and we're making it, we're almost there. Cassie coasts onto the exit. "Get through that light," I say. "Pull off at the first side street. Okay?"

She nods. "Bil, it's okay now. I'm not dizzy anymore."

But I keep my eyes glued to the road until she finds a side street and turns in. She drives halfway down the block. Then she pulls to the curb and parks the car. Her hands sink into her lap.

For about a minute there's no sound but our breathing, deep and together and fast. Cassie stares blankly out the windshield. One of her hands clutches a clump of her hair. The other lies palm up on the seat. "Billie," she says finally, her voice low and croaky, "I'm so sorry. That's been happening lately, I don't know why—"

Before I can stop myself, my fist crashes down on the dashboard. "It's because you don't eat! If you weren't starving yourself, that wouldn't happen! What are you trying to prove, anyway?"

Cassie's eyes focus on something out there, something I don't think I could see if I tried. "You sound like Daddy," she says.

"Fuck you!"

She looks at me then, her eyes puffy red slits, her hair standing up in places in spikes. She shakes her head. Then she turns and gets out of the car. Her door hangs open as she walks down the street, away from the car, away from me.

"Good," I say to no one. "Good. Go. See if I care." And for a minute I let her walk, just watch her get smaller and farther away. Her big black coat floats along, stick calves and dirty white sneakers poking out underneath.

But something stirs inside me, and for the first time I'm terrified of losing my sister. For some reason, I think of the picture I drew of her, years ago, that she still has taped next to her bed. Yellow-scribbled hair, magenta mouth, sky-blue skirt—her favorite color.

And then I think of her bed, neatly made, and me alone in my bed, next to it. And I get out of the car and run after her, high heels smacking pavement.

I catch up quickly and fall into step beside her. For a while we walk together. Large, shuttered houses move by us, their trees gray and bare as pencil drawings. "Where are you going?" I say.

She stops and looks at me. "I don't know. Nowhere. Right here." She sits down heavily on someone's lawn.

I sit down next to her, for once not caring whose property we're on or whether they see us there. The street is quiet, the sky still and silver, overcast. It seems like hours since we've left home. And it seems like years since Cassie's come home from college. It occurs to me how rarely I've seen Tiffany lately, and suddenly I long for her.

Cassie pulls her arms up into the body of the jacket, so she can hug her waist. The sleeves hang empty. She's shivering, even though it's not that cold. I watch her, thinking, She's beautiful and I'm not, but I'm warm and she's freezing. I look down at her sneakers. They seem pathetic somehow. It's drizzling now, and for a second I have the sensation that we're being cried on.

And then I do something I've never done before, or at least not for years: I reach out and hug my sister. My arms go all the way around both of hers, and I squeeze hard, so hard it probably hurts, even through all those clothes. And even through all those clothes, she feels like a skeleton. I think about the stuff I read about anorexia:

how your hair falls out and your skin breaks out in rashes, how you grow a fine fur on your body like a rat. "Cass, what are you gonna do?" I say. "You can't go back to school like this."

She shrugs, but she lets me keep hugging her. "I have to. Dad won't let me stay home, anyway."

"He would if he knew how fucked up you are. He'd have to."

She slips away from me then. "I'm not that fucked up. I'm not fucked up. Anyway, he won't. He won't admit something's wrong with me, and—"

"That's your fault. You keep telling them you're fine. Tell Mom, then. Tell her how much weight you lost. Tell her to take you to Dr. Morse. Or I'll tell her. You just have to back me, okay?"

She glances up at the sky. "It's raining. How long have we been out here? We better get back."

"You're changing the subject, Cass."

"Well, what do you want me to say?"

"Say you'll eat."

"Okay. I'll eat."

"You won't, though. I don't believe you."

"I will. I promise."

"When?"

She sighs. "Billie, I don't know."

"How about now?" I say.

"What. The grass?"

I think for a second. "McDonald's. A Big Mac. Right now, before we drive home and you almost kill us again."

"I can't eat a Big Mac. I hate Big Macs, Bil. You know that."

"Okay. A cheeseburger and fries. And milk shake."

Her fingers twitter. "There's no McDonald's around here, anyway."

I sit up straighter. "We can go to Five Oaks, then. We're right near it, I know I can get us there, if you drive. We'll sign Zelda's number on the bill. We'll ask for a table in back, so she won't see us if she's there."

I wait for her to veto the plan. Cassie's always hated the country club. "Okay," she says finally.

"Really?"

She licks her lips and looks at me tiredly. "It doesn't really matter where we go, does it?"

I hesitate a second, remembering Five Oaks' policy that guests have to be with members at all times, realizing we're far from dressed for the place.

But my sister has promised to eat. "No," I say, "it doesn't matter."

We find the club easily, with no other catastrophes on the road —though I'm ready to grab the wheel just in case. My sister drives in slowly, past the drained aqua pool and a dozen wet green tennis courts. Farther on, golf carts are lined up outside, their black tires glistening. "Remember when we stole one?" I ask, and Cassie nods and smiles a little. One night, while my parents were still inside at the table—we come for Mother's Day or Zelda's birthday, occasionally in the summer or on a Jewish holiday—Cassie and I went out and spotted a cart and jumped in and took off. We tooled across acres and acres of immaculate green lawn, around oak and red maple trees. The sun had just set; the air was turning deeper blue by the minute. "The dessert cart's coming now," Cassie said, imagining our family at dinner. "And Zelda's saying, 'Don'cha have the gonnolis? What's a matter? You always *used* to have gonnolis on the cart.'" She laughed and drove up onto a green, steering the cart in a gentle figure eight. "And now one of her friends is coming over, all decked in, like, bloodred lamé, and Zelda's telling her, 'They never have the gonnolis anymore,' and the friend is nodding and saying, 'Three times, I had to ask my waiter for more coffee! Can you imagine?'"

Now, Cassie passes the valet parking and parks in a space at the far end of the lot. I peer around for Zelda's car. If she's not here for a luncheon, she's probably here playing cards. "We have to hurry," I say, glancing at the clock as we get out. Cassie nods.

But inside, the first thing she wants to do is go up to the locker room and wash her hands. She washes her hands about fifty times a day; she can't stand to have any smell on them. I follow her up the spiral staircase, toward the locker room. She glances at the sign that says "Ladies." "I hope that includes *women*," she says.

The locker room is a maze of dressing rooms, bathtubs, a sauna, rows of tall painted metal lockers. We slink across peach-colored carpet thick as a sponge, past piles of lavender towels stacked outside shower stalls. Everything seems peach or lavender: color coordination times a million. "I like the colors," I say, and Cassie looks at me like I'm deranged. Mirrors, bordered by track lights, are everywhere. Our reflection surrounds us, white-faced girls with too-big coats and plastered-down hair, and I'm glad now that we've come up here. At least we can dry off first.

Except for a silver-haired woman polishing her golf shoes and two locker-room attendants talking in Spanish, the place appears empty, which is a relief. Cassie drifts from room to room, staring straight ahead as she walks—trying, I'm sure, to avoid seeing herself in the ubiquitous mirrors. She picks one of the smaller rooms to sit down in, then lets her coat fall from her shoulders. I sit down next to her, but I leave mine on. Vinnie's. I wonder where he is, whether he's called since I left. I didn't see him last night, and he seems miles away from me now, a person of my past.

In front of us, a counter spans wall to wall, covered with various appliances and neatly lined-up supplies—everything from nail polish remover to facial hair bleach. There are two blow-dryers, a set of electric rollers, and a hair-straightening iron. The room smells like hair spray and burnt hair.

Cassie's staring at the stuff. I pick up one of the dryers. "Come on, Cass. Wash your hands or whatever. We have to eat and get out of here. God, Mom's probably having a fit." I turn on the dryer and push hot air through my hair.

Cassie picks up a box. " 'Rectal wipes,' " she reads. She looks at me. "*Rectal* wipes?" She swipes at her hair.

I grab the box from her and slide it down the counter; it hits a mirror and falls to the floor. "Forget it," I say. I turn on the other dryer and hand it to her. Then I watch to make sure she does something besides just stare at it. I'm starting to feel like her babysitter.

Over the dryers I hear girls' voices and laughter, and seconds later three girls walk in. Two of them are in front, blabbing away. The third one trails behind. I recognize them all—they're about my age—and I know the third one's name is Beth because we've talked a couple of times. Usually, though, Cassie and I avoid the girls here, and they avoid us; they all know each other—from temple, summer camp, private school in North Berry. They dress in tennis clothes or preppy collared shirts, with lots of jewelry and short stylish haircuts.

I stare furiously at my reflection as they walk in, avoiding Beth's eyes. One of the ones in front is saying, "So he goes, 'Why?' and I go, 'Because I don't *want* to,' and he's like—" She stops when she sees us. Beth smiles. "Hi, Billie," she says. "How are you?"

"Oh! Hi, Beth. I'm okay. How are you?"

"Good. How's your winter been?"

"Good. How's yours been?"

"Good."

"That's good." We smile at each other for a second. The other two girls stare at us. One of them—sand-colored hair, pointy nose— is looking at Cassie, who's looking into the mirror, the dryer pointed mechanically at one section of her hair.

The first girl turns away from us and pushes up close to the mirror. "Ugh! I have so many zits, I could vomit up bile."

The second girl laughs. "At least you're not fat, like me." She turns around so her back is toward the mirror and stares over her shoulder at her butt. "I am so *fat!*" she says. "Fattest hog on the planet. Oh god, and these jeans make me look sick. How could you let me wear them?"

"Oh, shut *up*, both of you," Beth says. She rolls her eyes at me.

The first two girls laugh. They're dressed in baggy jeans and blazers, and neither is the slightest bit fat. In fact, the second one is almost as skinny as Cassie, and I'm thinking that Vinnie would never go for her. None of the guys in my school would. They like girls with something to grab, as Tiffany says.

Cassie turns off her dryer. Her hair is messy, blown all over the place. The girls are staring at her again, but she doesn't seem to care. She moves down the counter to a large lavender sink, turns on a trickle of water, and quickly washes her hands.

She looks around for something to dry them on. But the only towels are lavender paper towels, each one several layers thick. Cassie

frowns at them. Then she bends down and looks under the counter
and pulls out the wastebasket. On top is a half-used paper towel. She
wipes her hands on the unused half and drops it back in.

I feel the hair rise up on my arms. The girls are watching her
with horror. "Come on, Cass, we gotta go, see you, Beth," I say. I
take Cassie's arm and pull her away. Outside the room, I whisper,
"Christ, Cassie, can't you be normal, like, *once* in your life?"

But she doesn't answer, and I decide not to press it. I want to
eat and get the hell out of here. We move down the spiral staircase
and into the dining-room foyer, with its shiny piano, its large plush
floral couch. The ceilings are high as a kite, with ornate rafters
painted gold and cream. Handfuls of red and purple flowers explode
from a poster-sized urn.

Two women are ahead of us, waiting for the hostess to come
back. They're discussing a wedding they attended here last week and
whether the groom should be let into Five Oaks, since he isn't Jewish. The quieter one—a tiny tan woman in a red suit that matches the
flowers—thinks he should, but the louder one disagrees. "It's bad
enough they let the gays in now," she says. The first one shakes her
head. "Oh, Millie. What do you care what they do in the bedroom?"

The loud one shrugs and starts talking about some plastic gold-
fish she's bought her grandson. "You don't have to feed them, or
clean their bowl, or . . ."

I turn to see what Cassie thinks of their conversation. Her face
is green, and she's sort of swaying. "What's wrong?" I say, alarmed.

She shakes her head quickly. "Bil, I have to sit down." She falls
back against me. I catch her just before she hits the floor.

First the manager comes, and then Dr. Kaiser, one of the doc-
tor-members who's been eating in the dining room. By the time he
arrives—an elfish man with cottony white hair and a napkin tucked
in his shirt—Cassie's conscious again, sitting up telling everyone she's
okay. The doctor nods and examines her anyway, taking her pulse
and asking her a bunch of questions. People loiter nearby, trying to
catch a glance. I feel their eyes all over me, crawling up and down.

They help Cassie onto the couch and get her a glass of water.

Then they start questioning me, and I find myself telling them almost everything: how my sister hasn't eaten for days, how she almost fainted in the car on the way over here, how we're not here with my grandmother, just by ourselves, just to eat. I unload like a dump truck. The manager listens without a word, his pencil-thin moustache twitching slightly. Then he goes off to call my parents, and worried as I am about my sister and what my mother and father will say and everything else, the main thing I feel is relief. Finally, someone else besides me will have to worry about things.

Later, when we get home, my father takes Cassie's blood pressure and makes her get on the scale. From upstairs, I can hear my mother gasp, "Ninety-eight! Oh, Cassie, how could you?" Then they call Dr. Morse, their friend and our pediatrician, who says to bring Cassie over in a half-hour. My sister is sent upstairs to rest; my mother goes to the kitchen to make her some tea and cinnamon toast. And then it's my father and me, sitting in the dining room, him looking at me, not sure what to say. He doesn't seem mad, which at first makes me feel guilty but then starts to scare me. If he isn't mad, he must be incredibly worried. "Well?" he says finally. "What happened?"

Once more I start to talk, but this time I don't leave out anything. I tell him that Cassie's sadder than anyone I've ever known—that it's like she's put on a pair of thick glasses that tint everything with sadness. I tell him that she can't stop thinking, that her mind is relentless as a clock. That she paces the room, scrawls in her journal, stares out the window frowning. That she can't read, can't concentrate. That she hates everybody.

I tell him how she'll go through the refrigerator and eat only a rotting orange or a spoonful of peas so old that white fur grows between them—things she thinks she can save from becoming waste. How she'll dig an empty bag of Fritos out of the trash and finger-vacuum out the salt and the crumbs, then go in the bathroom and wash her hands six times to get the smell off. How she's hungry all the time—I can tell by the way anyone eating around her makes her nervous and alert as a rat—but she won't eat anything Mom serves. I tell him how I think she'd like to just disappear, that in fact she *is* disappearing; that under that sweatsuit, she's nothing but a twig.

My father listens as well as he can. He's never been much of a listener; if he's not interrupting you, he's shifting in his chair or tweaking his wedding ring. But he hears me out this time, his eyes focused on the table. At the end, he says, "Is there anything else I should know?"

I think a second, then shake my head no.

He stands up slowly, clears his throat. "I'm sorry you had to be the one to find out all that," he says quietly. "It should have been me."

Something tugs at my heart. I want to console him somehow. He turns to walk away. "Wait, Dad." I pull out my folded PSAT scores and hand them to him. "These came today. I did pretty good, I think."

"Pretty *well*. Did you?" He takes them, looking at me suspiciously, then at the scores. His eyebrows go up. "Seventy-three in verbal?" He looks at me again. "These are very good." He clears his throat again. *"Very* good."

I feel relief, and pride—and then, just as quickly, that same ambivalence I felt before. Am I doomed now or saved? I shrug nonchalantly. "I *told* you I studied."

"Maybe," he says. "And maybe you're just a smart kid. I know it offends you to think of yourself that way—"

"It doesn't *offend* me."

He laughs. "If you do this well on your SATs in six weeks, you might even get in somewhere decent—if you get your damn grades up. Hell, you might even—"

"Michael!" my mother calls from upstairs. "Should we go?"

My father drops the scores back on the table. He ruffles my hair. Then he turns around and heads upstairs, three at a time.

Five minutes later, the garage door rumbles down. It smacks the cement floor, and they all pull away: my mother, my father, Cassie. I sit at the table, one socked foot resting on Mollie's back, and let out breath it feels like I've been holding all day. The room is half-dark without lights, the edges of everything shadowed and blurred. My body feels melted to the chair. My head is emptier than it's been for weeks—filled only with cool dull air.

On the counter is my sister's cinnamon toast, cut in quarters like when we were kids—my mother's remedy for just about any ailment we had. I nibble a quarter, then devour it, suddenly starved. I toast two more slices, spread the butter on thick, dump on sugar and cinnamon. Then, plate in hand, I head upstairs to call Tiffany.

chapter
six

Slowly, painfully, over the weeks, it's becoming clear to me that Vinnie isn't the guy of my dreams—or if he is, then the girl I'm dreaming about with him isn't me. She looks like me, and she dresses and talks like I do, but she feels like an imposter somehow. Now, sitting in the back of the school bus with his big arm sandwiching my neck, I try once more to figure out why this is—and what to do about it. The thought makes me feel so bad sometimes that my eyes start to burn.

The front of the bus is full of wrestlers—silent somber wrestlers riding home in snowy dark after being slammed by a team they beat easily last year. The team that beat them is a good one, but that doesn't help much; it's the second-to-last meet of the season, and every wrestler except Vinnie and the 108-pounder were pinned.

Vinnie, for his part, pinned in the second period, and if he's sad for the team, he's also happy for himself. I can tell, just like I can tell he's happy the coach let me ride to and from the meet with the team —one of only four girls on the bus, and the other three are team managers. They're sitting up front with the rest of the guys. Vinnie and I are far in the back of the bus, rows from anyone, our thighs touching. At the window, I watch the snow fall and listen to the big bus wheels swish along the wet Jersey highway, rolling us closer to West Berry with each turn.

Vinnie squeezes me closer and plants a kiss on my cheek. "You smell nice," he says, burying his nose in my hair. "What is that, anyway?"

I shrug. "Baby powder. Or Herbal Essence cream rinse. That's all I have on."

"Maybe it's just you, then. I think it's just you."

I shrug again, nervously. Vinnie, I know, wants his hand down my pants, and I've said no one too many times already. It's time to shit or get off the pot, as Tiffany would say—to put out or get out. I don't want to do either. I don't want to hurt him, and I can't stand the thought of him hating me. I look out the window into the night, not really seeing it there.

Vinnie pushes my hair aside and kisses my neck. "You're driving me crazy, you know that?" he whispers. "You're killing me."

I inch away just a millimeter, wondering what's wrong with me. Vinnie DiNardio, pride of West Berry High, drool object for freshmen girls in the hallway. Sweeter to me than my own father. What more can I ask?

He feels me pull away, and—for the thousandth time—cuts me some slack; he lets his hand fall gently to my thigh, then leans back and closes his eyes. He's wearing just a clean white T-shirt and his wrestling warm-up pants; I've got on his jacket as usual. His biceps push at his sleeves. His hair is freshly washed, combed nicely back. He looks like a poster boy, smells like deodorant and soap—a smell I used to love. Why don't I anymore?

"So you're gonna come eat dinner with me, right?" he says, eyes still closed. "What do you feel like, huh? Meatball sub? Or no, raviolis. Swarming in sauce. Uh, man, the thought makes me cream." He opens his eyes, produces two squares of Bazooka gum, and hands one to me.

I tear it open, pop the gum in my mouth, and shove the wrapper, crumpled, into my jacket pocket. He unwraps his comic carefully and squints at it in the dark. " 'You are an artist, let your true colors show.' " He pushes the pink square into his mouth. "What do you think that means?"

"What do *you* think it means?"

It's the answer someone in my family would give—my mother, my sister—and I don't blame him for rolling his eyes. "If I knew, I wouldn't have asked you, would I?" he says. "You're the smart one around here." He squeezes my neck with two fingers. "So what does yours say?"

I pull the mashed comic from my pocket and hand it to him. He uncrumples it and smooths it as carefully as he did his. " 'Whether you choose love or fame, you'll be able to handle either or both.' Hm. That's a good one. Knowing you, though, you'll choose fame." He laughs, then hands the fortune back to me, working his gum. "So what's going on, babe, huh? Talk to me. You still going to see your sister Saturday?"

"Yeah, if she keeps the weight on." Even thinking about it makes me hyper; I haven't seen Cassie in almost six weeks, since she left for the hospital. "I talked to her last night," I tell him, "and she's still at a hundred. I don't see how she can lose two pounds in two days, so . . ."

"Easy," he says softly, and I feel pretty stupid then. In the past three days, Vinnie cut seven pounds to make weight—running miles after practice bundled in four or five sets of sweats, getting up at four in the morning to do push-ups to Bruce Springsteen. "No," he says, watching me, "don't worry. She won't lose the weight. Tell her to drink water before weigh-ins. Water and salt. It'll make her bloat up."

"Vinnie, she's supposed to gain *weight*."

"I know, I know, don't get nervous." He holds up his palms. "I'm just saying. I mean, the place sounds a little rough to me, you know? She can't even see her own sister?"

"It's for her own good," I say, but I half-agree with him, even though her program, at the Halley Psychiatric Hospital in Connecticut, is supposed to be one of the best on the East Coast—this according to Dr. Morse, who'd been able to get Cassie in almost immediately despite the long waiting list. Anorexics earn privileges

—phone calls, visitors—when they gain weight, and lose them if they lose it again. My sister took two weeks to gain her first half-pound, so my parents could visit. Now it's my turn, and I'm half-excited, half-petrified. When I picture the place, it comes out like *Night of the Living Dead:* zombie people all over the place, skin hanging off skeleton bodies like drapes.

"Who's going with you?" Vinnie's asking.

"What? Oh. Just my mother."

He smiles. "So you'll get to drive some of the way."

"Probably."

"You can practice what I taught you."

Last week, in the junior high parking lot, he showed me K-turns and parallel parking and reverse. Then we cruised out and around the streets, him coaching me. He was a great coach, patient and encouraging. A pang of guilt goes through me. And then it turns to distress: Maybe I'm becoming like my grandmother, thinking nothing's ever good enough.

"Well," Vinnie says, "I'm glad you're going for your sister's sake, but for my sake I wish you'd be here. I don't feel like going to this party alone on Saturday night." He looks at me. "No chance you'll be back in time, right?"

I shake my head no, though we might. "We can't leave till after I take SATs," I say, truthfully this time. "So we won't even get to the hospital till two or three. Then we'll probably stay for dinner, or something, so by the time we get home . . ." I sit back, examining my nails. "The party'll be good. You'll probably have more fun without me, anyway."

"Why do you always say shit like that?" I can feel him searching me. "You think I'm using you or something?"

I almost laugh. Surely there are easier girls to use at West Berry High.

But he's waiting for an answer. "Hey," he says when he doesn't get one. "I got something for you. You gotta spit out your gum first, though."

"Vinnie, I just put it in."

He cups his hand under my chin. "Come on, just do it, okay? Gum don't go with this."

I sigh and let the pink wad drop from my mouth into his hand. He spits his in too, then mashes the whole thing together and sticks it under the seat—something that would horrify Cassie. Anyone in my family, really. He leans down to rummage in his wrestling bag on the floor, his gold Italian horn dangling in front of his chest. On the back of his neck, the chain catches a ray of light hidden somewhere in the bus. I put my finger on the chain and move it back and forth. He laughs and butts my hand with his head. "Stop! What, you wanna wear it? Go ahead, take it. You wear it more than I do anyway."

I remove the chain from his neck and put it around mine, letting the horn fall down my shirt. "Found it," Vinnie says. He sits up, then holds out both fists, palms down, near his lap. "Pick one," he tells me.

I can see something shiny in his hands. I touch the left one.

"Wrong. It's both." He turns his hands over and opens them, revealing two tiny bottles of Southern Comfort. "I figured we could celebrate tonight, since you're not gonna be here for the party."

I smile weakly. I've never liked Southern Comfort—and then there's the fear that my father will smell it on me when I get home. But that's unlikely, since Vinnie and I are supposed to eat dinner first. Then I'm supposed to come home and study SAT words for two hours. That's the deal.

I examine one of the bottles, then hand it back to Vinnie. "Pretty cute," I say. "Thanks."

He nods, obviously pleased. "You know, I would've got disqualified from the meet if they found these." He twists open a bottle, sniffs it, holds it out to me again. "There's a reason, too, though. Guess what today is?"

I take the bottle again. It's pretty small, at least—a little smaller than my hand. "What?" I say.

"Think."

"Um—I don't know. What?"

He shakes his head. "Our three-month anniversary. Jeez, I thought the girl's supposed to keep track of that shit."

"I do, normally. It's just—"

"Forget about it, I'm only kidding. You got a lot on your mind, with your sister and everything." He brushes my chin with one finger. "So anyway, let's do a toast." He puts his hand around mine over the bottle. "To Vinnie and Billie DiNardio. Happy three months." He kisses me, then takes the bottle, tilts his head back, and drinks. When he's done, it's half gone. He hands it to me.

What can I do? I close my eyes and chug the rest, trying not to taste. It burns the back of my throat and down into my stomach. A slow warmth spreads through me, like I've swallowed heated honey.

Vinnie nods, impressed. "Thattagirl. I knew you could chug if you tried. Okay, round two." He opens the second bottle, and we drink that the same way.

I look out the window then, through dirt-streaked glass and onto a lighted highway. It looks surreal, like some electronic game. Cars roll by below us, hugging the ground—square, metallic, head-lighted blurs. Some have packed snow on their tops. Beyond the cars, snow blankets the sides of the highway. I feel better now—buzzed and swirling inside my head, my body not nearly as tense.

Vinnie's hand slowly massages my thigh. "You know some-thing?" he says. "You are so beautiful. I mean, even hotter than when we started going out."

I laugh.

"No, I mean it. I swear to God. I love your hair long, like this. And look at your eyebrows, they're like, perfectly arched." He kisses my forehead, then my eye, then my mouth again.

He is still a great kisser; that hasn't changed. I can taste the Southern Comfort on him, and I can feel it in me. Making me brave. I close my eyes and let Vinnie's hands wander all over me through my clothes. I'm sleeping and someone is giving me a massage, wak-ing up my body. That's what it feels like, and for the next few minutes, everything is a warm sexy blur.

And then Vinnie's somehow gotten himself down on the floor, his back mashed into the seat in front of us, his elbows jutting out, and he's got my pants unbuttoned and unzipped, and his hands are in my underwear. He's trying to get his face in there, too. "No—stop," I whisper, stiffening.

He pushes his hands under my sweater. "Why not, Bil? Come on! I want to make you feel good—"

"Vinnie, no! What if—like, what if someone sees?"

But that's lame, and we both know it; the bus is dark, and no one's coming back here—not that they'd be surprised if they did. Any one of the wrestlers would be doing the same thing, if he were Vinnie and his girlfriend were here.

"No one's gonna see," Vinnie whispers. His head sinks down again. His lips brush my belly as his hands burrow into my jeans.

I want to like it, and for a few seconds I try. But all the tempting feeling from before is gone now, and it's nothing but hands and fingers and lips touching me, touching my body in places no one has ever touched except in my mind, in my dreams. But in my dreams it feels nice. Now it feels disgusting somehow, like something crawling out of the toilet and touching me.

"Stop, Vin," I say, almost pleading.

He pulls away obediently, but slowly this time, slower than in the past. He slaps back hair that's fallen in front of his face. "You really want me to stop?"

I nod.

"Why?"

"I don't know. I just—I can't right now."

His eyes register something. "Oh. I get it." He climbs back into his seat, and I realize he thinks I have my period, which is okay for now. But his arm comes around me again, and his breathing is still heavy. And the next thing I know he's guiding my hand into his warm-up pants, and then his underwear.

My palm is stiff as a board, but he doesn't seem to care, and I tell myself, Okay Billie, just do this, don't wimp out again. I close my eyes and let his hand move my hand, trying to think about other things. I picture Cassie sitting in a white room reading a book, and then Tiffany making Jiffy Pop. I picture Dominick Zeferelli. Would I mind doing this to him?

Maybe not. Maybe I'm not a total prude, at least. On the floor across the aisle, someone has left a crumpled lunch bag, and I try to imagine what was in it. Vinnie is moving my hand faster now, his eyes closed, his breath deep and fast. And still faster. I close my eyes. He moans a little and jerks against my palm, and then my hand is wet.

Vinnie leans back, and after a few seconds he opens his eyes and looks at me. He takes a slow deep breath. "Oh, thank you, sweetheart," he whispers, moving to kiss me.

I yank my hand back and slide it fast across my jeans, furious now. "I want to break up," I blurt out.

The coach's voice rings through the bus then, almost as if he's heard me and thinks Vinnie might need to be comforted or something. "Hey, DiNardio, I'm comin' back there." Vinnie straightens his clothes and shoves more gum into his mouth to hide the liquor. A minute later, Coach lumbers back, smiling. "Hey, lovebirds," he says, winking at me.

He's come to talk about some move Vinnie used to pin his guy, something he did to the guy's legs. Vinnie talks to him calmly, as if everything's fine and he's perfectly straight, and I can't help but admire him for that. I listen awhile, then tune out. And then we're pulling back into school. We shuffle off the bus, avoiding the yellow-lit sections of the parking lot, heading toward Vinnie's car in the dark. Wrestlers call good-bye to us. A few congratulate Vinnie. He waves good-bye for both of us, not looking at me.

In the car, he puts in an eight-track and blasts it. The song is "Tainted Love," and I wonder if he chose it for spite. I look out my window, cracking my knuckles. He's driving me home; dinner seems to be off, though he hasn't mentioned it. For a second I'm embarrassed, and then I'm totally relieved. I wish it were five minutes from now so I were home in my room. I wish I were Tiffany.

But in front of my house, Vinnie turns off the music. He turns around and fixes his brown eyes on me. In the distance, I hear a horn honk—once, then again. "So is this it or what?" he says.

My palms are sweating even in the cold; I can't believe he's gonna make me say it again. "I don't know," I mumble.

He laughs a little. "Of course you know. Either it is or it ain't."

"Okay. It is, then. Okay?"

He flicks the crucifix on his mirror. "I don't get you. I treat you like gold. I do anything you want. I do everything. . . ."

I feel like something inside me has turned cold and mean, never to warm up again. My eyes start to fill up. "I know, Vinnie. It's not you. It's—"

"What?" He stares at me. "What? You're scared or something?"

I shake my head no.

He sighs. "Ah, just forget it. I should've known we wouldn't hit it off."

I turn to him, hurt. "What's that supposed to mean?"

"Nothing. Forget about it. Listen, can I have my horn?"

I slide it over my head and hand it to him, and he puts it back on. We both sit there silently then. I want to get out, but I can't seem to move. On the dashboard are stickers: *Girls play volleyball, boys play basketball, men wrestle. Italians are Numero Uno.* I touch the word *Italians.* "Are these yours or your brother's?" I say.

"What do you care?" His black eyes are buttons now, piercing my face. "Listen. You gonna sit here all night or get out of my face so I can go eat?"

His words sting like a slap. I open my door and push myself out. "Fuck you," I say.

He pulls away, his tires squealing a little as he goes, and it's not until he's gone that I realize that isn't at all what I meant to say.

Inside, Ethan licks me hello, and I hear Mollie whimper from behind a door somewhere upstairs. Otherwise the house is quiet, and all the lights are off except one in the den. On the kitchen table is a note from my mother. *Billie: We went to the movies with the Green-baums. Back around ten. Hope your dinner was fun. Love, Mom and Dad. P.S. Cassie called. She can't wait to see you.* I read it twice—the second time for hidden clues about my sister's health—then pick up the phone and call Tiffany. I'm still wearing my coat, Vinnie's coat. I'd forgotten to give it back, and he'd forgotten to ask. "Please be there, Tiffany," I whisper into the phone.

She answers on the seventh ring. "Billie?" she says. "Wait,

where are you? I thought you were going out with Vinnie. Did he win?"

"Pinned." I hold the phone away from my ear while she whoops with joy. "The rest of the team got killed, though. Anyway, I'm not going anywhere with Vinnie now. Tiffany, I have so much to tell you, I have to talk to you."

"You do? I have something to tell you, too."

"What?"

"You first. What do you mean you won't be going anywhere with—" Someone in her house picks up an extension, and I hear lots of voices in the background. "I'm on," Tiffany yells. The voices continue. "I'm *on!*" she screams.

Her sister Michelle giggles. "Oops! Sorry. Tiffy, honey, I need the phone, just for a sec." Her sisters always call her honey when they want something.

"Use the other phone," Tiffany says. "I just got on."

"I can't, honey. Daddy wants the line free. Just give me a few minutes, okay?"

"Jesus Christ. Hang up first, then." Michelle clicks off. "Tell me quick," Tiffany says.

"I can't, it's not a quick thing. Listen, let's just meet at the park, okay? In two seconds."

"Three," Tiffany says. She hangs up.

I grab Mollie's leash and run upstairs to get her, since I took Ethan the last time and I try to alternate. Ethan growls at her as we squeeze by him. I put myself between them till we get out the door.

There's no sign of Tiffany when I get to the park, so I head up the hill toward her house. Above me, glittery stars fill the sky, but I can't appreciate them. The events of the past hour are expanding inside me, like bread dough. If I don't tell someone soon, I'll explode.

I'm almost all the way to the Zeferellis' house when Tiffany appears on the street. I run toward her, Mollie's dog tags jangling. She's wearing new black hightops and a big faded jean jacket that I haven't seen before. Her lips are covered in frosty gloss; even in the night I see them sparkling. Her black hair is freshly curled. Just the sight of her makes me feel a million times better. "You look like a movie star," I tell her.

She laughs. "Oh, *please*! I didn't even put blush on. Hey, can I wear DiNardio's jacket? It would look sharp with this. You can wear mine."

I drop Mollie's leash and switch jackets with her, even though I'm wearing only a short-sleeve terry-cloth top—a shirt I've now outgrown, my mother reminded me this morning, but it's one of my favorite shirts, and anyway, tight is in. Tiffany's jacket is thinner than mine, and I shiver a little once it's on. It smells like cigarettes and perfume and something else. "Whose is this?" I ask.

"Dom's. Don't tell him I took it, he'll friggen murder me. Man, Vinnie's big. Don't you love this jacket?" She reaches down to pat Mollie. "C'mere, Moll-dog. Come here, Mollie bee."

I sniff the collar of Dominick's jacket, no longer cold, thrilled to be wearing something of his. For some reason, it makes me feel better about Vinnie, too—just knowing Dom is out there.

"So what did you have to tell me?" Tiffany says. "Come on, I'm dying. Wait, though, let's go to the park first. We can sit on the swings."

We run back down the hill like two twelve-year-olds, and for a minute I wish we were. The streets glisten like wet paint. At the park, we jump on the horse swings. Our feet dangle almost to the ground. I let go of Mollie's leash, knowing there's a chance she'll run and I'll have to chase her, but she just looks at me and then lies down nearby to wait. Ever since the fights with Ethan, she's not the same as she used to be—like she's grown old suddenly.

Over in the far bushes, a few kids are getting high; we can hear them talking and laughing, and I smell the nutty-sweet smell of pot. "Yo!" Tiffany yells, and someone yells "Yo!" back, but no one comes out, and I'm glad; I want Tiffany all to myself. "So?" she says, turning to me. "You gonna tell me or just bust my balls all night?"

I suck cold air into my lungs. My Southern Comfort buzz from before is all gone. And now that I've got Tiffany here, I'm half-scared to tell her. "I broke up with Vinnie tonight," I say, and a wave of fear washes through me. What have I done?

Tiffany smiles. "Get out."

"I am out," I say miserably.

She stares at me. "Why, though? I thought everything was going great. I thought he treated you like—I don't know. I mean, didn't he?"

"He did. He was totally nice. I almost wish he wasn't." I sigh. "I know, you think I'm stupid, right? You think he's perfect, and I'm a loser."

"Oh, come on, Bil. Get serious." A van passes by, the driver slowing down to look at us, then speeding up again. Tiffany takes out a cigarette and a purple Bic lighter. She lights up, sucking in her cheeks, and I watch her enviously, wishing I could smoke like that. "Listen," she says, shooting a puff of gray-white smoke into the night. "Do you regret breaking up?"

"I don't know. I mean, I don't wish he were here right now." I touch my horse's mane, yellow-painted metal. "I mean, how are you supposed to know, anyway?"

She thinks a second. "Well, let me ask you this. Would it skieve you to wash his dirty underwear?"

I laugh. "Yes."

"No, wait, forget that. Does he pass the wheelchair test?"

"What's that?"

"If he got hit by a car right now and was paralyzed for the rest of his life, would you still love him just as much?"

"I don't even love him now."

She laughs. "Well, case closed, then. You definitely did the right thing."

"You think so?"

She shrugs one shoulder. "Hey, you can't force it if the chemistry ain't there. You gotta go with your heart. Personally, I think the guy's a living doll, but I'm not the one going out with him."

For the first time, it occurs to me that Tiffany could want something I have. The thought amazes me, until I remember I don't have Vinnie anymore. Tiffany takes another drag, then offers the cigarette to me. I shake my head no. "Tiff," I say, "I gave him a handjob on the bus."

"No!" She laughs, flipping her cigarette with her thumb and two fingers. It sails over the fence and into the street. "Did anyone see?"

"No. We were in the back." I glance at her out of the side of my eye. "Would you have?"

"What, gave Vinnie a handjob on the bus? Probably."

"Tiffany!" I fake-kick at her swing.

"Well, you asked."

"Hey," I say suddenly, "why don't *you* go out with Vinnie?"

The minute I say it, I want to pull the words back. She turns away from me and swings her leg in a circle, making her horse fling back and forth like something burned. "Thanks, but I think I can find my own boyfriend without taking your leftover one. Anyway, if Vinnie wanted me, he'd have asked *me* out—not you."

"Probably thought he couldn't get you."

"Oh, right."

I start my horse up, too, wondering why every time I open my mouth lately, something moronic comes out. I never used to be like this. I used to say only complimentary things, stuff I was sure wouldn't cause trouble. "Come on, Tiff, I didn't mean it like that," I plead. I can't stand the thought that she might be mad at me. "Hey! What did you have to tell me, anyway?"

"Forget it, it's nothing."

"Oh, come on."

She smiles a little. "You're gonna die," she says.

"Tell me!" I say, filled with relief.

"Okay. Ready? My sister's PG." She nods, her black eyes bright in the night. "I swear to god."

My hands fall to my sides. "What? Which sister?"

"Bambi, fool! Michelle doesn't even have a boyfriend. Her and Ricky broke up again." She flips her hair back over her shoulder. "And get this. She's almost six months. That's why she eats half the friggen house every time my mother cooks. She was afraid to tell anyone because Tito's divorce didn't come through yet, but now—I guess she couldn't hide it anymore or something."

My swing has stopped altogether. For a second I wonder if my parents will have to find out about this. "So what's—I mean, what's she planning to do?" I manage.

She shrugs. "I think they might get married. After his divorce is all set."

I pull my coat tighter around me. My news with Vinnie is nothing compared to this. "What did your father say?"

"He had a fit." Tiffany laughs. "You should have seen him. He threw the toaster at the car—"

"*Your* father?"

"Yeah. But he's okay now, my mother told him to grow up. She was eighteen when she had Dominick, so how mad could he get? Bambi's nineteen, almost. Anyway, he calmed down after that. I think he's kind of into it now. As long as it's a boy." She laughs again. "Bambi wants a boy. She says it would be a tiny built-in worship machine."

For a long time, we don't talk. I don't want to say the wrong thing. She seems to be happy about this, like it's good news or at least not too bad. Am I supposed to be happy, too?

Tiffany reaches down to pick up a rock from the ground. She whips it side-arm across the park, near the trees where the smokers are. They've switched to cigarettes now; a hint of minty tobacco wafts toward us, and I see the orange tips of their cigarettes painting patterns in the night. Mollie sniffs in their direction, her nose in the air. I turn to Tiffany. "If it's a girl, maybe she can name it Cassie, since my sister'll probably be dead by then."

Tiffany smacks my arm. "How can you even say stuff like that, ya retard?"

I shrug, feeling sort of weird all of a sudden. Weird and sad. For some reason, everything seems sad now—the whole world, everything. I tell myself that maybe it's because I'm a little bit jealous of Tiffany, and for a minute, that seems possible. She's so happy, so carefree; no matter what happens, it's okay by her.

Tiffany turns to me again. "You still going to see her Saturday?"

I nod. "After SATs. If she stays at a hundred pounds."

"Shit. My baby toe weighs more than that." She swings awhile, silent, and I wonder if she's thinking about SATs, how I used to try to get her to take them with me. I don't, anymore; not since she threw out her PSAT scores and then told me she couldn't remember what she got. When she asked what I got, and I told her, she said, "You're so smart, I'm so *envious!*" but I didn't think she was, not at all. I asked her if she'd try again, and she laughed. "No way, sweetheart. Once is enough for me, thank you very much."

"So how's Cassie doing, anyway?" she says now. I tell her about the meetings Cassie goes to now once a day, sometimes twice. "My father thinks they're bullshit, but Cassie says it's helping, so . . ."

She listens, nodding, even though she hardly knows Cassie. "She'll be all right," she says confidently.

"How do you know?"

"I can feel it," she says, and I'm not jealous anymore, just grateful, to her and for her. "I know how we can find out for sure, though," she adds.

"How?"

"Ask the Ouija board. Me and Bam were just doing it. We asked it all about her baby, like if it would have a cleft palate or whatever. And I asked it about Danny." Danny's a friend of Michelle's who Tiffany has a crush on. "You want to ask it about Cassie?" she says.

"God. I don't know."

"Well, come over anyway. You can see Bambi's kid and feel it kick in her gut. I'm telling you, it's amazing. You won't believe she's been hiding this thing. It's like she swallowed a basketball. Her stomach's as tight as GLAD Wrap."

I push my thumb into my thigh. "Is Dominick home?" I can look at him in a whole new light now, now that Vinnie's not my boyfriend anymore.

"I doubt it," Tiffany says. "He's probably at work, as usual. Or at school."

I hesitate a second longer, wondering if they all know about my sister, or if they think my parents did something to make her like this. In a way, I just want to go home—climb in bed and read some more of *Wuthering Heights,* escape from everything.

Tiffany jumps off her swing, her sneakers smacking the dirt. "You coming?"

"I can't stay too long, though. I have Mollie, you know?"

"Of course," she says. She gives her swing a push, so the horse bucks up in back. "Come on," she says. "Let's blow this junkyard."

Bambi lies on the couch, a bubble-gut queen in pool-blue silk pajamas, one palm flat on her stomach. Her sisters crowd around her. "Honey, can you get me some chocolate milk?" she says to Tiffany and, to Michelle, "Shelly, can you bring my cigarettes over, please?" Michelle tosses her the pack, then leaves the room. "I'll get the chocolate milk," I offer, hoping the milk will counter the effects of the cigarette. I go out to the kitchen and pour her a big glassful. Tiffany's parents don't seem to be around. I go back and deliver the milk to Bambi.

"Thank you, honey." She beams. "Here, you want to feel the baby kick?"

"Oh—that's okay."

Bambi rolls her eyes. "Look at her, Tiff, she's embarrassed! How cute! Here, honey, give me your hand." She lifts up her pajama shirt and places my palm against her bulging stomach.

I'm embarrassed, but I'm also fascinated—not just that there's a baby in there, but that she's kept it a secret this long. Her stomach feels hard and very warm. I wonder what the baby looks like, and what position it's in. I wonder if it likes chocolate milk. I picture it smoking a tiny cigarette. "There!" Bambi says. "Did you feel it kick?"

"Um—"

"There! There, it went again. Did you feel it?"

"I did," I lie. "That's really neat. Thanks." I pull my hand away slowly.

"You should see my tits," she says. "They're like fucking water balloons. Want to see?"

I smile. "That's okay."

"Bambi, *please*!" Tiffany says. "Lord God!"

Bambi laughs, long and deep.

On the other couch, their grandfather sits quietly, staring at the television through his bottle-thick glasses. He's watching *All in the Family*. Canned laughter fills the room. I go over and sit down next to him. He smells slightly wine-y, slightly musty. "You're gonna be a great-grandfather," I say.

He turns to me and shrugs, then smiles. I smile back, wondering how much of all this he comprehends. Maybe nothing. Or maybe he gets everything and just takes it all in stride. After all, he created these people.

Tiffany goes off to get the Ouija board. She's wearing her short rabbit coat; she likes to wear jackets inside sometimes, when she isn't trying to show off her chest. I'm wearing Vinnie's coat, which Tiffany gave me back when we got here and put back Dominick's.

Bambi yawns and picks up the remote control and changes the channel to a disco-dancing show. I glance at their grandfather to see if he's mad, but he doesn't seem to notice. Tiffany comes back in. "I couldn't find it," she says. "This house looks like a bomb hit it." She plops down on the couch. "I'm pissed," she says. "Bam, do you know where is it?"

"What?"

"Ouija."

Bambi rubs her stomach through her pajamas. "No clue. Tiffy, would you make me an English muffin, hon?"

Tiffany stares at the TV. A man in a white suit and a black shirt is dancing in circles, arms over his head like an ape. "Make it yourself, wart hog," she says to Bambi. "Ooh, I love this song."

"I'll make it for you," I say, standing.

Bambi looks at me. "Really?"

"Sure. What do you want on it?"

"Oh, whatever. Peanut butter and fluff, if you can find it."

I go off to the kitchen again. For some reason, the refrigerator is empty, except for a package of cream cheese and two bottles of Tab. I find the English muffins in the pantry—which is also almost empty —and take one out and stick it in to toast. I can't find peanut butter, but I do find marshmallow fluff in the kitchen cabinet, next to a bottle of gin. I open the jar and dip out a knifeful of the white goo and lick it, waiting for the muffin to pop up.

"Good, huh?" It's Dom's voice, coming from directly behind me.

I turn toward him, embarrassed. "I was gonna take a new knife to do the muffin—"

"Sure, sure you were." He smiles briefly around a toothpick in his mouth, then reaches past me to get a spoon from the drawer. His arm brushes my shirt. My body goes hot underneath it. My face is hot, too, but luckily he's not looking at me. I back up a step to give him room. He opens the teapot, checks it quickly, then runs some water into it and turns on the stove. He gets out a jar of instant coffee and dumps two big spoonfuls into a mug. He glances at his watch. Then he pulls out the textbook he's been carrying under his arm, opens it to his bookmark, and begins to read.

He's wearing dirty sneakers and a leather jacket, which I can smell along with the scent of cold air and a hint of gasoline. I watch his amber eyes moving behind his eyelids, scanning the words—far-apart eyes, less round, more slanted than Vinnie's. He's taller than Vinnie, too. He moves the toothpick back and forth with his tongue. I hang back behind him, trying not to stare. "What are you reading?" I ask.

His eyes stay on the page. "Accounting. Got a test"—he glances at his watch again—"in forty-five minutes."

"Oh. Good luck."

"Thanks." He still won't look at me, and I realize then that he thinks I'm nothing more than Tiffany's little friend, not even worth a second glance. The thought makes me mad, and then, suddenly, determined. I want him to notice me here.

The English muffin pops up. Dom glances at it, then at me. "Yours?" he says.

"Unless you want it."

He laughs, just a breath, and his eyes fix on me. Finally. "That's okay," he says. "I don't have to steal your English muffin. I can make my own—"

"Actually, it's for Bambi." But I don't reach out to get it. I can

still feel where he touched me—a brush of skin, tingling, burning
through my shirt.

He raises his eyebrows. "She's got *you* making her meals now?
Nice." He shakes his head.

"I don't mind. I volunteered. I like to cook for people."

"Do you?" He's still looking at me. "That your boyfriend's
jacket?" he says after a minute.

"Ex." Now I'm thrilled this is true. I peel off the jacket and
hang it on the back of a chair, aware of my tight terry-cloth shirt. "I
don't really need it now, though," I say. "It's pretty hot in here."

Dom's eyes dart once fast down my body, then back up to my
face. I don't know whether to blush or grin. I cross my legs, standing, and lean back against the counter, trying to look sexy. "That my
sister's shirt?" he says.

My heart thumps. "No. Why?"

He shrugs. "It looks like something she'd wear, I guess."

For some reason, that doesn't feel like a compliment. The teapot whistles, and he turns away from me to pour water into his mug.
He takes out a plate and slaps the English muffin on it. "Maybe I will
have this," he says. "We'll toast Bambi up another one."

"Okay." I go to the pantry and get out another English muffin,
relieved to be temporarily out of his sight. But when I walk back, I
catch him glance at me again over his mug of coffee, like he's about
to say something. I wait hopefully.

The phone rings. Dominick turns toward it, but he doesn't
move to answer it. And then, from upstairs, Mr. Zeferelli yells down,
"Don't anyone answer that," which surprises me—both because of
how loud he's yelling and because I hadn't even realized he was here.

The phone rings again. Dominick scoops his muffin halves off
the plate and picks up his mug. "Well, I've gotta go. See you later."
He heads out of the kitchen, and as the phone rings for the third
time, I hear the front door slam.

Mr. Zeferelli is running downstairs. "Don't pick that up," he
yells, coming into the kitchen. He speeds by me toward the living
room, looking flustered and sweaty. "Don't answer that," he yells

again. The second English muffin pops up. I take it out of the toaster
and put it on a plate. The phone keeps ringing.

It rings five more times while I put fluff on the muffin and
another four while I carry it in to Bambi. Then it stops. Bambi and
Tiffany glance at each other. They're both sitting up now. "Thank
the Lord," Bambi says.

I put the plate down on the table in front of her, but she doesn't
seem to notice. The phone starts again. "Oh, *fuck,*" Tiffany says.

Their father bursts in through the door on the other side, from
the family room. He's running from phone to phone, making sure
no one picks it up. As if anyone would at this point.

"Daddy, *relax,*" Bambi says. "You're gonna give yourself a heart
attack."

Mr. Zeferelli stares at her, wide-eyed and panting. The phone
rings again. He turns and runs out of the room, back toward the
kitchen.

I have never seen him like this. I sit down next to Tiffany,
nervous now, too. "Why isn't the machine on?" I ask, but she holds
up one finger, like I'll tell you why in a sec, and that's when I know
something's really wrong here. Why would they avoid someone so
desperate to reach them? The phone continues to ring. The four of
us stare at the TV, and the rings are like sirens, going through me so
loud that I can't even think about Dominick.

I want to leave, but if I leave before the phone stops, it'll seem
like I'm being rude or deserting them. I count four more rings. And
then, finally, silence. "Twenty-nine," Bambi says. She takes a deep
breath.

I stand up. "Tiff, I should probably get going."

She stands up, too, and for once, she doesn't fight me. "I'll walk
you out," she says.

It's not until four in the morning, when I wake up alone in my
bed, that I remember that Dominick was about to tell me something
just before the phone started to ring. I try to imagine what it was,
but I can't, and for a while I just lie there, staring plum-eyed at my
old alarm clock. I can still hear the Zeferellis' phone ringing in my

head. I get out of bed, rinse my mouth with cold water, and go downstairs.

In the kitchen, I turn on the light and sit at the table, listening to the sounds of the night. Heat blows gently through the vents; the refrigerator hums away, and then there's the muffled marblelike click of the freezer pushing out ice. And then the whole thing clicks off and quiet fills up that space and my mind. The sounds of silence, of the world asleep except for me—or at least the part of the world I know about.

I go to the front door and crack it and step outside for a minute or two, and it's a different kind of silence out here, bigger and louder, much more vast—wrapping around me like a blanket, keeping me safe. Stars salt the sky, thick in some places and thin in others, and I think that it's awesome, and that someday I might like to capture that beauty somehow. But after a minute I start to get cold, and as the comfort disappears, my thoughts come tumbling back. Not just the Zeferellis now, but Vinnie, pissed and wounded in the car after I told him I wanted to break up, and then Cassie, standing miserably with ten other emaciated girls in some hospital hall. And then my parents. I'd heard them arguing, as I fell asleep, about the hospital plans: my mother wanted us, me and her, to stay overnight in Connecticut so we could visit Cassie again on Sunday, and my father didn't want us to.

Lying in bed, I'd urged my mother on mentally—not so much because she was right as because he always wins. She gets tired of arguing and he doesn't, or he yells louder and that's that. And he did this time, too, his voice rose as hers faded, and finally I heard her turn on water for a bath, and I wanted to go in and fight the battle for her. I didn't, though; I just stayed in bed and clapped the pillow over my ears, like a wimp.

I go back inside and drift past my parents' bookshelves. *Goodbye Columbus, Lolita,* a bunch of stuff by John Updike. I take down one of the *Rabbit* books and flip through it. Sex everywhere, some woman's breasts always flapping her rib cage under a see-through nightgown. It makes me think of Bambi, and then of Dominick. I think of her sticking his palm on her stomach the way she did with mine, and then I picture me instead of her, lying under his hand. Except that my stomach is flat, not pregnant. His hand moves down, moves all over me, and it's nothing like with Vinnie on the bus, not anything like that. I think of what his mouth would taste like. Cigarettes and coffee, maybe.

At the window, I open a curtain and peek out again, and this time I notice other things than I did a few minutes ago. Grass pokes through the snow in patches, like some big askew checkerboard. Behind the ear tree, our green garbage can is sprawled on its side again—the way the raccoons dump it almost every night now, despite my mother's efforts to keep them out with bungee cords. Squinting, I spot some orange peels, crumpled-up yellow napkins, a blue and pink tampon box. If Cassie were here, all that would bum her out, but I think it's pretty. The raccoons, too; my mother can't stand them, and I can't really blame her, but I know if I saw them, I'd find them beautiful, somehow. Above the garbage, through tree branches, the moon is an exact half-circle. The black air is starting to fade to royal blue. In not too long, the moon will be gone, and the air will become silvery.

I turn to go back upstairs; I want to try to sleep again. Sometimes I find being tired oddly comforting, but tomorrow won't be one of those days, between visiting my sister at the hospital and taking the SATs and remembering all the stuff that happened yesterday. Or trying not to.

Upstairs, I tiptoe past my parents' door and get into bed. Ethan is on Cassie's bed, snoring away. I flip over and close my eyes. But my mind won't turn off. I wonder if this is how Cassie feels—always thinking, her mind racing wild, like some runaway train.

I hear my parents' door open and close then, and my mother tiptoeing through the hall—I can tell it's her by the way the steps creak so gently as she pads downstairs. It's almost five now. I can't imagine what she's doing down there. I wait a few minutes to see if she comes back up; when she doesn't, I go down.

Through the slats of the kitchen door, I see her sitting at the table, under soft yellow light. She has a bunch of papers spread out in front of her, and she's sipping coffee and writing something with a green felt-tip pen.

I pull the doorknob gently and peek in. My mother jumps in her chair, then puts her hand to her heart. "Billie? You scared me! What are you doing up?"

"Sorry, Mom," I whisper, stepping happily into the room. "I couldn't sleep. Are you doing work?"

"Mm. My lesson plans for next week. I wasn't sure I'd have time later on."

I move to the table. "Mom, are you serious? It's not even Saturday morning yet. You have all weekend."

"Well, you and I are going to see Cassie today, and Daddy always has things planned for Sunday. . . ."

"What about after dinner?"

"*Masterpiece Theatre.* You know. And by the time that's over, it's ten o'clock, and then it's time to make Daddy's lunch for tomorrow. And mine."

I sit down across from her. "Tell him to make his own lunch. Tell him to make yours, too, for a change. And tell him you don't want to watch *Masterpiece Theatre,* if you don't." I sound like my sister. The Cassie of last year.

My mother shrugs. "I don't mind getting up. I like it. I work better in the morning, anyway."

I'm quiet a second. I know I should go back upstairs and let her work, but it's so rare I get to be alone with her like this—no one else in the room, no one calling, no one yelling from upstairs for her. I want to tell her what happened with Vinnie. Maybe she'll know what I should do, how I can get him not to hate me.

And she doesn't seem to mind me there, or if she does, she's not showing it. She stares down at the page, her arm moving in the sleeve of her big purple robe—a birthday present from my father last year. Her writing is small and round and flowery, nothing really like her. The part in her hair is slightly imperfect—like a sidewalk crack. Her dark-blond hair is threaded with silver. Once I'd suggested that she dye it, like Mrs. Zeferelli. She just laughed. "Maybe I like to look my age," she said. "Maybe I don't want to look eighteen."

I sit down at the table. "So what's the lesson?" I say. I take a sip of her coffee, then cringe. It's bitter and black.

"Well," she says, "Monday we're starting with the difference between *want* and *need*."

I smile. "*Want* and *need*. Like the Rolling Stones song. So what *is* the difference?"

She puts down her pen. "Needs are things we must have to live," she recites, "and wants are things we would like to have but can live without." She looks at me. "I'll name something, and you tell me if it's a want or a need. Ready?"

I nod.

"A new Barbie doll."

"Need," I joke.

"Wrong." She laughs. "There are only six needs, and Barbie is not one of them. Maybe you need to go back to second grade."

"I guess I do. What are they?"

"Air, water, food, clothing, shelter, and love."

"Love? That's not a need. People can live without love, can't they?"

She thinks a minute. "I suppose so. But not very happily."

"Kids without Barbie dolls don't live happily either."

She laughs again. "That's not true. You never had a Barbie doll, and you were happy."

"I didn't want one. I had a football."

She smiles, and before I can stop myself, I ask, "Are you happy?" It's last night that makes me ask it—their arguing voices still fresh in my head.

My mother frowns and rubs one of her fingernails. "Yes, I'd say I'm happy."

"What about when you and Dad fight?"

"We don't fight," she says, still looking at her nail. "We *argue*. And most people argue. Things get resolved through conflict."

"So what did you, uh, *resolve* last night? Are we staying in Connecticut or coming home?"

She looks at me, clearly surprised that I heard them. "Coming home," she says.

"Why? He doesn't want to pay for a hotel room, right?"

"Wrong. In fact, he said if you want to stay over and take a bus back tomorrow, you can."

"Why can't you, then?"

She puts down her pen. "Because Daddy likes me to be here on Sundays. He likes all of us to. You know that, Billie. He has surgery early on Monday, and Sunday is his day to relax."

"He can't relax without us for one day?"

She doesn't answer, so I say, "Then why does he spend half the time yelling, if it's so relaxing?"

She thinks a minute. "Well, he yells, and then he's sorry. He's under a lot of stress, Billie. It's not easy to be a surgeon. There are worse things he could do than yell once in a while."

Her loyalty amazes me—and disgusts me, a little. I stare at the table, wondering if I'll ever be this way about someone.

"He's right about this weekend, anyway," she says, after a minute. "I'll go back and see Cassie again on Wednesday with him. I'll take a day off school, that's all." She sighs. "Her doctor will be there then. Daddy wants to talk to her in person."

"Her doctor is a *her*?"

"This one is. She has a few."

I nod, wanting to ask more about my sister. "So am I staying in Connecticut tonight or what?" I ask.

"Do you want to?"

I don't, really. One day is enough. My mother sips her coffee. "Do you want me to make you some breakfast?" she asks then. "Oatmeal, or cream of wheat?"

"No thanks. I'm too tired to eat."

She looks at me carefully. "How long have you been up?"

"I don't know. Like an hour and a half."

"Really? I didn't hear you."

"Were you up, too?"

She nods and takes another sip of coffee. Her hand trembles slightly as she puts her mug down, and I notice then that her eyelids are sort of puffy, and tiny lines crease the edges of her eyes. There are more lines lower down, outlining her mouth—vertical lines, like the folds in a fan. I've never noticed them, and I wonder if they've been there a while or just recently—whether maybe my sister caused them.

I have an urge to say something nice to her then. "Mom, guess what?"

"What?"

"Bambi Zeferelli's pregnant. Almost six months. I felt the baby today."

She blinks. "Are you kidding?"

"Nope."

"That's absurd!" More lines form in her face: between her eyebrows, around her lips.

I pick up a pencil from the table. "Why is it absurd?" I say, tightening my hand around it.

"It's ludicrous. Whose baby is it?"

"Her boyfriend's, of course. They're practically engaged. Mom, what's the big deal? She's almost twenty. How old were you when you had Cassie?"

"I was twenty-five, and I was married, and Cassie was planned. And wanted."

"Her baby's wanted. God, they all can't wait for it."

"And who will take care of this baby they all want? Where will it live?"

"I don't know every detail, Mom! I just found out today. Bambi will take care of it. Maybe it'll live with the Zeferellis. They wouldn't care. They'd love it."

She doesn't answer.

"Bambi's boyfriend is old," I insist. "He already—" I stop before I blurt out that he already has two kids. "He's a nice guy," I say. "I know him. Tito. He'll rise to the challenge."

My mother stares at me. I touch the pencil point to the table. "What?" I say, finally.

She shakes her head. "Oh, they're crazy. Bambi never even graduated from high school, did she?"

"Well, guess what, Mom? A lot of people who don't graduate

from high school have babies! Anyway, she's taking her equivalency test next month. Then she'll have her degree."

My mother frowns down at her work.

"Mom," I say slowly, "how come you hate the Zeferellis so much?"

She sighs. "I don't *hate* them—"

"Okay, *dislike* them. What did they ever do to you?"

She cocks her head. "I don't dislike them. I just think you'd be better off with girls whose futures are more likely to be like yours. Girls more at your intellectual—"

"What future? What exactly *is* my future, Mom? Anyway, Tiffany's smarter than me. So's her brother. They all are." The point of my pencil, my mother's pencil, cracks off and shoots across the table, falls on the floor. "Just because they don't, like, spend every living second studying," I say. "Just because they know how to have fun once in a while. So their daughter is pregnant, so what? Yours has anorexia. Which is worse?"

My mother's eyebrows dart up, then back down. She stands.

"Mom," I say, my stomach slowly tightening.

But she's turned away from me. She walks around the counter, over to the sink. She plucks the coffee pot from its stand and begins to fill it with water.

I stand up too. "Mommy?" I haven't called her that in years.

"What." She still won't look at me.

"I wasn't trying to be mean."

She stares at the water.

"It's just—I get so mad you guys all hate Tiffany. She's the best friend I ever had, and I don't know why you all hate her. She doesn't hate you."

She turns off the water. The pot is full, full enough for ten cups of coffee, though my parents drink only one each and my mother's already had hers. But she slides the pot into the coffeemaker and leaves it there.

She goes to the refrigerator, opens it, and stands peering in. Inside her bathrobe I see the shape of her back—strong but narrow, a soft purple *V*. I think of her offering to make me oatmeal. I feel like crying. "Mom," I say lamely. "I want to hear more about your school. What's after *want* and *need?*"

She turns and glances at me, then away. "I have to get my work done now," she says quietly. "Go upstairs and get some sleep before your SATs."

The room is brightly lit with fluorescent lights, filled with tired but alert high school students. On the desk in front of me are two perfectly sharpened number-two pencils. "When I say 'Begin,' you will have forty-five minutes to complete the first section," says the prompter, a bearded man in a turtleneck and khakis. He paces up and down the rows, his rubber-soled shoes squeaking. "Do not at any time flip ahead or back to other sections of the test. If you have a question, raise your hand and I'll come to your desk. There is no talking." He looks at his watch. "You may begin."

For two or three minutes, I think about my sister—so nervous that her hand locked around her pencil, that when she read the questions all her mind registered was, "This is a test." I think about my mother and what I said this morning. I think about how much I despise SATs. As I sit there, my hatred grows, thick and deep.

I pick up a pencil. Without opening my booklet, I fill in the circles in various patterns on my answer sheet. First I do a daisy, then a heart, then my initials. Then I do a figure eight. I try to do a dog's head, but it doesn't come out too well. In the last column I do a huge zigzag.

I glance at the clock. Nine minutes have passed. All my circles are filled in.

I place my pencil on top of the booklet, then stand and walk to the front of the room. The prompter looks up from a book. "Can I go to the bathroom?" I whisper to him.

He stares at me. "Already?"

I nod.

"Hurry up," he whispers.

I walk out of the room and then out of the school, into a

freezing cold, cloudy day. The sky is the color of raspberries, the trees bleak and bare. I turn and head for Tiffany's, where I know I can hide for three hours. I feel light as whipped cream. Lighter than air.

chapter
seven

When I come home from Tiffany's—just the right number of hours after leaving for SATs to arouse no suspicion about where I've been—my parents are in the process of deciding that my father will come with us to Halley Hospital after all. His patients were quicker than he'd anticipated this morning, and he's found a doctor to cover for him this afternoon. "Good," my mother says, gathering stray dog food chips from the kitchen floor. "I'll call Cassie and tell her we'll be a little later than we'd planned, and—"

"Call and tell her we'll be a little later," my father repeats. "We'll eat lunch in the car. I'll have half a tuna, half a PB&J." He turns to me. "Hello there. How was the test?"

They both search my face until I mumble that it was fine a couple of times, but they're too busy, thank god, to stay on it. My father rushes to call someone, and my mother starts taking out bread and tuna and mayonnaise. There's no evidence of their fight from last night. And my mother seems to have forgotten my harsh words this morning—or maybe she's just too preoccupied to dwell on them.

I go upstairs and change to Tiffany's ankle-high spike-heeled maroon boots, tight jeans, and a V-necked T-shirt. I throw a sweater on over it, to make my mother happy, and then Vinnie's jacket, which I might as well wear while I can. Then I grab my big black tote bag and go down to the car.

In the garage, the cold of the floor seeping through the thin soles of the boots, I stare at the red Schwinn bicycle that was Cassie's years ago and then mine. I won't get to drive now, I'm sure; I'll be my father's car slave for two hours, and then we'll all be sitting in Cassie's room, talking about—what? SATs? The thought makes me cringe. My mother appears then, wearing a huge padded jacket, a scarf, and a wool hat and carrying the bag of lunches. She glances at my boots and my bulging tote bag—crammed with makeup and hair spray, two books, and assorted other stuff—but she doesn't say anything. And then my father arrives. He rushes us into the car, and when he turns it on, violin music sails through the air. I wait for him to turn it off or down, but he doesn't. I close my eyes and plug fingers in my ears.

But I fall asleep, and when I wake up, we're almost there. The music is turned down, and my mother and father are talking softly about my sister. "She keeps complaining about the vitamin supplement drink," my mother said. "She says it nauseates her." She sighs. "She wants you to talk to her nutritionist and see if she can skip it and just have the meals, but I don't know, Michael. I'm afraid she's just saying it to avoid the calories, and I'm not sure it's fair to change their rules—"

I lean forward, rubbing my eyes. "What if she doesn't drink it?"

My father turns halfway around. "Is your seat belt on?"

"No." I put on the belt, make it as loose as I can, and lean forward again. "What if she's not hungry?"

"She's hungry," my father says. "She's twenty pounds underweight."

"Twenty-five," my mother says. "For someone five-foot-seven. According to the Keller book."

"Twenty-five," my father says. His eyes stay on the road.

"But what happens if she doesn't drink it?" I say. "I mean, what if it's really thick or tastes bad?"

"She loses privileges," my mother says, glancing at my father.

"She can't make phone calls and things." She turns back to me. "Billie, it's *vitamins.*"

My father turns around again. "I *told* you to put your seat belt on," he yells.

"It's on! It's on! Okay? God." I sit back and tighten the belt so hard against my stomach it hurts. "Forget it," I mumble. "I'll ask her myself." Neither of them says anything. My father turns off the heat. And I remember my SATs, and I'm glad I did what I did.

We ride in silence until my father exits the highway. He makes a few turns—the roads getting smaller and emptier and prettier with each one. The hospital is at the end of a country road, in the middle of a snowy nowhere. On both sides of us fields extend out like white flags. A pair of cross-country tracks carve a large oval to my right. I follow them with my eyes. "This doesn't look like a hospital," I say, forgetting I'm mad.

"It's a private hospital," my mother says. "They want the patients to feel positively about it—almost like they're at camp." We approach a swing post with no swings, a frozen brook with a little stone bridge, a red jungle gym perched like a giant bug in the snow. My father pulls into a half-filled parking lot and turns off the car. For a minute my parents just stare at the place. And then my mother starts to unpack our lunches. Wax paper crackles; tuna smell fills the car.

I'm not hungry, but I make myself eat. My parents chew silently, facing straight ahead. My father's hair is starting to thin on the crown; a palm-sized pinkish *O* of scalp shows through, and I can't stop staring at it. My mother passes out grapes, but my father waves his away. And then, out of nowhere, he says loudly, "She doesn't need to have the vitamin drink if she hates it so much. They can give her something else in its place. I'll tell her nutritionist to take her off it when we get up there." Before we can respond, he opens his door, gets out of the car, and slams us in.

Now I wish I'd kept my mouth shut. I watch him walk away from the car—feet slightly splayed, as always—toward the row of squat snow-covered pines at the edge of the lot. He wears baggy green corduroys and his long winter coat, and he carries his hat—a small, stiff, football-shaped black hat that he's had for about a million years. After a few seconds he sticks it on his head, where it sits like some stiff dead animal, barely covering his ears. It can't possibly keep him warm. He sticks his hands into his pockets and stares out into the trees.

My mother watches him, too, her lips pulled in. "Want a cookie?" she says absently.

I shake my head no, but she holds out a Fig Newton and I take it anyway, and as her fingers brush mine, she says almost urgently, "Oh, why is he out there in this cold? He'll freeze!" Her voice startles me.

Almost as if he's heard her, he starts walking back toward us. He opens his door. "Are you finished?" he says. "Come on, let's go, it's already after two." We scramble into our coats and follow him in, through the dull-white snow, under a clay-colored sky.

I'm expecting something sterile and depressing, but the lobby is colorful and bright: flowery couches, a television, leafy plants hanging here and there. I glance around, trailing behind my parents, to see if anyone else looks anorexic. A twelve- or thirteen-year-old boy with bad acne is coming toward us, one parent on each side holding his hands. He's wearing some sort of helmet and thick goggles that make his eyes look as big as quarters. I move to the right to let him pass, but he stops—so his parents have to stop, too—and stares at me. "You're pretty," he says in a man's voice.

I look down, my face hot, pretending I didn't hear him, and start to walk past. But a second later he says it again, behind me: "You're pretty."

I turn and face him then. His parents are still holding his hands, but his head is turned around like an owl between them, looking back at me. "Thank you," I say quickly. I move ahead and catch up to my parents fast.

My father stops abruptly before the elevator. "I want to go to the gift shop first," he says. "Jane, I'll meet you up there. Will you take my coat, please? Billie, you come with me."

I glance out the side of my eye—the kid and his parents have gone out the front door—then follow my father silently, wondering what he's up to. He's never been the gift shop type—doesn't like getting ripped off, doesn't like spoiling us—and when he does bring home gifts, they're usually things the drug companies give him: a miniature desk kit that says Inderal on the case, or a capsule that expands in water into a capsule-shaped sponge marked Procardia. When there's only one, he devises elaborate sharing rules for Cassie and me.

Now, though, he strides into the gift shop, still holding his dead animal hat, and starts down the first row, picking up things as he goes —a glittery Yo-Yo, a plastic kaleidoscope, an egg of Silly Putty. He finds a Rubik's Cube, plays with it a second, then puts that back, too. I pull a heart-shaped key chain off a shelf. I think about stealing it—like some of my friends would—but I put it back, afraid of getting caught.

My father is holding up a wall calendar. "Would she like this?" he asks me.

I take the calendar and flip through it. It's big and slick, with a different dog on every page. I think of Cassie talking about how there's so much stuff, too much *stuff* everywhere. "Well," I say, handing the calendar back, "I would, if I was sick."

"If I *were* sick. Which you're not, thank God." He stuffs the calendar under his arm, then finds a box of pink-and-white-checked stationery and a pink felt-tip pen to go with it. By now, I'm pretty sure that Cassie won't want any of this. At Cornell her walls were bare, and when she wrote me, she always wrote on the back of paper with other stuff on it—rough drafts of her papers, or notices from her dorm that she'd taken out of the trash.

My father's at the register now. He frowns at his selection, and then he's back in an aisle again. I glance at a wall clock. We've been down here ten minutes already. He comes back to the register, the Rubik's Cube in his hand. "You're getting that, too?" I say. "For Cassie?"

He nods and reaches for his wallet. In front of him is a candy rack, and he scans it quickly, then pulls off a tube of Rolos. "She used to like these when she was little," he says. "Maybe she'll eat them." He plops it in the pile. Then he adds another, and then a third and a fourth.

I stare at him. I know from my mother that you're not allowed to bring food onto the Eating Disorders floors, and I know he knows it, too. But I don't say anything, and then he's paying for everything, thirty-two dollars plus tax—the same person who freaked out when I called home collect from a phone booth once, for fifty-eight cents, because I couldn't find a dime.

Back in the hall again, we both speed up, him finally realizing, I think, how late we are. I hold the railing as we jog up the stairs to the fourth floor, where Cassie is. But halfway up, he stops again. I almost say, What now? until I see his expression—like he wants to laugh but can't, quite. He shakes his head. "How can a girl not want to eat?" he says.

For a split second, I'm struck with pity for him, standing there with his stupid hat in one hand, his bag of gifts in the other. "You're asking the wrong person, Dad," I say softly. I take another step. But he keeps looking at me, as if I know something, as if I know the answer. So I say, "That stuff is good, Dad—what you got for Cassie." I nod at the bag. And then I turn and start walking again, my heart heavy, and after a second he follows me.

No one's in my sister's room, which is immaculately neat except for my mother's coat on one bed. I remember reading that anorexics like everything organized, that even a few things cluttered on a table can overwhelm them. My mother comes bustling in. "Oh, here you are!" she says. "I was just talking to a girl from Morristown —of all places—and she's *leaving* this afternoon! And she looks *good,* Michael! Well, of course, I don't know what she looked like when she got here—" She notices my father's bag then. "You bought something? Let's see." She holds out her hand.

But he shakes his head and hugs the bag against him, as if it shields him from something, and then my sister shoots in, almost crashing into my mother. She's wearing a powder-pink hospital gown that comes down to her knees, big white sweatsocks, and no shoes. Her hair has grown out a little from when she chopped it off at my grandmother's, and the blue circles under her eyes have faded slightly. Her collarbones still push at her skin and her face is still sucked in, but what I can see of her does look a little better—or at least not any worse. I feel myself fill up with relief.

"Oh!" she says. "Sorry! God, how long have you been waiting? I had to go up and weigh in—usually we do it in the morning, but the nurse was sick so everything got delayed." She seems out of breath.

"That's okay, we just got here," my mother says. She moves to kiss her. "How much do you weigh?"

"A lot," Cassie mumbles, kissing her quickly, reaching behind herself to clutch her gown closed. She kisses me, too, and I smell shampoo—just-washed hair. She rises on her toes to kiss my father over his bag. "Hi, Dad. You can put your stuff down, if you want. Hang your coats up. Or we can go take a walk. Do you want to walk? Wait, though, let me just take this thing off." Her eyes dart around the room, settling on the closet. She heads toward it. "They make us wear them for weigh-ins, because they know exactly how much they weigh and they don't have pockets we can stuff anything in, and if we wear the same thing every time—well, you know what I mean, it's always accurate and everything. . . ."

She's talking ten miles a minute. My parents stare at her. And then my father clears his throat and thrusts his bag in her direction. "This is for you."

She's reached the closet by then, still babbling, still clutching her gown closed in back. She reels around and looks at the bag. "What? What is it?" Her free hand flies up and pinches her neck.

My father smiles. "Open it and see."

Cassie eyes my mother, then me. She smacks something invisible off her cheek. "Oh. Oh. Let me just—can I just take this thing off first? It makes me feel weird. I'll be out in a sec, okay? Sorry. Sorry." She slips into the closet.

The door closes behind her. My father's still holding out the bag, like someone with a crying baby not sure what to do with it. I close my eyes and pray Cassie will come out and take the bag and say thank you—just be normal for once.

But she doesn't come out. We wait—three minutes, four—until

my father sighs loudly and yells, "What the hell are you doing in there?"

Silence a second, and then Cassie's muffled voice: "Don't *yell* at me. I'm trying to get dressed. I'm trying to—" Something crashes and tinkles. "Oh, shit," she moans.

The door opens, and she steps out and gets down on her hands and knees, peering back in. She's wearing too-big jeans and a baggy brown sweater that used to be my father's. She's attempted to pull her hair back into a tiny ponytail, but the short sides stick out all over the place, like a hacked-off spider plant.

"Don't touch it if it's glass," my mother says, rushing over. "What was that, anyway?"

But we can all see what it was: the hand mirror from our bathroom at home—the one I've been searching for all month.

Cassie glares at my father. "That's because you yelled at me."

He shifts on his feet. "I didn't yell at you. I asked what you were doing. You were in there a long time, we were waiting—"

"I was getting dressed."

He clears his throat. "I'm sorry," he says. "I don't think I yelled —but I didn't mean to upset you. Come away from the glass, before you get hurt."

"You *did* yell," she yells.

"Cass," I hear myself say, "he didn't mean to."

"I'll go down and get a broom and dustpan," my mother says. "It's not bad." She hurries out of the room.

"Unless you're superstitious," my father mumbles.

Cassie sits down on the bed. She looks miserable.

"I'll take the bad luck for you," my father says softly. "Okay, Cass?" He reaches out and pats her on the head, but she won't look up at him, and I know that she's trying not to cry. He always does this: yells and screams about nothing and then tries to apologize.

He places the bag of gifts on the bed next to her, and she takes it even though I know she doesn't want to. "What is it?" she says, doing a bad job of trying to sound cheerful. She pulls out the stationery, and I have to look away. She hates it. "Oh, this is nice, Dad," she says. "This is—you didn't have to—"

"I know I didn't." He's standing against the wall, arms crossed, coat still on, smiling. Oblivious.

She pulls out the Rubik's Cube next, and then the calendar. She leafs through it. "Those dogs seem so sad," she mumbles, flipping past a page of greyhounds. Finally she gets to the Rolos. She pulls out tube after tube. Her mouth twitches. She holds the candy toward my father. "Dad, these are yours, right? They're not for me. You can't bring food in."

He shrugs one shoulder. "Why not? You used to like those. Eat a few. They're good for you."

But his smile has changed, and his voice is slightly higher-pitched. He knows now that the gift is all wrong, and I feel that knowledge spread out and trap us there. "I'll have them if you don't want them, Cass," I blurt out. "I love Rolos." I pluck a tube from her hand and sniff the wrapper. "Mmm," I say, though I smell only paper. And then my mother comes back in, broom and dustpan in her hand, and we all concentrate on cleaning up the glass—silver shards, pointy broken reflections of all of us, piled in the trash.

My parents leave then to go talk to one of Cassie's doctors. Cassie watches them go. When they're gone, she picks up the Rubik's Cube. "I can't stand these things," she says softly. "There's no point to them. They drive me crazy."

I sit down on a chair. "Here. Give." I take the toy and move the colored squares around a little. "I like them," I say after a minute. Cassie gets up and lays the other stuff on her desk. She picks up the Rolos. "Do you want these?" she says.

"You don't?"

"God, no. I think I'd—"

"Throw up?" I take the candy and shove it into the pocket of Vinnie's coat.

Cassie smiles. "Shh. Don't talk too loud about stuff like that here."

"Oh, Are there a lot of . . ."

"Bulemics?" She sits back down on the bed. "Yeah. There are a lot of everything. Anorexics, bulemics, chew-and-spitters—"

"What?"

"You know, they chew their food, then spit it back out, so they don't get the calories—"

"Ugh!" I cover my mouth, then uncover it. "No, I mean, it's not that bad, it's just that—"

"Come on, Bil, don't patronize me. Of course it's bad. It's pathetic." She leans back against the wall. "Maybe that's why I'm gaining weight like a pig from hell. I can see it right here." She pinches skin under her chin, and then I know why she was messing with that mirror.

"But that's *good*, Cassie," I tell her. "You're a rail. You could gain a thousand pounds—"

She shakes her head. "It's not good, it's gross. I can't stand it, really, but it's the only way out of this place. Not that it's so bad. I mean, in a way, it's easier. Just a few simple rules. If you gain you're good, if you lose you're bad." She makes a circle around her wrist. "Well, depending on whose rules you follow. Sometimes it's the opposite. I mean, there's all this competition, you know? People notice everything. That's the worst part, everyone *fighting* to be sick. The one who wins is the girl who's as thin as a tissue and can't climb five stairs. It's deranged."

"I know." I think it's got to be great that she's saying all this.

She's quiet a second. "I should talk, right?" She shrugs. "Sometimes, you know, I look in the mirror and see the bones in my shoulders and the outline of my—my uterus, or whatever, and I feel so *good*. Like there's nothing excess, nothing I don't need. It's the purest feeling, like a drug. I think, if I could just stay here, just like this." She takes a Chap Stick out of her pocket and stares at it. "But then you go up and get weighed, and you've lost a quarter-pound from yesterday, and they tell you your bones are deteriorating, and your hair's falling out, and your blood pressure's down. And you take your shoes off and your feet are all swollen up like dead rats, and suddenly you're so *scared*. You know? Your rational side takes over, and you're completely freaked, you're like, 'What am I *doing* to myself?'" She shakes her head. "They take turns, your emotions and your sensible thoughts, and whichever one's there at the time seems so right. But if you don't eat, you could—well, you could actually *die,* Bil. You could actually kill yourself. I mean, a lot of anorexics *die.*"

I shake my head. "Don't talk like that."

She stares at me, her eyes glassy. "You know," she says softly, "I read this book about the Holocaust, and the author was talking about when he was in a concentration camp and he was starving, almost to death. He said he'd think about how, this one night, a few days before the Nazis invaded his town, he was eating this bowl of spaghetti and he didn't finish it—about what he'd give right then for that extra spaghetti, those few pieces he left in his bowl. I think about that, you know, and then I think that I'm sitting here starving myself on purpose, and I feel so—so, like, *ridiculous.*"

"You can't help it, though," I say.

"Sure I can. All I have to do is eat a meal, right? Eat a piece of bread and butter or something." She blows out air. "What a loser I am."

She's working herself into a state again, flinging her hands in the air and shaking imaginary bugs off her hair, and I want desperately to change the subject. "Guess what, Cass?" I say quickly. "I broke up with Vinnie."

She looks at me, only half there. "DiNardio?"

I nod.

"What happened?" she says finally.

I put down the Rubik's Cube. "He was—we were on the school bus, he wanted me to—he wanted to fool around, and I didn't want to. One thing led to another. . . ."

It's working. Cassie's face relaxes a little, concentrating on me. "You're not into him?" she says.

I shrug. "In some ways. Some ways not."

"Which ways are you?"

"I don't know. He's nice, he's really cute—" I hold up my hand. "I know what you're gonna say. Looks are twenty-five percent what you have and seventy-five percent what you do with it." I heard her say this once a long time ago.

She smiles. "What isn't, really? But actually, I was gonna say looks are irrelevant, and nice is only relevant if he isn't." She rubs her bottom lip with one finger. "I hope you didn't give in, anyway. I mean, did you?"

"Well, not really, but—"

"Good."

"Yeah, but now I feel like a prude. And a jerk. I mean, he treats me like gold."

"How, exactly, *does* one treat gold?"

"What?"

She sighs. "Sorry, Bil. I didn't mean that. It's just—it's not about being a prude; it's not about being *anything*. You didn't want to fool around with the guy, that's all. No big deal." She thinks a second. "Anyway, wouldn't you rather be a prude than a slut?"

"No. I mean, everyone's a slut. I feel like the only virgin in the whole school—"

She's staring at me. "Your friends are sluts, maybe. Mine weren't."

"You didn't have any friends. At least not any you really cared about. You had boyfriends, and you were into school. I'm not like that, Cass. The only class I really like is English—well, and history." I glance at her clothes, miles of sweater and jeans and, under it, her deflated body. I don't ever want to be like that. "I'm not sure I even *want* to go to college," I say. "Maybe I'll just work in the mall. I'll get a job at Puppy Palace. Or I'll be one of those people who puts makeup on customers. Michelle Zeferelli did that once, she said it was totally fun."

Cassie's looking at me like I'm some retarded lab animal she can't get to walk through a maze. "Yeah," she says, finally. "And then you can come home at night and drink beer and watch TV. And eat Ho-hos. And when you have a bad day, you can buy a new blender to cheer yourself up." She closes her eyes and shakes her head back and forth, as if she can't bear the sight of me. "I've got news for you, Bil. It's not gonna happen. Not in our family. Blue-birds don't raise blackbirds."

"What?"

"Think about it."

I don't say anything.

"You don't have to be a slut, Bil," she says softly.

Listen to you, I'm thinking, telling me what I don't have to be. "I'm not a slut," I say.

"Okay," she says. "Good."

"Good."

"Good."

I pick up the Rubik's Cube again. The last thing I want to do is argue with her. I move a row randomly. The reds are all lined up from before, but now all the yellows are a mess. Cassie's playing with her Chap Stick again, pulling the cap on and off, starting to get hyper again. Hyper-dermic, Vinnie would say. Someone knocks on the door. We both jump about a mile.

"Who is it?" Cassie yells.

A girl sticks her head in the door. "Hi, Cass. Oh, wow. This has to be your sister."

Cassie's breathing deeply. "*God,* Lisa, you scared me. This is Billie. Bil, my friend Lisa. Come on in."

Lisa drifts into the room, and I have to try hard not to stare. She looks like a tiny, stick-limbed doll. She has a long dark braid, even longer than Cassie's hair was, and a round little face, and she's wearing a black T-shirt, black tights, and a sweatshirt tied around her butt. She's like a snake-person, a balloon string dangling from a head. Her black ballet slippers seem to float off the floor as she stands.

"Hi," I say, looking directly at her face.

She smiles, an awesome straight-toothed smile. "It's nice to meet you, finally. I've heard a lot about you." Her voice is soft and sort of high, very sweet, and she has a slight southern accent. She looks about my age, though she seems older somehow.

"You have?" I say. I try to think of something else to say—how long have you been here, do you like it—but everything seems wrong. So I just smile back, then get up and stick the Rubik's Cube on the desk with the rest of the gifts.

Lisa checks me out, then the gifts. "Oh, wow," she says. "Did your parents bring all that?" She flips through the calendar. "This is beautiful."

"Do you want it?" Cassie says.

Lisa smiles. "*Yeah,* I want it. My mom never brings me anything."

"Take it," my sister says.

"Of course I'm not taking it, Cassie. It's yours. It's a gift."

"No, really. Please? I'd love it if you would. It would make me feel great."

"She hates it," I say. "She hates gifts."

"I don't *hate* it," Cassie says.

Lisa looks at me, then at her. "I'll take a few pieces of the stationery, then. If you seriously don't mind."

"Take the whole box," Cassie says. "We'll share it, okay? I'll come get some when I need it."

"Well, thanks, hon." Lisa smiles, weighing the box in her hand. "It's nice and small, too—nice short letters. I'll write and tell everyone I'm still alive." She slides down to the floor and sits against one wall. "I'll write my demented cousin Tricia. She keeps sending me these letters asking if she can come here and do research for some psych class she has. Do you believe that?" She looks at me, as if she's known me for months. "I haven't even seen the girl in five years. All I remember about her is that she was always *doing* things, she'd always *done* everything. Don't you hate that? People who have *done* everything? Like, you say, 'I'm going hang gliding,' and they go, 'Oh, I've done that.' "

I nod, laughing.

"That, and she was always drinking milk," Lisa says. She sticks out her tongue. "It was gross. Or eating ice cream."

"Milk's good for you, Lisa," Cassie says, smiling.

Lisa shrugs. "Yeah, well." She sighs. "So what all are y'all gonna do?"

"Nothing," Cassie says. "Just hang around, I guess. What are you?"

"I don't know. I feel weird today. Like everyone's looking at me weird." She shrugs and glances down at her legs, and I notice then how thin her hair is on top, near the part. "Maybe I'll write letters," she says. "It's too cold to go out, anyway." She touches the stationery. "Did you go out this morning, Cass?"

"For about three seconds. I froze. There's no sun."

"I like that, though," Lisa says. "I like gray."

We all look out the window. I can see some volleyball courts without nets and, beyond, snow and endless trees. "Less pressure to have a good time, maybe," Cassie says.

"Yeah, maybe. Or maybe I just got sick of the sun."

"Lisa goes to University of Arizona," Cassie tells me.

"You do?" I say, surprised she's that old. "What year are you?" She smiles. "I don't know. I was a sophomore, but . . ."

"Billie's taking SATs now," Cassie says, after a second. "Poor thing." She looks at me. "When are they, anyway?"

"Were. Today."

"This morning? You're kidding! How did you do?"

I feel a small pang of anxiety. "Horrible, I think."

Cassie rolls her eyes. "Oh, right." She turns to Lisa. "She aces her PSATs, and then she doesn't even want to show my father her scores. I, on the other hand, get about a hundred total, and he knows my scores the second I put my pencil down."

"That's because you're an 'oldest,' " Lisa says. "I should know, I'm an 'only.' We're sort of the same."

"No," I say. "It's because my father's obsessed with all that stuff."

"So I hear," she says. "Well, maybe he's learned his lesson by now. This place is pretty good for teaching parents a few things." She pauses. "And then there's my mom, who wouldn't know an SAT if it crawled out of her purse and bit her. The only letters she knows are *M, R,* and *S.* She's like, 'Baby, you don't want to get *too* educated. Men don't like a girl makin' them feel *inferior.*' " She says this with a heavy southern accent, drawing out the words. "One time," she says, looking at me, "she set me up on a date with this guy—her friend's ex-husband, of all things. He was thirty-three, but of course she didn't tell me that. She tells me, 'Make sure you invite him up for a drink after, so I can say hi.' Then when I do, there's this note on the counter—real big, bold, block letters, right?—saying, 'Honey, I went to go see your aunt Sally, she wasn't feeling real well, back tomor-

row, Love, Mom.' And here I don't even *have* an aunt Sally! She just
wanted him to stay over with me."

"Whoa," I say softly. That sounds horrible to me, worse than
anything my father's ever done. "So what happened?"

"Nothing. I booted the guy out on his lard-ass butt. Told him I
had my period. Realistic lie, huh? I haven't had my period in two
years." She laughs. "Poor guy. He wasn't half bad, really. Just another victim of Mom."

"Lisa's gonna make her mother happy, though," Cassie says,
"and marry Kenny the food-cart guy. Right, Lis?"

Lisa leans back and looks at the ceiling. "Oh lordie, he is buffed
as they come. A hunka hunka burnin' love."

I make a note to remember that one for Tiffany.

"Gotta do something first, though, right, Lis?" Cassie says.

Lisa nods. "Gotta get myself out of here." She turns to me. "He
won't do anything till I'm out, not even take me to the movies. He's
afraid he'll—what? Endanger his job."

"Jeopardize," Cassie says.

"Yeah. Talk about motivation to eat." She sighs. "Well, I don't
have the energy for a boyfriend right now, anyway." She pulls her
braid over the front of her shoulder, so it hangs down her chest like a
tail. She rubs her finger over the end of it. "Tell you one thing," she
says. "The day I get out, I'm gonna blow that boy away. I even know
what I'm wearing. Tight white shirt, baggy blue jeans. My mom
would approve. She says you should wear one tight thing, top or
bottom, but not both."

"Why?" I ask.

She shrugs. "I guess you don't want to look too interested."

I glance down at myself, glad I still have on Vinnie's jacket over
my skin-tight clothes. "Do you like Arizona?" I ask. I've never even
thought about a school like that—big and far away, not Ivy League.
I've always sort of thought it was Cornell or nothing. Now that
seems ridiculous.

"Oh, yeah, I like it," Lisa says. "It's a beautiful place. I like the
heat. Tucson, Arizona, at six o'clock at night, you feel like you've
died and gone to heaven. The sky'll be black with masses of white

stars on one side and streaked pink and blue and silver on the other, where the sun's going down. It's really spectacular. And you always know which way you're facing, north or south or whatever, because of the mountains on all four sides. Pastel mountains. All four of them look different. One's pointy, one's really round like a sand castle, one's all jagged, like glass."

It sounds amazing to me. "Is the school hard?" I ask. I wonder if my father would ever let me go there.

Lisa shrugs. "Depends what you take, I guess. It doesn't have to be. I took a lot of dance, so—you know, I was into it. Well, up to last year. Then I was *really* into it." She laughs. "Anyway, if I ever go back, I'm studying old people. Old people, they just amaze me."

I think of Zelda's voice on our answering machine, and then of Mrs. Mast, my old algebra teacher at school. She'd eat lunch during class, and yogurt and granola would fall out of her mouth all over the place as she taught, and all of us would be grossed out and laughing, and she'd be too deaf to hear. "How do they amaze you?" I ask.

"Oh, I just like how they look, all shriveled up, like gloves that got wet and dried. And I like their white hair. I love it. Sometimes they smell so good, too. Like vanilla. Did you ever notice that?"

Zelda smells like perfume. I look at Cassie. She's sitting cross-legged in her chair, still holding her Chap Stick, smiling. "Sure," she says. She seems calmer now.

"Mostly I just like to be around them," Lisa says. "They give me something to look forward to. I mean, just to look back and know you got there, you didn't get some awful disease or something. Or you know. To not care how you look anymore."

"My grandmother's the opposite," Cassie says. "She's a walking vanity freak."

"Yeah? My grandma died two years ago. She was a saint, I mean it. My dad's mom, not my mom's. I don't even know my mom's." We're quiet a few minutes, Cassie playing with her Chap Stick, Lisa playing with her braid, me pretending to play with the Rubik's Cube but really staring at Lisa. She talks as much as some of the people in my family, but with her I feel like I could listen for days. And she seems to soothe Cassie, too—maybe because she's so different from her. Except that they both weigh about as much as a grape. Lisa's worse, though; I can tell. "What's your last name?" I ask her.

She smiles. "Cooper. Why?"

"She's trying to find out if you're Italian," Cassie says.

"Shut up, Cassie."

"Italian, oh god, no," Lisa says. "I'm pure Polack. Well, *sort of* pure." She looks at me. "You all are Jewish, right?"

"Not really," I say. "We never go to temple. We celebrate Christmas and Easter."

"Easter?" Lisa looks amazed.

"We're Jewish," Cassie says. "Just not religious." She smiles. "My father thinks *he's* God."

Lisa nods and leans back against the wall.

"So when do you think you're going back?" I say.

"Hm?" She looks a little spacey suddenly. "Where?" she says.

"To Arizona."

"Oh. I don't know. When I get out of here, I guess." She rises up slowly, like a black stem. In the light from the window, next to all her black clothes, her face is too white, tinted slightly green. "Ya'll got me in the mood to talk to my old granny," she says. "I guess I'll have to settle for calling up Mom." She sighs. "I've logged way too much butt-time today anyway. Gotta get *motivated* here, right? *Do* something. *Make* something of myself." She takes a deep breath.

"Go for it," Cassie says. "No one'll be down there now."

Lisa nods. "I'll catch ya'll later, then. I won't say 'bye, because I'll be back." She waves and slips out of the room.

We watch her go, not talking. And then Cassie says, "She's gonna die."

I feel like I've been punched in the chest.

"She's been losing weight since she got here," she says.

"Then how come she can use the phone?"

"She can't. She uses Kenny's. She's got a key to his office in the basement. Although they probably wouldn't try to stop her anyway, after this long. She's been here like four months already. She's been upstairs three times."

"Upstairs?"

"The intensive-care floor. They force-feed you, pretty much. Intravenous and everything."

"Oh, *god!*" I shiver.

"It doesn't help, though, with her. She just loses the weight as soon as she gets back down here. Her mom doesn't even come anymore. She says it's too depressing—well, that's what Lisa says she says."

"I don't believe you." I feel like crying.

Cassie stands up. She touches my arm. "Let's take a walk," she says. "Let's get out of here."

But we run into my parents at the end of the hallway, coming back toward Cassie's room. My father motions Cassie aside. "Okay," he says. "You don't have to have the vitamin drink anymore. I talked to your nutritionist." He shifts from foot to foot, looking pleased.

Cassie's face spreads into a smile. "Really? That's excellent." She sounds like she used to, last year.

"Well, she wasn't very happy about it," he says, more serious now. "You're not supposed to discuss it with the other patients." He clears his throat. "Just make sure you eat, or I'll call and have you put on it again. And I'll send you some vitamin pills, and you're to take those every day. Understand?"

"Yes. Thanks, Dad." She beams. My mother looks at her and then away, and I wish, again, that I hadn't said what I said in the car, about the vitamin drink being gross. I know that Cassie should have it. But I understand why my father did what he did, too. If he can't help her, at least he can fake it. I think of Lisa again—her big smile, her bone body wrapped in black.

Cassie's chatting with my parents now, leading them through a tour of the place, her walk with me no longer in the plans. I follow them past a gym, a pool, a room full of exercise machines. We end up in a game room with a couple of pinball machines and a pool table exactly like the Zeferellis'.

The sight of it cheers me up. "Let's play," I say, thinking they'll probably all refuse. But my father says, "Come on. Stripes and solids." He racks up the balls.

I beat him first game, and he beats me second—only because I scratch—and then we play teams, Cassie and my father against my mother and me, and for once I'm the best, and everyone's impressed with me. My mother holds her cue like a pencil, so that it flies up when she shoots, and if she doesn't miss the cue ball completely, she sends a ball flying off the table, which cracks us all up—even Cassie, a few times. My father teases my mother and lets her shoot again a couple of times. At one point he tries to teach her to shoot. "*Good,* Fly!" he says when she makes a good shot. And I want to hold on to the moment, because for a little while it's perfect, just the way it should be. Like it was the day Ethan was born, and my father delivered the three puppies, and we all sat around the whelping box listening to them suckle, breathing the sweet milky smell of them.

After a while Lisa comes by. Cassie introduces her to my parents, and then Lisa and my father shoot a game. My mother and Cassie and I watch from the couch. Lisa's good, she's beating my father, but you can tell they're both having fun. I remember what Cassie said before, that Lisa will die soon, and I think that it can't possibly be true. She's laughing and flirting with my father, stretching all over the place to take her shots. My mother can't stop looking at her, though. Her eyes linger on Lisa's rubber-band body—her face bunched up with the worried look she's perfected since Cassie got sick—as if she's afraid that any second Lisa will lean too far over and snap in two. I think she's probably wondering, too, if that's what my sister looks like under all those big clothes.

By the time they stop playing, it's four thirty. My father leans against the table holding his cue; Lisa sits on the edge, her feet dangling, her legs hanging like two twigs. No one talks for a second. And then my mother rises, glancing at my father. "Lisa," she says, "we thought we'd take Cassandra out for dinner, and we'd like to invite you along. There's a French restaurant about twenty minutes from here that's supposed to be very good. Would you like to come?"

Lisa turns to Cassie, who looks at my father, tension pushing into her face like a stain. "The thing is," Cassie says slowly, "we're really supposed to eat here, Daddy."

He waves his hand. "That's okay, it's Saturday night—"

"I *like* to eat here, though," she says, a little louder. "And we have group meetings at night. I don't think I should miss it. I mean, I don't *want* to. Miss it." She gathers both sleeves into her palms, so her hands are hidden, and bounces on her toes, completely hyper again. Her hands tug at the back pockets of her jeans. It's like he's suggested we all go out and shoot each other.

Lisa makes some excuse and disappears from the room, and there we are again, just the four of us. And I hear myself say, "Actually, Dad, I'm not hungry yet either. Maybe we should just go home and eat." I'm trying to keep a scene from happening, keep my sister from getting more upset.

My father looks at me. He bounces his cue gently on the floor, and I know he's trying to decide whether to get pissed or just let it slide. I hold my breath. We all hold our breath and look at him.

"Okay," he says finally. "I'm not gonna force you all to go out to a nice restaurant, if nobody wants to. We'll just go home and eat there. Forget I ever suggested it." He tosses his cue hard on the table, for emphasis. And then he turns and walks out of the room.

We're not back in the car for ten minutes—me silent in the backseat, picking at my nails, wondering why it always seems to end up this way—when something incredible happens: My father pulls over to the side of the road, turns to me, and asks, "Billie, do you want to drive?"

My mother stares at him. She knows he hates being a passenger in a car, that he almost never gets in one unless he's the one driving it —and even when he is, he's tense and aggressive and obnoxious, like some kid full of hormones and beer. And she knows that if he wants to help me learn to drive, today isn't the day to do it. It's a terrible idea.

I know all that, too. But I think that some part of him is truly trying to be nice to me—doing what he can't for my sister, feeding me something I can appreciate—and I want to reward him for that. And I *do* want to drive. I accept his offer, and we shift places, so my mother's in back and I'm in the driver's seat.

I buckle my seat belt, then stare out the windshield, tense but thrilled. I've driven a little bit with my father before, but never a long distance like this and never on a busy highway. On the one we're about to get on, cars flow by in a colorful stream. I adjust the seat and the rearview mirror, checking myself out in it to stall for time. The minty eyes of my sister stare back at me, and for a second I'm startled at how much we look alike—not just the color of our eyes but something deep inside them, something I used to see in Cassie's eyes and now I see in mine, too. Determination, maybe—the desire to be in control. The same thing I felt this morning taking my SATs. There's something vaguely troubling about this, but I can't figure out what it is right now. I kick the idea out of my head. I *want* to be in control, for a change; I want to have some power. And I can have it, if I just go for it, just take charge. I grip the steering wheel.

"Come on," my father says. "Let's make it home in time for the news."

Despite everything, something in his tone makes me pause. "Dad, maybe I should wait. I haven't driven much on the highway—"

"You're fine," he says. "Just get on and go."

I take a deep breath and shift into drive. I remind myself that Tiffany has done this since she was fifteen—one hand lazily on the wheel, the other flicking cigarette ashes into the wind. I touch the accelerator.

My father coaches as I go—more insistent and demanding than Vinnie, but complimentary when I oblige. He tells me to move over a lane, to watch the car on the right, to get up past thirty ("We're on the highway, for chrissake!"), then tells me *"Good!"* or *"Very* good, Billie!" each time. My eyes fly from the road to the mirror to the speedometer. Forty, forty-five. "Faster," he commands.

I think then about how often he gets stopped for speeding, and how he never gets a ticket because he's a doctor. That always drove Cassie crazy; it's unethical, she said. I press the accelerator, my back rod-straight, my legs frozen in place. The dashes blur to one. We're up to sixty. "Good!" my father says, and I smile through my nervousness.

We pass a green station wagon, a blue van. And then something amazing starts to happen to me: I feel as if my foot controls not just the gas pedal, but my confidence. And the faster I go, the better it gets. I'm driving pretty fast now—not just around West Berry but someplace different, someplace real, far from home. I accelerate a touch more, feeling the rainbow of cars around me.

My mother relaxes a little after a while—she sits back, anyway—and my father asks her for the paper. I drive on while he scans the sports section, monitoring me occasionally, reading things out loud the rest of the time: some stadium in Chicago is closing down, some basketball player leads some team in slam-dunks. It occurs to me that he should have had a son, that a son might have cared. But he's always said he's happy with daughters.

I glance at him, then back to the road. The sky has darkened—it's almost evening—and I'm not supposed to drive at night with a learner's permit. "How much longer on this road?" I ask, but before he answers, I see the sign for West Berry. Five or six more miles, and we're home.

"Get in the right lane," my father says. "You'll be getting off on the right."

My heart starts up. It's getting on and off that's hard, speeding up and slowing down—not the stuff in between. "There's a car there, though," I say, eyeing a small red car with a sunroof. A girl with a slinky of gold bracelets rolls alongside us, mouthing song words.

"That's okay," my father says. "You're ahead of her. Pull in front."

I accelerate and steer over, holding my breath. The girl slows and lets me in. Piece of cake.

"Good!" my father says again, and I swell with pride. But seconds later the exit ramp is coming up on the right, and I'm neck-and-neck with a green car that wants into my lane. The driver inches in front of me, and I lift my foot, letting him in.

My father leans over me, his arm knocking into mine as he blasts our horn. "Dammit," he yells at me, slapping his thigh, "what'd you let that schmuck cut you off for?"

My hands tighten on the wheel as I follow the car off the highway. "I would've hit him if I didn't slow down."

"You wouldn't have hit him, he'd have come in behind you. That asshole." He makes a fist and touches the dashboard, but I feel it as if he's touched me. On the ramp, I pull up to a stop behind the green car. "Now come on, the light's about to turn green," my father says. "You want to turn left here."

I fumble for the left-turn signal.

"You don't need the signal," he says. "You're in a left-turn lane, you're just wasting it here. Go on, turn."

I turn left, then get quickly into the right lane. We're on a four-lane road, heading uphill. Above us, the sky is purple as a grape.

"Good," my father says. "Although you could have stayed in the left lane. You've got a mile, mile and a half, and then you'll turn right onto Highland. Pull into the left lane now, pass this guy in front of you. He's crawling."

I want to stay where I am. "Dad," I say, "maybe you should drive the rest of the way. I'm not sure—"

"No. We're almost there. You're doing fine. Keep going. Just don't let any more schmucks cut you off."

My mother's wool hat pokes forward, between us. "Michael," she says, "maybe you *should* take over, if she feels nervous on these streets—"

"She's fine," he interrupts. "What's she gonna do when she gets her license, pull over every time she's worried?"

"No, but when she gets her license, she'll know what she's doing. It's getting dark, and she didn't sleep well last night, and there's a lot of traffic now, and we've all had a long day, including you—"

"I'll worry about my state of mind, thank you," he snaps. He turns back to me, and I see his glasses next to my face, feel his hand near my shoulder, the heat of his breath. His eyes scan the road, looking for people to beat. Get ahead, get ahead. I think of my sister and what happened when she couldn't get ahead anymore. And suddenly I don't want to be here, driving along with him yelling at me. My body's stiff as a corpse, and my bra is wet with sweat. "Pass this car," he says again, and everything—my muscles, my brain, my feet—goes soft then. "I can't, Dad. I don't know how to pass."

"Sure you do. Just go by him."

"No. Dad—I can't." A whimper has crept into my voice, and I despise it.

He shifts impatiently. "Come on, Billie. Pull into the left lane and accelerate. You'll go right by him." He looks over his shoulder. "There's no one behind you, if you go now. Hurry up, you've got a green light up ahead."

I press the accelerator, but I'm afraid to get over. We move in on the car in front of us. My foot lifts instinctively.

"What are you doing?" my father yells. "I said to go!"

I try once more—my heart a sledgehammer now—and this time it works, I'm in the left lane, passing the car. But up ahead the light turns yellow. I start to brake.

"Go!" he screams.

For a good three seconds, my foot shakes wildly in the air. And then it smashes down and our car shoots forward, but by then it's too late. We reach the intersection just as the light turns red, and the red bursts through my brain as a sea of headlights speeds toward us. I scream.

When it's over—when we've made it through, and all three of us are alive and well and shaking like spilled-out mercury—I turn on my signal and pull the car over to the right shoulder and put it in park. My hands drop to my lap. I don't look at my father. I'm trying desperately not to cry, but of course I do anyway, and as I feel the tears well up and spill out, I wonder how I'd possibly felt sorry for him this afternoon, how I'd ever felt sorry for him. How I'd ever felt anything but this.

But it's not just fury I feel, even now; it's something else, too. Sadness, I think. Because he's tried to offer me something, a chance to drive, and we've both fucked up, both disappointed. I turn slowly and look at him. "Why did you make me do that, Daddy?"

His face registers something—maybe the same thing he felt when he asked me why Cassie wouldn't eat. Or maybe something else completely. "I'm sorry," he says finally.

My throat tightens.

"But"—and his tone becomes harsh and angry again—"if you'd gone when I told you to, that wouldn't have happened. Next time, *listen* to me."

And then it's hatred I feel, pure and sweet. I think of my sister, hyper and bony, wasting away. "There won't be a next time," I say. My voice is amazingly calm. I open my door.

And I get out and run. First toward some office building on the side of the road, its windows big and black and empty. Then, behind it, onto the unlit lawns of a red-brick apartment complex. My heels dig into the ground, until the left one twists in some snow and cold slush pushes into my boot. I right myself and keep going. Down a narrow path now, pine trees blowing on my left. Wind slaps at my face. Cold and dark surround me, and there's no moon, no stars anywhere. I turn around once to make sure no one's chasing me. No one is. But I don't stop running.

chapter
eight

I run until I reach the next main road, till my fingers and toes are numb, and then I know—suddenly—where I want to go, and what I want to do when I get there. I step into the street and stick out my thumb. The second car that drives by picks me up.

The driver—a balding man I put at about my father's age—drops me a block from Dom's Shell station, just like I ask. I want to approach the place slowly, on foot, in case Dominick's outside. And it turns out he is, pumping gas into a white Camaro. I hide behind a Jeep, shivering, until the Camaro pulls away and Dom goes back in the office—a small room lit with a single yellow bulb, its windows tinted orange from the Shell sign outside. He sits down at the desk and scribbles something, then drops the pen and blows into the tops of his fists. He's wearing his leather jacket over his uniform, and his dark hair pushes out the bottom of a baseball cap that says "Knicks" on it.

The sight of him loosens something deep inside me, like thread unraveling. I think of our conversation last night in the Zeferellis' kitchen, and I try to think of something good he said to me, something nice. But I can't think of anything, so I tell myself, Well, of course not. What did you expect, between last-minute cramming for his test and then the phone ringing like that? And I unsnap Vinnie's jacket and move toward the office, breathing gasoline fumes, feeling its heat already.

I knock on the door quickly, before I can change my mind. Dom looks up, surprised—used to people arriving in cars, I guess—and then gets up and lets me in. I search his face for signs of joy that I'm here. But he looks more confused than anything.

"Hi!" I say brightly, and I clench my back teeth, trying not to shiver. The place smells like stale cigarette smoke.

Dom glances outside, then at me again. "How'd you get here?"

"I walked." I flip hair out of my eyes, trying to look sexy. Vinnie's coat hangs off me. My feet squish inside my wet shoes.

Dom blinks. "What are you, kidding me?"

His voice is almost mean. On his desk is a fat textbook that says *The Fundamentals of Management III.* The TV buzzes behind him, Bugs Bunny or Popeye, just loud enough to hear.

I back up a step, my confidence slowly seeping out. "I got in a fight with my father. Um—can I use your phone?"

He shrugs. "Help yourself."

But I have no one to call. I pick up the receiver slowly. If I call Tiffany, she'll know I'm down here. Forget about Vinnie; he hates me now. I don't have Cassie's number and probably couldn't reach her even if I did. I start to push buttons randomly. To my horror, I feel a fresh batch of tears working up. I hang up the phone. "Can I use your bathroom first?"

Dom stares at me. "Are you okay?" His voice is nicer now. I feel a pinprick of relief.

I sniff once, hard. "I'm fine. Why?"

A car pulls in, and the driver honks for service. "It's over there," Dom tells me, pointing to the bathroom. "Have some coffee if you want. You look frozen solid." He heads outside.

The bathroom smells like mildew and lavender air freshener. I close the door and look for a mirror, but there isn't one on any wall. For some reason, the thought that I can't see myself makes me feel slightly frantic. I check under the sink, burrowing around in the dim grayish light, moving cans of stuff that look like they've been there for years. No mirror. I stand up and try to look at myself in the faucet, but I can't see anything but colors—nothing like my real face.

I turn on the hot water, hard, and run my hands under it. They're red as lobsters, defrosting from numbness to pain, and still shaking a little. I dry them with toilet paper, then rinse my face and my mouth. I take a deep breath and go back to the main room.

After a minute Dom comes in and heads straight for his desk. He sits and writes something on a receipt, then sticks it in one of the drawers. My hands dangle at my sides. Finally he leans back and looks up. "Did you get some coffee?"

"No—that's okay, though."

Dom gets up and pours two mugs of coffee from a half-filled Mr. Coffee pot. He dumps in sugar and white powder from two jars on the shelves, stirs them with a pen, and hands one to me. "Take your coat off," he says. "Stay awhile." He motions to the couch.

"Are you doing homework, though?"

He shrugs. "It'll wait." He smiles a little, and my heart soars in my chest. I put the coffee down on a table and pull off my coat, dropping it in a heap on the floor. I'm still not sure he really wants me to stay, but I don't want to go. And then I catch his eyes flick over my body—but quickly, like he's trying not to look or at least doesn't want me to see him looking, and I think that must be a good sign, a great sign. I sit down on the couch, which is ratty and maroon, and take a sip of the coffee. It's lukewarm, sweet as a Twinkie —not like the bitter stuff my mother drinks. "Mm. This is good," I say, surprised. I sip again.

Dom smiles.

"What?" I glance down at myself to see if something's wrong. In the light from the Shell sign, my hands look orange.

Dom shakes his head. "Nothing. So you want to talk about it?"

"Talk about what?"

"I don't know. You tell me."

"Oh, my father the asshole. Not really. You want to hear it?"

"Not really." He smiles again, and then he just keeps looking at me, not talking, till the silence makes me feel ridiculous. I shift in my seat. "I was gonna call Tiffany, but—" I can't think of how to finish the sentence. I sip my coffee a third time.

Dom removes his cap, drops it on the desk, and runs fingers through his hair, closing his eyes. His hair is mashed down on top—dirty, maybe—which gives me a little more confidence. "She's not home, anyway," he says. "They all went to the doctor with Bambi."

"*All* of them?" I picture the entire Zeferelli family standing around some TV screen, ooh-ing and aah-ing while Bambi lies on a table with her basketball belly. "Did your father go, too?"

"What do you think?"

"No?"

He laughs.

I'm starting to think he's making fun of me somehow. I stand up. "Well, I should get going. Thanks for the coffee."

"Where are you going?"

"What?" The truth is, I have no idea.

He sighs. "Listen. If you want to go home or wherever, I'll take you. I'll be off in an hour. Otherwise you can call someone to pick you up. But I'm not letting you walk out of here at night all alone. Especially in this cold."

Is this a good sign? I stand there, hands at my sides.

"Listen," he says, more gently now, "why don't you just relax awhile? Sit back, get warmed up. I'm not going anywhere."

My pulse beats faster. "Are you sure I'm not bothering you?"

He waves his hand around. "What am I doing? Pumping gas for a bunch of fools who have nothing better to do than drive around in the freezing cold. That's about it."

I sit down slowly, once more. Next to me, the soda machine hums. On its side, held up with a magnet, is a Playmate of the Year calendar, featuring a smiling girl with bronze hair and matching bronze crotch hair and huge round boobs and big square teeth. I wonder briefly if the calendar is Dom's or one of the other guys'. Nearby, an electric heater on the floor sends out small waves of heat. Between that and the coffee and Dom and everything else, my body is slowly getting warm, and with it comes a feeling of being slightly drunk, slightly buzzed. Dom flips through the pages of his book, not really stopping to read—like he just needs something to do with his hands. He glances at me, then back at the book. "How'd you do on the accounting test?" I ask.

He shrugs. "Okay, I think."

"That's good. When do you graduate?"

He shrugs again. "Maybe next year. Depends if I take two classes next semester or one." He sighs. "I get pretty burnt out working full time and taking two courses. No time to study."

"Why don't you quit your job?"

"Why? Well, it pays for my classes, for one. It pays for this book, which cost forty-five bucks."

"But doesn't your father—" I bite my thumbnail. Surely the Zeferellis have the money to put Dom through college.

"I don't mind this, anyway," he says after a minute. "It's easy, it's legal, it's"—he pauses—"it keeps me out of trouble." He swings his feet up to the desk. Work boots under uniform khaki pants. He closes the book. "So what do you do to stay out of trouble?"

Now that he's finally talking to me, I feel shy. "I don't know."

"Well, what'd you do today?"

"Went to see my sister."

"Where's your sister?"

"In Connecticut. In the hospital. She has anorexia."

"Does she?"

"Didn't Tiffany tell you?"

He shrugs. "I don't talk to Tiffany much these days. She's a little preoccupied. Well, I guess we all are." He sips coffee.

"Why?"

He puts down the mug. "You gonna make me say it?"

"Say what?"

He raises his eyebrows and watches me a long time. Outside, I hear a car pass by, and I see a flicker of lights. Next to me, Bugs Bunny falls off a cliff. "Say *what?*" I repeat.

Dom bites his lip from the inside. Then he stands up and comes over and sits on the edge of the couch, next to me but not too close. He reaches toward me, and I close my eyes, thinking now's the time, he's finally about to kiss me. But I feel a gentle tug at my hair instead.

I open my eyes. "You had something in your hair," he says. "I got it out." But he doesn't move away, just looks at me, his eyelashes thick and dark. His amber eyes are steady on mine, the color of light caramel.

I feel myself blush under his stare. I can smell him next to me, gasoline and coffee, and I can see him under his gas station clothes—the outline of his legs, of his knee. Dirt pushed up under his nails. My heart pumps away.

But he stands up again quickly. "Well, I should do a little more work. Make yourself comfortable. There're some magazines over there. Or change the channel, if you want. I'm not watching this crap anyway." He steps back to his desk and sits again.

Now's my chance to do what I came here for, and I know if I don't take it, it might not come again. I get up, feeling like I'm in a dream, and make my way over to Dominick's chair. When I get there, I kneel down on the floor and put my palm on the crotch of his pants.

"What are you *doing*?" he says. But he doesn't sound mad, and he doesn't push my hand away.

I look down then, at my hand—I'm afraid if I see his face, I'll lose courage, or he'll try to stop me. I move my palm gently, then a little more firmly, until I feel him get hard beneath it.

For a few seconds he doesn't move, and I keep going, holding my breath, my hair in front of my face. And then he leans back and spreads his legs a little, and that's when I know he's given in, and I want to laugh with happiness, to stand up and hug him. Behind him, I catch sight of the light switch, and I reach out and flip it off, so no one outside can see in. Then I fumble with the top of his pants, but I can't get the clasp, and after a second he reaches down and helps me. I unzip, still not looking at him. His pants come open. White underwear. I move it gently, and he springs out, bigger than I expected.

Somehow I know what to do this time, and I'm so nervous—and so thrilled he's letting me do this—that I'm not grossed out when I close my mouth over him. He's breathing harder now, his chest moving in and out. His hand touches the back of my head, guiding me. I close my eyes. I'm the one in control, the one with the power. Now I see what all my friends see in this.

He moves faster and faster, pushing against the back of my mouth, almost to my throat. I concentrate on his breathing, and his excitement keeps me going. I open my mouth wider, afraid to let my teeth touch him, and after a minute I hear him groan. And then he jerks and comes into my mouth, again and again.

I want to gag and spit it out, but I know I can't, you're supposed to swallow. I close my eyes tighter and force the stuff down my throat. It's hot and salty, almost unbearable. But only for a second, and then it's done, and a part of him, Dom Zeferelli, is inside me.

I hold him in my mouth until I feel his breath return to normal, which seems like a long time. Then I pull away and wipe my mouth on the back of my hand and look up. I'm waiting for him to pull me up and kiss me and hug me, tell me I'm the best, tell me he's been waiting for this. Tell me I'm the love of his life, or at least the love of his week.

But he stares straight ahead, not even looking at me. And then I get it. Of course he doesn't want to kiss me; who would, after what I just did? I stand up, so I'm looking down at him, towering over him. "I want to go all the way," I say, my voice confident.

He looks up at me. His eyebrows dart together, then back apart. He touches my arm and sighs. "No, you don't, hon."

Hon! I nod. "Yes, I do. I do." I fumble with the snap of my jeans. Somewhere in the back of my mind is the thought that I could get pregnant, but I push the idea out of my head.

But Dom shakes his head. "Come here, come down here." And he pulls me onto his lap, my legs straddling him. His arms come around my back, underneath my hair. And he kisses me—finally— once on the mouth. Soft, but fast.

My body relaxes. I open my mouth and move toward him again, determined to get him, to not let him get away, and he lets me this time, he kisses me longer, opening his mouth, too, letting my tongue in. His mouth is warm, a hint of cigarettes and coffee, just like I knew it would be. I touch his hair—beautiful dark-brown dirty hair. His tongue touches mine. I reach down and unzip my pants.

"What are you doing?" he mumbles into my mouth, but his breath is heavy now, and I keep on kissing him. In one quick motion, I pull my shirt out of my pants and push his hands up underneath it, and then I reach around and undo the bra clasp for him. His fingers come up under the material, his palms warm on my breasts. His touch is slightly rough, rougher than Vinnie's ever was, but I like it, I love it, because he's given in. I stand and yank my pants down to my socks and place one of his hands between my legs, against my underwear.

This is the truth: I think of the movies then, of how the girls act, and I copy it. I move my body around under his palm, pressing him to me. I close my eyes and let my breath get harder and heavier, like with Vinnie—but this time I want him to go through with it, this time I want to give in. There's something else different about this time, too: I can't really feel his hand. I mean, I can feel it there, but I'm not thinking about it, I'm thinking about *him*—what I'm doing to him, how I can make him want me, how I can have him. And it works. His hands start to move on their own. And then it's him doing things to me.

Somehow we get over to that grungy couch, and he lies down on top of me. Both of us are still wearing shirts and shoes; my pants are gathered in a clump on one foot, and his pants are still on both his legs, but pulled down to his feet. I slide my hands up his shirt, then unbutton it and kiss his chest. He smells like sweat and a hint of scent —powder, or deodorant—and he tastes like tart oranges. I kiss his chest, sucking his skin, trying to make him crazy, and it's working, he's starting to moan and he's hard again. But he stops. "Wait a minute," he says. He gets up and hobbles toward his desk, opens a drawer, and comes back with a Trojan. I turn away while he puts it on—in case he's embarrassed, but also because it makes me feel a little sad. I had hoped he wouldn't use one. But I don't have time to be sad for long, because then he's back on me, trying to get inside. I close my eyes and help push him harder, till a knifelike pain pierces through me and I have to gasp.

But it's a joyful pain, too, because I'm the one causing it, and I know I want to. For a second I wonder if this is what Cassie feels when she refuses to eat: the power of being in control dulls the pain. But I still feel it, the pain, and I know she must, too. Cold sweat breaks out all over me. He moves faster now, and after a while he's coming again. I hold my breath, tightening my muscles, and it seems to go on forever—thirty seconds, a minute—till I think I might break.

But I don't, and somehow I even manage to relax my body a little at the end. When it's over, I lie there, the throbbing between my legs slowly fading. In the distance, I hear cars going by, and it occurs to me only now that we could have been caught, we would have, if someone had come in for gas. I open my eyes. The room is still and dark. Dom lies over me, his chest moving up and down. He's shrinking inside me now, a balloon leaking air, and I want to hold on to him. I'm aware of an odor, the musty couch and something else, the smell of sex. I look up at him, smiling.

He glances at me for just a second, his mouth open partway. Then he looks away. "Shit," he says.

My stomach folds a little. "What?"

"You've never done that before, have you."

It's a statement, not a question. Was I that bad? I look down at his chest, avoiding his eyes. I feel the wet spot under me on the couch, still warm but cooling fast.

Dom takes a deep breath. He slides out of me. He pushes up and off the couch, then turns away from me to take off the condom. He pulls up his pants, then glances outside, squinting. Then he says, "I'll be right back." He goes in the bathroom and closes the door.

Outside, the orange Shell sign lights up the lot. I stand and pull on my jeans, then touch the wet circle on the brown couch. My finger comes up wet. I sniff it. Blood. What color was the couch?

The toilet flushes, and for a second I panic. I turn the pillow over quickly and sit down on it. My hair falls in front of my face, and I let it stay there once more, hiding behind it. Hiding in that dark room.

Dom comes out of the bathroom. In the dark, I see him look at me. "Listen, I'm gonna turn the light on now, okay?"

"Okay." But I close my eyes, just for a second. He flips on the switch. I open my eyes.

Dom grabs his coat from a hook on the wall. "I've had it," he says, not looking at me. "Want to get out of here?"

I don't move. It occurs to me that he's done this a million times. A million girls. I don't get up, don't move, don't say anything.

He turns off the TV, then looks at me. "Are you okay?" he says finally, and this time I wonder if I am. He watches me a minute. Then he comes over and sits down next to me. He puts his arm around my neck and kisses me on the cheek. And for that second it's okay again, for just that second everything's great. I lift his hand to my face and kiss his fingers. I lay his palm flat against my face.

He pulls it gently away. "Come on," he says. "I'll take you to my house. You can wait for my sister up there."

Somewhere deep in the back of my mind, a little voice tells me to just ask him to take me home—or better yet, to go out to the street and stick my thumb out and take it from there. Instead, I climb on the back of his motorcycle and ride in the cold to the Zeferellis' with him. And when we get there, against all better judgment, I wait around while he goes in the kitchen, and not for Tiffany but for Dom. I linger in the foyer, waiting for him to sweep me into his arms and tell me he loves me, tell me everything's okay.

He comes out a minute later with a coconut-covered doughnut. He moves past me, up the stairs. At the top, he calls, "Make yourself at home. I'm gonna take a shower, so . . ." I hear him go down the hall to his parents' bedroom and close the door behind him.

In the living room, the big wood clock ticks away. I stand and listen to it, yanking on one thumb and then the other. No TV is on and no phone is ringing, and I think I've never heard their house this quiet. The lights are off, too.

Something inside me feels weird—my stomach, my head, my throat—but I think it must be the combination of first-time sex and running around in the cold. After a while I go up to Tiffany's bathroom. I know I need a shower, but I don't want to take one, I want to smell like I do, like Dom and me mixed. In the medicine cabinet is a bottle of Bambi's perfume. I dab some of it on my wrist. With a black makeup pencil, I draw a thick black rim around each eye. I wander out.

Their parents' bedroom door is still closed. I go back downstairs. In the kitchen, I remember Mrs. Zeferelli's gin in the cabinet next to the marshmallow fluff, and I open the door and take it out gratefully. I take a huge swig, then another and a third. Tears burn my eyes. I take another swig for good measure, then pour myself half a tall glass. I add ice and replace the bottle, then tiptoe into the hallway. Warmth spreads through me, and I feel better already. I'm starting to see the attraction of liquor. Ice clinks in my glass.

Still no sign of Dom. I move to the stairway—and I freeze. Mr. Zeferelli is sitting at the dining-room table, in the dark, directly in front of me. He's looking down, focused on the top of the table, but I know he knows I'm there, and I realize he saw me go by the first time, too. It occurs to me—with something like amazement—that he doesn't want to see me right now any more than I want to see him. Just keep walking, Billie, I tell myself. But my feet don't seem to move, and finally he has to look up. He forces a smile. His eyes are puffy as wet bread. "Oh hi, honey," he says weakly. "How you doing?" The table is empty. He's been sitting there doing nothing.

Words tumble out of me then—how Tiffany said I could sleep here, how I've just come downstairs for some ice—but he's not listening, he's looking down again, nodding. "That's okay, honey, why don't you just go on up, I'm sure she'll be right back."

I thank him about fifty times and get myself halfway upstairs, out of his sight. And then I struggle to put everything together: the phone ringing and ringing yesterday, and no one allowed to answer it. Dom telling me how preoccupied Tiffany's been. Mr. Zeferelli sitting here doing nothing, looking worse than I've ever seen him. Something's wrong. I hug myself, suddenly afraid. A drop of gin spills on the carpet.

The liquor is allowing the events of the day to creep back into my mind: my sister, the car ride from hell with my father, the gas station with Dominick. But it blurs them, too, almost like they happened to someone else. Or like I dreamed them.

I go up the rest of the stairs, swaying a little as I walk. All the lights are off in the hallway. I take another sip of gin, then sit down on the carpet in the dark. Down the hall, the parents' bedroom door opens, and Dom comes out, a towel wrapped around his waist, and goes into his room, not seeing me.

After a minute, I place the glass on the floor, get up, and tiptoe unsteadily down the hall. His door is partly opened, and I can see him lying face-up on his bed, wearing pale blue boxer shorts. His eyes are closed. The lights are off, but his TV is turned on to some clappy game show, throwing a purple haze on the room.

I stand there a long time, just looking at him. Gin waves roll through my head. Dom seems to be asleep. I push the door open gently and go in.

I kneel down next to his bed, holding my breath, letting it out only when I'm all the way down and he still hasn't moved. I lean close to him. I can still smell a hint of gas, though now it's the clean version: tinged with soap and shampoo. In the purple light, his black hair curls around his ears, still a little bit wet. I lean closer. Walnut peach fuzz blankets his inner ear. His cheeks are slightly wind-burned, and the lower part of his face and neck are covered with soft, even stubble, like a tiny black carpet. I almost giggle.

He's breathing loudly, through his nose; he has allergies year-round, like Tiffany. I move even closer, so my face is almost touching his, but I hold my breath so he won't feel me there. On his shoulder is a tiny almond-shaped birthmark—not unlike Cassie's. I can see now that his chest is smaller than Vinnie's—softer and rounder, not as pumped. A line of black hair curls down his stomach and disappears into his underwear. His big hand rests on one thigh, too big for his body.

I move my face down to his waist and sniff deeply, and through my drunken haze I tell myself that I want, more than anything, to have him inside me again—though some part of me knows that what I really want is for him to let *me* in. To let me into his world, the Zeferelli world, and take me out of mine.

Quickly, I remove my clothes—first my sweater and T-shirt and bra, then my shoes and pants and underwear. I drop it all on the floor and climb onto the bed. My head is throbbing. Dom blurs before me. I lie down and push my dirty naked body up against his warm, clean, almost-naked one. I close my eyes.

Immediately, the bed starts to spin. I open my eyes. Dom bolts up in bed. His hand flies to his hair. "What are you *doing*?" he yells. "Jesus Christ, you scared the shit out of me!"

I shrink away from him. "Sorry. Sorry. I was just—"

"Jesus!" he yells again, panting.

I sit up, aware of my bare chest. Aware, and then amazed . . . and then horrified. I throw one arm over myself and reach down for my clothes with the opposite hand. But I can't quite touch them. I roll off the bed, get to my knees, and attempt to pull on my underwear.

But my eyes won't focus, and my hands won't move right, and I can't seem to get anything on. After what seems like an hour I get my underpants on my legs, though when I yank them up, they're on backward. I grab the rest of the clothes, drop my bra, pick it up, and run, with the pile, out of the room.

I run smack into Mr. Zeferelli, who's standing in the hallway. Time stops then. I stand there, half-naked and breathing hard, and he stands there staring, too stunned to move. "Oh god, I'm sorry," I whisper finally.

By then, Dom's at his door. I stagger toward Tiffany's room in my underpants, both of them watching me. I close her door and get my clothes on fast, blood pounding in my head. And then I open the door and get myself out of there.

I walk toward our house in a fog, tripping twice on the way, the second time scraping my hand on the curb. When I get there, the front door is open. I let myself in and walk straight past my parents, who are reading the newspaper in the den. The dogs follow me.

"Billie!" my mother calls, starting to get up, but my father mumbles something to her and she doesn't call me again. I walk upstairs, holding the railing for support, and close myself in my room, locking the dogs outside. I don't turn on the light, just kick off my shoes and pants and slide in bed, still wearing my T-shirt.

I close my eyes and wait then, marking the seconds, for my parents to come upstairs and deal with me. Vaguely I wonder if they'll realize I'm drunk, and if they'll be more pissed about that or that I ran from the car. That seems like days ago now, weeks. I wonder if they worried at all while I was gone, or just assumed I'd be back. If they tried to call Tiffany's to see if I was there. If Mr. Zeferelli answered or just let the phone ring.

I hear my father say something, and then the springs of his chair creak; he's getting up. I brace myself. But the TV goes on. And then I hear the springs creak again. He's sat back down. He's settling in.

I open my eyes. They aren't coming up. For a second I'm relieved—almost vindicated. But then, slowly, slow as the sun going down, a different kind of anxiety comes over me. I *want* them to come up, I'm *waiting* for it, wondering what's taking so long. Because anything my parents could say or do, any way they could punish me, would beat lying here thinking about what I did.

But they don't come. I flip over onto my stomach and pull the covers up over my head. Then I hug my arms crisscross over my chest and let Mrs. Zeferelli's gin sink me, sick and mortified, into sleep.

chapter
nine

I wake up with a headache and a heaving stomach and a fever of 103. As if nothing ever happened—as if it's any other day of our lives —my mother makes me tea and turns on the vaporizer and brings me an extra blanket, and my father feels my glands and listens to my chest with his stethoscope.

All day long I drift in and out of sleep, sweating and dreaming horrible things: I climb a pastel-colored mountain in Arizona with Lisa, only to watch her hurl herself off and float away like a kite; I'm making out with a boy who has Vinnie's body but when I stop and look at him, he has no face; I'm late for my SATs and burst into the room, realizing, as I do, that my underwear is on outside my clothes and everyone's staring at me. When I'm not asleep, memories of Dom and last night start to creep back, and then I feel even sicker. Tiffany doesn't call me all day, but I'm too spent to worry much about it.

I worry a little more when she doesn't call the next day, and a little more the day after that—though I'm still pretty sick, and it turns out I have more than just a hangover. My father brings me drugs and a pillow-backrest that says Motrin on it and a copy of *The Phantom Tollbooth,* my favorite childhood book, and tells me if I don't drink something every hour, he'll put me in the hospital. So I drink every hour, little cups of tea and orange juice and liquid Jell-O my mother brings. Otherwise, my life pretty much stops for a week. I lie in bed, aware a little more with each passing day that neither Vinnie nor Dominick nor Tiffany is among the people who call me. Vinnie and Dom don't surprise me, of course, but after a while the fact that Tiffany hasn't called starts to fill me with a sort of panic. I'm sure she knows everything about me and Dom at the gas station, and I'm scared to death to face her—and even more afraid she won't give me that chance.

By the time I feel well enough to pick up the phone and call *her,* though, I've lost my nerve. For two days I start to dial about fifty times but don't press enough numbers to get through. On the third day I connect but nobody answers, and I'm almost glad. My mother has collected my homework from school, and I dig into it with a sort of relief, glad to have something to do besides think about my life and what I've done to it lately. Cassie calls once, sounding distant and edgy. She hasn't lost any weight, but she hasn't put on any more either. I ask her how Lisa is. "She's—well, she's okay," she says. "How are *you,* though? You never get sick. What happened?"

I tell her I don't know, maybe I was due. I don't tell her about Dom. I can't bear to talk about it yet, and I think that maybe I never will. Maybe it'll be my secret, my own personal humiliation.

It's not until my parents declare me cured and I drag my sorry butt back to West Berry High that I find out Tiffany hasn't been in school the past two weeks either. Chris Paroni tells me this, munching a salami sub at his locker, next to the one Tiffany and I share— the one her stuff is still inside: a few books, a few vials of lip-gloss, her lavender mirror on the door above the poster of Ray Charles, who she loves. "We thought you two blew town together," Chris says, breathing vinegar on me. "We had you in Vegas by now. Want a bite, beautiful?"

"No thanks. Chris, can I borrow a dime?" I collect it and run to the pay phone and call Tiffany again, this time praying she *will* answer, this time not caring if Dominick or her father picks up. I let it ring until I'm almost late for homeroom. Then I hang up and run to class.

I try again next period and the one after that. No answer, no machine. Meanwhile, I pass Vinnie twice in the hall, and both times he acts like he doesn't see me. The second time he's with this girl, Tina Villardi—a tough curvy senior with black nail polish, a gutter mouth, and a big, tight-assed sexy butt, the kind I wish I had. She's asking him about the regional wrestling tournament this weekend; while I was sick, he won the Districts, the first step toward the States. I slow down enough to hear him tell her that the tournament is all day Saturday at Valley High. She catches sight of me lingering and looks away smiling, and I think, He can't be *with* her, can he? But I know too that she'll give him what he wants in a second; he'll barely have to ask. And I wonder if he'll like that or not—if he'll like her more or less afterward. Certainly making a slut out of myself with Dominick didn't exactly make him love me. On the other hand, he didn't exactly love me before I did it either. The whole thing changed nothing for him. Only for me.

After school I have teachers to see, and then my mother picks me up and takes me straight home. I call Tiffany once an hour all afternoon, and the same thing all the next day. I tell myself, half-heartedly, that the Zeferellis must have packed up and gone to Hawaii or Jamaica or somewhere for a couple of weeks—some free excursion or great deal her father got from a friend, maybe. I picture them lined up in bikinis on beach chairs, wearing neon sunglasses and sipping red drinks. A radio is on, and Donna Summer is singing: Someone left the cake out in the rain.

Saturday morning, I sleep in until eleven. When I wake up, I find a note on the kitchen table from my mother: *Gone to see Cassie, didn't want to wake you. How's your cough? There are fresh bagels, lots of fruit. Make yourself a good breakfast. We'll be home by dinnertime. Love, Mom and Dad.* I stick a bagel in the toaster oven and start to scramble two eggs, but while I'm cooking, the phone rings and I run halfway to the den, spatula in my hand, in case it's Tiffany. My grandmother's voice squawks onto the machine. "Oh!" she screams. "Oh, I would have hung up, but your answering service picked up so fast! Boy, how do you have time to answer the phone if you're at home? Well, don't call back, I'm on my way out to play bridge. I'm just calling to ask if you want rye bread tomorrow night or whole wheat. King's has a sale on the whole wheat, but I'm not gonna buy it if no one'll eat it but me. . . ." She sounds insulted suddenly. "Well, I'll try you later, I suppose." She hangs up.

I finish making my breakfast, feeling slightly guilty for screening her call, then sit down and eat it slowly. It's a still, slate-colored day out, not sunny but not raining or snowing either. I open the newspaper and read the comics and the advice columns. My horoscope says, "Let an old friend help you with a new problem." I push my plate away, Tiffany's absence burning like a hole inside me. Then I go upstairs, where I get dressed in about a minute. I glance at my high heels but decide to put on sneakers for a change. I throw on a scarf of my mother's and Vinnie's coat, since I haven't yet managed to return it and he's been too busy ignoring me to ask. Outside, I lock our front door and head for the Zeferellis'.

I jog with my head down to avoid the cold wind, my hands deep in my jacket pockets, and more excited—and nervous—with each step at the thought of seeing Tiffany again. But when I turn onto her block, I have an odd feeling that none of them will be home, and as I approach their house, I see that in fact there are no cars at their place. Nothing in the driveway. Michelle's car was already gone—someone came and took it last month because she wasn't making the payments, Tiffany said—but I can't imagine where the rest of the cars are; even if they went on vacation, Bambi's should be here. I jog toward the house, slowing down as I get there, hugging my jacket tighter around me. The windows are dark. Outside them, the leafless bushes dance like skeletons.

Through the mail slot I see only dark. I ring the bell and, when no one answers, reach down for the key they always keep under the heart-shaped doormat. It's gone, so I go around the house and climb in the bathroom window, like I once saw Tiffany do.

Inside, the first thing I see—after the pink seashell soaps and the pink bathroom rug—is a rust-colored, spike-heeled sandal, one of the ones Mr. Zeferelli was selling last year. It's lying on the floor outside the bathroom, and it fills me with hope. I pick it up and hold on to it.

There are dishes in the sink—a stack of plates, a coffee mug that says "I Hate People," a big bowl filled with reddish water. Congealed tomato sauce clings to its edges. In the fridge is a half-full bottle of Tab, a jar of spicy mustard, a hunk of chocolate cake in plastic. I touch the plastic. The cake is hard as a brick.

I notice then that the house is cold—almost as cold as outside. I move through the downstairs, still holding the shoe, my hope fading a little with each step. On the couch in the den is their crumpled white blanket; on the table, nail polish. Next to it is a *TV Guide* from two weeks ago.

I can't quite bring myself to go upstairs—my last trip up there is still fresh in my head—so I go down instead, to the basement. The pool table stands in full kelly-green glory, and I have an urge to rack up the balls and shoot a game right there—as if shattering that perfect triangle of colored balls in a million directions might help me figure out where the Zeferellis are, where they went. But I don't do it, and the house stays so quiet, it's spooky. Across the room, a pile of clothes overflows from the top of the dryer onto the floor; scattered around it are a few random shoeboxes, some opened, some closed but crushed. I toss the shoe I'm holding toward the boxes, and when it hits, it sounds unnaturally loud. I think of Dom's voice in the gas station: "You gonna make me say it?" I think of them moving here less than a year ago, slapping pink paint on the house. I think of Mr. Zeferelli at the table, staring at nothing.

I remember, then, the afternoon last month when the silver Cadillac pulled up at their house, and Tiffany grabbed me and told me to be really quiet. The two of us peeked through the blinds as a man came to their door, his partner waiting like a big wax dummy in the car—big men, with greased-back dark hair, smoke-colored jackets, pinky rings. The one rang the bell a few times, and we listened nervously to it chime. "We didn't pay the gas bill yet," Tiffany whispered, and I knew she was lying but didn't press it. And then the guy got back in the car and they drove away, and that was that.

I pick out the cue ball from under the table and blast it toward the corner pocket with my hand, suddenly furious at Tiffany—at all of them, really—for leaving me like this. The ball smacks in the pocket, so hard the whole table hums and vibrates, and then it disappears. I wait for silence to settle again. But instead the basement phone rings, shrill as a siren in that room, and for some reason it scares the hell out of me. I stand motionless, paralyzed by fear. Someone is calling the Zeferellis. Someone's on the other end. And I'm the one here.

It takes four full rings—each one louder than the one before—before I can move. I bolt upstairs, tear through the kitchen, and hightail it out the front door.

Back home, I sit panting on the carpet in the den, trying to sort out my thoughts. The dogs wander over, nudge each other out of the way, and I hold my breath a second, thinking they might fight. But they settle down without so much as a growl. I kick off my shoes and rub my hands over their velvety jowls. When did they stop trying to kill each other? Was it sudden, or did it happen gradually?

I lean back against the wall and close my eyes, thinking about Tiffany, until a car door slams outside and both dogs scramble to the window, collars jangling. They rise up on their hind legs and stick their heads under the curtains. I get up to see who's out there.

It's my grandmother Zelda, teetering up the front walk, her brown fur coat clutched tightly around her, a matching round hat on her head. She carries a formal black purse. I can see the wind blowing her, making her sway a little bit. I open the front door to let her in.

"Oh!" she says when she sees me. She holds her cheek against mine and kisses air. Her cheek feels like cold soft leather, and I inhale her perfume, the familiar smell of her.

"I was in the neighborhood," she says, taking off her hat. "My bridge game got canceled, so I went to the hairdresser instead, and then to Shop Rite, and I thought I'd stop here a minute on the way back. You're all so busy these days, I never see any of you. I called this morning but I got your answering service again. Anyway, I thought I might catch someone here—"

"Well, you caught me." I smile, sort of glad to see her. "I got your message. Here, want me to take your coat?"

"That's okay, I can only stay a minute. I wasn't gonna go to Shop Rite either—I like to go Sunday—you know, so everything's fresh when you come for dinner—but then I remembered it was double coupons today. Did you know, if you've bought something and haven't opened it yet and it goes on sale, you can bring it back and they'll refund the difference?" She's making her way into the den, the dogs trailing her, me trailing them. I picture her hauling back jars of mayonnaise, cucumbers, cans of tuna fish. The check-out girls rolling their eyes.

She drops onto the couch. "Ugh!" she says, sighing, as she takes off her hat. "This wind wears me out so. I can hardly get anywhere these days."

"I know. I wish spring would come." I sit down on the floor again. "It's supposed to be here already."

"It never comes on time." She smiles. "So how do you feel, sweetie? Here, don't you want to sit on a chair?"

"No thanks. I'm fine, Zelda. I'm all better. Thanks for asking."

"That's good. Your father was worried, you know. Between you and your sister . . ." She glances around. "Where is he, any-way? Oh, they must have gone to see Cassandra, it's Saturday. That's right."

I wait for her to complain that my parents never take her along to Connecticut so she can see Cassie, too, but she just says, "So what were you doing?"

"Me? Nothing. Just—getting ready to study, I guess."

"Mm. For your SATs?"

I shrug. No point in telling her I already took them. Or that, last week, without telling anyone, I signed up to take them again in May—just wrote a check from my mother's checkbook and filled out the form and sent it in. It made me feel good, for about a minute.

"Whatsa matter?" she's saying. "You don't like to talk about school anymore? You used to love to tell me your grades."

"Really? Well, I don't, anymore."

She laughs. "Okay. We won't talk about it. I don't really blame you, anyway. I always hated those damn tests."

"You did?" This surprises me.

"Mm. They made me so nervous. And I always did lousy on them. I never understood how your father did so well on everything. I guess he got it from your grandfather's side—"

"I didn't even know they had SATs in those days," I say.

"Well, maybe not exactly *that* test, but they had similar things." She sits up straighter. "In those days, though, it wasn't so important for a girl to be so smart. In those days, other things mattered more for a girl."

"Like what?"

"Oh, looking nice, and acting properly, and taking care of your family, and doing volunteer work. That was very important, volunteering. One wanted to be charitable. And of course finding a nice man. I was engaged by the time I was your sister's age and married the following year. These days, I think half the girls don't even want to marry as long as they have a career. It's very sad. Marriage is a good thing, you know. A girl should feel very lucky to find someone who loves her and takes care of her." She scratches at a tiny spot on the collar of her coat. "These days girls don't even care how they look, for the most part. Don't you think that's true?"

"No," I say.

"No?" She stops scratching and looks at me. "Well, your sister certainly doesn't care. If she did, she wouldn't let herself get emaciated like this."

I stare at her. "She's not doing it on *purpose*," I say finally.

She raises her eyebrows. "Well, she doesn't get physically sick when she eats or anything, does she?"

"No," I admit.

"Well, so." She shakes her head. "I guess I just don't understand it, that's all."

I don't either, but I won't admit that. I don't want to be in the same category as she is right now.

Zelda shifts in her coat. "Am I disturbing you? Go back to whatever you were doing. You don't have to entertain me."

"I wasn't *doing* anything, Grandma. I was sitting here. I just came home from my friend Tiffany's house."

"Oh? And how's she?"

"I don't know. She wasn't there."

She pats her hair tentatively with her palm, like she's making sure it's still there. It's gold, almost the color of Mrs. Zeferelli's, and sprayed like a ball around her head. "Well, where was she?" she says.

"Probably halfway across the country by now." The minute I say it, I know it's true.

My grandmother's hand stops patting. "What do you mean?"

I debate a minute, then decide to go for it. "Her family—well, they owed money to people, I think. And they didn't have it. So they left. That's what I'm guessing, anyway."

She stares at me. "*People?* What *people?*"

"I don't know. The mob. The mafia or something."

She smiles patiently. "That couldn't be, Billie. Why would you think that?"

"I just do."

"You know for sure they're involved in the mafia?"

"No. I just *think* so."

"And you still went over there?"

I feel my neck muscles starting to stiffen. "Zelda," I say, "Tiffany was my best friend."

"That's even worse. Then you're involved, too. What if something happened to them when you were there? Weren't you afraid?"

"No," I say, but I think of running up the stairs, just an hour ago, to get out of Tiffany's house. "It wasn't dangerous or anything," I say. "Especially for me."

She turns up her nose. "How do you know? You don't know that, Billie. One can never be too careful these days."

"I *am* careful." My voice is louder now. "Anyway, she was my best friend. I don't care if her family owed a million dollars. It's just money. What do I care?"

She frowns. "Well, you *should* care. And you shouldn't be so cavalier about money. You won't be, once you have to worry about it. Money is important. It's terrible to owe people." She shakes her head. "Aren't there any Jewish girls at your school?"

I stare at her, furious. "What's that supposed to mean?"

"Nothing. I'm just asking." But she sounds defensive, as if she knows how horrible she's being.

"What does it matter if there are or there aren't?" I say. "I picked Tiffany for a friend, I *love* Tiffany. And she picked me." I shake my head. "That's what's different about now from your time. No one cares what anyone is now. And we stand by our friends, they're like family. They're *paesanos,* if you know what I mean."

I know she doesn't. And I know, too, that what I'm saying is absurd. I'm talking about the way I want it to be, not the way it really is. Tiffany's family probably doesn't even like me—and why should they? As for Tiffany, she's gone without so much as a phone call, and I'll probably never see her again. That's how much she cares about me.

My grandmother sighs. "You're wrong, Billie. Friends are never like family, not really. In the long run, your family are the only ones there for you."

I shake my head. "That's ridiculous."

"Well, it happens to be true. You'll see."

I tug hard at my socks. My grandmother watches me. "What's come over you?" she says after a minute. "You used to be such a sweet little girl. Your sister was the one with the sassy mouth, not you. You were the quiet one." She smiles. "You'd sleep over with me and tiptoe out of bed at the crack of dawn to go watch your cartoons."

I don't answer. I don't feel like being nice to her now. I just want her to leave.

She picks up her hat and places it back on her head, and I think, meanly, that it's a stupid hat, as stupid as my father's. I wonder if he got the idea from her, and if I'll be wearing one in twenty or thirty years. I hope not.

My grandmother stands up slowly. "Well, I guess I should let you study. Ugh, this coat weighs a ton. I shouldn't even wear it anymore. I bought it when Grandpa was around to help me on and off with it."

I get up then, move with her to the door. The dogs follow,

sniffing at her hands. "Well, I didn't mean to bother you," she says to me. She pats each dog once on the head.

"You didn't," I say. But I wish now that she'd never come. Instinctively, I lean out to kiss her.

Again, her perfume overwhelms me. It's the same kind she's always worn, strong and flowery, as familiar as my bedspread—a smell that, when I recognize it in a store or someone else's house, always surprises me and makes me think of her.

The door is open now. Gray light seeps in from outside, revealing brown age spots on her skin. I can see that she's tried to cover them with makeup, and somehow, despite everything, that makes me sad. She opens the door. "Well—good-bye," she says. She steps out. The storm door slams behind her.

I watch her, still angry, as she hobbles down the steps. The wind has picked up even from an hour ago, and again she seems to sway. Her legs poke out from under her big coat, skinny calves and ankles covered in expensive stockings, leather shoes.

I start to close the door. But just before I get it shut, I see her hat fly off her head. It blows to the ground and begins to roll down our front walk on its side, like a quarter. Her hands fly up. She staggers after it, but the wind pulls it along—rolling it toward the street, keeping it inches ahead of her.

For a few seconds I just stand there and watch, almost glad. It serves her right—for trashing my friends, for being so prejudiced. Let her see how loyal *her* family is.

But a car is coming, and the hat is almost to the street. My grandmother waves both arms frantically, trying to alert the driver to stop. And before I can stop myself, I open the door and run out and grab the hat as it reaches the curb. I pick it up and brush it off. "Here," I say, handing it to my grandmother. I'm breathing hard. The car passes us, moving fast.

To my amazement, there are tears in her eyes—same eyes as my father's, navy-blue as the ocean. "Grandpa gave me that hat," she says. "I love that hat." She takes it from me. "Thank you, sweetie."

For a second I can't speak. I almost let the hat go; I almost didn't catch it for her. I take her arm then and walk her to her car and open the door. She settles herself in, and I close it again. She smiles through the window. "You're a good girl," she says. And she turns on the motor and drives away.

I watch until I can't see her car anymore. And then she's gone, and I'm all alone in the street. Above me, everything is silent, unmoving—as if time has stopped momentarily. Through my socks, I feel the cold concrete on my feet.

Up the street, a cat darts across the road, sleek and silver. Running somewhere. I watch it until it disappears behind a house. Then I turn around and walk slowly back in.

chapter
ten

My mother calls at four o'clock. "How are you?" she asks.

"Fine. I'm reading *Fear of Flying*. Where are you?"

"We're still at the hospital. I called to tell you we won't be back until ten or so. So you'll have to make yourself some dinner."

Something tightens inside me. "How's Cassie?" I say, and then, "Mom, tell me the truth."

"She's—well, she's not great. She's lost a pound and a quarter—"

My voice vanishes, then returns. *"Why?"*

She sighs. "That's what we're trying to find out. Daddy's waiting to hear back from one of her doctors, but she's just on her way over now, so—wait, hold on a minute." She covers the phone, and I hear muffled voices. "She's here," she says. "I'd better get off. There are hamburgers in the freezer, and you can open a can of baked beans to go with it—or make yourself a frozen dinner. Or some soup, if your throat is bothering you, there's chicken soup in the—"

"Dammit, Jane, get off the phone!" This from my father, in the background. I want to reach through the phone and smash him.

"I've got to go," my mother says quickly. "We'll see you later."

"Mom?"

"What?"

"Tell Cassie I love her."

She pauses for the quickest second. "I will," she says.

There are a bunch of extra keys in the change cup in the kitchen cabinet. I take them all, then slip on Vinnie's jacket and go down to my mother's car. The third key I try turns it on.

Valley High School is only a few minutes' drive, though it takes me a while to find parking once I arrive. Cars line both sides of the street, wrestling bumper stickers all over the place. I look for Vinnie's car without finding it. I park carefully and go in fast.

At the gym entrance, though, I stop and stare. The white-lit room seems nearly twice as big as West Berry's gym, and matches are taking place on five or six mats simultaneously. Sounds rise up from all of them and converge over the room, almost amplified: a frantic, jumbled mass of wrestlers' grunts and refs' shrill whistles and hordes of fans chanting boys' names. Wrestlers dressed in different colors—blue, gold, green—crawl all over, ubiquitous as bugs: pacing, grappling, getting rub-downs from their coaches. In their tight skimpy singlets they seem practically naked; their muscles spill out all over the place. The room is warm—almost balmy—and smells like fresh sweat and Ben-Gay and leather coats and hair spray, and the whole thing feels like some sexy feverish carnival. I step inside, breathing it in.

But once I'm there, I'm not sure where to go. No West Berry wrestler besides Vinnie has made it to this tournament, and I don't see him anywhere. I scan the crowd. After a minute I spot Sharon Cicalese, a girl I've gone to school with since kindergarten. I head toward her set of bleachers. She waves when she sees me and motions me up to sit next to her. "Who's wrestling?" I ask, sliding in next to her. Two smallish guys—one in red, one in gold—are circling the mat, their heads lowered like alley cats.

"One thirty-two," she says. "The guy in the red's from Glen Ridge." She tells me she came here to see her cousin Joey wrestle, but he lost in the last round. "My family all left, but I'm staying. I love this shit."

I smile. "Me too. So what round is this?"

"The semis. The finals are later, at eight. Are you staying?"

"I don't know. . . ."

"You should! I'll look for you, we'll sit together."

"If I can. Hey, did you happen to see Vinnie wrestle?"

She closes her eyes, turns her face toward the ceiling dramatically, then looks back at me. "I mean, was he incredible, or was he *incredible?*"

"I don't know. I didn't see him." I feel pretty stupid saying that.

"You *didn't?*" She glances at my jacket. "Oh, wait, I did hear you broke up with him, now that I think about it. Is it true?"

A cheer rises up around us. The red guy has taken the other guy down. "Sort of," I say. "It was mutual, though, really."

"Too bad. You were a cute couple." She smiles, then yells encouragement to the Glen Ridge guy, who's got the other kid in a spread-eagle now, grimacing in pain. He breaks away, finally, and Sharon turns back to me. "Anyway, Vinnie did great. He pinned his first two guys no problem. The third match was really close, though. He won, but he was really beat at the end. I mean, forget about it. And they had to pack up his nose halfway through when it started bleeding." She makes a grossed-out face. "But he made it to the semis—in fact, he should be wrestling any minute. There, I think." She points to the mat across the room. "I'm coming over right after this."

I thank her and make my way around to Vinnie's section, watching nervously for him. I don't really want him to see me, at least not yet; I want to climb the bleachers and blend into the crowd and watch him beat some guy to a pulp. I want to watch someone I know, someone I'm involved with—or was, at least—win at something for a change. Then, afterward, I can congratulate him, and he'll have to at least acknowledge me. He'll be glad I came, too—even if he won't admit it.

I step into the stands and begin to walk up, noticing the group of West Berry wrestlers extending across the top row. I wave to them quickly, then look away before they feel like they have to invite me up. I'm about to sit down when someone thumps my back. I turn sharply. Tina Villardi—Vinnie's sleazy new girlfriend—stands behind me, snapping a wad of pink gum, one hand glued to her hip.

"Excuse me," she says loudly, "but I couldn't help but notice you have something on that doesn't exactly belong to you." Next to her, her friend Patti Reinhardt snickers through her nose.

A couple of people glance at us. On the mat, the two 145-pounders are getting ready, fastening their headgear. A man a few rows above us calls out, "Can you sit down, please?"

I move up a row and sit, feeling sweat break out on my back. Tina glares at the man for about half a minute, then steps up and stands in front of me. "You gonna give it to me," she says, "or make me take it off you?"

"I don't know what you're talking about," I hear myself say, and I'm amazed at my boldness. Tiffany's legacy, maybe.

Tina rolls her eyes. "Let me put it bluntly, then. That jacket you're wearing? Well, it's Vinnie's, and he wants it back. So if you don't mind, you can take it off now, and I'll, like, *deliver* it to him." Next to her, Patti laughs again.

I think about saying, What if I *do* mind, you sleazy little pig-faced bitch? But I peel off the jacket and hand it to her. "Fine," I say. "I was planning to give it back to him today anyway."

She sneers, chomping her gum like a goat. "Well, now you won't have to. How convenient. Because you know, he really can't stand the sight of your face."

Is that true? Behind Tina, I see the wrestlers down on the mat, preparing to start, and I concentrate hard on them, trying to stop shaking, trying not to think about what she said. Above us, a woman yells, "Girls, would you please sit down?" The ref's whistle trills for the match to begin.

Tina's eyes find the woman, then narrow into staples. "Would you hold your fucking horses?" she says, adding, *"Please?"* Then, slowly, she turns and maneuvers down the bleachers in her heels, shaking her ass as she descends. Patti follows her, practically blowing snot out her nose with how hard she's laughing.

When they're gone, I let out a sigh of relief, which quickly turns to fury and humiliation. If Tiffany were here, that never would have happened. Tina probably wouldn't have come up to us at all, since everyone likes Tiffany, but even if she had, Tiffany would have set her straight: told her off or, more likely, said something funny and just made her laugh. I open my clenched fists, wipe my sweaty palms on my pants. That slut. That little bitch.

Around me, people are cheering for the wrestlers. "Come on, stick him, Rory!" one guy yells. The ref holds up fingers to indicate points. I watch absently. If even Cassie were here, Tina wouldn't have said all that. Or at least the Cassie of before. There was something about her that always kept people from bothering her. Maybe the fact that she never bothered with anyone, just avoided people and did her work. Or maybe just her beauty. People were intimidated by it sometimes, I think.

I shift in my seat. Cassie still wouldn't be picked on, but it would be for a different reason now: it would be because she's sick, a patient in a psychiatric hospital. Sickness wasn't just ugly or annoying; it was repulsive and scary. Tina would probably stay as far away as humanly possible from someone with anorexia. She wouldn't want to risk touching her, breathing her air—though of course she'd talk behind cupped hands or, later, to her clique of other sluts in the schoolyard at night. "Did you see Cassie Weinstein? Her neck is a needle, and her head looks bigger than her body. And her hair is all weird and thin—oh god, it is so *disgusting!*"

On the mat, the wrestlers are stalling, leaning into each other, arms intertwined. A pound and a quarter she's lost. I tell myself that's really only one good meal: a hamburger and fries, maybe a hot fudge sundae to top it off. I could get her to eat it, too. I'd force her, stuff it down her throat, scream at her until she finished. Hell, Vinnie probably lost six or eight pounds for this match alone. He'd put it back on in an hour. A pound and a quarter is nothing.

I see him then, standing on the sidelines. His headgear is on but not fastened. His upper body looks great, but his legs are thinner than ever and his face is pale and tense. The sight of him fills me with excitement and nervousness and longing all at once. I think of Tina saying he can't stand the sight of my face, and the back of my throat closes up. Vinnie extends his hands straight out in front of him, and

Coach shakes them so his arms go up and down in waves. On the other side, another coach is doing the same arm thing to the kid Vinnie has to wrestle—a shorter, stockier guy with a shaved head who stands like he has a bowling ball stuck between his legs. He looks scary; all he needs is an earring and darker skin, and he could double for Mr. Clean.

Vinnie breaks his hands away from Coach then, and I see him take some deep breaths. Once he told me he gets so nervous before a big match that the whole room spins like a record. Then he'd be sick and dizzy for the first minute or two he wrestled. Even at a couple of the matches I went to, someone had to bring out a bucket because he thought he might throw up, though he never did, at least not when I was there. Anyway, I know he's that nervous now, and my heart goes out to him. I say a silent prayer—to Whoever—to please let him win.

The match below us is in its last period, but I can't concentrate on it. I see Tina slide into the front row of the stands. "Get psyched, Vin!" she bellows, and again I wonder if he's just using her for sex or if he could really like her. I picture her slimy little hand digging into his pants, clamping itself onto him. Around me, cheers break out. "You got it, Rory, you got it!" someone yells, and the ref blows the whistle and raises one guy's hand. The match is over.

In the past half-minute, Vinnie has somehow disappeared, and people are starting to look around for him. Someone yells, "Where the hell *is* he?" and someone else calls out "Jesus, let's go, already!" The ref goes over to Coach and says something. Coach shrugs and looks at the clock, then points toward the red-lit EXIT sign.

And then Vinnie comes running through it, toward the mat, his headgear on and fastened. He looks completely different than he did three minutes ago; the nervousness is gone, and he's totally pumped up, wild and wired. If I didn't know him better, I'd guess he'd gone out and done drugs. But that's not his style. He's just psyched; he's going to the States and he knows it. He springs onto the mat like a small kangaroo.

The stands explode in cheers then, much louder than for the last match, and the wrestlers up top start to chant Vinnie's name and thump the stands with their feet. I look around in awe, amazed that all these people are here for Vinnie. Who are they? Some of them must be his family; one woman could definitely be his mother. She's small with the same black hair, young looking and wearing a turtle-neck and a cardigan sweater. And soft pearl-pink lipstick. For all that Vinnie and I talked about it, I never even met her.

Vinnie and Mr. Clean are out in the circle now. Vinnie bounces on his feet, his legs like springs. The ref leans over and speaks to him, and Vinnie nods and keeps bouncing. The ref speaks to Mr. Clean, too. Then he blows the whistle, and my fingers dig into my thighs as the guys begin to circle around.

If the last match seemed like it was going in slow motion, this one's just the opposite. Within seconds, Vinnie dives for the guy's legs and takes him down. "Two!" the ref yells. The wrestlers above me drum the stands with their shoes. Mr. Clean flips over quickly, so his stomach's to the mat, but Vinnie flips him again. The crowd thunders. Clean is on his back now—not a minute into the match— and flipping around like a fish, straining to keep his shoulders off the floor. Vinnie holds him awhile, racking up three more points. But he can't quite pin him, and after a few more maneuvers the whistle trills the end of the period.

Next period, Vinnie starts out on top—like he did to me that day in the wrestling room. And in less than a minute he has Mr. Clean on his back again, floundering. He scores two, then two more. Clean flips onto his gut, and Vinnie lies over him, the front of him pressed against the guy's back, his arm wrapped around the kid like a bear. He's starting to lose steam; he's breathing heavily, but so is the other kid, and the score is nine–nothing, favor Vinnie. All he has to do is hold on. "Come on, Vin," I whisper. Their bodies rise and fall in unison. I close my eyes and think of me under there instead of Mr. Clean—lying flat on the mat with Vinnie's hot body pressing into me. Now I would go all the way with him. Now I would do it, but now I don't have the chance.

The ref warns the guys they have to keep moving, they can't just lie there like logs. Mr. Clean manages to crawl them both out of bounds. His headgear is undone, and he takes his time putting it back on until someone yells, "Stall!" and other people join in. "Whaddaya think this is, the country club?" Tina yells. "Get out there and wrestle, pussy."

This time Mr. Clean starts on top, his white body gleaming with sweat. Vinnie's pink finger marks show on his arm like a burn. Vinnie stands up quickly, Clean still clinging to his waist. He breaks Clean's hands off him and turns to face him.

The crowd goes wild. I rise with the people around me, chanting his name, feeling the rush of watching him wrestle. And I wish that I could soak up some of this thing Vinnie has and give it to my sister, the thing that makes his life seem so simple, so matter-of-fact. He knows what he wants and he knows how to get it. And if it's not easy—because I know it's not easy—it's still simple in a way. As simple as holding some guy's back to a mat. Then he wins, and he advances a step with each win, and it's the ultimate when he reaches the end—it's the best it can be, and he can sit back and enjoy it, bask in his glory and his life for a while.

And afterward? Well, sure, there'll be *something,* but he doesn't have to worry about it right now. I hear my sister's voice telling me I'm being simplistic, that I'm reducing a complex thing to something too easy . . . but I don't want to think about Cassie. Not right now, anyway. I watch Vinnie enviously as he works to pin this guy. As long as he wins, there'll be a logical, concrete next step. The finals are tonight. And the States are just around the corner, waiting for him. Calling his name.

What I don't think about, as I sit here envying him, is what happens if he doesn't win. Three-quarters of the way into the third period, leading a million to nothing, Vinnie is suddenly on his back. His neck is purple as he fights to keep it off the floor, his back is arched, his legs strain with every muscle in him. But his fight is gone, and ten seconds later, he's pinned—sprawled on his back, eyes closed, mouth open in agony. The crowd is dead quiet. And my breath is sucked away.

Later, at home, I sit on my bed and dial Vinnie's number. I want to tell him I saw the match, that the loss was a fluke and he did great anyway. I want to tell him how beautiful he looked out there. I want to tell him how sorry I am.

His mother answers the phone.

"Can I please speak to Vinnie?" I ask.

"Who's this?" she says.

In the background, I hear Vinnie's voice, and then a girl laughing. Tina.

I hang up before his mother can ask again who I am.

chapter
eleven

My parents are fighting, though it's my father's voice I hear clearly—rising and falling, gathering anger and volume and speed. It rises above the dishwasher, above the TV, up through the floor of my room. Through my desk and the pages of my book, *Tess of the D'Urbervilles,* so I can't see the words, can't concentrate.

"I want to talk to my daughter," he yells. "I'm sick of this bullshit. I pay a thousand dollars a week so they can tell me I can't speak to her unless it's an emergency? It would be one thing if they were helping her—"

"How do you know they're not helping?" my mother says in a voice loud for her. "It's a long-term program, Michael! Dr. Watson told us that at the beginning—"

"Dr. Watson can shove it."

"Oh, Michael."

"What?" Silence. *"What?"* he yells louder. "I don't think it's helping my daughter to be taken out of society and locked up like a prisoner—"

"Well, she got *sick* in 'society,' and I don't see how it can make her any worse to try to get some treatment—"

"She got sick at Cornell—if you want to call it 'sick'—because she was under stress and she didn't like the food and no one was telling her to eat. She thinks—"

"Oh, come on, Michael! You know anorexia has nothing to do with liking the food."

I sit up straighter. Is this *my* mother?

"Don't 'Oh, come on' me, Jane!" he says. "I *don't* know that! I know what I read, which is a bunch of conflicting theory about where it comes from and how to treat it. Joel Robbins says if his kid had anorexia, he'd keep her home and just put the whole family through therapy—"

"Joel *who?*" says my mother.

"Robbins. The chief oncologist at Summit General."

"Well." I picture her furiously wiping the kitchen table, slapping her pink and white rag all over the place. "You wouldn't do family therapy anyway," she says. "Would you?"

Silence, and then, "I don't know what I'd do. All I know is my daughter's not getting any better at Halley, where they treat her like some goddamn victim of—" He pauses, and I see him now, searching for words, his eyebrows lowered, his mouth in a frown. His blue eyes beam through his horn-rimmed glasses. "I think she should come home," he concludes. "She should be here, where I can take care of her. Where we both can."

I open my door to hear my mother's response to this, and it's good I do, because she says it softly. "What if she gets worse here, Michael? How would we deal with that?"

"She won't get worse."

"She could. Lots of girls get worse when they leave—"

"Well, those girls are screwed up. Cassie's not. She's a smart healthy kid who let a little freshman-year stress get completely out of proportion, thanks to us. If we'd all stop catering to her illness, she'd stop acting like she *has* one."

Even I've read enough to know he's completely wrong about this, and I suspect he knows it, too. But I have to admit Cassie doesn't seem to be getting a whole lot better at Halley. I think of her pencil wrists, her razor-sharp jawline, the peach fuzz that's grown on the back of her arms. And haven't I, too, been mad and frustrated that I can't even talk to her on the phone anymore? Haven't I felt that if only *I* could get at her, I could get her to eat better than those doctors?

And yet in the back of my mind, I still think she's better off at Halley than at home. And while I'm glad my mother is standing up to my father for a change, I also don't want them to fight anymore. Their voices make me wilt, like a plant. I go out to the top of the stairway and lean forward, listening. My father has turned off the television. I hear only the hum of the dishwasher, and I wonder if my mother's silence means she's starting to be swayed to his position or she's just given up. I tiptoe halfway downstairs. Above me, the ceiling light flickers briefly, like the bulb is starting to burn out. And then my mother says, "Why don't we let *her* decide, Michael? She is eighteen, after all."

I want to cheer for her. I barrel down the rest of the stairs and into the kitchen. "That's what I think, too," I say. "Why don't you ask Cassie what *she* wants to do?"

My father, standing against the oven, turns and observes me like I'm a fly that's buzzed in. And then his expression softens ever so slightly. Obnoxious or not, I am the healthy daughter, and that's worth something these days. "I don't ask Cassie," he says, folding his arms over his chest, "because I don't think she's equipped to make the best decision right now."

"Well, who is?" I say loudly. "Are you?"

For a second he just stares at me, like he's not sure whether to smack me or admit that I'm right. And then, finally, he answers: "Yes. I am." He turns to leave the room, but he looks back at me. "I'm her *father*," he yells.

Later, brushing my teeth with the door open, I hear him apologize to my mother in their room. He tells her he's sorry he got pissed off before. He jokes about something, calls her Fly, tries to make her laugh.

And she does laugh, after a minute, and I know she's forgiven him then—because that's their pattern, and because she loves him, and because she knows he loves her. And now for a day or two he'll be extra nice and she'll be a little snotty to him, and then he'll find something else to be pissed at and it'll start over again.

Thinking about it now, it seems that love is the worst reason for her to forgive him, not the best. That love should be able to do better than this. That, if you love someone, you should do it without making them feel bad all the time.

And then I think about how he loves Cassie, too—about how we all do. And I wonder if that's what made her sick, and, if so, whether it'll be enough to save her again.

Weeks later, when I go in to take SATs again, I do what everyone else in there does: I read each question carefully, pick the answer I think is correct, and fill in the corresponding dot with my pencil. I'm not really nervous—just a little numb, maybe—and most of the questions seem pretty easy; in fact, I'm sort of surprised at how well I know most of the words. When I finish, I leave quickly, beating the crowd down the hall and to the door and outside. I squint into dazzling sunshine. It warms the May air, filling an endless blue sky with its rays.

I head up toward the fenced-in tennis courts, where my sister used to play first singles for West Berry's team. Inside, I sit down, cross-legged, on the ground. Past the courts to my right is the empty football field, its new grass seed just starting to sprout. To my left are four courts and then a gated, newly repaved driveway: shimmering black tar, sparkling white lines. There's a pickup truck parked on one side, but no one appears to be inside it. No one appears to be anywhere.

In my back pocket are a pack of matches and my unopened SAT scores from last time—the day I used my answering sheet as a doodle pad. That was over two months ago now, though it seems more like years. I inch the stuff out of my pocket and place the sealed score sheet on the ground in front of me. For a second I'm tempted to open it. But I resist, like I've done since I intercepted it from the mail three days ago and hid it in my sock drawer. There's no point in looking. The scores are part of my old life, the one with Tiffany and Vinnie and Dominick. I will see the old scores when today's scores come, together on the same sheet. And then, like the colleges, I can look at the scores and try to figure out what they say about me.

Unless, of course, my father calls the testing service first to ask why my first scores haven't come. Somehow, though, I have a feeling he won't, that he'll just wait for the new ones and keep his mouth shut. Lately he does, more, with me, which is sometimes great and sometimes sort of unsettling.

The matchbook says "Rocco's Tuxedos" on it. It makes me think of Cassie's senior prom, of the strapless gown she wore and her long hair done up in a pile, a few pieces cascading out like ribbon. I remember being simultaneously proud and jealous of how cool she looked. I remember, too, that she went to the prom with Steve Zucker, that he came to take her after she broke up with her latest boyfriend. I think briefly about calling him when I get home, to find out how he's doing.

But he'd ask how Cassie is, and then I'd have to say it: She's lost another pound, she's not allowed to talk on the phone anymore. I pluck out a match, strike it, and touch it to the envelope, watching the whole thing melt into an orange-blue flame. When the flame gets close to my hand, I drop it and let the paper burn on the ground the rest of the way.

The dogs are wired when I let myself in the house around one thirty, and even though I've just walked a mile from school, I take them each out for a run—first Mollie, then Ethan. I time the walks, forty-five minutes each, so neither one of them feels cheated. When I get back with Ethan, my parents are home. And Cassie's with them.

When I see her, the weirdest thing happens: My body takes over and does what it wants, so I feel almost like I'm watching myself. I run to Cassie and fling myself at her and hug her so tight, she laughs. Then I let go and look at her. Her hair is longer and thinner, almost below her ears, and her face is dry and patchy. She's skinny and washed out and white and pathetic. I burst into tears.

Cassie smiles. "And I thought you'd be *glad* to see me." She gives me a squeeze then, presses me to her bony chest and hugs her string-bean arms around me. My parents stand there watching, their coats still on. My mother's eyes are filled up with tears. My father looks, somehow, both happy and sad. His vinyl lunch sack hangs from his shoulder—the one my mother bought at Woolworth's for him, in the kids' department.

Later, after my mother asks a million times if we're sure we'll be okay, my parents go out to the movies with the Greenbaums. Cassie and I sit on the couch in our pajamas, she with a sweatshirt over hers, and socks and slippers. Me in just a T-shirt. We watch old reruns: *The Brady Bunch, The Partridge Family, Carol Burnett.* I tell her about the Zeferellis, and her eyes widen. "Where do you think they went?" Her voice is soft and slightly hoarse, like it always is now. The voice of a girl with no energy.

"Who knows?" I answer. "Maybe California, or Canada. Or Italy." I go into the kitchen and get a container of ice milk and two spoons. "Want some?" I say, coming back in. I scoop out a huge spoonful, then put the carton on the coffee table, where she can reach it. "It's lowfat. Coffee."

"No thanks. So what's up with DiNardio?" She doesn't look at the ice milk, or at me eating it.

I tell her he's with Tina now, that he doesn't talk to me any-more. She blinks at me, eyes wide, lips still peely-red. "You've had a fun semester," she says sarcastically.

"It hasn't been that bad, though." Saying that, I realize it's sort of true. I should have lost it by now, for all the stuff that's happened, but somehow I feel okay.

I ask her about Lisa. She shrugs, avoiding my eyes. "I guess she's all right. Just, you know, getting through the days." She pushes up a sweatshirt sleeve and scratches her wrist. She has a slight odor now, slightly sour, and I've realized it's the smell of an empty stomach. "To tell you the truth," she says, "I didn't see Lisa much by the end."

I swallow ice cream from my spoon. "What do you mean? I thought you two were good friends."

"We *were* friends. But the people there, they're not—they don't let you get too close. They're so competitive. They can't help it. And someone like Lisa—well, let's just say you saw her on a good day."

I hold my spoon out for Ethan to lick. "So how was she on a bad day?"

"Dark, moody, absent. . . . She kept her distance. I don't think she could ever really trust anyone, after what her parents put her through. I didn't blame her. So I gave her space, and she took it. Toward the end she was in intensive care a lot anyway."

"She got worse?"

She shrugs. "You get worse, you get better."

"But she's out of there now, right?"

"Yes."

I regard her a second. "Are you sure?"

She turns to me and sighs loudly. "Yes, Billie. I'm *sure.* Okay?"

It's a sign of her bitchy old self—it didn't all disappear with the flesh—and I want to cling to it, even if it's mean. After a minute, I say, "You were never up there, were you?"

"Intensive care? No way."

"Not even close?"

She shakes her head, and I wonder if I should believe her. "Did you want to come home?" I say then. "Did Dad give you a choice or make you?"

"Well. He made it sound like a choice, but you know what that means." She smiles a little. "I knew it was coming, anyway. He's been losing patience with Halley ever since he got in a fight with Yvette—"

"Yvette?"

"My shrink. My therapist."

"Oh." I close the ice cream and place my spoon on top of it. On TV is a commercial for Pepto-Bismol. "Was he horrible?"

"In the fight? Sort of. I mean, he said appalling stuff, and every-thing—but, you know, what else is new."

"Like what?"

"Well, like he didn't think I was getting better at Halley, and he didn't like some of their policies, and he wanted to be allowed to talk to me on the phone whenever he felt like it. Yvette said she couldn't do that, it wouldn't be fair to other patients and it would be destruc-tive to me. So he told her to go to hell." Cassie smiles. "And Yvette said, 'You can say anything you want to me, Dr. Weinstein, but it won't change the rules.' Then he just stood there fuming. I think he was amazed that anyone could ever say that to him."

Cassie reaches for the afghan on the arm of the couch and pulls it over her legs. "Anyway, I felt kind of bad for him then, if you can believe that. He's so clueless."

"He's not clueless." I say this instinctively, nothing to do with what I really believe.

"No?" Cassie shoots me a knowing look. "Then what would you call him, Billie?" She sighs. "Anyway, Yvette wasn't surprised. She knew he'd act just like that eventually. She's been hearing about him for months now. And she's seen much worse than Dad, really. She says his bark is worse than his bite."

"That's what Mom says."

"She says if I could just learn to not let him get to me. . . ." Her voice trails off. She seems less angry than last time I saw her, less hyper, and more—what? Resigned, maybe. For some reason, this bothers me. "Do you mind being back here?" I ask.

Cassie crosses her legs. They rest on the coffee table, like broomsticks. "I don't know. I'm not thrilled about being home for too long, but you know. I couldn't stay there forever either. It was costing a fortune."

"So what? Dad has the money."

"Well, I'd rather not have it spent on me, if I can help it." Neither of us talks for a minute. Then she says, "Just as long as they don't try to make me eat."

"Of course they will, Cassie. How can they not?"

From the side, I see her face tighten. "Well, it won't work. I'll just leave if they do."

"And go where?" It comes out harsher than I mean it to. But I don't like the idea that she can just up and ship.

"I don't know," she says. "Back to school, maybe. I think"—she doesn't look at me—"I think I could do better, now, there. I mean, I've learned some stuff."

Not how to eat, I think. I bring the melting ice cream back to the freezer. Ethan follows me into the kitchen and back again to the den. When I sit, he lays his fat square head down on my knee. I pat him, thinking about Lisa. After a while, I say, "The dogs haven't fought lately. They just, like, *stopped* one day."

"Really?" Cassie glances at Mollie, lying under the table. "Come here, Mol," she says.

Mollie lifts her head and wags her tail, but Ethan pushes past her and goes over to be patted instead, and Mollie puts her head back down on her paws. "Go on, Mollie," I say, but she ignores me. Cassie sticks her tongue out at Ethan. "I didn't ask for *you*, bug," she says. She pushes him away. Then she yawns. "Oh god, I'm so tired. I can't believe how long we've been sitting here." She stretches. "I think I have to go to sleep."

"Just stay till the end of Carol Burnett. Please? I love Tim Conway."

"He is pretty funny."

"He's a pisser."

She laughs hoarsely. "You still talk like Tiffany, even if she's gone." She yawns again. "I gotta go up, Bil." She drags herself off the couch, the blanket draped around her. She climbs the stairs slowly, one step at a time.

"Wait," I say, "I'm coming." I turn off the TV and follow her. And the dogs follow me. A small procession.

Cassie doesn't wash her face—maybe because her skin is so dry —and she doesn't put toothpaste on the toothbrush, so her whole bathroom routine takes about six seconds. She spreads three extra blankets, doubled over, on her bed, then climbs in and burrows deep. Her tiny head sticks out, like a lollipop. Under the covers, her body is almost nothing, barely a lump. A worm between sheets. "Aaah, my own bed," she says softly, smiling. She closes her eyes and takes a deep breath.

I know she wants me to leave, but I don't want to. "Cass?" I say after a minute.

She doesn't answer.

"Cassie, I know you're up. I have a question."

She doesn't move.

"Are you dead?"

She smiles. "Yes."

I laugh, relieved she's not. "Who's the first guy you fucked?"

She opens her eyes and smiles. "Why the hell should I tell you that?"

"Because I want to know. And I'm related to you."

She closes her eyes again. "Ask me in the morning. We'll play Twenty Questions."

"Okay. But did you like it?"

"The first time?" Her eyes stay closed. "Of course not. It gets better, though. Why, who'd you do it with?"

"No one."

"Liar."

"Okay. Dom Zeferelli." It's the first time I've even said his name out loud since that night, and I feel my heart speed up slightly.

Cassie's eyes open halfway. "You didn't!" she breathes.

"Why?"

"Billie, did you?"

"Maybe."

"He hit on you? At their house?"

I don't answer for a minute. I could just tell her yes and be done with it. But that would defeat the purpose. What I want is to tell her exactly what happened and then have her tell me it's no big deal, my life will go on. And then I can tell her that hers will go on too, she'll be fine. And both of us will be right.

"We did it at the Shell," I say.

"Oh my god." She smiles. "Well, was it fun, anyway?"

"No. It was humiliating. He used me—no, I used *him*. I sort of threw myself at him, to tell you the truth."

Her eyes are open all the way now. "Oh, Billie," she says sadly. *"Why?"*

I shrug. "I was sick of being a virgin. I wanted to see what the big deal was. And—well, I thought I liked him. I thought he was nice, like the rest of his family. He's not. He's a jerk."

"In what way?"

I plop down on my bed and reach for the copy of *The Catcher in* the Rye on my night table. "I don't know." I open the book and pretend to read.

But Cassie's eyes aren't closing. "You know," she says, after a minute, "it's really much better if the guy likes you."

"I know."

"And it's better the second time, too."

"I know that, too." And I *do,* somehow. I sigh. "I just wish I'd done it with Vinnie instead."

"No, you don't."

"Yes, I do. He's so—he would have been so sweet. I don't know why I didn't."

"Because you didn't want to. Or you weren't ready. God, Billie, you *are* only sixteen."

"So what? I feel like a mutant or something."

She laughs.

"Anyway, I'm almost seventeen." I turn to her. "Anyway, how old were *you?*"

"Sixteen. But I was ready."

"So am I."

"Well, so—go for it."

"As soon as I finish this book."

She laughs, then lifts her head up to see, and I hold it up so she can. "Oh, I love that book," she says. "I should read it again."

I glance at the books on her night table that she had my mother borrow from the library for her: *The Science of Garbage, How to Save the Planet in 365 Days, The Age of Greed.* "So why don't you?" I ask.

She shrugs and lets her head fall back down on the pillow. "Do you like it?"

I close my finger in my place and look at the cover. "I like it, but—well, Holden Caulfield is so . . . pathetic."

Cassie smiles. "That's what's so great about him."

"Why is that great? It's sad, though. It makes me sad."

"It's *supposed* to, Bil." She watches me. The room is dark, a muted smoky sort of light that comes from my little bedside lamp.

"Well, I'd rather be happy," I say, but then, feeling like I might have offended her, "I'm only on page twenty-three, though. I'm sure I'll like it better as I go."

Cassie watches me, her straight hair tucked behind her ear. "I wish I were you," she says finally.

"No, you don't." But I'm flattered a little.

"Yes, I do." She turns her face away from me. The back of her hair is a soft brownish-gold, darker than it used to be. On the wall, her shadow is giant-sized.

I close my book. "Want to play a game?" I glance at the old games stacked on our shelves. "Hey! Want to play Triple Yahtzee?"

"Bil, I'm so tired," Cassie mumbles. "I can't play a game."

"Then let's do *something* fun, at least. Let's call someone. Let's call Steve Zucker!"

"We'll call him tomorrow," she says after a second.

"Okay, then who can we call now? I know—Lisa! Let's call Lisa at Halley. Cass, she'd probably love to hear from you—"

Cassie turns to face me, suddenly awake. "No," she says.

"Why not?"

Something flickers across her eyes; I see it before she can hide it. "They won't let us talk to her."

"We'll call that guy she knew, the one who worked there. The food cart guy." I reach for the phone and pull it onto my bed.

Cassie sits up. "Don't."

She is keeping something from me. My stomach folds over. "Tell me," I demand.

"Tell you what?"

"Why you won't let me call her." I stare at her. "*Tell* me!"

"Okay! Stop yelling." She takes a deep breath. "She's not there anymore. I should have told you before, but I don't—I didn't want to upset you."

I stare at her. "What do you mean she's not there anymore. Where is she?"

"I don't know. One morning she was gone. When I asked, they told me her mother checked her out."

I can't stop staring. "Do you believe that?"

"I don't know." She stares at her bedspread.

"Well, her mother wouldn't have checked her out," I say. "Would she?"

"She might have. I don't know, Billie. I don't know what I believe."

"Well, can we call her at home then?"

"I don't have her number. And it's unlisted."

"She never gave it to you?"

She shakes her head. "She didn't. I swear, Billie. Why would she? I was right there." She lies back down slowly. "Sorry, Bil," she says. "I miss her, too." She closes her eyes one more time.

I look up at the ceiling, completely frustrated. Once more, I go over the stats in my head: Forty to fifty percent of anorexics never recover completely. Up to fifteen percent of them die—or five percent, depending on what book you read. In the stack of books about eating disorders that clutter my mother's room—some she's bought, others she's borrowed from the library five or six at a time—I found one that said only five percent die. That's what I believe. That ninety-five in every hundred of them live.

Cassie's breathing deeply now. I read a few minutes longer, until I think she's asleep. Then I get up and pull the phone out into the hallway, closing the door on the cord. I pick up the receiver. I will start by calling Halley and demanding to know where Lisa went. Then I'll call wherever that is and just *ask* for her. If she's not there, I'll try somewhere else.

I listen to the dial tone a second, then place my hand on the hang-up button, realizing I don't have the number for Halley in here. But I can't call information; my father has a fit if we do. He'll see it on the phone bill and want to know who called. . . .

"Tough shit." I say this out loud, and then I take my finger off the hang-up button. I'll call anyway. But instead of a dial tone, I hear a girl's voice. "Hello?" she says.

My heart jumps a beat. "Who's this?"

Tiffany laughs. "Who do you think, fool? Michelle, do you believe it?" she calls into the background. "Billie forgot my voice already!"

★   ★   ★

She is calling from Texas, though when I ask her where in Texas, she's vague. Near San Antonio, but not in it. They're living in a two-bedroom condo until they can get their feet on the ground, but it's heaven there, hot every day, and no huge hills, like in West Berry. And Mexican food to die for. It's humid, yeah, but she goes to the pool and lays out every day. She's not in school—she decided to wait till next year and then just start junior year over again—but she's meeting people anyway, at the pool, at the store. Mostly guys. There are cowboys all over the place. One of them is Warren, he's nineteen and beautiful and drives a yellow pickup truck, takes her anywhere she wants. "And ladybugs, there are all these ladybugs where we live, they keep smashing into my sunglasses . . . oh yeah —God, I can't believe I forgot to tell you—Bambi had her baby! Anthony Joseph Tito Rackinelli. She couldn't decide between the two middle names, can you handle it? And Bil, I'm not just saying this because he's my nephew, but he is the most gorgeous kid I've ever seen. Bambi might audition him for infant modeling. You can make like two hundred bucks an hour or something—"

"Tell her about his pecker," Michelle says in the background.

Tiffany laughs. "Oh yeah. His little penis is *huge!* The doctor said lots of babies are like that at first, then it shrinks to normal size after a while. But we think he takes after his father."

I hear Michelle snickering.

I picture a miniature Tito, huge penis lolling between little fat legs. "Is Tito down there?" I ask.

"Not yet, but he's coming. Next week, I think. Next week, right, Michelle?"

"What?" she yells.

"That Tito's coming?"

"How the hell do I know?" she says.

"I don't know," Tiffany says to me. "He might drive down with Dominick—"

"What do you mean? Dominick isn't with you?" The mention of him makes me nervous—as if, just by saying his name, I'm confessing that whole night to her.

But if she knows anything about that night, she spares me from

knowing she knows. "He didn't come with us," she says in a normal
tone.

"So, like—so he's still at your house?" Could he have caught
me over there, peering in their refrigerator, slamming pool balls on
their table?

"No," Tiffany says. "We had to get out of that house. Long
boring story, I'll tell you it another time. Anyway, he lives in Black
Berry, of all places, with his girlfriend—"

"They got back together?"

"I think. I'm not sure, though. Well, you should ask him, he's
closer to you than to me. He's still at the Shell. Of course. He's
married to that place. He'll probably own it someday. You should go
by and see him when you get your license—hey! One month from
today, right? Sweet Seventeen, babe! That sucks, though, your birthday is after school ends, so no one can make a big deal over you."

"Yeah, but I can lay out."

I'm goofing, but she takes me seriously. "This is true. And then
you can go out that night with a fresh burn. Are you going out with
Vinnie?"

"Not quite. He doesn't even talk to me." I tell her about the
wrestling match I went to, about watching him get pinned, about
him and Tina the Pig. And then I tell her other things. That I went
to her house that night looking for her. That my sister's back here
but still not doing so great, to tell the truth.

Before she hangs up, I ask for her number. "I can't give it to
you," she says. "My father won't let us give it out. But we're moving
soon, to a house, and I'll call you from there, okay?"

I think about this for a second. And then I say, "Why didn't you
call me sooner, Tiffany? I was worried. And—I missed you, you
know?"

"I missed you, too," she says. "A lot. I would have called if I
could. My father was a lunatic, he wouldn't let us call anyone." She
pauses. "I'll tell you all about it next time. Anyway, tell your family I
say hi, okay?"

"Yours, too."

"I'll call again soon. I'll call you on your birthday. If not sooner. Okay?"

Somehow, I don't think she will. But somehow—maybe just because she called once—I can deal with that now.

I stay there on the floor, the phone still on my lap, until I hear the garage door crack open. A car door slams, and then I hear footsteps coming up—and then Frannie's voice. I hang up the phone and go downstairs.

In the kitchen, Frannie can't stop shrieking. She screams and squeals while my mother grinds beans for coffee, warms a crumb cake, pours milk in a pitcher. Before I can figure out what she's going on about, my father motions me into the den. "How's your sister?" he says.

"Fine. What's Frannie yapping about?"

My father ignores my question. "Did she eat anything?" he asks.

"Cassie? Um—no. I tried to get her to have ice cream, but she acted like it was a time bomb or something."

His eyes linger on mine a minute. He looks tired. "Okay," he says. "Thanks."

"For what?"

But he goes into the kitchen then. I follow him. Frannie's husband, David, and my mother are carrying plates into the dining room. Frannie follows with silverware, still blabbing away.

My father cuts the cake and places slices on plates while my mother pours coffee for everyone. She pours me a cup, too—by mistake, I think, but I take it anyway. "He's a hero!" Frannie's yelling. "I'm telling you, Billie, it was professional macho redefined. Here we are, and the movie is playing away, and the entire audience is watching your father, and—"

"I wouldn't quite call it 'entire,' " my father says. "There were all of twenty people in the place." He hands Frannie a piece of cake, grinning.

"Pass the sugar, please," David Greenbaum says to me. He's smiling, and I realize I'm holding the sugar spoon in midair. I dump a few spoonfuls in my coffee and pass it to him, smiling back. I've always liked him. Then I turn back to Frannie. "Tell me from the *beginning,* please. And talk *slow*!"

"Slow*ly,*" my mother can't resist.

Frannie's eyes shine like stars. "Okay. Some man—he must have been, oh, around sixty-five, right Jane? Sixty at the oldest. *Maybe* sixty-one. Anyway, this man, I guess he had some sort of heart attack at the movie, and someone ran for an usher, and the usher yells, 'Is there a doctor in here?' Well"—she sips her coffee, makes a face, opens her bag and finds three packets of Sweet'n Low and pours them all in at once—"by that point they've turned up the lights, and your father gets up and rushes over to the guy. He gets him out of his seat and down into the aisle, and then he does CPR and mouth-to-mouth and all that stuff, and the guy—well, he just, like, he just *came back to life*! I was absolutely flabbergasted. I mean, his face had been all gray and horrible, absolutely ghostlike, and all of a sudden it was pink again, and he opened his eyes. It was absolutely inconceivable, Billie. People burst into applause. And the man's wife! Well, she was crying, and she couldn't stop thanking your father, and he was just trying to calm her down, and then the ambulance came, and—"

I turn to my father. "Is this true?"

"One person may have clapped," my father says. "And I missed half the goddamn movie." He takes off his glasses and rubs his eyes, but he's smiling.

"Oh, pfuff," Frannie says. "Just go back and ask them to let you see the movie for free. Hell, they'll probably let you in free for the rest of your life. In fact"—she glances at her watch—"if it makes the eleven o'clock news, you'll own them. Ugh, I cannot wait to tell Dean, this could be the straw that actually makes him apply to Yale Med—"

"Oh, it wouldn't make the *news,*" my mother says. "Would it?" She looks at my father.

"No," he says. He forks a bite of cake. "Well, I don't know. Maybe. I don't think so, though. No, I'd say it wouldn't."

"It should," David says.

My father glances at him. He forks another mouthful. "You think so?" he says through his cake.

"I do," David says.

"I'll go turn it on," I say, getting up, even though it's only 10:50. Frannie follows me in. "I can't miss this," she says. "I don't want to miss it. I am absolutely—" She stops midthought. "Oh, I have to call Dougie this instant and tell him to turn on the TV."

The news starts then, and the rest of them come in, and the five of us watch together. I wonder if Cassie's listening secretly from upstairs. She must hear Frannie. She must be up. "Drama at the movies," the anchor says then, and Frannie screams. "This is it!" "A local doctor, surgeon Michael Weinstein of West Berry, saves a moviegoer from near-death. Apparently the man, Nathan Paul, had a heart attack at a revival of *Amarcord* at the Union Theater. Dr. Weinstein, who was attending the Fellini movie with his wife and two friends, performed CPR until the man was breathing again. Mr. Paul is now resting comfortably at Fairmont Hospital, where he's listed in stable condition. And that's it for tonight. . . ."

"I was *there!*" Frannie screams, and all four of us laugh. The phone rings then. My father goes to get it in the kitchen, and after a minute we can tell it's Aunt Nancy, who's seen the broadcast. After a second my mother gets up and goes to the kitchen, too. David goes off to the dining room for more cake, leaving me and Frannie still watching TV. She seems, finally, to be all shrieked out. She leans back on the couch and smiles at me. "Well," she says. "What a night, huh?"

I nod. "The whole day. I didn't know Cassie was coming home, either."

Frannie nods. She seems to be considering something. Then, in a lowered voice, she says, "Does she look okay, Billie? Your father said she looks much better."

"He did?"

"Mm. He thinks she'll be fine. He said he thought the whole thing was mostly the stress of school, and putting her in that place just made everything worse, and—"

"I know what he thinks," I say meanly.

Her mouth snaps shut, and she looks at me, suddenly sober. "What. You don't agree? Tell me. You think she looks bad?"

"It's not that. It's—well, it is that, I guess. I mean, she does look bad. She *is* bad." I don't know why I'm telling this to Frannie Greenbaum. "I'm glad she's home, though," I say. "Maybe she will be better here."

She's watching me. Her face melts. "Oh, honey," she says. She moves over and hugs me.

Her touch makes me want to cry, and even the joy of Tiffany calling can't stop the sadness. I choke it back. "No, I know," I say. "She'll be fine." I inch away from Frannie.

And now her face spreads into confidence again. "Billie, your dad's a pro. I'm telling you. I wish you could have seen him tonight —not just saving that guy but comforting his wife afterward. This poor scared old thing . . ." She shakes her head. "He's such a good man, Billie. And he knows exactly what he's doing, you know. He's got such a good reputation—"

"I know."

She watches me a minute longer. Then she sighs. "I know, but this is different, right?" She takes a deep breath. "I guess it *is* ironic. I guess it is." Another deep breath. "You know, Billie, it's so different when it's your family. It really is. Dean got sick once, and . . ." Her voice trails off. She shakes her head. "It's like when people let their own parents starve home alone while they're off feeding the elderly for charity. It's—sometimes it's impossible to see it, when it's your own family. Sometimes you just *can't*—or you don't want to. You want everything to be perfect, you don't want to believe you messed up. It's too painful to face the facts. . . ."

I nod, waiting for her to finish, waiting for her to say, "But *your* sister will be fine." But she just looks at me, her mouth closed tight for once. And then my mother walks in. She sits down lightly on the coffee table. From in the kitchen, we can hear the men talking, and then my father's laughter, and then David's. "More coffee?" my mother asks.

"No thanks," Frannie says.

For a minute we just sit there. Then I get up and turn off the television. The room is dark then, but I don't turn on a lamp. Moonlight bathes the curtain from behind. Gentle rain patters on the leaves of the ear tree.

My mother turns to me. I think of telling her Tiffany called—to lighten up the moment, to feel good again. But before I can say it, she says, "How was Cassie?" And she looks at me hopefully.

So I tell her what she wants to hear. What Frannie couldn't tell me before. "Cassie's fine," I say.

I wake up at four fifteen, tears streaming down my face. In my dream, I was performing a magic trick as a demonstration for my speech class: I would put someone in a booth and close the curtain, and the person would disappear. First I did Tiffany, then Vinnie, then Lisa. Everyone clapped. Then I did my grandmother, and then the dogs. And then Cassie wanted to try. "For the finale," she said. I told her I wanted to get the other people back first, but when I tried to, I didn't know how. Cassie was getting impatient. "Come on," she said, walking into the booth. I grabbed her arm, trying to hold her back. But she wouldn't listen, so I started crying. And here I am.

I sit up in bed and wipe tears off my face. Then I get up and go over to Cassie's bed and kneel down next to it. I put my hand in front of her mouth and hold it there until I feel her breath, warm and smelly. I touch her forehead with one finger to make sure it's warm, too. She stirs and turns away from me. I watch the covers to make sure they rise and fall again and again.

Then I get up and step away from her. The house is dark and quiet; outside, it seems to have stopped raining, and I can hear the wind blowing gently. I get dressed fast, jeans and a sweatshirt and sneakers from the pile on the floor near my bed. I check Cassie once more. Then I go down to the kitchen for car keys and then down another flight, to the garage.

I cringe a little as I press the door button, knowing it might wake my father—but the truth is I don't really care. By the time he could get down here, I'll be gone. I back the car out carefully but fast. I'm pretty good at driving these days.

I'm still crying a little by the time I get to Vinnie's, which makes me mad. I wipe my face and take deep breaths, then drive around his block trying to chill out. Then I park across the street from his house. In the glove compartment I find my mother's flashlight, and I take it with me when I get out.

All the lights are off at Vinnie's house, both inside and out, and there are no stars or moon to help light up the sky—but a streetlight a few houses down from Vinnie's keeps the block from being totally dark. I cross the street and stand on the sidewalk in front of the DiNardios', staring up at Vinnie's room. It's cool out, and the air is still damp from the rain, but I don't feel cold. I turn on the flashlight and shine it on the ground, looking for something to throw up at Vinnie's window.

I find some pebbles and a couple of acorns, all small enough—I hope—not to break anything. I position myself on the lawn and toss the first one up softly. It doesn't even reach the house. I toss the second one as hard as I can. It sails over the roof, and I laugh. Am I really doing this? I toss another one up, then a fourth. I'm getting a little closer, at least.

The sixth one hits. I wait a minute or two, my heart beating fast, but no one comes to the window. It occurs to me that maybe Vinnie's there but I just can't see him in the dark room, and then I think that maybe he can't see me either. I turn on the flashlight and shine it on my face for a while, but nothing happens.

I throw more pebbles and shine the light on myself again. Still nothing. I aim the light at his window, then. I toss more pebbles until another one hits.

But this is so stupid. I start to turn to go back to my mother's car. As I do, out of the side of my eye, I catch Vinnie's light go on behind me.

I sit down on the lawn to wait, not realizing until my jeans are soaked through that the grass is still wet. I put the flashlight in my lap and drop the rest of the pebbles, which I've been holding tight. I wipe my clammy palm on my pants. What will I say to him? At home—and on the way here, in the car—I had it all planned. . . .

The light outside the DiNardios' front door goes on then, and Vinnie steps out under it. He's wearing sweatpants and a white zip-up sweatshirt jacket and sneakers, untied, over bare feet. He glances toward me. I turn on the flashlight and shine it on my face. "It's me," I say, smiling. "Billie."

He blinks and squints, looking not at all thrilled to see me. "Billie?" He walks over slowly, shuffling his feet.

I lower the flashlight to my neck, feeling my smile fade out. Vinnie stares at me a second. He licks his lips, then glances at the flashlight. "Are you nuts?" he says. "Are you retarded?"

I turn off the flashlight. Well, what did I expect? But the tears start to push up again—hot, hard pressure in my throat. Big mistake, coming here. I stand up and turn away from him, my hand blocking my face, so he won't see me crying. "Sorry," I say. "I'm leaving. I didn't mean to wake you." I spin around and walk fast toward my mother's car.

"Wait a minute!" He jogs to catch me. One palm comes onto my shoulder, and the other hand clamps my upper arm. He turns me around gently. "What's the matter?" he says. "Are you crying?"

"No." Again I put my face down, so he can't see it. I push my hair back with one hand and sniff.

He sighs. And then he pulls me into him, just like he used to. His hands come around to my back. "C'mere," he says. "Come on. You know I can't stand it when girls cry."

I can't even answer, he feels so good. I let my arms come around him, too. I hold my breath, trying to swallow my sobs. And I tell myself, Remember this.

He holds me a long time, until I'm not crying at all. But I still don't want to let go of him. His jacket is unzipped partway, and I can feel the warmth of his skin. I close my eyes and lean on his shoulder. "I'm sorry, Vinnie," I tell him. "Really sorry."

His arms loosen slightly. "For what?"

"For everything. For hurting you—"

He lets me go quickly, then laughs. "You didn't *hurt* me. I'm not some fucking wimp, Billie. I'll survive without you. Believe me."

"I know. I didn't mean it like that. I just meant—" I look up at the starless sky. "I meant, I'm sorry about how it ended. I didn't want it to be—I wanted us to be friends."

He picks up a pebble and tosses it down the street. After a while, he says, "Who says we're not friends?"

"*You.* You don't even talk to me at school. You don't even look at me, Vinnie."

"Well, I wouldn't worry myself about it, if I was you."

"Well, I would. I am."

"Well, don't."

"Okay! I won't anymore."

He picks up another pebble and tosses it back and forth between his hands. He lets it go, watches it drop on his sneaker.

"I saw you wrestle that day," I say. I want to say something nice to him. I want to leave on good terms. I think I'll do anything to have that happen, whatever it takes.

"What day?" he says.

"At Valley. At the Regionals."

He looks up at me. "You were there? Where were you sitting?"

"Near the team. Near your new girlfriend, *Tina.* Didn't she tell you?"

He laughs. "She's not my *girlfriend.*"

"No? You could've fooled me. So could she."

He laughs again. "Don't act jealous. It doesn't become you."

"I'm not *jealous.*"

"Good. You shouldn't be."

Is that a compliment? I'll take it, anyway. I smile a little. Vinnie looks at me, and he's smiling, too. And for a second I think he might kiss me again, and I'd love that, I really would.

But he doesn't, just clasps his hands together and raises them toward the sky and stretches. He yawns. "Well, listen," he says. "I should go back in and sleep another half-hour, if you're all done bawling. I have to get up and go running at six—"

"What for? Wrestling's over, isn't it?"

"So what? I still gotta stay in shape. I've already put on eight pounds since the Regionals." He laughs. "I might be coaching at wrestling camp this summer, too. I can't show up like a slob." His tone has changed a little. Slightly harder, more determined. He's had enough of me.

"Okay," I say. "I'll see you at school." I turn once more to leave. "Thanks for coming out. Sorry I woke you."

"Forget about it. Come on, I'll walk you to your car." He walks with me, not touching me. When we get there, he says, "You all right now or what?"

If I wasn't—if I *weren't*—I wouldn't tell him now. That wouldn't be fair. He wouldn't want to know, anyway.

But the thing is, I am okay. Pulling away in my mother's car, I feel like something heavy that's been inside me has lifted out. I turn the corner and accelerate, rolling down my window. Cool air rushes in. I face it head-on, tasting spring on my tongue, feeling it sift through my teeth. I think about the dream that brought me down to Vinnie's. It was silly, it was just weird. No one's disappeared. People are farther away, yes. But they're still here.

And I can drive now. I signal to turn onto our street, even though no one's behind me—just to waste the signal a little to spite my father. But as I turn the corner and head toward home, I feel something pricking at my high—trying to bring me down. "Okay," I say out loud. "She could die. She might not get better. Just face it, Billie."

I turn into our driveway and pull the car in slowly. In the garage, I turn it off and sit for a minute, very still. I half-expect my father to rush down in pajamas and start yelling at me. But no one comes. I get out, leaving the car door slightly open so I don't make any noise. I leave the garage door open, too. No one will steal the car, not here. I tiptoe upstairs.

In the kitchen, the clock says 5:49. Amazingly, the house is still quiet and dark; if they've heard me, they've decided not to say anything—or to deal with it in the morning. I deposit the keys back in the change cup in the cabinet and head up the second set of stairs.

In the bathroom, I stand in front of the mirror and examine my face. I'm looking for my parents in me. I look hard, trying to be objective, but I don't see them in there; I never do, even though people have told me I look like both of them. I do see Cassie in there, though; more and more now, my face is like hers—but with eyes a little less round, nose slightly wider, mouth a touch more severe. I'm not quite as soft and pretty, I look tougher than she does. And the truth is, I like it that way.

On the counter is her hairbrush, stuffed with yellow hairs that come out in clumps every time she puts the brush to her head. I take a comb from the drawer and use it to pull out the hairs. I dump the hair in the wastebasket and put the brush back out again, clean.

When I open the door, Cassie is standing there. I jump back. "You scared me!" I whisper, but I'm thrilled to see her.

Cassie rubs her eyes. "What are you doing dressed?"

"Nothing. I went to Vinnie's."

"What?"

"I drove there. I talked to him."

She looks at me like I'm crazy.

"Did I wake you?" I say.

"Not really."

I glance at my parents' closed door. Now that I'm up here, I don't feel like going to sleep. "I'm going downstairs," I whisper. "Come with."

"Okay." She goes back to our room and comes out with her pink comforter wrapped around her. She follows me down.

But outside is where I really want to go, into the fading hours of the night. Cassie follows me again. Neither of us turns on the light, though probably for different reasons: She doesn't want to waste energy, or to *use* anything, and I want to savor the dark. I sit down on the front steps, the butt of my jeans still damp from Vinnie's grass.

Cassie debates a second, then sits down next to me. She tosses me a corner of her blanket, and I throw it carelessly over my legs. I'm not cold, but I don't want to refuse her offer either. For a long time the two of us sit there, not talking. The ear tree stands regally, its limbs lightly swaying. The leaves are damp from rain, and every so often I see one gleaming in the dark, like a tiny oil slick.

Next to me, Cassie wraps her half of the blanket more tightly around her, and as she does, I swear I catch the night lighten a shade,

from navy black to navy blue. I bend down to untie my sneakers.
"What are you doing?" Cassie says.

I kick my shoes off and stand up, not answering her. I want to
walk in the wet grass. I want to feel the wet grass on my feet.

"Where are you going?" she says, but I move onto the lawn, still
not answering. Cool wet grass tickles my soles; its smoky-sweet smell
rises up to greet me. Nearby, I can smell the tomato plants my
mother just planted, their strong, salty stems already taking root. I
raise my hands to the sky, and then I close my eyes and spin around,
and I keep spinning, not thinking about anything.

I spin until I step on an acorn. "Ow!" I say, and I tumble down
dizzily in the grass. A car is coming down the hill. I watch its headlights approach. A station wagon sails slowly by.

When it's gone, though, I'm still watching the spot in the street
where it passed me; something out there has caught my eye. I get up
and take a few steps toward the street. And it happens again: a quick
flash in the fading dark, like dimes or jewels. Silver coins.

I move to the curb, and then out into the street. I can't see
anyone or anything. I look up and down. "What are you doing?"
Cassie croaks. Her hoarse voice fades, swallowed up by the air.

And then I see it: from inside the sewer, tiny silver eyes peer out
at me. I move closer. Raccoon eyes! And not just one set, but—I
count quickly—ten eyes! Five sets. A raccoon family.

I turn to my sister and motion her over with my hand. The light
is coming, the night is fading away, and I can see her clearly now.
She's just sitting there. I motion again, almost frantically. And this
time she rises slowly, her blanket draped around her. She drops the
blanket. It sinks to the ground, and she steps over it and walks toward
me.

I turn back to the sewer and take a step closer to it. I can make
out five pointy snouts now, five little black and white triangle heads.
Paws clamped over the grate. I wonder how they can hang on like
that, all crammed together in there. What's underneath them? Or
maybe they're just hanging in nothing, in air. Holding each other up,
somehow. Three of them are just babies, I see now, heads no bigger
than a kitten's.

Cassie comes up behind me. "What?" she says, and then she sees, too. "Whoa," she whispers, touching my arm.

But another car is coming, a yellow sports car, speeding down the hill much too fast. We back up to the curb, and I cringe and grab Cassie's arm this time as the car roars down the hill. The driver honks as he passes. He's a kid, not much older than us.

When he's gone, so are the raccoons. "Damn," I say softly. We wait a few minutes more, watching the sewer. But they're gone.

I turn to my sister, expecting her to say something about the driver—what an asshole, what a jerk. But she's smiling, she doesn't look angry. She looks almost normal. *Happy,* even.

I stare at her face, because it's been so long since she's looked like this. And I think, It's the bones. It's her bones, just like Zelda said; Cassie's always had good bones. And isn't that what's most important? As long as the bones are there, she can always get back the rest, can't she?

For a second, I allow myself a fantasy: I apply to the University of Arizona and get accepted with flying colors. My father wants me to go to Cornell—where I also get accepted—but I tell him I'm going to Arizona no matter what he says, and he realizes he has no choice anymore, that now it's my life, it's up to me. So he agrees to let me go, and then Cassie decides to come with me, and he agrees to let her go, too. When we get there, she eats like a pig and gets happy and fat. For exercise, we climb mountains together—pastel mountains, like Lisa said. At the top, we eat tuna fish sandwiches and watch the sunsets. We talk about Lisa, who, we've found out, has become a Broadway dancer. . . .

Next to me—in reality—Cassie teeters a second, then steadies herself. "I'm going in now, Bil," she says softly. She turns around and heads toward the house.

Above her, the sky is lemony, streaked with red. "Wait," I call out. "I'm coming, Cass."

I make one stop—at the garbage can, to pull off the bungee cord my mother puts on to keep out the raccoons. I wrap it around my hand. And then I dash up the steps and follow my sister inside.

Cathi Hanauer

HAS WRITTEN FOR SUCH NATIONAL PUBLICATIONS AS
McCall's, Mademoiselle, Elle, AND *Seventeen*. SHE LIVES
IN NEW YORK CITY WITH HER HUSBAND AND DAUGHTER.

Made in the USA
Lexington, KY
06 December 2010